SON OF THE SALT CHASER

SON OF THE SALT CHASER

THE SALT CHASERS DUOLOGY

A. S. THORNTON

CamCat
Books

CamCat Publishing, LLC
Fort Collins, Colorado 80524
camcatpublishing.com

Hardcover ISBN 9780744306132
Paperback ISBN 9780744306071
Large-Print Paperback ISBN 9780744306378
eBook ISBN 9780744305678
Audiobook ISBN 9780744306170

Library of Congress Control Number: 2022941017

Cover and book design by Maryann Appel
Map illustration by Maia Lai

5   3   1   2   4

For E,

I would watch the moon cross the sky every night for you.

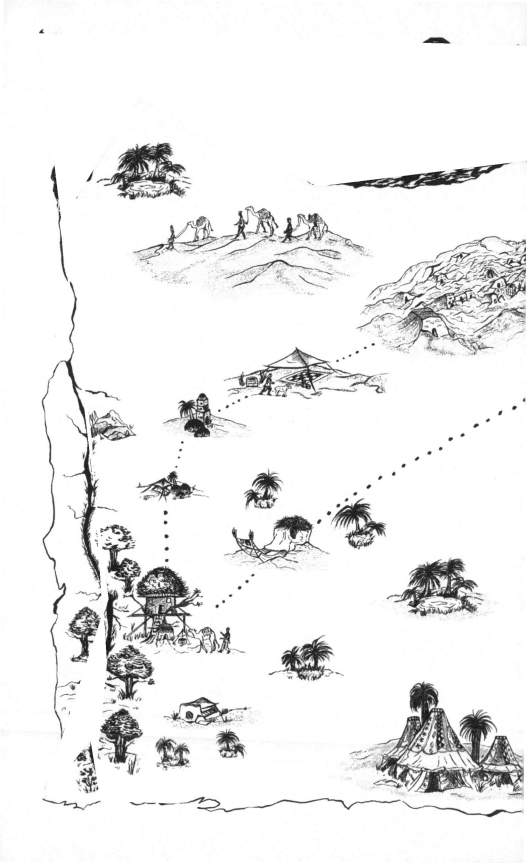

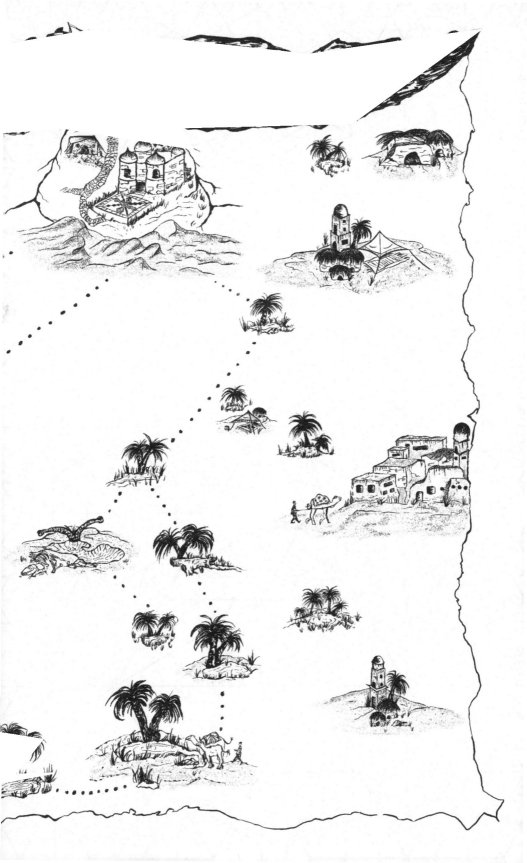

I.

DECEPTION

—— ··· ——

ALKHIDAL

Tahira,

Papa won't look at any of us. Mama won't stop crying. I know you are angry, but it won't do to stay there. We can help you take care of it. They only want their daughter back. And I want my sister, my friend.

Our caravan moves southeast in two nights. It will be the quarter moon of winter's end when we arrive. We will stay for three dozen days. This should reach you in time, so please come back to us. I have heard Ibrahim seeks another wife. The king's son! A better man than that animal who took your future with his fine clothes and gleaming crown.

Do you know what those sea-people call us? Salt chasers. As if that is what we want! They can't understand that we don't wander to pursue riches; we journey to chase our desires. And we always get that for which we hunt.

If you don't come home, I will search for you. And him.

Zahar

—Unopened letter, found deep under sand

1

EMEL

The moon was only a sliver, and I was grateful I could not see the dunes around us. Watching them shift from the wind's hands would drive me to madness sooner. Already I was sure I could hear the hatif whispering, telling me to turn back. The bones of my knees, my feet, my spine, all agreed.

Instead I focused on the sounds: creaking barrels and crates stacked on grunting camels, the swishing of weary travelers' robes, the tinkling of tack on royal horses.

The ache in my bones would diminish when our journey stopped at sunrise, but there was another pain that would not stop when my feet did. It slid its fingers around my ribs and pulled so hard that, at times, breathing seemed impossible. It was incessant, because it was grief.

Tavi was silent beside me, her breath coming in soft huffs as we walked in the long caravan.

It was the third night of our journey to Madinat Almulihi, and already I regretted the decision to leave home. Without a camel to carry food and water, I would not survive on my own if I turned back. I was trapped in the middle of this desert. What a foolish plan it was to leave everything behind, hoping to find my lost love in a sparkling city by the sea. Stretching open my eyes, I tried to see the man who rode his horse at the front of the caravan, King Saalim. I saw nothing. The darkness had swallowed him completely.

I chewed my cheeks and stared at the blue-black sand, focusing on each step forward. That was the only direction I could go: forward. There was no going back to the life I'd once had.

My mother and father were dead. The rest of my family—my half-sisters, other mothers in the harem, full and half-brothers—were all to be dispersed into the settlement to try to find their way without their father or their husband. Without the Salt King. And there was no Saalim. At least, not the Saalim I knew. The careful jinni with strong hands. Enslaved just as I was—with cuffs of magic instead of silk—he was kind and thoughtful. That man I loved was free. I should be overjoyed, but now he was someone else.

Saalim was a king who belonged in Madinat Almulihi, his life could not intersect with mine. I had promised I would find him, though. I'd promised we would be together again. I could not give up.

Would it have been better to stay an ahira, bound to a life of seduction and submission, and for Saalim to remain a jinni, no less a slave? If my hand hadn't been forced—if my father hadn't determined to send me away to live as the whore of Omar, a cruel and despicable man—could we have found happiness? It was not a perfect life, but its familiarity was a comfort. And I would still have Saalim.

I shook my head against my traitorous thoughts. *No.* There was no part of that life that we deserved. At least now I had freedom.

The caravan slowed. Murmurs met my ears.

"Thank Eiqab," Tavi whispered as we stopped. "I am so hungry." She sank slowly, achingly, onto the ground and dropped her head onto her knees.

Forty days, they had said, to reach Madinat Almulihi. After tonight there were thirty-seven more. We could not survive this.

Tavi and I had been foolishly confident when we ventured on this journey. We had nothing to lose, the world was at our fingertips. At least, that is what *I* had thought. Did Tavi believe it only because I did? Did she resent me and my role in her choice? Guilt pricked at me.

"I'll be back," I said, and set out after other villagers and soldiers toward the front of the caravan to collect our rations. The hope that I might see Saalim at each stop gave me strength.

Slung across my shoulders was a sack containing my things from home. The gentle clatter of those objects was a balm to the ache in my legs and chest. I touched them through the fabric with the delicacy of a mother with child caressing her belly.

"Your name?" the man said as I handed him my empty goatskin.

"Emel, and my sister is Tavi," I replied, taking my now-full skin and giving him Tavi's. He was generous with our water ration. At dawn we would arrive at an oasis where our water stores would be filled.

He nodded. "Emel and sister Tavi. Parvaz."

It was this way every time. They asked our names, told us theirs. It was strange they bothered at all.

I followed the crowd to the man who handed out our meals. My heart thudded as I leaned around the line of people, hoping to see Saalim.

The man—whose face was shadowed beneath his guthra—gave me two handfuls of dates and two thin slices of dried goat's meat. We could not risk lighting a fire at night to cook, alerting opportunistic nomads to our presence. It was why we traveled at night, slept during the day.

That, and the fact that a foot journey like this would take twice as long under Eiqab's draining sun.

"Emel!" the man said, and I recognized him as Amir.

Behind him, several men were seated with legs crossed in quiet discussion. Their boots were off, set beside them, and their horses were tied to the trunk of a nearby tree. These were men of Almulihi. King's men. At Amir's exclamation, one of them turned toward me. Even in the shadows I knew that man's face. *Saalim.* My stomach flipped; my breath shallowed.

"We should be at the oasis before the sun has lifted from the ground," Amir said. "Don't forget to find me."

Dragging my attention from Saalim, I smiled, pleased Amir had remembered his promise to me.

"I will." I was nudged out of the way by a hungry traveler before I could look once more at the seated king.

Amir had promised to help me with my map when we arrived at the oasis tomorrow. On the first night of our journey he had shown me his bawsal when I asked him how they knew the way. The glistening gold direction-teller pointed north—to Almulihi—as if by magic. I had shown him my map in return, and he'd tutted at its blankness.

My sister was sitting with my friend from home, Firoz, and his lover Rashid when I returned. All were silent in their fatigue. Firoz and Rashid walked further back in the caravan and often only joined us for meals. Rashid was the one who said it was better if we were separated, so we might learn different things about Almulihi.

I was still cold toward Rashid for taking Firoz from me since undertaking our journey, as we might otherwise have lent one another some of our will to move forward, but I no longer had the strength to feel betrayed.

Tavi nibbled at the dates. "Oh yes," she said. "This is the best one I have had in my whole life."

Smiling, I turned to Firoz. "How has your night been?"

Smacking his lips after a long drink of water, he shrugged. "Quiet."

"That's good, eh?"

He didn't reply.

Rashid nodded. "It is good. No sign of nomads, no sand-winds, no hatifs." He peered around as if checking to ensure it was indeed still quiet. I scowled at Rashid before looking away, the date in my mouth suddenly losing its sweetness. It was Rashid who had poisoned Firoz with fear.

Firoz was my dearest friend, and like me, had always dreamed of escaping the stifling life of our settlement. But the Firoz I knew and loved seemed to disappear more each day—growing uneasy and taciturn. Did he, too, regret coming on this journey?

After Saalim—not *my* Saalim, the jinni, but this new and distant stranger— had slain my father, the infamously power-hungry Salt King who controlled the salt trade as a means to rule the desert, he told my family we could join him on the journey back to Almulihi. Villagers were welcome, too. I worried it would be impossible for Firoz. He lived with his mother and younger siblings, eking out a life selling coconut juice at the marketplace. There was no extra coin to support Firoz's desperate dream.

But Rashid had found the money. I did not ask how, nor did I ask Firoz what his family thought of his leaving. I saw his siblings' tear-stained faces when they said goodbye. It was unlikely Firoz would ever see his family again. Did he, too, sometimes regret this journey?

"Sons, my feet hurt." Firoz slipped off his sandals and foot wraps. His knuckles kneaded the curves of his soles.

"Like I've been walking atop a carpet of scorpions," Tavi agreed.

Rashid rubbed the back of Firoz's neck until Firoz leaned into him, dropping his head onto his shoulder. Jealousy hit, and I looked away. Regret would not lurk so near were I taking this journey at Saalim's side.

But Saalim did not remember me, so it mattered not that he was nearby. And none knew what nor whom I had lost. Magic had stolen those memories from everyone. None knew the ahira had fallen in love with a jinni, and both had found everything in their freedom. Except each other.

That I was alone with those memories made the pain all the worse.

"It will get easier," Rashid said.

I looked at him, confused, before I realized he spoke of the journey.

"Yes," Tavi agreed with too much enthusiasm. We knew nothing of long journeys, but hope was our only companion.

"It will," I said. "Our feet will ease into this; our bones will quiet. It will be worth it." I hoped they did not hear my doubt.

"We have been talking about a plan for when we arrive in the City," Rashid said as he looked to Tavi and me. Why did I hear hesitation? "It seems best if we find the baytahira."

I spat a date seed into the sand. "No." The baytahira was where the whores did their work. It was the only place I would have found coin, should I have been cast out by my father for refusing to serve as ahira to gain him powerful allies.

"I don't like it," Tavi said.

Rashid at least looked ashamed. "I know. But it's not for long. It's an easy place to find work."

"Work?" I huffed.

He ignored my heaving chest. "We're likely to find somewhere to stay for a few nab."

Firoz saw my fury. "It's just an idea. Until we can figure out something better. Nothing is settled."

Back home, Rashid and Firoz had spent much of their time in the bay-tahira. There, they were free to be as they were. There, people knew how to keep secrets. Perhaps they were not completely wrong for reaching for what was familiar and safe.

Exhaling slowly, I picked up my last date.

Rashid continued. "We can't show up in the bazaar expecting someone to have work for us."

Tavi asked, "How do you know they have a baytahira?" Then, she looked at me and pointed to the date in her mouth, raising her eyebrows like it really was the best one yet.

Rashid huffed and stood. "Because desperation fuels fortune, and Madinat Almulihi is a city of wealth." With his teeth, he tore off a piece of dried meat and walked away.

We had so many days left in our journey. Things could change. I would not argue this now.

But I refused to leave my life as an ahira only to settle somewhere else and do the same.

<hr />

When the sun had barely risen, we saw the oasis.

"Not much farther now," I whispered to Tavi.

Sand had found its way between the folds of the cloth wrapped around my feet, the grains digging into the raw parts of my foot left exposed by my sandals.

I looked ahead at the copse of trees that protected the water at its center, and counted the steps until I could lie down and finally sleep.

Though I wanted to crawl into a shady slumber right when we arrived, we all assisted where we could to get the caravan settled: guiding the camels to the trees to be tied and fed, leading the horses to water and sparse grass, helping to unload the cargo from the animals' backs.

This oasis was much larger than the one near my home, and once the animals were tended to, the people spread throughout the trees that circled the dark blue pool. Some sought bits of privacy—a lost luxury. Some rushed to the deepest, clearest water and filled their goatskins, drinking heartily. Others waded into the shallow areas to splash their faces and cool their feet. Tavi and I found a large patch of shade and lay down on our cloaks. I did not bother to search for Rashid or Firoz.

So tired, I did not even search for Saalim.

"I don't know if I'll get used to this," I said to Tavi through a yawn, pulling my scarf over my eyes.

"Hmm?"

"Sleeping at day, waking at night."

After a long pause, Tavi said, "I remember when the hardest part of my day was pretending to be more interested in the muhami than the trays of food." She laughed. It was sputtery—little puffs of air.

"Or the wax. I thought it was the worst pain I'd ever felt."

We spoke slowly and breathlessly, our words working their way up through our fatigue.

"Hadiyah. Adilah," Tavi whispered. "I wonder what they're doing now?"

I wondered, too. If I were home, I could go and see them. I regretted speaking aloud of the zafif and our attendants. It only served to bring back the gnawing ache of what I'd lost.

It's already done. There is no turning back.

When sleep found me, I dreamt of a bird with two broken wings flapping sadly at the bottom of its cage. It had soft gray eyes that pleaded with me. People watched as I pulled it from its cage. Speaking softly to it, I ignored them. Then,

I clamped my fingers over its neck, fragile and soft. It thrashed as if begging me to stop. But I didn't. I didn't stop until it was lifeless in my hands.

When I awoke—my face wet with tears—I was still swimming through the question: Had I ended the bird's suffering? Had I done any good at all?

Leaning back onto my hands, I pushed my feet into the cool water. My raw, blistered skin welcomed the relief.

"What do you think they're doing?" Firoz asked, nudging me with his own submerged foot.

Soldiers from Madinat Almulihi stood across the large pool. I would have assumed they were cooling themselves, too, but the longer I watched, the more I saw that there was a pattern—almost a rhythm—to the way they dipped their hands into the water and pressed it to their brows, wrists, and necks.

"Praying," a voice said from behind me. A voice so achingly familiar it took all of my strength not to jump from the ground and rush to him.

Slowly, I turned to Saalim.

In our few days of travel, I had come to understand that he and his men behaved differently from my father and his court. It still surprised me that their king—my king—could appear so unlike a royal. His dark sirwal was rolled at his calves, his feet bare. He wore no weapons, and the black tunic across his chest was dust-covered and almost tattered at the edges; the guthra that loosely wrapped his face, equally worn. Had Saalim himself not told me tales of the wealth and allure of Madinat Almulihi, I would not believe that it was a city worth seeing at all.

"Eiqab will strain to hear," Firoz said.

Saalim looked away from his soldiers down to Firoz. "We worship the giver, not the punisher."

"Wahir," I said. How strange it was to see someone praying to the lesser god. How wrong.

Saalim's gaze met mine.

A rush of cold and hot, longing and desperation, and . . . Sons, how didn't he feel it? Couldn't he see me as I saw him? I felt as I had the first time he looked at me after he became human again, when he had killed my father and his eyes locked on mine. I stared back, willing him to feel, to remember as I did . . . the set of his jaw hard beneath my fingers, his lips against my own, his breath warm as I pulled it into my lungs. His hands so careful against my skin, his heart beating against my breast, the tremor of his voice as he said my name.

"Emel, isn't it?" he asked.

The memories scattered. I bent my head to the ground, not wanting him to see my grimace. He felt nothing, remembered nothing. Sons, he did not know me at all.

Masira was a devious goddess, giving so much but taking as much in return. Damn her magic that she unfurled like a woven rug! Something beautiful to cover all of the ugly scars and secrets, to distract from them. But that was all the magic did, wasn't it? What it tried to remove, it did so sloppily. Everything still lay underneath the threads.

"Yes, she is Emel," Firoz said loudly.

I looked back to Saalim, brushing away my thoughts like sand on my palms. Saalim continued. "Today, you and . . ."

"Firoz," he said.

Saalim paused at the name, his brow pulling together slightly before he continued.

"Firoz. I am still learning. You both will help with the cook-fires." Then he turned from us and continued around the water's edge.

"Well, I at least know food is cooked *on* a fire. What do you know about cooking?" Firoz chuckled. His mother always cooked for his family, and I had had no business working in the palace kitchens as an ahira.

I forced a laugh as I watched Saalim walk away.

"What bothers you?" Firoz asked.

I shook my head.

"He's just a king, Emel. Same heart that can be pierced by blade." He stabbed the air with an invisible blade.

Pressing my lips together, I rose. "Tavi will help me with the fires. I'm sure she'll be awake soon."

"No, let her rest. I'll help."

I shook my head. "She will want to be with me. You find Rashid."

Firoz winced at the sharp way Rashid's name fell from my tongue. I walked away, regretting any mention of his name.

Firoz followed me. "Why does he anger you?"

Walking as swiftly as I could, I said, "You don't know?"

"The baytahira is just an idea. Besides—" He put his hand against my arm as he caught up to me. "There is work there that isn't bedding others. I wouldn't let you do that."

I grunted and continued walking.

"I'm no fool, Emel. I'm still your Firo. Your *friend!*" he called after me as he slowed. "I know something is not right with you. You can tell me."

I stopped, letting him catch up. I did not want him to shout any louder. Already people were turning in our direction.

"We left together, remember? As we promised each other we would. This was *our* plan," he said, his voice quieting as he closed the space between us. "I know that something has changed with you. I can see it. *Feel* it. You are going to have to trust me . . . trust Rashid. Trust people, Emel. You can't do it all alone."

I could say the same of you, I wanted to tell him.

I had told him everything. When I had accidentally freed Saalim—I had told him what I had done, whom I had loved, how I had ruined everything with a wish. It was right before these soldiers tore through our village. Right before my father was killed, and we were freed.

He had never mentioned what I told him. Did he not believe my words, not believe that a jinni was real? Did he think I was crazed? Or like Saalim, had he forgotten as the ripples of Masira's magic spread?

On the horizon I imagined I saw the sharp peaks of my village jutting out from the sand. I wished I could turn back, not to what I had hated there, but to what I had lost in my pursuit of freedom.

A wind blew, and in its breath I thought it whispered *patience.*

2

SAALIM

Travelers we had met on our journey warned of worsening sandstorms in the east and of nomads who sought out kings. One group of traders insisted they'd found a skull so large someone could live in it. "There was a si'la inside. Stay clear; it's on your path," the man told Amir, pointing at his map to a place where no route existed. Stifling laughter—there were no such things as shapeshifting creatures that lead nomads to their death—we sent the crazed men on their way.

Sixteen nights left of our journey, and we had encountered nothing. Wahir had blessed us, or all nomads were indeed mad. Under the moon's light, I saw more travelers approach from the north. While I had no expectation that their tales would differ at all from those who had come before them, I could not help but notice that they were different. They drew near so quickly, they were surely on horseback. They had not come from far.

"What are your orders?" Nassar said.

"Stop the caravan. I will go to meet them."

Nassar called back to the soldiers and villagers behind us. The message carried through the people like a hatif.

With my mare Farasa's reins in hand, I met Tamam at the front. Tamam was my best soldier, and swiftest with his blades. Broader than the palace bricks and taller than me by a hand, he intimidated with presence alone. When he saw me, he broke the line without a word and mounted Hassas.

There were three travelers awaiting us up ahead, all in dark cloaks with faces hidden in shadows. Their hands, too, were covered as they gripped the reins. Their mounts were a small desert breed, used to sparse grass.

"What do you seek?" I asked.

"Ah. A sea citizen, then," the man at the center said, ignoring my question. The two who flanked him hummed with interest. The man's voice was deeper than I expected from his small stature, and though I could see no weapons on either him or his companions, I placed my hand on the hilt of my sword. I could not discern where they were from.

Farasa was calm beneath me, but Tamam's horse grew agitated—swishing her tail and moving her head from side to side. I loosened my fingers on Farasa's rein, willing her to ignore whatever it was that Hassas found disturbing.

"Who are you?" I pressed.

"Desert dwellers, slaves to the sand. *You* might call us salt chasers." He hissed the words.

Their act was leaving me with little patience. "You can see my face, but I cannot see yours. Respect would have you lower your hood."

The flanking travelers moved to show their faces, but the man at the center raised his gloved hand to stop them. "I am the one who speaks." He threw back his hood.

He did not appear as someone of the desert, despite his claim. His skin was as white as the polished stone in the throne room. As if he'd never seen the sun. His hair had been shorn to the scalp, and in the dim light, I could see the deep scars that arced across his skin with intentional design.

I wanted to turn from him, his face and bearing twisting my gut. "Why have you come to us?"

The man smiled now. "To see if you, too, bring promising accounts." He turned to the rider at his left and nodded.

I was surprised to see that it was a woman who lowered her hood. She was more repulsive than the man—her scalp scarred and shorn the same, but she was so thin I felt that it was a skull I peered at in the night. Tamam whispered to Hassas as she backed away from the foreigners, growing more agitated. Their own horses stood still. Had I not seen their narrow chests heave, I would have thought them to be of stone.

"She doesn't like us," the woman said, watching Hassas. Her words rasped against her tongue and grated against my ears. Even Farasa chuffed at the sound.

Tamam grew impatient. "Promising accounts of what?" he asked.

"The return of the goddess," she said, a smile leered across her hollow face. "We have been waiting for her. She told us to keep it safe until she has returned." The words spilled out of her like blood from a slaughtered goat. "We've kept it safe in the keeper's hands—we have done what the goddess has asked. For lifetimes, we have kept it safe waiting for her! And now we hear—"

"Kept what safe?" I asked.

She did not hesitate. "The box."

"Ghurab!" the man in the center said, turning in his saddle to glare at the woman. She cowered.

"They could not take it, Wahas," Ghurab said, finding again her will as she leaned toward him, scowling. "Even if they wanted to, they could not find it." She smiled again, seeming pleased with what she had done. I cared not what they hid and what they sought. Ghurab continued, "People say the goddess walks amongst us again."

Wahas turned to me. "Elders speak of a cricket that climbed into a treed nest and became a bird. At the desert's edge, a man saw a griffon dive into the waves. She never resurfaced. A thirty-year ruler was lost in the south, and the sands shifted. What have you seen?"

I bristled. South was Alfaar's settlement. He had been a thirty-year ruler. The "Salt King," they had called him. His settlement was under my rule now—or Usman's, who acted as ruler in my absence. Had these people been there, or, Sons, was that where they were headed?

"We have seen nothing," I said. "So if that is all you seek, it is time you leave us."

At last, the third traveler spoke. He did not remove his hood. "Can you spare some water? Or perhaps, something to eat? Our journey home is long."

Nothing about their appearance suggested that they were incapable of fending for themselves in the desert, in spite of what they said, and their manner left me even more suspicious of their purpose. Tamam and I backed our horses away. Tamam shook his head. "We have nothing to spare."

I tightened my grip on my sword, waiting for them to depart.

"We are poor travelers," Ghurab said, her boasting transformed to begging. "Anything small."

"No," I said, lifting my sword from my waist. I edged forward, feeling the need to take blood, to protect my people and home. "Do not ask again."

Wahas's eyes widened when he saw my blade. "He does not carry the scimitar," he whispered. "He is from the City."

Ghurab said cheerily, "Madinat Almulihi."

"Madinat Almulihi," the hooded man repeated.

Wahas looked beyond me as if seeing the caravan for the first time. "If you are from the City . . ." He considered me, then Tamam. He looked south. "You must be the ones they spoke of. The slayer of their Salt King." Wahas laughed. "Then the king is amongst you now." With the slightest press of his heel against his horse, he moved closer.

"Do not come any nearer," I said, again flashing my blade. Farasa moved toward him at my command. One swing and Wahas' life would pour from his neck. Another and Ghurab would follow.

"*You* are the king." Wahas whispered it, leaning toward me.

"Leave us," I said, the tip of my blade a fist away from his cheek. Tamam followed suit and aimed his sword.

Finally, Wahas nudged his horse back.

"It *is* the City's king!" Ghurab hissed.

I should kill them now. The moon glinted off the flat of my sword.

"Is there none upon the throne, then?" the hooded man asked gleefully. "When the king crosses the desert . . ."

I will kill them. Farasa stepped closer and closer.

"The goddess has returned! We must go back," Wahas said finally, turning his horse. "Make haste!"

In a few breaths, their backs were to us as they fled.

Tamam waited for me: I felt the question. Do we kill them? His blade was still ready, Hassas's muscles trembling as she waited for Tamam's call.

"We let them go," I said finally. Regret filled the space the words had left behind.

~~~

"I should have killed them," I said, hating myself for seeking Nassar's approval, but knowing I needed it all the same.

Nassar had an uncanny ability to understand the motives and ways of salt chasers. It was why my father often sent him for negotiations with those people. I would use Nassar for the same.

"They are no threat," Nassar said when I finished telling him what had happened with the nomads.

"They left talking of the empty throne."

"It is not empty," Nassar said patiently. "Azim is there with your army, and he would sooner die than let anything else happen." Like the death of my family.

My brother, who had always been quick to settle disputes with blade, would not have been so lenient with them. They would be dead, and I would be left without worry. His tactics might not be so barbaric.

"Saalim," Nassar warned, as if he knew my thoughts. "These are salt chasers, not the army that attacked Almulihi."

Ignoring Nassar, I squinted ahead. I could almost make out their silhouettes. It was not too late; I could follow them still. "I would rather not lose more civilians, nor the head of my army."

The longer I considered it, the more I realized Nassar was wrong.

"We go now," I called to Tamam. "They cannot live."

"Careful," Nassar hissed at my back as we left. "This is a mistake!"

Ignoring him, Tamam and I rode into the night, following their trail.

Though Nassar was angry, when I glanced back, he had lit the guide light. We would know where to return to when the deed was done.

Though I thought I could see them ahead, the faster we rode, the more trouble I had finding them. Staring at the ground, I saw three lines of hoof prints. We followed the trail until . . .

No.

Their tracks were gone. The sand looked as though it had never been touched. I stared at it, confused. A sand wind could not have passed through; we would have felt it. I had failed, and now the nomads were gone with the knowledge that Almulihi was without a king.

I could not be responsible for more blood lost. This was too soon after the attack on Almulihi. The attack that had stolen my parents from me—the king and queen—and my sisters and brother. Was it these people who had tried to bring my home to its knees, who thought to steal from us our fortune? Visions of my home being invaded, of civilians and soldiers falling to the ground, and blood pooling between bricks clouded my mind.

"We will shorten our passage," I said to Nassar when we'd returned.

"It is impossible."

"We will find a way." I went to the head of the caravan.

Although I wanted to believe Nassar's plea that they were no threat, the nomads left threads of unease pulling at me.

Thinking of all I had lost brought to the surface a loneliness that clung like a shadow. It had been there since arriving in the Salt King's settlement. It called to me—the fathomless darkness. Arriving home would settle it, at least in part. It had to.

We needed to expedite this journey. No matter the cost.

When we stopped at daybreak, the people talked. Some had seen my hurried chase across the sand, and they were drunk with curiosity, asking questions about who had come, what had happened.

"They have spent two dozen nights staring at sand and sky. This is a bit of excitement when there has been no change for so long," Amir said, seated across from me. He stared at his map, the edges held down by piles of sand. Sighing, he said, "There is nothing we can do to safely speed up the journey."

"We must." I thought of Helena, who was set to arrive only days after we did. What would her family think of their daughter being queen of a threatened city?

Amir's narrowed eyes angled at me briefly before returning to his map.

"There is a small oasis here." He pointed to an isolated, marked area. The arcing lines that indicated the long-trusted trade routes did not cross through it. "But I do not know its condition. Going through this oasis might save us two or three days, but there is great risk if it is dry."

"We take it."

Amir exhaled, pouring the sand from his map, and began to roll the parchment. "I do not think it wise."

"We tell everyone to ration food and water, to prepare if need be. There should be enough for us and for the horses to get by."

He shook his head. "We'll have no opportunity to fill stores before the change. If we're to shorten the passage, we change course tonight. There's nothing left to ration other than what remains in our barrels. People could die. Horses could die, even your Farasa."

Our eyes met. He knew where to strike as Farasa had been given to me by my father when I was a young man, but I could not be swayed in this. "We will make do with the water stores we have left. We take the shorter route." I rose and looked to the caravan. It was a calculated risk: Almulihi or these people. I could not place Almulihi's value beneath my soldiers, these salt chasers, nor myself.

"It is reckless," Amir called at my back.

More villagers than I expected had chosen to make the crossing to Almulihi—close to thirty. I could not blame them; their settlement was ragged. I had never seen so many worn and weary people in one place. Their numbers left us little room for mistakes. We had additional barrels for water stores, a number of extra camels, and enough preserved goods to make the planned journey decent for everyone, but still, it was not much. My soldiers had grown thin, and I, too, was tying my belt more tightly.

The sun had barely risen and already I could feel the sweat at my brow. It would be another miserable day. If it wasn't worthwhile to make a swift return to Almulihi to safe-keep it from potential invaders, then at least we would sooner return to where there was movement to the wind, salt in the breeze, the coolness of stone streets. And no damned camels.

Walking down the caravan line, I checked that my men were comfortable. Those resting had made tents with their cloaks and sticks—the villagers had shown them this clever trick when they couldn't find shade—and were sleeping beneath them.

My gaze traveled past the soldiers, and I searched each villager closely. Though I knew I should go back to my station, I did not.

I wanted to see her.

"Emel," I whispered to myself. I liked the sound of her name when I said it.

After I had slain Alfaar, his family had wept and writhed and peered at me like the predator I was. Not Emel. She looked at me not with anger but with curiosity, almost an understanding. It was like she knew me. Why did she watch me that way? What was she seeing?

I thought I would never see her again, but then I learned she would join our caravan. Inside, I was excited as a boy when I saw her at our departure, but after all this time, I still found it impossible to approach her. I was a betrothed king, and she was the daughter of the man I'd conquered.

So far, she also maintained her distance from me. Did she think me an abject king? But the way she watched me created a palpable closeness—as if we shared a history—like I could reach out and examine whatever it was.

I clenched my fists.

Why did I think of her at all? Sons, she was just a salt chaser! Being drawn to her felt out of my control. Like there was something I was not understanding. This was shameful. I resolved to call for Dima as soon as I was home. A few nights spent with her would settle me until I wed Helena.

I tried to shake it off, shake *her* off, but it was an unquenched thirst, and it would burn until I could sate it.

Just beyond a cluster of yoked camels, Emel sat with her sister. I relaxed my fingers, watching her stare at her hands, her mouth downturned. I wanted to touch her, press my thumb to the edges of her lips.

A nearby soldier looked up from the horse he fed. His thin, shadowed face told me he was tired, hungry. "Is all well, my king?"

I shifted from foot to foot. *King.* That was my father. It was not me. Not yet. I still needed to earn that title after I had proven such a failure to my family, to Almulihi. How else could I fail? I thought of my decision to change course. "You heard of the planned route change?"

The soldier nodded slowly and glanced to the goatskin on his hip before looking back to the horse.

I turned from the soldier and strode toward Emel despite my better judgement. My heart quickened.

"Did you hear?" I asked, too loudly. At my question, the camel nearest to me startled and rose to its feet, the others following suit. I staggered back from them.

"Woah, woah," Emel called, scrambling to grasp their lines. They tossed their heads and opened their mouths. I felt a fool as Emel tried to settle them herself. It was clear she did not have much more experience working with them than I had, and another salt chaser soon ran to take Emel's place. He handled them with experienced hands, tutting and whistling, and pulled them from the line to settle.

Emel and I stood staring at each other. It felt as though it was just us standing there. I wanted it to be just us.

"I'm sorry, my king," she said.

I stepped toward her. "Saalim."

"I know." Her eyes stayed on the ground.

Then say it. "Will you be able to ration?" I pointed to her goatskin.

She shook it. It was nearly full.

"You've drunk almost nothing. We've traveled all night."

"It is easy to conserve when it's cool."

"Cool is not how I would have described last night."

She smirked. "This is tepid compared to summer." With dark, heavy robes she looked to be more comfortable under the high sun than I felt in my thin clothes.

I balked, imagining summer. Dirt layered on sweaty skin, the scent of dust and camel dung, buzzing flies sticking to my hands and face. No respite. I hoped I would never experience it myself.

She said, "But then, I was born to endure this."

What else had she endured? I could not imagine her life as a daughter of Alfaar. The man had whored up his daughters to power-hungry men for his own gain. My sisters' lives in Almulihi had been so different, so easy by comparison.

With effort, I said no more and continued down the caravan, checking on the soldiers.

As I walked back to the front, I tried to see Emel again. She was beneath her cloak tent, face in shadows, so I could not see if she watched me as well. Disappointed, I continued by. *Pathetic*, my brother would say if he were still alive.

And he would be right. Almulihi could be my only focus now.

Being out of this damned desert would clear my mind. I would build Wahir the grandest temple in all the world if it meant I would never have to step foot on this sand again.

3

EMEL

"Almost there," we whispered to ourselves with cracked voices and sagging shoulders. The oasis was just past the dune ahead, and we stared at the dune like it was a pile of treasure. Its surface appeared so smooth, I imagined it a pile of salt in my father's throne room. The largest pile in the world, stolen from a jinni.

Stolen by magic.

As if by the same magic, the oasis was not there when we passed the dune. There were no trees, no bushes, no water, nor a smudge of a shadow anywhere that signaled respite lay waiting for us.

It must be too dark to see it; the sun not yet risen. Once it grew lighter, we would see it.

So this was the life of a nomad, to chase wealth regardless of the consequences. Though that was too simple, too superficial. It was not wealth we chased today, not salt. We were seeking water, refuge. We were chasing life, because if we stopped, death would catch us.

As we ventured closer, the travelers began murmuring—a sweep of whispers that rose into loud confusion—all seeing the same thing as I: There really was nothing.

Death would catch us.

Saalim had taken a foolish risk, and he had failed. My shoulders sagged, suspecting what he was feeling, remembering the guilt he'd spoke of when he failed his city.

"A mistake. It is just a little farther," Tavi said hoarsely. Her water was nearly gone. She had conserved what she could, as had I, and that left us both thirsty and weak.

"I am sure," I said. There was not enough water left in the barrels to get us to the next oasis.

As the sun crested the horizon, an irregularity against the sand drew my attention—the oasis! Hope flooded me and I took stumbling steps toward it.

But no. It was only to be a piece of dry wood. My fingers knocked against it: hard and hollow. There were others like it, and the gladness slipped away like water through rocks. Thin cracks spliced the ground, and the sand here was hard as stone.

Was this where water had once been? Where Wahir had once stepped? If so, Eiqab's sun had destroyed it.

Silently, the caravan stopped moving. People stared at the desiccated wood, the dry earth. Few spoke. A sob broke through the silence behind me. Wasteful tears. A woman dropped to her knees, face pressing into the sand. She mumbled a sad prayer, but the sand was too cool for skin to sear. Eiqab would not listen, so her prayer would blow away in the wind.

"Do you have any water?" Firoz said coming up beside me. Shame hushed his words.

I held my breath, wrapping my fingers around the vessel at my hip. I shook my head, careful that the water did not slosh against the sides to reveal my lie. I was too thirsty to share what I had left with anyone. Even Firoz.

Firoz glanced to Tavi, to her goatskin, but he said nothing. Rashid was beside him, staring at the ground. Their eyes sunken, lips dry.

Ahead, Saalim was huddled with his soldiers, a map held open between them. He was standing still, arms tightly crossed over his chest. The men around him were equally still, all watching the king as he peered at the map. I did not need to stand amongst them to know they were as scared as we were.

They spoke for a long time. No villagers approached the men, no one moved from where we had stopped.

My mouth was sticky, my lips cracked and sore. I wanted to take a sip of my water, but I could not now that I'd lied to Firoz who still stood nearby. The world was spinning like I had drunk two goblets of arak. I shivered against the breeze and closed my eyes.

"—two days away. We have nearly two barrels of water that we will divide amongst us. Ration."

Slowly, I opened my eyes, my head aching and body hot beneath the rising sun. I blinked away my sleep, and the man who spoke to us became less of a dark smudge. It was Parvaz.

"Will it be enough?" Rashid asked, hoarsely.

But Parvaz had already moved to the next group. His steps were slow and measured, and every moment the sun pulled more moisture from his body. Soon even he would be dry as the trees.

Death caught us.

Two villagers died that day. They would be left behind for Masira's birds. The travelers talked to comfort themselves, explain why it would not happen to them—the dead had been old, irresponsible with their water. A wife and a brother mourned them, crying without tears. How many more would be unable to rise come the night?

The water was divided amongst us. My goatskin was full. It was to last until the next oasis, two nights away. Before, I was allowed to drink three each day.

I took a long drink and still felt thirsty.

Yes, more would die.

When the night came and the journey was to resume, I rose slowly. My head pounded as the world tipped and turned. My heart raced. With little strength, I helped Tavi up. Standing, we were like the wooden puppets our mothers used to make dance for us—movements jerky, threatening to collapse. I could barely look at her, for each time, guilt ripped away at me. If I had not fed Tavi fantasies of a city by the sea . . .

"Don't," Tavi whispered. She shook her head. "I made this choice, not you."

Pressing my lips together, I reached for her hand. *Thank you, sister.* She took it between her fingers and then let go.

We walked forward, listening to people around us trying to rouse their companions from their stupor. When they could not be roused, when there was the strength, the unconscious were slung over camels' backs. But there was not always the strength, nor the companions. I did not look back. I did not want to see the scattered people that had fallen from our line like the red autumn leaves Saalim once told me of.

The night was a blur. I was hot and then cold, and then hot again. I would wipe my brow, but there was no sweat. Tavi was the same—I'd hear her teeth chatter then see her dropping her cloak from her shoulders.

The journey was taken one step at a time. It felt unending. When I glimpsed Saalim his head was always held high, but his shoulders sagged more and more, his steps smaller and smaller. I tried to wonder about him, what he thought and felt, but I did not have the energy and my eyes would again drop to the sand. The caravan stopped many times, and each time we began again, I felt less of a desire to rise. My gut felt as if it were rolling in on itself, consuming my bones, chewing them to shards.

Sometime in the night, a horse died. Some drank its blood—or did I dream that? Someone had the strength to carve the animal. I sucked at the meat like a piece of fruit Saalim had once conjured from nothing.

Then it was day again. Everyone lay down. Never had so many been so silent.

We were not going to make it to Almulihi. This realization came with a wave of comfort, warm and pleasant. We *were* going to die. Death would serve me far better than stone buildings with climbing vines, a palace with tapering domes. I rolled to my side, letting my face fall into the sand. I closed my eyes and prayed to Eiqab that the end would come swiftly.

Saalim lay near—just beyond my reach. Behind him, brass lanterns flickered orange against the tent wall. At first, the fires pleased me in their warmth. But then they were hot. They burned my throat. I tried to gather sand so that I might douse the flames but my fingers hit a woven carpet. I looked to Saalim— *get rid of the lanterns*—but his eyes were closed. His hands were by his head, and on his wrists were golden bands with edges that seemed to melt into his hands, as though they had been forged from his blood.

He was a jinni again. I moved to wake him, but I was too tired. Staying where I was, I watched him breathe. His face was smooth in his sleep, always so relaxed when he was away from my father.

But the burning in my throat became too great. I needed him to get rid of the fires.

"Please," I whispered.

Saalim's eyes opened. "Emel, what is it?" He sat up, his face creasing in concern.

"The lanterns are too hot."

"They are gone." And so they were.

"Come closer," I said. He came, lying beside me, and I draped my arm over his chest. His heart beat fast like mine. Breathing him in was like gulping in relief. My hand fell along his ribs and I closed my eyes. I would never move from here.

"What else do you need?"

"My throat still burns."

"Water, then?"

Sons, yes. That *was* what I needed. I nodded.

"Then you will have it."

I waited. Nothing came.

"What else?" he asked.

"There is no water."

"There will be. Is there anything more?" Saalim moved to rise.

My father must be waking soon. He would expect Saalim at his side. "Is it time already?"

Saalim nodded. "Hurry, tell me your final wish."

The untethered longing washed through me. Could he feel it?

"I wish for you." I tried pulling him close, but I could not, weak as I was. I pressed my hand to his skin, feeling his breaths.

"I am here."

"I wish for you even when you are not."

Sadness swirled in his eyes, unsaid words waited on his tongue. He held up his hands, and the golden bands were gone. "It is too late," he said softly. "I am just a man."

Suddenly voices clamored outside. I closed my eyes, wishing away the world that threatened our peace. I could not say goodbye to him again.

My eyes opened to blistering sun. The tent was gone. Saalim was gone. Only the voices remained. And the burn of my throat. *No.*

"Saalim?" I said weakly. I already knew he was not there. I was in the middle of the desert with the caravan scattered around me, waiting for death.

The voices drew my attention—loud in their vigor. People were sitting, the bottom of their vessels turned to the sky as they poured water into their mouths. I sat up as quickly as I could. Why were they being so reckless?

As I moved, I felt my own goatskin heavy at my side. Heavy as though it were . . . full? In my hands I felt the liquid move.

"Water, Emel," Tavi said from behind me. Her voice was smoother, not so fragile and dry.

"Water?"

She nodded. Opening the goatskin, I slowly tipped it to my lips. "Bless Wahir," I said. I allowed myself two long drinks, then held the water at arm's length, resisting the temptation to drink it all at once. Tavi was doing the same. We knew what came if Eiqab saw us drink Wahir's gift too quickly: He would take us in his fist and shake us. Sometimes until we died.

"Where did it come from?" I asked.

She shrugged. "Barrels are full. No one knows. No one saw."

"We were all sleeping."

Tavi nodded.

A chill swept through me as I remembered my dream. Had it been magic? Saalim was not still a jinni. Was he?

What if he was?

I shook my head and turned to where Saalim's men were clustered. I could not see him. Did he still wear the golden cuffs that bound him to Masira? My fingers flew to the sack at my side, feeling the hard golden cuffs within. It was impossible.

Suddenly eager, I attempted to stand. But the haze had not yet left my mind, and I wobbled on hands and knees before I sat back on the ground.

As the day progressed, the questions only multiplied. No one understood, and the soldiers were not forthcoming with answers.

"Where did the barrels get filled?" I asked one as I scooped kuskus—finally stewed now that we had water again—from the iron pot. I glanced to the water stores. People were lined up, waiting to get more. There was more than enough to take us to the next oasis.

He shrugged. "King Saalim has not said."

No, he would not have. Especially if he did not know.

The more the water washed away my confusion, the more unsettled I became. What explanation was there other than magic? Magic did not come freely. What would Masira want in return for the water? Shivering, I pulled my arms across my chest as if to protect myself from the goddess.

I had toyed too much with magic when Saalim was a jinni. Too many wishes that had gone awry, too many threads loosened by what we had done, people who were changed.

Saalim had told me that when he granted a wish, none would remember what had been except the one who wished and the jinni who granted it. But he was wrong, because people did not forget completely. It was why Firoz had been so strange after my wish rescued him from a hanging for his collusion with the secretive Dalmur. It was how my father knew Saalim when he looked into his face, before he was pinned to the ground by Saalim's sword.

My wish for freedom from the Salt King had freed Saalim from being a jinni and resurrected a city of stone by the sea. That magic spanned the desert.

Had something horrid come from my tampering? The fear of it had sworn me away from magic for good. It no longer had a place in my life. Even though it had brought me some of my happiest moments, it too had caused some of my most tragic.

Sabra. No, I could not bear to think of my older sister, of what consequences my wishes had visited upon her. I turned to my younger sister instead: Tavi was wiping the remains of her kuskus with her finger and bringing it to her lips. Already her eyes were brighter. She looked down at her bowl.

"How do you feel?" I asked.

"Much better. Still, I am not eager for our journey tonight."

Silently, I watched her.

Her gaze met mine. Did she see my worry? She said, "I will only regret all this if we don't make it to Almulihi." The corner of her mouth turned up into an almost smile. "Miss out on all that food, eh?"

I stared at my empty bowl. "If I hadn't—"

"Stop," she implored, the levity gone. "We are heading toward a new life. We cannot look behind us."

Through the length of our journey our roles had reversed. Now, she did not need me like I needed her. Despite her fatiguing body, the farther away we got from our home, the stronger she became. My baby sister was like my mother.

"Think what you will about my being here," Tavi continued. "But I only feel relief." She looked around us slowly. Her eyes were soft, her body relaxed, as she leaned back onto her hands. "Every day, I am somewhere I wasn't before. I'm no longer a prisoner in that tent." She said *tent* with such malice. "What would I be doing now that Father's court has been picked apart? I know nothing other than being an ahira. People would not have accepted us in their lives. I would rather be here." The words tumbled out of her now. "I had not realized how much I dreaded that life. Hated it. Muhami who cared more for our father's salt than me, pulling me to bed. You taught me that I deserved more, Emel."

I remembered when I finally convinced her to sneak from the palace as I did. She saw the village for the first time, saw the horizon.

Tavi sighed. "I am weak and exhausted, but too, I am glad."

I felt flickers of happiness, listening to Tavi.

"I am grateful," she said after she took a drink of water. "For this." She held up her goatskin. "And that our lives as ahiran are gone from us. We never have to face it again, eh?"

But that wasn't true. Rashid planned to find us lodgings in the baytahira. After nearly perishing beneath Eiqab's sun, I knew I would do whatever it took to survive in Madinat Almulihi. I was sure that the need for coin would be stronger than our resolve. After all, we were experts at leaving our pride behind.

I shivered beneath the sun.

4

EMEL

The dunes encircled Madinat Almulihi like a nest, and I could not climb them fast enough. I thought of Rafal, the defiant storyteller who had been executed at my father's command. He said the city was surrounded by stony cliffs that could not be traversed by camel. But there were no cliffs, only smooth slopes of sand. When Saalim was freed and Madinat Almulihi was restored, the desert had changed, too.

Finally, I saw the city. At first, it appeared as scattered piles of salt bricks. The white stone buildings gleamed dully under the sun. But it was not the city that held my attention, nor that of my companions. It was the immense stretch of blue sparkling beyond it.

The sea.

Tavi did not believe that it was water, convinced that it was Eiqab's trick again. We had seen so many of them as we traveled—inviting pools swirling on the sand's surface, only to disappear as we neared.

"How can you be sure?" she asked me with wide, hungry eyes.

"The legends say so," I said, unable to tell her the truth. I had once been here and had walked across crumbled stones with Saalim. I had run across the shore as the ocean licked my heels. I had watched mewling white birds—*gulls*, they were called—soar above the sea and sit atop fallen walls. I had lain with

Saalim, our limbs entwined together, our breath in each other's lungs. She would not believe it. Magic was not real, after all. I had not believed in magic myself until it knelt before me in the form of a jinni, washing the blood of slain men from my hands.

Seeing Madinat Almulihi ushered the swift return of those memories and with it, all of my worries. I had gone on this journey to see if King Saalim shared more with the Saalim I remembered than his golden eyes. I knew it was foolish to think I could charm a king, coax the answers I hoped to hear out of him. I was a castoff king's daughter, a tired ahira—used, soiled, unworthy. And if he did not want me? If I came all this way to find that Saalim did not know me from another salt chaser? I sucked in a breath, imagining life in an unfamiliar place without the person I wanted most.

As we neared Madinat Almulihi, it emerged as if it had been forged by gods. It was a beacon of wealth, of dreams. Stepping on the stone streets after so long on the sand felt like waking from a daze. Suddenly, we were somewhere real.

At the entrance to the city, Saalim was met by two riders. He and several of the soldiers left us behind as they rode away with him.

"Has something happened?" I asked Kofi, a nearby soldier. My voice rose in worry.

"Nothing," he said, frowning at me. "They are returning home."

To the palace. My steps faltered. So that was it? He was gone from me so suddenly. I do not know why I expected something more, one last opportunity to speak to him. There was no way our paths would cross easily. How would I find him again? I bit my cheek and stared ahead but saw only all I had lost.

"It is like nothing I imagined," Tavi whispered.

Blinking, I finally saw the city we walked through.

We passed stone homes covered with wooden rooftops, many of them alongside livestock enclosures. Lines with clothing told me that these were peoples' homes, and the green plants that crept across the walls and filled crevices between bricks told me that this was nothing like my settlement. Here, life flourished.

We traveled down what seemed like the main road. It was wide, and we shared it with people carting goods, children chasing chickens, and unfamiliar soldiers on horseback. If it had not been evident by our dusty clothes and weary limbs, then it was abundantly apparent by our awe that we were from elsewhere. The soldiers, eager to get home, tried to hurry us along, but we were slow with curiosity, gawking at this, elbowing each other to talk of that.

Residents stood in their doorways watching us, frowning with arms crossed and eyes narrowed. Where there were no people, there was a carved piece of wood that served as a door. For privacy, Saalim had explained to me once. I marveled at the luxury. There were little holes I remembered Saalim called windows, too. They let in the wind and the light, he had told me. Some had pots hanging in them, green spilling from the edges. Others had delicate fabric coverings. And some had tiny faces with curious eyes that watched.

This place was nothing like the deserted, crumbled ruins I remembered when the jinni Saalim brought me here. It felt so long ago, but it had not even been half a year.

A gust of wind blew across my face. I inhaled and smelled the sea—the wet life—whirling with the dryness of the desert.

As we walked further into the city, the buildings grew larger, the homes and shops closer together, the people louder and more jubilant. But, too, bolder in their displeasure. I could count on both hands the number of times I heard someone call to us that we should return to where we'd come from.

The bitter reception did not diminish our enchantment with the city, though I cringed with each insult.

At a wide intersection, down one street stood an impossible number of shops with beautiful storefronts. They had brightly painted walls and swinging signs each more elaborate than the next. People swarmed between them, but movement from a rooftop stole my gaze. There, atop the busy shop at the corner, was a woman standing alone on the flat roof. She leaned on the edge as we passed. Something about her was familiar. The robes she wore were thick and long like mine, but it was her face that held my attention. She looked at us warmly, almost welcoming. A stark contrast from the others.

"It never ends," Tavi said in awe, untroubled by the jeers. Her eyes darted from the buildings, to the wide stones underfoot, to the bright plants that crept down the stone walls. She touched a wall carefully, as if it would break, then gently brushed her finger along a leaf. "It's so soft."

I felt it, too. We giggled, the surreality heady.

"What're you doing?" a woman with a shrill voice said as she stepped out of the home we were touching.

I stammered incoherent sounds.

"Nothing for you here. Mind your hands and keep moving." She jutted her chin forward, and we both looked away, hurrying to the middle of the street so that we would not be tempted again. As we walked away, she mumbled something about salt chasers.

"They are unhappy to see us," I whispered.

Tavi shrugged. "They don't know us, eh?"

In the cracks between the stones grew flowers I recognized—their petals closed tightly in the sun.

"Moon jasmine." I pointed to the flowers. "They open at night."

Tavi looked at them swaying in the wind and smiled.

Behind us, I could no longer see the desert—only the low dunes that swelled above the city. The deeper we traveled into Madinat Almulihi, shepherded along by the soldiers, the more apprehensive I became. I knew the city was large, but I had not expected to feel so small.

"Where are we going, do you think?" Tavi asked.

I shrugged, wondering the same. Those from my settlement were gathered together. The further we walked, the closer we huddled. Our home was childish by comparison, small and fragile. Shame burned my face as I thought of the pride my family—and sometimes even I—felt of our home. The largest in the desert, the center of the salt trade! The Salt King, the most powerful man! My father thought himself a god sitting atop a throne of salt. Now more than ever I understood that he was a feeble man with stolen treasure and only an illusion of power. That village had been my whole world until Saalim had shown me there was so much more to it. Now I was seeing the world. And I was not ready.

The people of Almulihi continued to stare. They appeared unusual in their bright clothing with open necks and bare faces, hair whipping up with the wind, and they all spoke with the same melodic cadence to their words.

Firoz and Rashid came toward us from farther up the line. Firoz's smile stretched to his ears.

"We know how to get to the baytahira," Firoz said, walking at our side as he continued to explain. "Amir said we'll be able to get there on foot quickly. We've already passed it, actually."

Rashid continued the explanation, but I did not listen. Why had they asked Amir? What if he told Saalim? He would think me so soiled, he'd never let me step foot in the palace.

"We need to find a woman called Kahina, the proprietress of the baytahira. She'll find us a place to stay and work," Rashid said.

My stomach turned. "Good," I said. "Everything is working out, eh?"

Firoz and Rashid agreed and began discussing what they would see and do in the city, unbothered by our cold welcome.

". . . heard the game-houses are huge. People serving drink and food until dawn!" Firoz's smile grew impossibly wider.

Rashid said, "We're in a real city now."

Tavi's pace had slowed, and she fell behind them. "I don't want to," she whispered, staring at Rashid's back. It was like she waited for me to give her the alternative, the other secret option I'd been holding behind my back this whole time.

"I don't either. But what else is there? We can't separate." Where would Tavi and I go in this enormous, hostile place? "It's just for now. We need somewhere to sleep and . . ."

"Work," she spat.

"I'm sure this Kahina will know other ways to get coin." I could not meet her gaze.

Tavi stared straight ahead, her mouth flattening into a tight line.

I pressed on. "We have to stay together."

"I know."

"Well," Rashid said as he and Firoz came to a stop. "Are we going?"

I had no good reason to delay, but I had to try. "Not yet. I want to see where they take us."

Where were they taking us?

When the sky began to purple, we arrived at a break in the crush of buildings. Smooth swaths of stone were punctuated with gardens that led to wide stairs. Smaller structures surrounded the expanse like children at their father's feet. At the center of it all was the palace.

My shoulders fell back, my fists relaxed. *This* was what legends told of Madinat Almulihi. Glinting domes perched atop white-washed towers. Windows with flickering light sprinkled the walls. Wide balconies stretched over the palace like crossed arms.

And somewhere inside was Saalim.

The steps ahead were lined with soldiers who waved when they saw the caravan approach. It was an unexpected gesture of welcome. Those whom I assumed were servants rushed from low, open-walled buildings adjacent to the palace. They went to the animals, hauling the barrels and wares away. The camels were gathered and led back down the street while the unloaded horses were taken to the buildings whence the servants had come.

I gasped. "They're not kept there?" The walls were as pristine as that of the palace, and the floors were cleaner than my father's halls. Fine quarters indeed for work animals.

Tavi said, "Perhaps we can stay with the horses instead of the whores."

We continued forward, stepping slowly up the stairs as we took it all in. The walls lining the stairs were the smoothest stone I'd ever seen. In front of the palace were more gardens with flowers so bright, I could see them at dusk. Groomed trees lined the entrance in perfect symmetry.

Though I could scarcely see them, I knew the windows and doors were bordered with small, decorative tiles, one of which lay in my sack.

Where in the palace was that tile missing now?

My gaze continued upward to the domes that towered above us. When Saalim and I found shelter in one that had crumbled to the shore, it had seemed immense, but seeing it atop the palace was even more unbelievable, as if they were placed by Masira's hands. We must be near the sea now . . . yes, I could hear it.

The rush of waves was incessant in its song. I searched for the sea, longing to see it again now that we were so close, but buildings obstructed my view.

"Keep moving!" Parvaz yelled, swinging his arms toward the stairs. "We're all hungry!" He repeated it over and over. I empathized with his urgency. If a meal was promised at the end of this journey, I wouldn't want to be shuffling us around. We moved very slowly, every turn revealing something new and fascinating. For once, our eyes were hungrier than our stomachs.

"Come on," Firoz said, grabbing my elbow and tugging me back down the stairs.

I shook my head, yanking free from his grip. "No. First, we go the palace."

"Do you know what they call the man who tries to keep me from food?" Tavi said grimly. "A vulture's meal." Her smile could not hide her irritation.

"Yes, we all should eat," I agreed. Perhaps Saalim would be inside. "We will go after."

Rashid said, "We shouldn't arrive too late. Kahina may be hard to find at night."

I lowered my voice to a purr. "Aren't women in the baytahira *only* found after dark?"

He said nothing.

I took Tavi's elbow. "Come. First, we eat."

We were led into a large room with an arched, elaborately tiled ceiling. At its center, Amir stood with Nassar. Two disconcertingly vacant thrones sat behind them. A few soldiers lingered beside them. I searched for Saalim, but he was absent.

The floor was layered in the dust our clothes and shoes carried in, and I could almost see it in the air. We did not belong in this glistening palace. In the

immensity of the room, with most of Saalim's soldiers having left us, I understood finally how many we had lost on this journey. There were perhaps half of
the villagers standing with me than had began the journey.

"Welcome to Madinat Almulihi," Nassar said. He did not speak loudly, so
we were forced to silence our whispers to hear. It was strange seeing Nassar here.
For years, I had known him only as my father's vizier. I'd even hated him. But I
did not know he had been trying to sabotage my father—to find Saalim—all that
time. Now, he was Saalim's advisor. I tried to slow my rapid heart and relax my
arms by my side. *He is no threat*, I told myself over and over.

Nassar went on. "As you have a new king, your loyalty to him will be shown
in your respect for our city and customs. You will earn your keep here, as we do
not tolerate beggars."

Kofi scoffed and glared at our group.

"You are invited to one last meal provided by King Saalim, after which you
can rest for the night in our guest quarters should you have nowhere else to go.
You are to find your own place in the City by morning." Nassar directed us to
the next room, equally large but much less extravagant.

Long tables were set with piles of food. Behind them, fires and counters
held still more food, tended to by palace staff. The feast reminded me of my
father's winter and summer festivals—only, if this was for poor villagers, I could
not imagine a feast for nobles.

"We will remain here, along with Nika and Mariam, should you have
additional needs." Nassar gestured to two women who stood at the periphery
of the room. Their clothing was soft and flowed with such delicacy, it had to
be the thinnest fabric in the world. They had wide scarves, equally delicate,
draped over their shoulders. They were so elegant, they looked to be a queen
and princess of legends. One had wide, dark eyes and a soft smile. She was
much older than the other, whose eyes were narrowed, scanning us as though
taking count.

I turned to Firoz. "Let's stay until morning." I might have one last opportunity to see Saalim. I vowed to myself that I would speak to him.

Rashid overheard. "We go tonight."

"It's foolish," I said, trying to hide the fury that thrummed through me. Why the rush? "We know we have a place to stay here. We don't know what to expect—"

"Emel. Tavi." It was Amir. "Come to me." He beckoned us, eyeing Rashid and Firoz warily.

"We have work for you in the palace," Amir said when we were near.

We gaped at him. The palace? I bit my cheeks to hide my smile. Eiqab be praised! Tavi's hand gripped mine.

"Ah," he said as if understanding. "It requires work to earn coin, see. The coin you use to buy what you need—"

"No," I said perhaps a little too harsh. "We know how coin works." I looked around, unsure how to ask the question. "But why? We are . . . unskilled."

He nodded, understanding. "Honor. Children of a slain ruler should be provided for."

That was not the desert way. Children of a slain king obeyed the new king lest they face death. But I would not dwell on the differences between the people of the sea and those of the sand. He said they had work for us.

Tavi and I did not have to go to the baytahira! We did not have to face our past to find our future. Relief washed over me like cool water. I looked to my sister and saw she understood the same.

"What will we do?" I said, turning back to Amir.

"You will be housed and trained by those who work for the palace. They are people the king trusts." Amir leaned in and smiled warmly. "And I do, too. They are good people. You will find that, with them, you are welcome."

It was too much to believe. Tavi and I, *together* and *safe*. We would be working for the palace. Perhaps Masira was not so devious after all. Saalim's path and mine would cross with certainty! I pulled her arm into my side, squeezing her hand even harder. It was everything we hoped for, and I felt like the threads, finally, were being pulled together.

There was a tapestry of a future I could see. The image appearing before me was bright and beautiful.

This is why we had made the journey. It would be worth it in the end.

"Emel," Amir said, "you will find lodgings with Altasa, the palace healer. She is old and tired. She said she needs strong arms and an even stronger will. When I told her about you, she thought you would serve best." He grinned.

"Tavi has arms even stronger than mine. We will serve her well," I said.

Amir shook his head, frowning behind his beard, and looked to my sister. "You will live and work with Saira. Her husband is a great fisherman, and he supplies us with most of our fish. Enormous hauls when he comes ashore. The best seabream. Saira said she would happily take help."

"Where will we live?" I asked, trying to envision where a healer and a fisherman's family would find a shared space.

"Altasa lives on the palace grounds, of course. In the gardens. Saira lives along the west canal. It's an easy walk from here."

I shook my head slowly. "Amir," I said, my voice weak. "While I am grateful for this, we cannot be separated. She is my sister. Is there somewhere we can stay together?"

"This is what has been arranged. If you will not have it, then do what you please." He shrugged sadly. "Altasa and Saira are good women. You will be treated well, fed, and have a place to sleep. You will have plenty of opportunity to see each other. Do not fear." He lifted his arm as if to lay it on my shoulder, but then he reconsidered and dropped it back to his side.

Tavi said, "It is our only offer?"

Amir nodded.

I spun to face her, "We'll figure something out. We stay together."

Tavi looked from me, to the tables laden with food, to Amir. She glanced behind me, where Rashid and Firoz were waiting. To the ground, she said, "Not much choice, eh?" With immense resolve, her gaze locked on Amir's. "I would be happy to help Saira." Her words were as solid as the ground we stood upon, but I could hear the fear that pressed against the floor, searching for the cracks in which to take root.

Amir stared at me, waiting for my response. My mouth hung open. This was not what I wanted.

Slowly, I nodded.

"Good!" Amir clapped his hands together. "Nika will make introductions after we eat. Now, come join us."

He went to the table and piled his plate high, as though making up for the long journey.

"There is another way," I said, cringing. *The baytahira would not be so bad, would it?*

"I'd rather be away from you than to be *there*. Besides, he said we'd only be a short walk away from one another." She smoothed down her robes. "Now, I'm hungry." She followed Amir, not looking back at me once.

Finding Firoz and Rashid, I told them our plan.

Firoz drew back. "How quickly you abandon us."

Rashid pressed his hand to Firoz's back.

"The baytahira . . ." I began, unsure of what to say. Firoz looked at me with so much anger, I wanted more to put out the flames of his fury than give him a meaningful explanation. "This will be better, see, because we will get coin and we can all find a place to stay together sooner. We'll have a job right away, and—"

"We were supposed to do this *together*." Firoz spat the last word. "Nothing has changed, has it? You belong in the palace. I belong in the streets." He turned from me. Rashid looked at me sadly, then followed Firoz without another word, without a meal.

As quickly as they had come together, the threads of my future were coming undone.

5

EMEL

On my insistence, Nika took us to Saira's home first. It was not far
from the palace, but the path was convoluted, especially at night.
One winding street after another. The roads grew narrower, allowing for two or maybe three people to walk side by side.

"Most of us live here," Nika said. The ground, slick from the misty air,
glowed orange from the light inside the homes. They looked to be warm inside. I pulled my cloak around me, wishing I could be by a fire, too. These
homes were smaller than those at the edge of the city. They shared walls and low
rooftops. Like the others we had seen, their belongings were everywhere—hanging from doorways and windows, strung across the streets by rope. We edged
around people drinking in chairs tucked under their windows, cloaks wrapped
around their shoulders against the damp air. Sweet-smelling smoke—different
from the Buraq rose—was puffed into the air by drowsy men.

We emerged from the narrow lane walled by homes to a street where the
homes faced a wide strip of water. Tavi and I faltered.

Nika smirked. "The west canal." She pointed as she spoke. "That way to
the sea, and this way to the city."

Though I had never seen a boat, Saalim had described them well enough
that I understood they were the vessels I saw bobbing atop the water. Tied up

alongside the canal, most were empty, gently swaying with the invisible heart-beat of the sea. One man stood in a boat, rocking with it as he picked up full crates and set them on the road. A young boy ran to the crate and pulled it across the road through the open door of a nearby home.

We stopped in front of a doorway that appeared the same as all the others, except that large barrels were beside it. There was a sharp, foul odor coming from them, and when the woman who lived in the home walked out to greet us, I smoothed my frown.

"Two of them?" she asked Nika, nodding toward us. The woman was tall and thin, with high cheek bones that cast deep shadows on her cheeks in the firelight. Her hair was braided tightly against her head.

"No, just one. Tavi."

Tavi took a tiny step forward, her fingers toying with her robe.

"I am Saira," the woman said with a tired smile. She narrowed her eyes and looked at me.

"Her sister," Nika said. "She'll be with the palace healer."

Saira nodded, then turned back to Tavi. "Well, come on. I'll show you your bed. Keep quiet. The children are asleep."

Tavi and I embraced for a long time.

"Save your coin," I whispered into her ear. "I'll visit you often. As soon as there's enough, we'll find a place we can live together, eh?"

Tavi hummed agreement, and I heard the tightness in her throat, felt the tremor in her hands at my back. Did she feel the tremor in mine?

"It'll be fine," I said, not believing myself one bit. "I'll come tomorrow."

Nika interrupted. "I need to take you to Altasa before it gets any later." She sounded bored.

I separated from Tavi and watched her walk into Saira's home. I tried to move away, to follow Nika down the road, but my feet were rooted to the ground. I was abandoning the only family I had left.

"Find your own way, then," Nika called down the road. I looked at her retreating back, the bright fabric flashing out from under her cloak, before looking again to Saira's closed door.

"Good," Nika said when I caught up to her, though nothing sounded *good* coming from her. "Altasa has been working for the palace longer than I've been alive," she said as we walked. "She knows everything that happens. Nothing slips by her." Her gaze shot to mine when she said this.

We turned onto the large road, nearly empty aside from a few people. They leaned on each other and drunkenly sang a song about the sea. After we scurried across the road, Nika asked, "So why did you come here?"

"I wanted to see the ocean," I said.

"You had not seen it before?" She did not hide her surprise.

"It is something of legends where I am from."

"And where are you from exactly?"

I told her of my village in the middle of the desert.

"Ah, that's right. The 'Salt King.'" Nika raised a finger as though it had caught on a memory. "He had a reputation."

I nodded. "He was a longtime king." He was a ruler for nearly thirty years—unprecedented when younger and stronger men were constantly challenging him for his throne. Of course, no one knew he had a magical jinni that kept him in power.

"That is not what I mean. I heard he sold his daughters to nobleman."

She must not have known I was one of those daughters, and I did not want it revealed with an explanation of how exactly he used the ahiran.

"And that he would host parties where he would . . ." Her voice twisted with gossiping pleasure. "Bed his wives under the watch of guests."

Thinking of something to discuss that might serve as a distraction, my gaze stayed trained on the palace. As we traveled up steps, I said, "I have the sense people here don't like those from the desert."

Nika laughed.

Upon entering the palace, we passed through an enormous room called the atrium—with an actual fountain of water!—before we were outside again. The path we took sat between flowering shrubs and long, rectangular ponds. The soft splashing told me there were even more fountains here. The two arms of the palace cradled these gardens.

Off the stone path, a spongey plant covered the ground. Nika walked on it without hesitation, so I did the same. It felt strange, though, to be walking on something so precious. The leaves touched my feet through my sandals. They were sharp and cool and made my toes itch.

Nika stepped over a small brick divide that went up to my shins. Had I not been watching her, I would have tripped over it.

"Altasa's gardens," she said without flourish.

We had certainly left the manicured palace grounds. Here, there seemed to be no order. Treetops loomed into shadows overhead, the garden torches lighting them just enough for me to know they were full of leaves. Curls and tangles of plants writhed across our path, and I crunched through them as Nika did. Lambent light peeked through the tree trunks before us.

"There's a path, you twit!"

The voice came from the direction of the light.

"These weeds would have me believe otherwise," Nika yelled back.

Leaves rustled, and the shape of a tiny woman took form. I could only see her silhouette—her body and wild hair. A gnarled finger pointed to the ground. "It is here!" She ushered us to the side, and though it was indeed mostly covered in plants, I was standing on a solid path.

Nika sighed. "This is Emel."

Altasa's stare held me fast. "The salt chaser they promised me?"

Nika nodded. "If you've no other need for me, I will go." She hesitated, and when Altasa said nothing, she turned to leave. "Wahir watch over you," Nika whispered to me as she passed. It did not sound like an invocation of goodwill.

"Follow me," Altasa said. "And keep to the path!" Then she mumbled something about my needing to clear the path tomorrow.

I bunched my cloak in my fist as I looked at the house. It was close quarters to be sharing with someone who cared more for the plants than me. I prayed

Tavi received a warmer welcome. Behind me, the palace soared up through the trees, white walls glowing orange. Somewhere within those walls, Saalim slept.

"You're not a princess anymore. Get your eyes off that palace."

So she knew who I was.

"I'll show you where you sleep." She poked at the door with her cane, and it swung open. The smell of spices and smoke wafted out along with an intense heat. Using the wall for support, Altasa stepped inside.

The room was small, mostly occupied by shelves stacked from floor to ceiling. Reminiscent of the healer's home in my village, they were covered in jars containing various powders, liquids, chopped plants, and other things unfamiliar. Some were marked with scratchy letters, but most were not. Corked vials of all shapes and sizes were scattered amongst them.

Hanging above me were dried plants and flowers tied in clusters. I arched my neck, staring at flowers I had never before seen. I could have studied them all day.

A drop of sweat fell down my temple, and I looked at the roaring fire tucked in a brick alcove. There was no smoke inside, despite the large fire that burned. How could that be?

"I need a moment . . ." Altasa took several shaky breaths. "Before I show you the house."

The healer was frail, the shape of her bones visible through her hands and arm. She walked bent nearly double so that her unruly hair, kept in some kind of long braid, lay nearly flat on her back. Her thin lips would have been unseen if not for fattened cheeks that pulled her lower lip down into a pout. But her eyes creased in a way that suggested she had once been happy.

With her cane, she nudged a chair out from the wooden table at the room's center. The tabletop was stained with reds, browns, and greens, and had various tools strewn across it. When she was finally seated, she laid her head back and breathed heavily.

"Just got back from a long trip, see." She took deep breaths. "My body isn't what it used to be. Water's there." She pointed to a black kettle beside the fire. "Sage is there."

"Of course," I said, hurrying to the kettle, looking in the direction of the sage, hidden somewhere amongst the shelves. My head spun with childhood memories of watching my mothers prepare tea. As an ahira, I had never made it.

The kettle was heavy as I carried it to the fire.

"Are we to drink hot water?" Altasa said.

Setting the kettle down, I stood and went to the shelves. Humiliation kept me from looking at her. I stared at the jars, but saw nothing. If I couldn't even make tea, how would I be of any use to her? I couldn't let her see how little I knew. If Tavi resolved to live with Saira, I would do the same with Altasa. There were dozens of bundled herbs and plants. Picking them up one by one, I smelled them and prayed I would remember the scent of sage. Finally, I found a thick bundle of soft leaves. This was it.

About to dump the bundle into the pot, Altasa snapped, "Sons, only a few leaves!"

"And the honey?" I asked, proud I remembered. Oh, how I loved the sweet sage tea when my head ached after a drunken night with a muhami.

She chuffed. "You really are a salt chaser, aren't you? Here, we don't need our tea sweet. We have cakes and pastries to satisfy the tongue."

With a delicacy that belied my frustration, I placed three leaves in the pot. Picking up the kettle, I moved to set it atop the flames.

"Planning to lose that hand?" Altasa asked. "A good idea if you don't want to have to do anything around here."

Hesitating, I looked around.

She groaned loudly. "The hook is there. Use it to hang the kettle over the flames."

I picked up a thick metal rod with a hooked end and clumsily used it to attach the kettle above the flames. Kneeling down, I saw a large hole that the smoke escaped through. I bent lower to see where it went.

"It's a chimney. Smoke travels up it and goes outside," Altasa said. Her voice softened. "I have forgotten what it was like."

"What it was like?" I asked as I stood.

"Being in the city for the first time."

I waited, staring at the flames.

"I was a salt chaser, too." She watched me carefully. "Everything is different when people live behind stone walls, isn't it? You can't hear voices on the other side. What are they hiding?" Tilting her head toward the table, she said, "Sit."

In front of me, a pestle lay on its side, its end coated with sticky orange. The mortar had been wiped clean. There was rolled parchment, one piece loosened just enough that I could see it was a correspondence of some kind. I squinted to see if I could make out the words, but my reading was too poor and the light too low.

"Like you, I lived under camelhair wool and wooden posts, searching the horizon for windswept dunes and trees that marked an oasis."

"If you are like me, then you know we are not all salt chasers, eh?" I leveled my tone to hide the anger in my voice.

She laughed, and it sounded more like a dog's bark. "Bah! It's in your blood. You may not have traveled for riches, but your father did. And his father, too. We of the sand," she waved her gnarled fingers between us, "are born knowing one thing: comfort, power . . ." She took a slow breath. "They're bred from wealth. Just look at where we are." She waved her hand.

Altasa was not wrong. My father and his ancestors had been nomads seeking salt mines. If mines were not found, they at least hoped to find others with whom they could trade for salt. Salt was rare, and it was essential for life.

Only when my father found the oasis that hid Saalim did he end his travels. With a wish, he was given enough salt to make him the most powerful ruler of the desert. He had been a salt chaser until he found it. Then, he was the Salt King.

She continued. "Why have you come here, if not for wealth? For a life better than the one you left?"

"Not for coin," I said.

"For love, then." She said it like she knew it to be true.

Ignoring her, I said, "I don't need an excess of salt nor coin to find a better life."

"It will help you find it faster."

"Perhaps. And you?" I asked. "Did you come for the salt?"

Slowly, she said, "Revenge." She flashed a crooked smile.

I did not veil my disbelief. "Did you find it?"

"Almost."

Suddenly, she banged her cane onto the tiled floor. I jolted, tearing my eyes from the dancing flames. She stood more swiftly than I thought possible and grumbled about showing me where to sleep. Then, "If you don't take that pot off now, we won't be drinking anything tonight."

I hurried to unhook the kettle and set it onto a metal trivet before following her through a closed door. She led me into a hallway so cool and fresh by comparison I hoped it was where I slept. Then she pushed open a door and directed me in. This was where I would sleep.

She pointed at one of the other closed doors in the hallway. "Wouldn't nose around in there unless you've plans to see a naked old woman."

I thought I would sleep like a babe after milk, but when I finally lay down, my eyes would not stay closed. After nearly forty nights of traveling in the darkness and begging them to remain open, they finally decided to obey.

And, too, the bed was so soft that when I finally dozed, I dreamed the ground was swallowing me, and I startled awake.

Giving up, I went to the window. It was as wide as my shoulders and as tall as my chest. I drew back the curtain and stared out at the blackness, feeling the wind and listening to the leaves and sea.

⌒〜ℓ⌒〉⌒〜ℓ⌒⌐

When morning came, I sat at the edge of my bed, staring at the room and disbelieving it was all mine. The walls were white and smooth, the floor red with cold ceramic tiles. My eyes fell on the table beside my bed. Pulling open the top drawer, I peered at the pieces of my life I had carried with me across the desert.

The golden manacles that had cuffed Saalim's wrists shone dully. His vessel—his prison—was there. It rolled forward when I opened the drawer and clinked into the manacles. The empty vessel in my hands was one of the last things my father had seen before Saalim plunged a sword into his back.

My fingers continued their survey of the drawer, ensuring all was there. My map, tucked to the side. The piece of cloth that wrapped the smallest treasures: a blue tile whose color matched the sea, a golden necklace that once belonged to my mother, and a plucked moon-jasmine that Masira's magic kept alive. If I took it out, its petals would tightly close as it saw the daylight. Last in the drawer was the broken toy soldier who held a straight sword.

It had been Saalim's when he was young. I do not know why I carried it still, but I could not part with it. I could not part with anything that once was his.

A thunk echoed through my room and jarred me from my reverie.

"Medicine won't make itself!" Altasa yelled through the door.

Fastening my mother's necklace around my neck, I swiftly closed the drawer in a muted clatter.

I stumbled into the main room, smoothing my fustan down over my front. "I am sorry, we slept during—"

Altasa proffered a basket in my direction without a glance. Instead, she surveyed her shelf, scanning the jars and vials and pulling the ones she wanted. I took the basket, and she tipped her head toward the small pile she had already stacked on the counter. Carefully, I placed them inside.

"Crush equal parts cardamom and cumin until powdered. Take the fennel petals and add to the mixture after. Maybe six, seven. Enough to wet it into a paste."

I looked at the seven jars in my basket—two of which contained flowers— and looked back at her, the feeling of inadequacy returning. "I don't know . . ."

She set two more jars in my basket and leaned in so close, I could see gray ringing the brown of her eye. "Who are you exactly?"

"I don't know—"

"Exactly!" She spat. "You don't know anything. What salt chaser doesn't know the tapered cumin seed? The green of a cardamom pod? I will forgive the flower. Who raised such a witless child? Princess or not, I expected better."

Anger burned in me, consuming the shame for fuel. She was being unfair. I put my shoulders back and leaned toward her. "I was a daughter of the *Salt King*." Altasa's brow raised in mock surprise. I continued. "We had servants who handled these things. What business had I learning cumin from cardamom?"

She narrowed her eyes at me and slowly worked her gaze down my neck, to my shoulders, my chest, and to my feet. Eventually, she nodded. "Kept in chains. It's no wonder . . ." She continued nodding as she turned back to the shelf of ingredients, mumbling inaudibly. Several times, she turned back to me as if making some connection.

As if she understood something at last.

SAALIM

The food kept coming out on trays, and the wine was flowing as if from a fountain. The people talked loudly and laughed even more loudly. They faced each other with piles of meat and bread and fruit in between. With so much joy to be had, why did I worry?

"Have you learned anything more of those that killed your family?"

What small joy I had fled like mice in the shadow of a falcon. Omar, tactless as always.

"No," I said. "But our guard remains. We will find them soon."

"We've a pack of louts, too," Omar said, licking the wine from his lips. "They left their marks all over my city. Black hands."

Ah, yes, Omar. Your little pack of vandals who mark your city are certainly equal to the men that assailed Almulihi and killed my entire family.

Unclenching my fists, I reminded myself that the man meant well. It was not his fault his father indulged him.

"What does Ibrahim think?"

"That they are waiting for—you, there!" Omar raised his empty goblet to a servant who advanced into the dining hall with a decanter full of arak.

"Ibrahim's settlement is not alone," Gaffar said as Omar watched his goblet fill. "I have heard of similar sightings in other settlements."

"More hands?" I asked out of politeness, growing wearier with each sip of wine.

Omar slammed down an empty goblet, drops of the arak dregs splashing onto the table. "Come back!" he shouted to the servant.

"It will hit you quickly," I said, sliding mine out to be filled.

"Exactly," he said. "No better way to welcome my friend to his throne." Omar was never one to miss a party.

Everything had moved so swiftly after the attack on Almulihi, we barely had time to mourn my family before we heard news of Alfaar. Thinking his hunger of power reason enough to attack my home, I'd left in a hurry to see if the rumors of the Salt King were true. Though it was confirmed that he had as much salt in his tent as we did in the palace stores, and was indeed a threat worth ending, it was evident he'd had no hand in the ambush of my home.

So I returned to a waiting throne and uneasy people with no new information. And tonight we celebrated my acceptance of the crown.

Everything felt wrong.

The guests grew rowdier as the night wore on. Amir stood and pounded the hilt of his sword against the table until everyone fell silent. I watched him, thinking of our earlier discussion.

There had been no unusual sightings at the city's edge since we arrived and no word of suspicious behavior in Almulihi. I shifted, remembering the foolish haste I demanded of our journey.

How many died because of my blindness, my insistence of taking the wrong path? Men patrolled the city's borders night and day looking for suspicious people in black cloaks, for soldiers, anyone or anything that might tell us who had attacked our city and on whose behalf the three suspicious travelers might have approached us during our journey. Were the events related? Nassar insisted they were not.

I could not admit aloud that I wondered the same.

"We are glad you all have joined us to welcome our king," Amir said. "Though we still keep in memory the royal family, tonight we celebrate King Saalim. We are here not for sadness but for triumph. Bathe in Wahir's water, and pray with his gift." He dipped his fingers into a shallow bowl of water that rested beside his plate.

Doing the same with my bowl, I said a quick prayer for peace and resolution. I pressed my fingers to my opposite wrist. Others did the same.

"Now," Amir continued, reaching for his wine, "to King Saalim's homecoming! And since she has joined us, to the future queen!"

With escorts lurking behind her, Helena sat several seats down from me. Despite her pallor, she was worthy of viewing. She had broad shoulders, a full mouth. Her waist appeared small beneath her dress, her hips, though, did not seem much wider. Helena's eyes—green like the sea—met mine, and she studied me like she knew my thoughts. She smiled. I nodded in return, my goblet held aloft.

Others echoed Amir's sentiments while I gazed at them through a blur.

"A song! A song!" someone shouted.

Gaffar jumped onto his chair and began clapping and stamping his feet into a familiar rhythm. Others jumped up, clapping, and with Gaffar's lead, they sang the words we all knew:

O! You who braves these shifting sands.
To venture t'ward more salted lands.

If amongst the dunes a skull you find
Flee fast that cursed corpse, if you can!

For in tusked-skull a si'la dwells
Exiled, her love torn from her hands

She studied the darkest magic arts
Her power beyond the grasp of man

The goddess weeps to look upon
One who freed herself from fate's plans.

She'll steal your soul and cast it out
A feeble whisper upon the sands.

Magic. It was a word I once laughed at. Edala had believed in it, and I had always thought her a fool. It was perhaps the only matter my brother and I agreed on; our sister was starry-eyed and stone-headed, always searching for the goddess' gifts.

But then there had been water in barrels. Water from nothing. And why, when I thought of magic, did it feel different now? Like peeling back a curtain to reveal something real. I stood from the table and walked to the archway, where Omar and Tamam stood looking out onto the night-lit balcony.

"Saalim honors us with his presence!" Omar yelled, slapping my back.

Tamam, surely still on his first and only cup of wine, watched me with clear eyes and a furrowed brow.

Buildings in front of the palace had darkened with the evening, with slices of light peeking out from them. Bright like iron to be forged. Beyond the city was Wahir's greatest gift: the sea. I could smell it in the air—the brine and wet sand.

"My, this one is different. Straight from the desert," Omar said, and I knew that tone. He saw a woman. "Is that how you like them now?"

Laughing, I looked back to see what poor palace servant Omar had his eyes on now. The man had married recently, but Sons, it had not quelled his enthusiasm.

The drink made her hazy, but I could see she was as beautiful as any of the ahiran here. I leaned back on the balcony railing and said, "Mariam sent you, then?"

She had stopped completely beneath the archway that split the dining hall from the balcony. It framed her in such a way that it looked like she belonged there—like my mother had when she walked these halls.

"Altasa," she said, and when she spoke, I knew her voice.

The smile fell from my face, and I pushed myself away from the railing to stand upright. In that loose dress, I had not recognized her. It was something a woman of Almulihi might wear, senselessly embroidered and brighter than the flowers in the garden. With no scarf covering her head and face, my eyes traveled greedily from her mouth to her neck to her chest. Her hair and eyes blacker than the night. My blood stirred and pooled, and I felt myself moving toward her.

"She sent me to give you this," Emel said sharply.

Something was not quite right, and it distracted me from the image of her naked legs twisted with mine. Her voice had a hard edge to it, and she was not looking at me but beyond me.

At Omar, like he was a scorpion in her bed.

I cleared my throat. "What is it?"

She held out a lumpy sack. "The medicine."

For the aches that persisted still from our journey. "And you deliver it tonight?"

"She said it must be delivered on a first quarter moon."

I exhaled and rubbed my brow. All healers were the same. I remember my mother complaining when servants would interrupt their sleep to deliver tonics sent by Zahar. "Of course. A servant could have brought it." I should have just taken the sack, but instead I continued to talk. She dropped her arm, the bag dangling by her side.

"It was your servants who directed me here. I did not know there was a party."

No, but the servants did. A cruel joke for the salt chaser.

Taking the medicine from her, I said, "Thank you for bringing it."

She nodded briefly and turned to go. Tonight she was different, closed and reticent.

"Won't you stay?" Omar asked her.

I bristled.

"I'm alone tonight." He laughed.

"Omar," I warned.

He looked at me, surprised. "Who is this? Become king and suddenly you're too good for a whore?"

In my periphery, I saw Emel flinch. I closed my eyes, sobering quickly and willing patience with my friend. We had fun, in part due to his boorish behavior, but tonight I had no tolerance for it. "Go inside," I said with my hand to his back, my fingers slipping on the silk.

"Come now." He stroked his beard. "I can't have any fun?"

I looked back to Tamam, who was watching us like he watched everything—alert and wary. Leaving his goblet atop the railing, Tamam led Omar inside.

"He is drunk," I said to Emel. A poor explanation, and I regretted it immediately when I saw her frown. I was alone on the balcony now. Emel still remained under the archway as though an unseen barrier prevented her from coming closer.

"I need to return to Altasa," she said, making to leave.

"Please wait." It was out of my mouth before I could stop myself. Grasping for some reason to have asked her to stay, I blurted, "Have you seen the ocean yet?"

"I have."

"But not from here. Come and see." I gestured to the view, then realized it was night, and there would be little to see. My hand dropped.

Emel took maybe two steps onto the balcony and stopped. "It is lovely."

It did not sound as though she thought it lovely. She sounded terrified, and I said as much.

"We're quite high up." Her eyes darted to the balcony's edge.

Resting my hands on the railing, I said, "But it offers the best view of Almulihi." I saw it from her eyes—seeing my city for the first time, how beautiful and impressive it must be. And I, its king. Pride lifted my chin and chest.

"I've not been up high like this before."

I dropped my head, looking down at the rooftops. Of course she had not. She had lived in a village of tents. My silver-tongued mother would not have erred so. "There is nothing to fear. It will hold," I said finally, pounding the balcony with my heel. She flinched, moving closer to me. I could almost reach out and touch her.

She watched me carefully. *What is it you see?*

"Emel means ambition, does it not? In the old tongue?" I asked.

"I was told that once." She stood next to me now. Her fingers slowly stretching out to the railing.

"Not that I speak much of it. Tutors tried, but I was too stubborn. Didn't understand the value. Now, of course, I am reliant on translators to read the old scripts and laws." I was rambling.

"But that is appropriate for a king, is it not? My father had Nas—" She stopped and looked at me. "Men that helped him."

"It is, but a king should have help because he has too many tasks, not because he can't complete them on his own." I thought of Azim fighting the invaders I was too cowardly to face. "Dependence is weak."

She was leaning over the railing now, bolder by the moment. The scarf draped over her back could not hide the curve of her spine into her hips. I wanted to pull the scarf away, trace my fingers along that sloping line.

Another raucous song started inside, but it felt so far away.

The wind whipped up, swirling around us and fluttering the dress around her ankles so that I could just glimpse that she wore slippers on her feet. No sandals. She pushed back from the edge with the gust, fear widening her eyes. Her hair was fashioned similar to my sisters', who used to spend far too long with their reflections, twisting their hair and placing it just so. It had seemed like such waste to use time so frivolously, but seeing Emel with her hair spun around her head and dress swept down around her like a bird's plumes made me reconsider. Perhaps it was not so needless. Another gust of wind, and the scarf fell from her shoulders.

My eyes, greedy for more, dropped to her shoulder. I paused. Stretching over her skin were dark scars, shining in the light. The trails of at least five lashes. They were not the scars of a laborer, someone who had been in a horrible accident. They were the scars of disobedience, put there intentionally.

I gasped. What could a daughter of a king have done to warrant the punishment?

She looked at me suddenly. When she saw my face, her brow furrowed, and she reached up to her neck, fingers closing over the tapering ends of the scars.

Slowly, she backed away, pulling the scarf tightly over her shoulders, just as my mother used to do. But my mother had not been hiding scars.

"Was it worth it?" I asked.

Her face softened. What was she remembering? It wasn't the pain of the whip, the itch of the healing wounds. No, she was remembering what she had done to earn them.

"He is," she said, before she walked away.

Anisa flew back swiftly, prey dangling from her beak. I held up my hand, luring in the golden eagle with bloody meat. She landed with a soft thud, dropping the mouse onto the ground in a frantic hurry to get the prize. She took the meat in my hand and turned away from me, shielding herself with her wing. I watched her fondly, listening to Nassar and Kofi speak at my back.

"And who were these travelers?" Kofi asked.

"People from the east," Nassar replied.

Kofi scoffed. "I doubt they can be believed."

"What motive would they have to lie?"

Anisa finished her meal, her ocher eye flashing to me.

"They bore you, too?" I whispered. Anisa was my best huntress. I was pleased, but not surprised, when she returned to me after the ceremony with Alfaar. She was more loyal than most.

No, she was not loyal. She was lazy. She knew who provided her meals.

"Saalim!" Nassar said, voice raised.

"I have no interest in travelers who say they were lured from their journey by a strange woman."

"Helena's family will want to know that you take all matters seriously," Nassar said flatly. "It could be a test."

"Ah, then please, tell me more."

"They say she was there one moment, gone the next. Found her by a skull larger than any animal that lives."

"In the east they must also sing the song of the si'la and drink too much arak," I said. Kofi grunted in agreement. Anisa fanned her wings when she finished, as if she knew how beautiful her feathers were.

"Then you will not care to hear what they said of the black-cloaked people they called the Darkafa."

Black hands.

Nassar continued. "They described them as you did."

"As I did?"

"The ones we met on the journey."

The travelers that approached us had hands gloved in black. The *louts* Omar described left painted black hands throughout his city as if it were some message.

Were they the same, after all?

Quietly, Nassar said, "Saalim, you will want to hear this."

I sent Anisa to the sky and walked back to Nassar and Kofi. "What did they say?"

"The Darkafa claimed to have found the goddess, and now they search for the Sons."

Losing my patience, I sighed and turned to watch Anisa soar. These Darkafa sounded addled. But it was always the addled ones that were the most worrisome.

Nassar went on. "'When the king crosses the desert, the goddess will return. She will unleash the second-born Son to put the first-born to death.'"

I cursed my poor memory of the Litab Almuq. "Which of the Sons was born first?"

"Clerics debate this; however, most believe it to be Wahir," Nassar said. "If the Darkafa believe the same, then I fear they will travel to Wahir's kingdom so that he can be destroyed."

Silence, save for wind. I stared at the horizon, where Almulihi looked like a stone cracked in half.

"To Almulihi," I said.

That evening, there was another party. The people who had traveled far to welcome me home would not leave quickly. My father's gatherings were the same—night after night of elaborate dinners and drinks, guests long overstaying their welcome. My mother never tired of it, or if she did, she hid it well. She would bring in men to spin fire and women to swallow swords, singers and bards, dancers and tellers of fortune.

When I was young, I would tiptoe down the steps barefooted so none would hear me. A child eager to be king so I could have parties every night and stay awake until sunrise. Now, I preferred to be the boy sent to bed at dusk.

Tonight Omar was sharing, as he often did, the details of his nights spent with women in Almulihi. Thankfully, Helena left to her quarters early in the night so she did not have to hear his lewdness. Always tactful, she had the makings of a fine queen. She would be returning home tomorrow to finish preparations for the wedding before making her final journey to Almulihi.

"You are certain that the salt chaser was not available?" Omar asked me through the loud stories other men shared.

I shook my head and chuffed. No matter how hard I tried to think of anything else, my mind swirled with images of Emel. Of her breasts and waist, her back and legs. Of scars that hinted of things I wanted to know.

Tamam sat quietly. I leaned toward him. "When are you going to find yourself a woman, eh?"

"Long ago I had a woman I loved," he replied, "but a soldier's life is one of duty. A scabbard has only room for its sword; there is no space left to carry love or soft things like that."

There was nothing Tamam loved like he loved his sword. Stoic and silent, I could hardly imagine a gentle woman in his arms.

He almost smiled. His lips parted as if he were going to say something more, but then thought better of it and sipped his drink, looking away.

I regretted dragging him into the talk. "It is late. My bed awaits."

"And surely a woman, too," Gaffar said.

"Wahir knows you won't be alone tonight!" Amir called. "Will it be Dima or someone new?"

"Dima! Always Dima!" someone called from behind me.

The clattering dishes and scraping chairs gradually quieted as I retreated. Away from the party, the palace was silent at this time of night, most of the servants had gone to bed or were tending to the partiers. The day-guards had long ago left their posts to sleep. Now, only night-guards flanked the palace perimeter. I took the stairs up to the tower slowly, my hand steadying me against the wall. The moon was bright through the windows. It was late, indeed.

When I turned into my room, Mariam was still there ensuring the fire was fed and the bath kept warm.

"Go to sleep, woman," I said fondly.

"My king." She dipped her silvered hair toward me. "Have you any other needs?"

"Dima."

She nodded before she took one more glance at the fire and scanned the room. All was satisfactory, I assumed, as she left quickly, closing the door behind her. She had been in the palace since before I was born, tending to my father and perhaps even my father's father. Her familiarity with this palace and my family did not strip her of her formality, however.

I pulled off my tunic and tossed it onto the ground as I sat on a nearby chair.

Like a tethered ship, my drifting mind snapped back to the water that filled our stores on our journey. Nassar had searched desperately, trying to find accounts or explanations that would help us understand. But drunk men talking about a woman who lured them from their path was getting us nowhere. I wanted to accept there would be no explanation, but no matter how I tried to let it be, my mind pulled me back.

The fire was enormous, whirling in quiet thunder. The gauzy netting suspended from my bed's tall frame swayed from the wind that came in. I followed the wind out onto the small balcony. This view was my favorite—overlooking the sea, the docks, the horizon. The salt-laden wind whipped up the tower. I inhaled, letting the wetness of it sober me, letting the coolness carry away my thoughts of magic and the woman whose black eyes haunted me.

Finally, a knock on the door. After stumbling through the seating room, nearly tripping on the leg of the desk, I found Dima waiting in the doorway, dressed in the color of red wine with her long hair braided over her shoulder.

"Again? You flatter me," she said as she walked past me to stand before the fire with hands outstretched.

She was not wrong. I had been needy since our return from Alfaar's. I had hoped all of that *emptiness* would be gone when I arrived home. But it had not left, and if anything, seemed to grow worse by the day. It had been how many moons since my family was taken? Since Almulihi was given to me? Four? Five? I thought by now the loneliness and the confusion and longing . . . I stopped myself.

I went to the edge of the bed, sinking into the feathered mattress. "Come here."

She did as she was told, as she was supposed to. But just once, I wanted her to say no, to refuse, to do something else. But she could not. This was her work.

Tonight, I was not interested in pleasantries, in sharing drink or lingering touches. I was drunk with muddled images of Emel in my bed that needed to be washed away. Pressing my mouth to Dima's, I pushed the dress from her shoulders. I untied her top, poorly it seemed, as it did not slide off easily until her deft fingers intervened.

Sons, the woman was soft. I pulled her to me as I lay down. My hands ran the length of her back, to her thighs and up again. I closed my eyes, thinking of Emel's skin beneath my hands. Dima removed my clothing until I was stripped to skin. Her hands were so perfect they felt wrong, and each night, they felt more wrong than the last. They were only there to touch, nothing more, nothing deeper. She swung her leg over my hips and there was no more thought of her hands.

I was barely aware of Dima. She was just a woman I clung to and thrashed against. A woman who had lips, breasts. Someone soft who tasted like sweet fennel seed. When it was done, I lay beside her and pulled her to my chest.

I wrapped my arm around her waist and pressed my lips behind her ear. She pressed back into me. She would stay until I told her to leave.

"Tell me," she said. When I said nothing, she continued, "You do not call an ahira to your bed this often because you want to bed. There is more."

"Hmm." I pressed my mouth to her hair, her braid wrapped loosely in my fist.

"I am here, should you need someone to tell. You know I can keep a secret."

The palace ahiran were tested and tested again with false and scandalous secrets before they were allowed to stay. So yes, she could keep any secret I asked her to. It was her job.

"Is it Helena? She will suit you well."

"Helena is fine."

"It is something else."

"I am so tired."

"Then sleep, my king."

I pulled the blankets over us. Despite the woman that lay sleeping beside me, the friends that lingered in the dining hall below, the future queen that slept in a neighboring tower, I still felt the nagging hollowness.

I still thought of Emel.

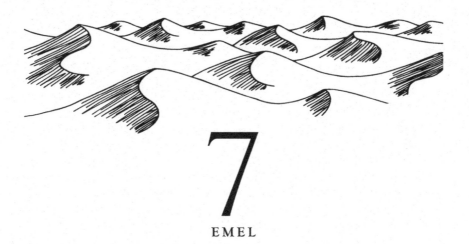

7

EMEL

It was the first time Altasa trusted me to go to the marketplace alone, and I wished she had not. I ran through the list of things she needed in a beat that matched my footsteps. If I forgot something, she would be furious.

Well, feigned fury. It came and went too quickly to be real. The corners of her eyes turned up when she barked at me, as though she could not completely hide her fondness. And fond she had grown. Perhaps it was that I was of the desert, like her. Or perhaps it was my patience with her on the days she was too weak to do anything at all and would hole away in her room. Today was one of those days.

She told me before I left that a ship had just come in with tulsi grown on the deck. I must get to the shop before they clipped it from its stems to dry.

The marketplace was not far from the docks, so I knew to follow the streets to the sea and turn in the direction of the ships. The differences between Almulihi and my settlement surprised me less every day, but the marketplace still stole my breath in terror. Stalls of goods seemed unending, each differentiating itself from its neighbor with loud shopkeepers or flamboyant signs.

A boy rushed up to me with a bag full of something dried just as a horse clopped by with enormous sacks flung over his rump.

I startled when he shouted, "The finest ginger crystals!"

In his fist were large pieces of soft yellow. I had never seen anything like it. Altasa had warned me not to sample anything. "They target salt chasers. Latch like a barnacle, and you'll never finish what you need to get done."

The boy saw me glance to his hand and raised his fist closer to my face. "Six fid for the palmful, but you can try it first and see if it is to your liking."

Altasa was not here today. What would it matter if I tried it? I reached for the smallest piece, pressed it between the tips of my fingers—firm but yielding—and popped it in my mouth. The boy nodded and smiled, waiting for my delight.

My face twisted as my teeth bit through the chewy fruit. It was spicy and strong and—I started to cough. I chewed more quickly, trying to hide my displeasure, and swallowed.

"Does it not satisfy you?" The boy grabbed my hand. "We sell other things at Papa's shop, come with me. We will find much you like."

I tried to pull away, but his grip was firm. "Oh no," I said after coughing more, the flavor still singeing my tongue.

"Yes, this way!" He pulled.

We blew past a man with arms outstretched, scarves draped over them. "Silk from across the sea!" he bellowed at me, ignoring the shop-boy pulling me along.

Another woman, modeling bracelets of silver and bronze, tried to get between the boy and me, brandishing the glistening jewelry. "The best price in the souk!" But even she could not separate the boy from my arm.

We turned down another lane with more stalls. I was so very lost, I would never find my way out. A small crowd filled most of the street we had turned down, and the boy slowed to navigate through them. The crowd faced a woman who waved her arms about, wearing bright colors and adorned with even more jewelry than the bracelet-seller. That she could stand with all that weight, let alone walk, surprised me. When I saw her face, I realized she was the same woman I had seen standing on the rooftop. Yet the clothes she wore now told me why she had seemed so familiar.

I came to an abrupt stop to watch her, my arm slipping from the boy's grip.

She was the same oracle who had told Raheemah her fortune back home. The one Saalim had conjured from magic so he and I could spend moments alone. My mouth hung open as I stared at her. Had he known her from his life here? Or was there magic at play now?

"This way," the boy said, wrapping his fingers around my wrist. "Almost there."

I shook my head, not breaking my gaze from the oracle. It was so obvious that she was from the desert, like me. Her skin like mine. Even the shape of her eyes, the arch of her brow. Being a foreigner in Madinat Almulihi made me so aware of people *like me*. It was a comfort, an easy breath, an understanding. I wanted to speak with her just so I could hear home in her words.

The boy did not care of my curiosity, determined as he was. Grunting, I yanked my arm from his grasp a second time.

"No!" I said, drawing the attention of a few spectators at the oracle's. "Leave me."

He did not relent. "But you have not yet sampled Papa's other dried goods. He has many. You will find much that you like." More pulling.

Shaking my head uselessly, I looked around for anything that might help me rid myself of him.

I needed to see this oracle.

"You!" A woman stomped toward us wearing a scowl that made me cower. She was a mother, of that I was sure. She reached out her hand and with a swift movement, slapped the back of the boy's head. "Find someone else. You're wasting valuable time on a useless customer."

The boy frowned at the terrifying woman, let me go, and ran back from where we had come.

I raised my hand in gratitude.

She ignored me and turned back toward the oracle. Perhaps she had been helping the boy instead of me. "Thank you," I whispered, nonetheless.

"—only a few nab. To know your future, a single dha. To know your fate, it will take more than that." Even the oracle's voice was the same, now that I could hear it clearly.

"Ah, but that will cost you," she said in answer to a question.

Finally, a man stepped forward and slid coins across the smooth table scattered with crystals and vials and urns. She swept them up and stood, leading the man into the curtained stall behind her. She took one look at us, her eyes briefly meeting mine, before she slid the curtain closed.

I waited with a few others. After some time, the curtain opened. The oracle had a grave look on her face, and the man left paler than when he had entered.

"Will you stand here and gawk, or is there someone who would like to know his fate?" she asked us.

"Do you travel?" I asked quickly.

"Travel? To the desert?" She gave me a knowing look. My accent.

"To settlements there?"

She shook her head. "My husband did. I've no interest in leaving Almulihi. I might consider it for the right price. What is your offer?" She patted the table, inviting coin.

"Oh, no . . . I just thought . . ."

I retreated, and the oracle looked away from me to the others who stood waiting, taking the next customer behind the curtain.

After many stops asking for help, entertaining numerous questions about where I was from and why my accent sounded different, I found the seller of tulsi. The leaves had already been cut when I arrived, but they were bright green and soft and so fragrant I did not think they could be any fresher than if I had cut them with the shears Altasa had sent.

I thanked the shopkeeper, ignoring her questions of my origin, explaining that I must quickly return to the palace to deliver the ingredients. At the mention of the palace, her mouth clamped shut, and she nodded.

With Altasa, I was never questioned. Though clothes could not hide the angles of my face, the darkness of my skin, the way I watched everything as though I were an infant seeing it for the first time, they knew better than to discuss anything other than business with Altasa around. Alone, they had no such misgivings.

Finally I acquired all that Altasa had requested. I found myself at the edge of the marketplace where stone streets became wooden planks that stretched out to the sea. The docks stood on alarmingly slim stilts above the waves, and tied alongside were boats with sky-high masts and tangles of ropes and slack sails. I watched the people move atop the ships for only a breath before my legs nearly collapsed and I had to turn away. How could someone feel safe standing on wood when water below threatened to swallow them?

Tavi lived nearby, so I followed the canal to her home. In front, a man in a narrow boat hauled a large crate onto the ground, then another. A younger man dumped the crate's contents, scattering silver fish all over. Small children fluttered out from the house to chase the birds away. Then I saw Tavi, crouched down and sorting through the fish. Some she tossed in a basket, others into a bucket, and some, finally, to the crazed gulls that were soaring overhead. A more effective distraction than the children.

There was laughter, and I looked from the cacophonous birds back to Tavi. She and the young man watched each other, their shoulders shaking as they giggled. She seemed, unbelievably, happy. Nodding in my direction, the man drew Tavi's attention to me. She looked at me then back to the man who shook his head and shooed her toward me.

"Emel," she cried, beaming. "Look at you!" She hugged me, smelling of her work. Did I smell of mine? She drew back, and I drank in her face. It glowed, and her eyes were rested and eager. Her hands smoothed over my clothes and hair just as our mother's used to. Her smile widened, and I saw that she had already gained back the youth she had lost on our journey. "You look like you belong in Almulihi," she said finally.

Almulihi. She said it like she belonged here. Her hair was braided around her head like mine. The neckline of her long tunic was embroidered with flowers and vines—so detailed it was something our mothers would have worn. Here, it belonged to a simple work-woman. Even the sirwal that cuffed just above her ankles were stitched with at least a dozen different threads, and her sandals were new and stiff. I flexed my toes in my worn sandals. They were old, but they had been mine for so long.

The slippers Altasa gave me were no good for walking these streets.

"—tried to visit, but they did not let me. Are you alone?" She looked behind me.

Visiting Tavi had been harder than I expected, as I was too nervous to leave the palace alone. This was only my third time seeing her, and we had been in Madinat Almulihi longer than a whole turn of the moon. The first two times were short visits, Altasa huffing with impatience as Tavi and I embraced.

"Let me show you where I stay. You can meet the children. Follow me." Tavi was talking quickly, still smiling. She beckoned me into her home.

The front room housed the kitchen and seating area. Despite the windows at the entrance to the home, it was dark compared to the palace, and a fire provided most of the light.

Saira sat at the table with two children slicing fish and removing bones. Though she had seemed austere on the night we arrived, she was now welcoming.

"Sit," Saira said warmly and gestured to one of the two remaining chairs at the table. They were mismatched, one leaning to the side.

Shaking my head, I said, "I can't stay long." I held up my sack of goods by way of explanation.

Tavi introduced me to the children, one of the little girls babbling to Tavi immediately. Tavi listened with unwavering attention, all serious eyes and nods, before excusing us.

As we stepped down the narrow hallway to the back room, Tavi whispered, "She says I am her big sister."

"Oh."

The back room was larger than the front, with several folding screens placed to divide the mats on the floor from the others. Tavi pointed to one corner of the room, hidden by the largest screen, saying that was where Saira and her husband slept. The children's beds were at the room's center, and to the right, behind another, smaller screen was Tavi's.

"It's all my own!" She said excitedly as she took me there.

I thought of my room—stone walls on all sides, a bed raised off the floor, tiles beneath my feet—and said nothing.

Beside her bed was a shallow bowl filled with water. Next to the bowl was a small plate with a smooth red stone swirling with orange and a rough, dark blue stone.

"What is this?" I asked, kneeling down to peer at the dark, clumped material the stones sat upon. I picked it up between my fingers. It smelled strongly of frankincense. I dropped it back onto the plate. That scent would always remind me of Mama. How it clung to her clothes and hair.

Tavi knelt beside me. "It is for Mama and . . . Sabra."

"What do you mean?"

"Have you not seen these?" She cocked her head. "They are in everyone's homes."

How many homes had she visited? How many people had she met and befriended? People scowled at me. Who welcomed her?

"Does Altasa not have one?" She looked surprised.

I shrugged. Perhaps in her room, but I had not been in there. Again, I looked around their shared space.

"It is a way to remember those that have died, to ask Wahir to shelter them from Eiqab's sun, to cradle them in water." As she spoke, she stood and went to the fire that burned in a similar alcove as Altasa's. It, too, had a chimney to suck away the smoke. She returned with a piece of wood alight and touched it to the dark clumps beneath the stones. Now I could really smell the frankincense.

"I chose that for Mama."

I smiled.

Tavi lifted the blue stone and gently dipped it into the water, treating it like it was a baby bird. She held it above the water, letting the drops fall back into the bowl. *Plunk, plunk, plunk.* Then set the stone back onto the burning incense. There was a quiet sizzle. "It is topaz. Saira told me topaz is gentle. I thought Mama would like that." She lifted the red stone and repeated the motion. "Fire agate," she said quietly. "For strength. For Sabra." When she set the stone onto the incense, it sizzled more loudly.

"You pray to Wahir now?" I asked sharply.

She sighed. "There is no rama here."

No, Madinat Almulihi did not have sand hot enough for prayer.

"A poor excuse." The words came out of me before I could stop them. I did not pray to Eiqab, either. Why was I fighting with her? I could not stop. "Have you forgotten home already?"

"Forgotten home? I do this," she waved her hand over the small shrine, "every day so that I don't forget them. So that I don't forget our home and where we came from."

"Well." I stood. "I need to return. I've been gone too long."

I gulped in the briny air—that which did not smell of frankincense—as soon as I was outside.

Tavi followed me out. "Please visit soon. I want to see you more. Maybe I can come to you?"

"Maybe," I said as I fussed with my tunic.

"We can visit Firoz and Rashid. How are they? Or we can do something else. Yakub knows his way around the city well." She nodded in the young man's direction who had taken over sorting the fish.

He looked over after he tossed a fish to the crazed birds. "Say my name?"

"Everything isn't about you," Tavi called, her words curling with glee.

I listened to the two of them, stewing with guilt. I had not yet seen Firoz and Rashid. I thought of them often, but fear kept me from going to the bayta-hira. "They are well. I'll return when I can," I said with a quick hug.

As I walked away, I heard Yakub speak. "Everything well?" he asked Tavi.

"Yes," she said quietly. I stopped briefly, pretending to adjust my sack. "She is very sad, I think. There is much she misses."

She knew so much despite knowing very little.

Tavi, smelling of sea and salt, already had found more joy in her life flinging fish than I did living within the palace walls only a breath away from Saalim.

Altasa was still in her room when I returned. Tossing my sack on the table, I retrieved the kettle.

Midday was fast approaching, and my diversion in the market made me late to prepare medicines. I hurried across the now-cleared path and went to the fountain gardens. Leaning over the edge, I held the kettle beneath the fountain—a vase that perpetually spilled water into the pond. Men's voices echoed inside, but they soon stopped. I heard a chuckle as footsteps clapped on the tiles outside, and I turned to see Saalim approaching. Today, he was dressed like a king. Resplendent robes, thick and sparkling with golden thread, hung from his shoulders, and a glistening crown with blue stones buried in its side was seated on his brow. I could not tear my eyes from him. Cold water splashed onto my arm, and I hastily righted the kettle.

"What are you doing?" he asked.

"Collecting water for the medicine," I said, wishing the kettle would fill more slowly.

"From the garden fountain?" Pulling the kettle away from the spout, I turned. He looked as if he was trying not to smile. "I've always preferred my water from the aqueduct. Cleaner, I think. But Altasa knows best. Should she decide she wants something . . . different, you are welcome to use the fountain inside."

Many people filled at the fountain in the atrium. I assumed that was the palace source. This fountain had slick green growing on its sides, and the water in the cistern was so dark I could hardly see through it.

My cheeks warmed. Altasa had never told me where to fetch the water. "Well, who are we to question what she asks for?" I said, setting the kettle on the lip of the fountain. "You look like a king today." The words slipped past my tongue before I could stop them.

"I must look the part when I see the people."

"An address?" I asked.

"Court."

"Which you should be on your way to," a familiar voice called from inside. Beyond Saalim was Nassar. A chill crept down my back, remembering the moment Nassar handed my father the whip.

Saalim nodded. "Tell Altasa I'd like more of the salve."

"I will."

When their footsteps were inaudible, I dumped the water back into the fountain and went to fill the kettle in the atrium.

Altasa was at the counter examining the shears she had sent with me when I walked into her home.

With the sharp ends, she pointed to the tulsi leaves. "These were not cut by you."

"No," I admitted, suspending the kettle above the flames.

"Why not?"

"I was late." I would never hear the end of it if she knew I had fallen prey to a shop-boy. "The leaves are fresh. What does it matter how they were cut?"

She spun the point of the shears into the wood countertop. "Every single thing on these shelves was prepared exactly as I needed them to be. They won't work otherwise."

"Work how?"

The shears fell onto the table. "I don't want to know why you were late, but I do expect that you won't be in the future. There are others who would happily do what you are doing for less."

"But then who would you talk of home with, eh?"

"Myself, like I've always done."

Lonely old woman. "When do you go back to see your family again?"

"My family?"

"Was that not who you had visited before I arrived?"

"My family is what brought me here, and now they're gone." She picked up the tulsi, examined the leaves, then let out a great sigh before dropping them back onto the counter. "You weren't flirting with merchant men were you?"

"I saw an oracle," I said.

"That imposter?" Altasa spun surprisingly quickly and faced me.

Her rest this morning had done her well—her face brighter, eyes less tired. She tutted.

"Why speak to such a fool? She makes enough coin as is, yet feels the need to go sputtering on about fortunes and fates, lying to people about what will befall them. People flock to her like she is the source of all magic."

The vehemence surprised me. "And you think she can't use magic?"

"Of course she can't. Did you see her use it?"

"She did everything behind a curtain."

"And how did she appear after?"

I stammered. "Appear?"

"Did she seem tired? Weak? Changed?"

Shrugging, I said, "I don't think so, but there were so many people." Saalim was never weak after using magic.

Altasa raised her eyebrows and nodded, as if this proved everything. "Know this about magic, so you're never conned into giving coin for a show: True magic requires sacrifice, and takes from the user when it is wielded. That woman is no magician, harnessing what Masira has gifted—" she gestured to her wall of ingredients "—to manipulate that which is around us." She moved toward me slowly, despite her improving limp.

Stepping around her to fetch the kettle from the fire, I said, "You believe it real, then?"

"Of course it's real. It's how Masira speaks."

I grunted my disapproval.

"What do you know of magic?" She laughed, and I wanted to tell her just how much I knew. More than she would ever know.

"Enough to know that I want nothing to do with it. No one should have anything to do with it." No longer wanting to speak of magic, I said, "The king requests more salve."

She chuffed. "Why don't you convince him to take the tonic? It's easier to make and works better."

"I'll ask when I deliver the salve." Pouring a bit of water into a bowl, I reached for the tulsi leaves. "Are these fine to use or not?"

She grabbed them from my hand. "No. You will do what I asked when their ship returns in twelve days."

She went to the fire and threw in the leaves.

A few days later, I looked through Altasa's recipe book, seeing if I knew enough to prepare more medicines without guidance. Though my reading was still weak, it had improved since I began reading Altasa's Litab Almuq, using my memory of the stories my mother had told me.

The healer appeared to be feeling better, and the better she felt, the more often she was gone. It did not bother me, though, to see her less. She asked me so many questions of my home and my life prior to Almulihi, I was beginning to worry that she would catch me in my lies.

I pushed the anise around on the mesh sieve, letting the steam coat it and hoping to get more drops of oil than I had so far. Carefully, I flipped through the thick pages. Turning to an unmarked page, I read the recipe for treatment of some bumps of the skin—cumin seed was used and another ingredient I could not understand. There was a recipe for festering wounds. And then one to . . . change an unborn child? I must have read that wrong. The next was a list of ingredients to chew for an aching tooth. I turned the page again and paused. Dhitah. I sounded out the word, nearly certain it meant death. Why would a healer need something for death?

But then I thought to those days on our journey when water was nowhere to be found. When death would be the kindest end. Perhaps Altasa helped those who felt the same. I remembered my dream of the broken-winged bird that I had killed in my fist. Sabra who died without pain. Could death sometimes be a mercy?

<hr />

The trees' shadows stretched across the gardens and ponds. I closed my eyes against the bright orange light that slipped between the leaves. Altasa's front door was open when I returned from the souk, her cane sitting against the table, cloak hanging over the chair. Murmurs hummed down the hall from her room. She must have been talking to herself again.

As the door closed loudly behind me, I heard a man's whispered voice. The door to Altasa's room opened and shut again, and she shuffled into the room.

"You're back," she said.

"Who is here?" I asked, noting that she stood nearly straight. I smiled. "A man?"

She cackled. "I am too old to bother with! Men would do better at the baytahira, eh?" Altasa was so amused by my question, laughing and shaking her head, that I could not help but smile, too.

"Where *is* the baytahira?"

Her eyes narrowed. "Not paying you enough?"

"Altasa!"

She laughed again and sat down, stretching her legs out in front of her.

"Your back is feeling better?"

"My medicines work!" She leaned forward and rubbed her knee. "Now, why do you need to know the whereabouts of the baytahira?"

"I have friends who went there when we arrived. To find work and a place to stay. I would like to visit them."

"Do these friends have names, or are you keeping that a secret, too?" Her eyebrows waggled.

I told their names, and she told me how to get to there. She said I could go that night despite the thyme needing to be cut right at sundown.

"You're well enough to do it on your own." I slipped on my sandals.

"But what am I paying you for if not so I can sit around?"

"*You* don't pay me at all." The palace paid my coin.

"Bah! You really are the best worker I've had. I don't pay a damn thing, and I work less."

The baytahira was further away than I anticipated. By the time I arrived, the sunlight was gone, and I had to pull my cloak a little more tightly around my shoulders. When I turned the corner, I realized we had passed this street when we entered the city. It was nothing like the baytahira at home, mewling people with loose limbs and tired eyes scattered in front of tents.

Loud and rowdy people filled the streets, hugging each other and drinking from chalices and goatskins. Others slumped against the walls, smoking or dozing. Buildings with enormous, open windows lined the street, and I could see that inside, too, they were filled. Most seemed like gathering places—friends laughing and eating and drinking, cards and coin between them. Smoke billowed out of windows, fogging parts of the street.

What I did not see were the men and women who bedded for coin. I looked for them—people dressed like their clothes were to be removed, those who looked as though perhaps they were keeping most of themselves hidden away—but I saw none.

At the end of the baytahira, it was quieter, with fewer people. Shops became homes. Turning around, I walked down the busy street again. And again. Back and forth the lively stretch. I had no idea where I would find Firoz and Rashid.

"I imagine you're lost," a woman said to me.

Following the direction of the voice, I saw her sitting in front of a brightly lit home. Beside her home was a quiet business with dim lighting. She sat with a man much younger than her, cards stacked on the tabletop.

She must have seen my gaze as I peered through the windows of the shop at silhouettes seated atop cushions. Inside was smoke so dense, it reminded me of the Haf Shata and the Haf Alsaf, my father's winter and summer festivals. I smelled it—charred honey. My fists clenched, battling my body's desire to breathe in more.

"My Bura-den," she said, tilting her head toward it.

"Bura?"

"Buraq rose. One of the only flowers that grows in the—"

"I know." Named after the flying steed, smoking it could make a person feel light enough to fly. Many nights I had inhaled the sweet smoke before seeing a muhami.

"You have passed here several times now. What are you doing?" She stood from the chair, and in a moment, was beside me.

I recognized her.

"You are the oracle."

She smiled and bobbed her head, the thick chains around her neck jingling with the movement. "Kahina," she said. "I've seen you. You're from the sand, too."

I shifted and looked down the street at a cluster of people arguing. "I am looking for my friends. Firoz and Rashid."

"I figured as much. You are Emel?" I nodded, and she cocked her head to the side, peering at me. "Every outsider comes to me when they arrive." She pointed down the road. Fabric billowed out beneath her arm, undulating with golds and reds and silvers and greens. "At least those who aren't told to keep away."

Pulling my gaze away from her glittering clothes, I asked what she meant.

"I remember what it was like to be like you. Foreign. How I was treated. When I met my husband and we opened the den, I wanted to make sure we were a place that welcomed all. Now, I own half of these businesses. Those that aren't mine belong to people I've helped. People call me the keeper of outcasts. That is flattering, but it gives me more credit than I deserve. I simply don't want people to feel unwelcome."

"Oh," I said dumbly. "Why would people be told to stay away?"

"We're a bunch of wild salt chasers. Watch your purse! We might take it." Her eyes were wide and bright, and she winked. "Things have gotten worse since we were attacked—especially with the deaths of civilians and the royal family." She pressed her fingers to her wrists. "People trust foreigners even less now. The baytahira is a stain on the city, I'm told. I disagree. I am simply giving a home to the people who would find one wherever they could. The palace streets would not be so beautiful if Bura-dens lined them, would they? At least, here, these people can be who they are."

"Such as an oracle?" I asked.

She laughed. "It's good fun, but it also allows me to find the lost people who haven't found me yet." Suddenly she clapped her hands together. "That was enough about me! Apologies. I like to give my speech to the newcomers." Kahina pointed across the way, her finger glinting with golden bands. "You can find your boys in the jalsa tadhat."

The spirit home.

Between two loud gambling houses was the jalsa tadhat, dark with a single small torch beside the entrance. There was no garish sign that told the passerby what was inside, and its windows were covered with dark fabric. Like many of the buildings on this street, there was a second level, and although those windows, too, were darkened, I could see firelight shifting inside.

When I stepped in, a young woman rushed toward me so quickly I nearly screamed.

"Shh!" she whispered. "They are summoning now."

Behind her, a half dozen people sat in a circle with a small fire between them. They were speaking quietly in a language I did not understand. I stared, wide-eyed, before the woman grabbed my hand and led me up the stairs. There were a number of doors that led off the narrow hallway, and she walked me through one of them. It was a bedroom. I panicked, and backed away from her, shaking my head.

"No, no," I said. "I am not interested in . . ." I pointed to the bed. "I am looking for a friend. Firoz is his name. Kahina said—"

She looked exhausted by me and took my flapping hands in hers. "This is my bedroom. I live here. Not work. You almost ruined the arwah. Odham would have been furious."

Wary, I asked, "What are they trying to summon?"

"Eh, only a hatif. There are newcomers."

I opened my mouth to ask more when something thundered from down the stairs. There was a crash, a slide, then groaning.

The woman sighed and ran out to the hallway. "Get up!" she hissed. "There is someone here to see you."

Moving swiftly, I stepped out of the room and peered over the railing. Firoz lay in a clumsy pile in the middle of the steps.

"Firo!" I said happily.

He looked up at me in a daze, and I hesitated.

"Blemel!" He cried, slurring my name. He stood, wobbling, before he fell and proceeded to crawl up the stairs.

When he was standing in front of me I could tell by the sweetness of his breath and the glaze of his eyes that he was as drunk and drugged as my father often was.

"Come with me," he slurred, taking my hand and attempting to pull me down the hallway.

I recoiled and pulled away. "Perhaps now is not a good time."

"Blemel no, now's perfect!" He was shouting.

Ahead, I saw a door open, and Rashid walked out in a rush. When he saw me, he looked surprised, but smiled nonetheless.

"Emel!"

The anger I felt toward Firoz shifted to Rashid. I gestured at Firoz, who was babbling about the arwah, which apparently had finished. Rashid asked me to wait, took Firoz into what I presumed was their room, and after a long moment, came out by himself.

"Join me?" When I hesitated he said, "Firoz should lie down."

Instead of going back downstairs, Rashid held open a curtain that led outside. There was a sturdy wooden ladder leaning against the wall that Rashid climbed up. From the small balcony, the backs of other homes were so close I could nearly reach out and touch them. Testing the ladder, I carefully followed Rashid.

My knees grew weak when I reached the roof of the jalsa tadhat. We were high up off the ground, only now there were no walls to contain me should I fall.

"It is safe," Rashid said, giving me his hand. I scrambled onto the flat roof.

Rashid seated himself at the edge, his legs dangling over the side. I chose a spot at the center—well away from the edges. From here, I could see the palace emerging from the city like a ship at sea—glowing a pale orange against the deep blue night.

"I am glad you have come. Firoz misses you," Rashid said.

"Does he?" Somehow I doubted that.

"We can't come to the palace, you know. He tried early on to visit." Tavi had said the same.

A stirring of shame. "So this is the life you've found? Summoning spirits?" My lip curled.

"It is all in fun. We could not all be handed palace work by the king."

"Fun? Hatifs might be harmless, but what will you attempt to summon next, an ifrit?"

"They try."

I gasped.

"Really, Emel?" He looked at me with unveiled exasperation. "Only children believe in those things. Children and the fools who pay us to summon them. Odham rattles bells and waves palm fronds to stir the air and everyone feels it was worth their coin."

He did not remember that he once believed a jinni would free the desert.

"You're fools to meddle in it," I said. What would happen if they summoned something real? I shuddered to think of the repercussions.

He shrugged. "The baytahira attracts people who talk, you know. It is why I wanted to speak with you." He scooted close to me and lowered his voice. "Some are whispering about a gathering of people with plans to upend Madinat Almulihi. Maybe the ones who killed the royal family . . ."

He waited, knowing that would snag my interest, but I was not going to let him take me down the path of conspiracy. Rashid was the one who had told Firoz about the Dalmur, who got us both tangled in that web. It was not something I wanted to deal with here. After all, it was meddling with rebellion that had almost killed Firoz.

"Does Firoz drink like this often?" I asked.

There was a sharp intake of breath. "He does. Since we arrived."

Rashid told me that Firoz took quickly to their life in the baytahira, to his freedom and his pocket of coin. "I'm sure when the newness wears, he'll slow his indulgence."

Kahina had directed them to the jalsa tadhat the same night I was introduced to Altasa. Firoz helped with the arwahs. Rashid worked in one of Kahina's Bura-dens, but lived with Firoz in the jalsa tadhat. I would not admit it to Rashid—Sons, I could barely admit it to myself—but I envied them. Rashid and

Firoz living together, enough wealth and time to spend it frivolously. I considered that Tavi and I could have lived together, too, serving drink or food or whatever else people did here that was not bedding for coin.

I brushed hair from my face. "Well, I came to see Firo, but it is clear he is occupied." For good or ill, everyone's life seemed to tumble ahead while I dug my nails into the ground, trying to hold on to that which I had so desperately left behind.

"Don't be so quick to cast your judgement." Rashid watched me, and I knew he saw my anger. "He has not been the same since everything happened in the settlement."

"I know." The scar left behind when he was to be executed, when I wished for him to be saved. He *was* saved, and though magic muddied his memory, he still felt the traces of an almost-death. "Turning to drink or Buraq doesn't help. You're only making it worse for him by allowing it."

Rashid was staring at the jagged lines of rooftops when I got up to leave.

Back on the ground level, I looked into the room where the arwah had taken place. The woman who had ushered me upstairs was now sweeping sand from between the cushions. Two people lingered, leaning against the wall. One was cloaked and turned so that I could not see him. The other was a small man with scars on his face, deeply shadowed by the firelight. The hair on his head was shorn to the scalp.

The way he spoke to his companion—almost with a sneer, his tongue sliding over his lips and glinting teeth—unsettled me.

Arguing voices from outside the door drew my attention away from the men. The woman dropped the broom with a loud clatter, groaning about "this again," and ran out front. I followed.

"Not here!" she shouted at two men who appeared to be arguing. "Not now! There are patrons inside!"

They were both very tall, and one was much older than the other.

"It is not any business of yours," the older man said.

"You don't know what you're playing with—trying to summon spirits," the younger man spat. He was different than many of the men I had seen in

Almulihi. Although he dressed and had mannerisms of a seaborn, there was something about him that was unusual.

"Odham," the woman said, pressing her hands against the older man's forearms. "Come inside. Ignore this fool."

"No!" Odham said and shoved his face a mere fist's distance away from the younger man. "I will not have people like this come and tarnish my work because they think they know better than me."

The young man scowled at Odham. Heavy silver bracelets clanked as he shook his fists at him. "Masira will not sit idle while you try to pull the strings of her power. She will have her say, and you will regret what you're doing here."

Unthinking, I nodded along to the young man's words. It was a surprising relief to hear what I was thinking spoken aloud by someone else. I edged closer to him, facing Odham and the woman.

"He is right," I said. They all stopped and looked at me, and when I saw the young man's face straight on, I hesitated. He was almost familiar, but I knew I had never seen him before. He had an arcing scar that stretched from his brow to his temple. I would not forget something like that. Looking back to Odham and the woman, I said, "There are consequences when you ask Masira to grant you things. She does not give without taking. And she does not give kindly. You dare summon an ifrit or si'la, you may bring this city to the ground."

Odham scowled and leaned toward me. "Fools," he hissed and looked between me and the strange man. "Are you children? That is stuff of legends! Of fire stories!" His voice grew louder.

"Odham . . ." the woman warned quietly. "Some are still inside."

As the woman pulled Odham away, the young man hissed, "If that is so, I'd rather be a child. Adults see things and think they see everything, but children know to look in the spaces between, and even when they have seen all, they still search for more." He turned to me. "Come. We have warned them. Let them learn what happens when they call on the goddess."

He beckoned me and I followed. It felt as though we were the only two sane people on the street.

8

EMEL

"**W**here are we going?" I followed the man down the street through the clusters of people. He took enormous strides.

"I don't know yet," he said. "It's just so . . ." He threw his hands out beside him. "Infuriating." Suddenly he stopped and turned to me. He pushed his hair off his brow and grimaced. "Sons, I have not even introduced myself." He nodded his head. "Kas."

"Kas," I repeated, looking up at him. "Emel."

His smile broadened, and I warmed, just a little.

"How would you like to get something to drink? To forget the fools that don't respect Masira. Or, are you hungry? We can go to my favorite place."

I shook my head. I had eaten my fill of dried, honeyed apricots before I'd left. "Not hungry, but a drink, I think I need." The last time I *needed* a drink, I was being prepared for a muhami. Tonight's drink was not to wash away my pride but my past. Although I had only just met him, already being with Kas felt effortless. The promise of this easy evening with Kas was almost a relief after everything with Firoz.

We went to the opposite end of the baytahira to a shop where people crowded both inside and out—it had walls that opened up like a market stall. Men and woman handed goblets across a low wall in chaotic order. There were tables and chairs scattered outside and each one was filled, some chairs even held two people, one sitting on another's lap.

"They serve wine from across the sea. The best there is." He smiled and fanned his fingers. "The grapes grow to the plucking of a guitar." Guitar? Did he mean sitar?

Kas went to find a place for us to sit and told me to wait by the street. I decided I would count to forty and if he had not returned by then, I would go back to the palace. But before I got to twenty, he was leading me toward an empty table with two chairs. Smiling despite myself, I followed him.

"I didn't think you'd find us a place," I said, sitting down.

"Just cleared," he said. "Let me fetch our drinks."

It was a cold night, and I wrapped my cloak tightly around my shoulders. I touched the camel fur gently, relishing its softness.

With a loud clunk, Kas set two goblets of heavy brass on the table. Thanking him, I took a long drink.

"So." He raised his eyebrows at me. "What does the maiden think?"

"Grapes enjoy music, too, it seems."

He laughed and took a drink himself. He watched the people around us for several breaths before he said, "Odham is a fool, always has been. Doesn't know what he's doing."

"A friend works there. He helps with the arwahs."

"You should tell—"

"I did. He won't listen." I had drunk half the wine already. "Where I'm from . . ." I began, then paused. It occurred to me that he hadn't asked. He hadn't faltered when I spoke to him or when he saw me, wondering at my foreignness. I warmed to him even more, my tongue loosening. "You can't even say *jinn* without everyone shushing you."

"Really?" he asked, slapping a hand to the table.

"Yes!" I said, smiling. Already, he felt like a friend.

"They are smarter than the people here."

"I don't know about that."

"Here, they're spoiled by peace."

"But it has not been all peaceful, has it?"

Sighing, he looked down at his clasped hands. "I try to forget. That was not peace, no. Enough time has passed since the attack that people are already forgetting. So quickly we take safety for granted."

"And now there is a new king."

"There is."

"Is he a good king?" I wondered what the people thought of Saalim.

Kas shrugged, and interlocked his fingers. "He is not King Malek."

The wine loosened my tongue. I said, "My father was the king of my settlement. He was killed."

He let out a long breath and met my gaze. "I am sorry."

"It was for the best, I think."

He cocked his head, and I began to explain who I was, where I had come from. It was easy, trusting him. "He was cruel. He kept my sisters and me locked away. To him, we secured allies. Made him powerful." The people at the nearby table stood, their chairs scraping across the stone. I watched them.

"Look at us." He grabbed the table's edge. "Talking of ignorant people and lost kings. This is not what we need and certainly not what I had in mind when I invited you along. Apologies." He offered up his palms and shrugged. "Perhaps we can try again?"

I smiled at him and pulled my cloak high over my neck as another gust of wind ripped through the street. "The wine was good. And the people are entertaining." I nodded to the rowdy crowds that surrounded us.

"I will make up for it at the gambling house."

Absently, I pressed my fingers against the small pouch at my hip. There were only a few coins, and I was not eager to gamble them away. It was strange to think that I had been so much wealthier back home. Granted, Saalim had given me all the salt I carried then, but still. Now I had less than a handful of coins that I protected fiercely. Wealth did not come by magic anymore.

"Come on," he coaxed, smiling. "Think about it like this—you're paying for the fun." He saw my face. "Do you have a fid?"

I fished out my pouch and searched for a silver coin. I had two.

"Promise me just one fid for the night, and I promise you I'll make up for the poor start to our evening."

"Just one."

We stood and left the table. Once I was clear of the crowd, I turned back, realizing we had not returned our goblets.

"What is it?"

I could not find our table. I told Kas, and he laughed. "Here, you pay for the wine and for someone to take the empty goblet when you're done. Now, shall we spend that fid or would you like to clear more tables?" He walked away from me, talking about how thrilled the shopkeeper would be to have someone do the work for free.

The gambling house was enormous inside. The ceilings were so high over our heads I could believe I was in the palace. Inside, it was calmer than the street had been, but there were still rounds of shouting, speckled cries—of happiness or lament, I could not tell. There were gambling dens back home—clandestine places hidden from the Salt King in plain sight—but I had never visited them. They were not where I wanted to spend the little freedom I had.

Nor the salt.

Kas led me to a table surrounded by a large crowd. Nudging people aside, he pulled us up to the front. There was a wooden carving of a coiled snake, its head at the center of the coil. Painted cowries were scattered across the tabletop, some seated within the deep grooves of the snake, while others lay around it. Three people played this round. They were tense, holding their shoulders up to their ears and their fingers in tight fists as they waited for the other to throw his cowries. A man did, and one of the red ones landed on the neck of the snake, the other off the board completely. The other two cheered, and the next man threw his cowries.

"Have you played?" Kas whispered. His breath touched my ear.

I shook my head.

"It's called maha—you feed the snake. Land as many as you can on him. The ones closest to his mouth get you the most points. Land one on his nose, and you win."

The nose was rounded in a way that landing a shell there would take in-credible luck.

The round finished, and the points were counted. When the winner took the money, others began to hold their bronze out, ready for the next game.

Kas spoke. "How about a fid for this round?" Those clutching their nabs withered, but a few others took their place and within a moment, my silver coin was in the middle of the table, and my palm was full of black cowries.

When it was my turn to throw, I took three of them. You could throw as many as you wanted on your turn—one at a time, or all at once—depending on your strategy. I had no strategy, so I simply tossed.

Two bounced to the outermost grooves, near the tip of the snake's tail. The other landed on the center of its neck. Kas nudged me, and I grinned.

The next player went. He cupped his blue shells and said into his palm, "For King Malek's soul, may Masira guard it."

"With wings spread wide," others said in unison.

The man threw his shells.

An older woman standing nearby absently watching the game leaned into her neighbor. "King Saalim is in a dark shadow."

"He can't be what his father was," a man replied.

My throat tightened at the disapproval in his voice.

"You think he's not fit?" the man throwing the blue shells asked as he wait-ed for the player with the red to go.

"Of course he isn't," she said it as if it were obvious. "He is arrogant, too."

"Both boys were." The man shook his head gravely, his gray beard swaying. "The daughters were good girls. Masira protect their souls."

Kas stiffened.

Horrified that they would disparage the royal family in such a public place, I poked my nail into the cowrie's cleft like I was fascinated by its shape.

"I have heard whispers of replacing the king," Kas said. "Come time for the Falsa Mawk."

Gasps. Even I stopped fussing with the shell.

"So soon?"

"Who?"

"How?"

Kas began to explain, and I stared at all their faces. They had forgotten the game and watched him eagerly. I dropped my fist to the table, letting the shells fall on the surface.

"Forfeiting your hand?" the man with the blue shells asked, eyes dancing between my coin and the cowries.

"Yes," I said, backing away.

"Wait," I heard Kas say to the people around the table. His hand was hot on my shoulder, and I turned around. "What is it?" he asked.

"I won't be associated with maligning the king or his family."

Kas made a face that looked as though he'd tasted something awful.

I said, "I can't risk losing my place here."

His eyes widened, and he laughed, shaking his head. "This is not some settlement, Emel. They cannot punish me for speaking words."

Now I made the displeased face.

"Please, will you come back to the game? I promise we will talk no more of politics." He rubbed his hands together and frowned.

"If you hold to your promise," I said. Together, we went back to the table. I picked up my shells. "Let's finish then."

When the people asked Kas to go on, he shook his head and said it was all meaningless gossip anyway.

The other two had tossed all their cowries, knocking my black shell from the neck. Peering at the hungry snake, red looked to be winning with two shells near the head and four on its body. Blue had only three on its body.

I picked up the remaining shells and with a gentle swing, tossed them. They dropped to the board like rain.

A woman laughed across the table from me. "It's no wonder you played the fid."

One of my cowries lay, impossibly, on the tip of the snake's nose. I stared at it, disbelieving it possible. We all stared as though waiting for it to slide off. It held.

Like magic, my one silver coin suddenly was three.

"Again?" Kas asked.

"No," I said, holding tightly to my silver coins. "I don't want to lose fid because there is a breeze in the room."

"It is not all luck. There is some skill in how you throw them."

"No," I said again. "I want to play something that I can control."

"Gambling is mostly luck, Emel."

"Then you play, and I'll watch. If I lose my money, I want it to be because I failed. Not because it was fated from the start."

In the way he narrowed his eyes, I knew he was making a decision about me. "This way," he said.

We strode up to an open circle of people around a low table. Kas gestured to an empty cushion, and with reluctance, I sat down. Five faces peered at me curiously.

"Buying a hand?" an older man asked me. His voice was sand ground against stone, and his hands looked equally worn.

"Just one," Kas said from behind me. Then he mumbled, "Have to see if the lady approves."

I smirked.

The hands from the previous round were laid out in front of their players. Beautiful illustrations were painted brightly on the thick vellum. I could see a drum filled with water, a dune of sand beside a single palm, a trio of vultures soaring in a circle, an urn of fire . . . my smile widened.

"It is my favorite," I said eagerly.

"You know ghamar?" Kas asked, surprised.

Nodding, I set down my fid at the center of the table. The old man took it and scooped up the cards. He shuffled them and dealt me my hand. I knew this game well. Though we did not call it by the same name, my sisters and I had a similar worn deck that we gambled with days and nights to pass the time. We had no coin, of course, but our cowries and chipped beads served the same purpose.

I studied my cards: a scorpion beside a dead rat, a silver chain wrapped around a thin wrist, a desert cave, and an enormous wave hovering above a small boat. The last card gave me pause. Ghamar was a game of power and storytelling. The goal for each round was to place the most powerful card to win the hand. There was no one card that was necessarily more powerful than the other. It depended on the player and how convincing they were in their storytelling. With my sisters, there was no explanation needed. We knew what we would say for each card—we had heard each other's stories one thousand times—so it was a quieter game. We knew which cards would win each round just by seeing the image.

The deck at home was the only one I had ever played, and I knew those cards well. Seeing this one now, I realized decks could be different. While it did not surprise me to see a card with the sea, I did not think that I would be able to win any hand with that card. What did I know of water?

The players began to lay down their cards: a snake with its jaws stretched over a fox, a sword with blood on its edge, a glistening, empty chalice, and a woman who cried into her hands—that was a throw away, I was sure. I looked back at my cards and reached for the card with the cave.

"Do you not think this one instead?" Kas pointed to the chained wrist.

I shook my head.

"If you're not playing, then you cannot speak," the old man said. I understood now he was not playing either. He was the keeper of our money, the dealer of the cards, and the judge of our game. Quickly, I placed the card on the table, excited to convince the others of why mine was the best.

"A sword takes a life with ease," the man sitting to my left said.

"But a snake is silent, and though its bite is small, it is deadly," a woman with a green scarf draped over her shoulders replied.

The man who played his sword shook his head, about to speak, but the scarved-woman continued. "A sword meant to kill must be precise and strong. It depends on who wields it. A snake is born with that power. He simply needs to sink his teeth once."

"Does drink not give you power?" the other man said, pointing to the empty chalice. "Wetting the throat of your enemy will always allow you the advantage. Especially when they see three of you." He chuckled.

"No, no," the woman in red said, shaking her head. "There is nothing more powerful than a crying woman, eh?" She raised her eyebrows and looked and me and the other woman. "A few tears, and we get what we want. I think, perhaps, being a woman is the most powerful thing of all."

Kas laughed with the other men. I smiled as I knew I was supposed to, but I was too excited to listen closely. This was too easy.

"You all speak of mundane power. Yes, these things can be strong, but what I have is ethereal, see."

"A desert cave?" The scarfless woman scoffed.

"It is no ordinary cave," I said quietly, becoming absurdly serious as I drummed my fingers against the table. "It is the home of a si'la. The strongest magic in the desert hides in this cave. The si'la can alter her appearance, convince nomads to do anything she wishes, and send people to the sky with the wave of her hand. She does not need a sword nor wine. Snakes nor tears. She has the providence of the goddess."

There was a grunt of approval behind me, and I allowed myself a small feeling of satisfaction. But I had not yet won. The card keeper would have the final say.

Without pause, the old man shaped his hand like a crescent moon and pushed the coins toward me as the others groaned. Then he tapped the table. "Coins for the next hand."

I threw in another fid, and Kas did not again suggest my play.

Although the moon was high, people did not seem to be thinking of home in the baytahira. They still milled here and there as if it were the start of the day.

"Is it always so busy?" I asked Kas as we left the gambling house, my coin purse notably heavier.

"Until the sun rises, and even then, sometimes it continues well into the day."

"I can find my way back," I told him as we left the baytahira.

"Oh," he said, stopping. "This is your way of telling me to leave, eh?"

I smiled weakly. "But it's also true. I know my way."

"You'll have to be careful going home."

"Why?"

He cocked his head as though it were obvious. "Not every person you meet on the street will take you to drink wine and a gambling house and expect it ends there."

My cheeks heated. "Of course. I am careful."

More people now were cloaked and covered. I passed two leaning against a wall with hoods pulled so far over their faces I could not see where they looked. I thought of the pair at the jalsa tadhat. Had I been foolish to follow Kas?

Kas said, "My night would not have been the same had I drunk wine by myself and gambled away coin. And I probably *would* have gambled it gone. You are the best ghamar player I've met. Though I haven't met very many. It's not my game of choice."

I raised my eyebrows. "You prefer testing Masira's charity."

He laughed loudly, and I couldn't help but laugh, too.

"I've spent many evenings at the jalsa tadhat, trying to convince Odham to stop what he's doing. It ends as it always does—unsuccessfully. Tarnishes the whole night. Never has someone walked out of that place agreeing with me. It was an unexpected but welcome change."

He had been kind tonight, and now that we were parting, I found I was not ready to say goodbye. I recalled something he said earlier in the evening. "What is the Falsa Mawk?"

"A day parade, night party. A celebration of the Sons. It goes until daybreak the next morning. Sometimes longer." A crooked smile slid up one cheek.

"When is it?"

He did not hesitate. "Just over two moons. Right before the king's wedding."

With his last words, Madinat Almulihi disappeared. I was suspended in the middle of nothing, the words echoing around me like a bad dream.

The king's wedding.

Could Kas see my face? Did he feel the panic that beat through me like a drum?

"The king will be married?" I tried to keep my voice level, to sound as if this was simply the curiosity of a woman who enjoys love. But the words came out breathy and shaky.

"Of course. To a woman from across the sea."

Gathering myself, I said, "How lovely." I pressed my hands to my chest, willing my heart to stop pounding. "I should return home." This man did not need to witness my coming apart completely.

We stood in the middle of the wide road off the baytahira. The palace soared up over the rooftops. Light sparkled from the windows. Saalim was in there somewhere, waiting for his queen.

We said goodbye. I had not gone more than one hundred steps when I heard fast footsteps clapping toward me. Turning around, I saw Kas running.

"Sorry," he said. "But I think we should do this again."

"This?"

"Yes," he said. "I can show you other parts of town. There is a great place we can walk—spectacular views of the city and sea. Or if you don't want that we can try this cook-house near the water. Fish come right from the nets. Or we can go back to the baytahira if you want to win more coin at ghamar."

His sheepish grin slowed the chill that was spreading fast through me. "And if I say no?"

He shrugged and ran a hand across the back of his neck. "You go home. And we had a fun evening."

I had come to Madinat Almulihi for Saalim. Though I'd vowed I would fight for him, he was set to be wed to someone else by powers much greater than mine.

Did I think I could convince a king a salt chaser was worthy, because I was marked? Because Masira had *chosen* me? I pressed my hand to the golden smudge on my chest, nearly laughing aloud. What a fool! The mark meant nothing.

I meant nothing.

Grappling with the revelation that Saalim would never be mine would have to come later. Perhaps in bed, knees to my chest, tears spilling on the softest pillow.

Saalim wasn't the only thing I'd wanted when I wished for freedom from my father, I reminded myself. I wanted a life that was all mine, that I had chosen for myself.

Tonight I had found that. Tonight was *fun*.

Firoz and Tavi had built new lives without me.

Saalim would never have me.

And Kas was standing here *asking* for me. The answer was obvious.

"When?" I asked, and he smiled.

II.

YEARNING

— ⦁—

LUQAT

M asira, great in power, was unconcerned with the Life that inhabited the desert. She left, in her wake, traces of her power that the People discovered and turned to their own purposes. In this time, there were many such magicians and conjurers that made gardens of the dunes and drew great wealth from the sands.

This amused Masira, and she thought, If they deign use the dregs of My power, I shall make sport of them; as they take from Me, so shall I take from them in turn.

In this way, the fruits of the gardens tasted of ash, and the gold of the sands crumbled to salt.

Wahir was appalled and admonished his Mother that she should punish man for making use of the gifts she left behind. Eiqab, too, disagreed. Why should man be allowed to wield the power of the goddess? Better to leave him to scratch his place from the stones of the desert.

Masira considered her sons and recognized their wisdom. To Wahir, she said: You are right. Those common Magics used by man, Love, Music, Speech, may be used henceforth without retribution. And to Eiqab, she said: You are right, as well. Those acts of higher Magic with which man rivals My Sons, I shall withdraw from the desert, excepting from those who are willing to sacrifice much. For to wield the greatest power, one must sacrifice all.

—Excerpt from the Litab Almuq

9

SAALIM

Beside me, Ekram walked down the dock with his ledger open in one hand and a piece of dried meat in the other. We could have been sitting in his storehouse back at the shore—the assembly of guards that trailed behind me would have preferred it as they eyed every passing stranger—but he knew I preferred to be out with the salt and wind, and I knew he felt the same.

"Shipments from the north are up, which is good, hm? Falsa Mawk helps. So does Helena." He tore at the strip of meat with his teeth. As we walked, people came and went from the ships like ants on a stick, slowly and methodically. "I've been sending out more salt to the east, but they've not been sending very many goods back. Linen is down. Maybe not so good of a price here?" He was staring at his list of numbers and words, not paying attention to the wooden planks under his feet as we passed the moored ships. Still, he managed to step over a plank that jutted out above the others. "Thali said her sugar and flower suppliers will be finding more fields, so we should receive enough by the time of the festival."

Even the docks couldn't distract me from the Falsa Mawk today.

It was an old tradition in Almulihi—a celebration for Eiqab during the day and Wahir at night. At first, it had been a quiet party shared between neighbors and families, but my mother loved the different displays and dances and games so much my father had transformed it into something as grand as he could—a citywide parade. He only cared that he was king, he told me once, because with that crown he could give my mother everything.

I think it was in his guilt for his past that he had found his commitment to give her the entire world.

Each year's Falsa Mawk seemed more elaborate than the last, with more and more of the city joining in. Now it was an extravagant quilt of celebrations that showcased the people who lived in the city. If it was my choice, I would not have it at all. It would be agony to watch the displays going by the palace. These people had once spent days pinning dried petals and leaves to wooden posts or practicing synchronized twirls and dips with their absurdly ornamented costumes, just so my mother would smile and clap. And she was not here to see it this year.

And then there was the wedding that would conclude the festivities. Thali and Mariam were handling the event with deft hands. They both had prepared the marriage of my father to my mother. Though the wedding would be easy by comparison, it would only deepen the loss I felt. That aching hollowness that would not go away.

"Here again," Ekram said. In the direction he stared was a familiar old woman talking to a young man.

"Altasa?" I asked, squinting against the sun.

"Mhmm." He chewed loudly.

I scanned those in her group. Was *she* with them? I exhaled, the question leaving with my breath. Emel was there, standing beside the healer, peering down at the dock. A flat wagon with two crates rested beside her.

Ekram continued. "Altasa has been here—"

I raised a hand to Ekram and excused myself.

Several of the shipmen saw me—or, they saw the retinue of guards behind me—as I approached, and they scurried back onto the ship, pretending to be busy. The healer turned, annoyed by my interruption.

"Altasa." I nodded. "Emel. What business have you on the docks? There are people who can do this for you." Though she had evidently regained some of her strength, Altasa still seemed only held up by her bones, and even then, barely. The enormous ship rocked up and down behind her. I could not imagine the pair carrying their things all the way back to the palace.

"Can't trust some boy to run my supplies for me. Barely can trust this one." She pointed her elbow in Emel's direction.

Emel frowned at the healer. Using her distraction to my advantage, I surveyed her. Emel's hand, gripping the wagon's handle firmly, was stained red. Altasa's hands, I noticed, were clean. Emel's arm was not as thin as I remembered. Her face, too. She was softer now. I wanted her to look at me, but she had turned toward the ship and watched its hull as if it were the most fascinating thing in the world.

I turned to Altasa. "Tell Nassar if you decide otherwise. The docks are no place for women."

Altasa scoffed and looked at my clasped hands. "Nor soft hands."

Ignoring her, I asked, "Has more salve been made?" Though the aches of the journey were behind me now, I kept requesting more, hoping Emel would deliver it.

"Take the tonic! It's quicker to make—"

"Finished preparing it last night," Emel said. "I planned to deliver it to Mariam today."

"Bring it directly to me after midday." It came out of my mouth before I could think of an excuse for why I might need her to deliver it personally. "The last time one of the jars, ah, was missing."

"You see!" Altasa pointed her finger. "And you expect me to have someone do this for me? Your own steals from you! Take care, Saalim—" She was the only one who managed to make the use of my name feel like an insult. "—people in your own palace could be against you." With her penchant for the dramatic, Altasa reminded me much of the old palace healer, Zahar.

───────

"Shall we clear it first?" The guard asked as we approached the low temple.

There were more windows than walls, and I could see a number of people circulating inside.

"No. Let them pray." Leaving the guards behind so as not to disturb those inside, I passed through the arches, the squares of sunlight through the windows spreading across my shoulders like a warm blanket, and found myself inside the temple.

The tedium of my meetings with Ekram used to send me to furious boredom, but I had seen the consequences of inattention and impatience. I would not make those same mistakes. So I listened, had him repeat that which I misunderstood or did not hear. I showed Ekram and the seamen that I was to be taken seriously, that *they* were to be taken seriously. But now my mind hummed with numbers and goods, and I needed something to calm it.

This temple was the largest and most ornate in Almulihi, but there were many more scattered throughout the city. It was a large room with a round, shallow pool at the center—wide enough for ten people to lie across, head to foot. Echoing around me was the sound of trickling water from the fountain at the edges of the room. People were kneeling at the pool, the fine reflection of the sun creating webs across their bodies. They pressed their hands into the water, then against their shoulders, their brow, their wrists.

None took notice of me. When people were in Wahir's temple, they thought only of him.

I walked to the fountain—a tipping of vessels fed by the aqueduct and then by each other. I held my fingers under the stream, letting them fall against the weight.

The Darkafa planned to destroy Almulihi because it was Wahir's city. They wanted Eiqab to reign to the edge of his desert. So it had to be salt chasers who wanted me dethroned. When a war wasn't fought to place a new king on the throne, it was fought to put a god there.

When the king crosses the desert, the goddess will return. She will unleash the second-born Son to put the first-born to death. My family had been attacked before I journeyed to Alfaar's, and I could not remember the last time my father had left Almulihi to travel inward. He had long used my brother for those errands. The

Darkafa seemed an obvious explanation for the death of my family, yet their augury suggested a different timeline.

Pacing around the room, my fingers following the trail of the water, I prayed.

I needed only one opportunity to prove I could rule like my father had. That the crown he had given me was not in vain. His blood was half of me, I reminded myself. I was of a king, and I could be the same. Though I felt myself to be a husk of what a king should be.

My knees sank into the cool water as I pressed my palms to the bottom of the pool.

A murmur came from across the room, an echo like the splash of water. I refrained from peering up at them. Talking was not forbidden, but should the whispers drown out the sound of water, it was frowned upon.

"The child carries it still."

"But has not the goddess been found?"

The goddess.

"Yes. But the child still has it."

"Why hasn't the goddess come for it?"

"She came once."

"To the cave?"

"I was not there, but I heard she took it, then gave it back to the child."

A woman hissed from across the room. "This is a temple, not a Bura-den."

When I noticed the whispering pair's appearance, I swiftly left the temple, water leaving a dripping trail behind me.

The guards waited for me outside and stood upright when they saw the urgency with which I approached. I told them what I had just seen and heard. "They are cloaked and hooded. I want to know where they stay, and why they are here."

They nodded. Kofi and Tamam pulled the guthras from their heads and the blue belts that held their swords from their waists, handing them to the others. Tamam was reluctant, as I knew he would be. He did not like to be without his defense. But they could not wear what marked them as king's men while maintaining discretion. Now they looked like civilians. They slipped beneath the archway of the aqueduct that fed the temple, waiting to follow the men.

I wished to have been the one to follow the Darkafa. My hands itched to grab their throats. *Murderers.* They had to be.

When I entered the palace atrium, Nika rushed up to meet me.

"King Saalim," she said in a hurry. "I am sorry to disturb you. There is a visitor here." She stared at the tiles.

"Not now," I barked. Primed by the men in my temple, anger ignited easily and spread through me, liquid and hot.

Nika was still as a statue. "I told her you did not like unexpected visitors. She said she was expected . . ."

Incredulous, I stared at the vines behind Nika that still swayed from her rushed entry. Right now, I wanted to rip the vines down, let their pots come clattering to the floor.

Nika flinched. Had I moved? "Where is she?" I asked more gently. The Darkafa, the death of my family, was not Nika's fault.

"The dining halls."

"Thank you, Nika," I said.

Nika let out a quiet breath as I departed.

My mother had warned me many times to temper my ire toward the servants. Since returning from Alfaar's, it had become less difficult to remember. Maybe it was that I was now king. Or perhaps things had changed after I had seen that pathetic man pretend to be a god over gullible people.

The dining halls were normally bright this time of day, but clouds had rolled across the sun. Emel stood alone in the room. Hurriedly, I waved away the guard who had followed me in.

"Emel?" I asked, stepping forward quickly. The pinch of guilt and anger releasing when I saw her. "What is it?"

She held the sack in her hands toward me. "What you requested."

"Of course." I had forgotten. As I took it, my fingers lightly brushed against hers. She pulled her hand away so quickly, I nearly dropped the sack. "Thank you. Please sit," I said, pointing at the empty dining table.

After pulling out a chair for her and myself, I said, "I have been meaning to speak with you for some time. Sons, it has been two moons now, hasn't it? Time has slipped by me. Do you have everything you need?"

Emel nodded.

"Is Almulihi to your liking?"

She looked away from me, staring at the long tapestries that hung from the ceiling. "That which I have seen, I enjoy. I have not seen much. Altasa keeps me busy."

"Is there somewhere you would like to see?" My father's insistence on propriety clamored loudly in my ears—this was a palace worker, a salt chaser. I kept talking to drown it out. "I can take you. Or if I cannot, I can have it arranged." I couldn't take her.

What was I thinking? Why did I keep talking?

She smiled weakly and shook her head. "I have a friend who can show me." The sun briefly peaked through the clouds behind her. She looked to be wreathed in gold.

Twinges of jealousy. "Friends from your settlement?"

Suddenly she frowned. "King Saalim . . ." She looked down at her fingers, distracted by her nails.

My name from her lips.

I urged her to continue.

"My friend has told me he has heard rumors . . ." she paused again.

"Of?"

"He said people are talking about a new king who will try to take the throne during the Falsa Mawk."

Leaning back, I said, "My father warned me that there will always be someone who sees himself a better fit for the crown. People will talk. It does not often mean sedition. Do not fear."

"I do not fear for myself."

Her eyes were as dark as ink and fathomless as the sea. I wanted to see their depths, know what she was thinking. "Who told you this?" I asked. I wanted as little known as possible of the threat of the Darkafa. It would serve poorly to have that knowledge permeate through the people. What boastful fool was telling everyone he met? Unless he was one of them . . .

"My friend."

"But who was he? Where did you meet him?"

She shook her head. "The baytahira—"

I shot forward. "Baytahira? Emel, don't waste your time there." It was not a place for foreigners, easy prey for coin. As a child, I'd snuck away to the street often. It was forbidden, of course, so it was always exciting. So many times, Kahina and her friend walked me back to the palace, holding my hand as softly as Mother. I never understood how people so kind could be found in an area forbidden to me. "Have you even seen all of the palace? It is the most beautiful place in Almulihi." I gestured around us, considering whether or not this was true. "Perhaps second only to the temple." The sun was gone again, and it grew darker outside with each breath of wind.

"No." Emel looked out to the balcony. "The sea is the most beautiful."

"Someone once told me they thought the water seemed angry."

Her face snapped back to me, eyes wide. In a rush, she asked, "Who?"

I thought about it, trying to recall who had said it. I could not remember one single detail from that conversation other than those words. I told her so.

She nodded, seeming as though I disappointed her.

There was a *pat, pat.* It started slowly, then increased in its frequency.

"Rain!" She ran to the balcony and spread her arms, face turned up.

Enchanted, I followed her out, unable to take my eyes from her. She laughed, letting the drops fall onto her face and hands.

"What are you doing?" I asked, laughing with her.

She spun, her clothes sticking to her as they became soaked. "The finest gift Masira can give."

I had never considered rain to be so wondrous. It helped to fill the water stores and cleaned the dust off of homes, but I did not feel the need to dance beneath the drops.

"Come," she said, watching me with bright eyes. She pulled my hand, tugging me outside so easily that it felt like we had done this one hundred times before.

With eyes closed, face tipped up again, she said, "Back home, everyone ran outside when it rained."

Of course. She was from the desert. She soaked it in, her sandals leaving wet, brown footprints on the balcony with each turn of her feet. Suddenly, she slipped on the slick tile, her arms flapping to prevent her fall. I caught her shoulders, and she spun toward me, gripping my tunic as she steadied herself.

We stood there beneath the rain, staring at each other. So close, I noticed the dip in her lip looked just like Anisa's wings when she soared.

Her shoulders rose and fell with her headiness, and though she was stable now, I did not let them go. And she did not take her hands from me. There was the gentlest press of her fingertips to my waist, her palms curving around my sides.

"Saalim." It was a whisper so intimate I took the smallest step toward her.

"You almost fell."

"You did not let me." She tilted her head, her lips parting like she was asking for more. Drops of rain slipped into her mouth, onto her tongue.

Oh, to be that drop.

A longing, deep and heavy pooled, and I slid my hands down her arms.

Misunderstanding my movement, Emel backed away. "Thank you," she said, her liquid gaze clearing as she pulled her hands away, leaving me cold and wanting. Her mouth closed as she adjusted her sopping fustan.

Clearing my throat I said, "Well, if you are done with your dance, I would like to show you the palace."

10

EMEL

Tiles on the floor swirled with blue paint. Small squares in every color marched along the borders of every door and window. Sheer curtains billowed into the corridor from the rainy wind, and torches quivered at the disturbance. I distracted myself with these things as I walked with Saalim, because otherwise, I would stare only at him.

Each time I would linger, letting him get a stride ahead of me so that I might stare at his back or survey his hands, but he inevitably dropped back until he was beside me.

He had been in my arms. I had been in his. Everything was shifted into its proper place for only a moment, and now I wanted it back.

He is betrothed.

It was foolish of me to follow him as I was, hoping he would take interest in a salt chaser.

But then why did he ask me to follow him?

"There are so few guards," I said to him as he took me through another room filled with plush pillows and wooden chaises. There was the occasional guard inside, but there were so few compared to those that stood outside.

"Too many would make it feel even less like a home." He brushed aside a vine for me to pass through.

"Less?" I walked around the room, touching the soft fabrics that covered the chairs.

I could smell the rain in the cold wind.

"My mother and father."

"You miss them."

He looked out a window that overlooked the gardens. "Yes. And my sisters. Even my brother. I would give much to have them back."

Of course he did not remember how much he *had* already given to save Madinat Almulihi. No matter how much is sacrificed, there will always be more to give, because there is always more that is wanted. Satisfaction slips through fingers like water.

Altasa's home was just visible, smoke sliding into the sky from her chimney. The rain had slowed. I said, "But soon you will have someone. A queen, eh?"

"Yes." A long pause, then, "Helena."

"Helena."

"I cannot say if it will change how I feel . . . I am sorry." Saalim's voice changed. The hard, formal edge was there again. "It is unacceptable to say such things."

"To say that the place where you live feels empty without your family? It is not unacceptable to say that you miss them. That without them, you are not what you were."

His eyes—still golden, though now without the glint of magic—met mine. "I forget that you do not have family either."

"I have my sister. She is not far from here."

"But you had many sisters."

"Yes."

Without another word, he led me down the passage. Saalim said finally, "Let me show you the towers. I have tea in mine. We can warm there for a bit and talk of things that make us laugh."

Saalim's tower? My pulse sped as we began up the stairs. Now would be my chance to—

A woman practically flying down the steps tumbled into Saalim.

"Oh!" she shouted, righting herself quickly, hand pressed to her chest. "Saalim! You startled me." Her chest heaved with deep breaths. She had called him Saalim.

"Dima," he said. "What are you doing here?"

Dima looked beyond Saalim at me. Her eyes dropped down to the clothes I wore—wet from the rain—as if that would tell her who I was. Did she see the stains on my hands? She looked away quickly, her face unchanged. She wore a beautiful fustan—the embroidery across the throat depicting fruit of all kinds. I could not fathom how much time must have been spent sewing it.

"I was waiting for you. Mariam suggested perhaps . . ." Her eyes flashed to me again. "Said you were at the docks today." Her voice was soft and sincere. I liked her for her concern, glad there was someone who fretted over him. Was she like Mariam, flitting around the palace pointing her fingers and beckoning people to follow?

"Ah," he said. "I do not need you." Why did he sound so uncomfortable?

"Very well." She nodded her head and began to move down the stairs past us. The strong scent of oud fluttered behind her. I would never forget that scent—it was the most expensive oil I had ever seen. It came from very far, the shopkeeper had told me when I asked him why it had cost as much as a camel's ride from my settlement to Madinat Almulihi.

When she was several steps beyond us, Dima said, "If you change your mind tonight, send word."

Tonight.

Now, I understood. She was an ahira. Nausea roiling, I watched her descend the stairs, her black hair shining in the gray day. Jealousy sank its teeth, and an understanding like venom coursed through me. She shared Saalim's bed. She knew him like I had known him—or, at least, as I knew him as a jinni. I did not know him as a king.

As a man.

Rooted to the stairs, I was still as a palm without wind. Dima lived in his palace. Walked through his halls like they were her own. She was bathed and fed and beautiful. When I was an ahira, I had and was none of those things.

"It is late," I said, staring at his boots, which shined like Dima's hair.

"But you have not yet seen the best view," he said in a rush. There was a pleading that I could not understand. He held his hand out as if he wanted me to place mine within. I began to reach out, but when I glimpsed my reddened palm, I pulled my hand back in.

Loud footsteps echoed up from below as two men approached. Kofi and Tamam.

"We found them," Tamam said. His gaze darted to me before returning to Saalim. Kofi stared at me without hesitation, a sneer curling his lip. Did he remember me from our journey? Or was it my face that told him I was a salt chaser?

Sons, what were they doing to me here? I was no salt chaser.

"Did you learn something of use?" Saalim said, eager.

They nodded.

"Very well. Emel—"

"It is no trouble," I said hastily, relishing the impending dismissal. "Thank you for all you have done." I carefully went down the stairs, steadying myself against the wall so as not to slip in my soaked sandals.

"Before you go," Saalim called. "There is a camel race." He must have seen my confusion, because he shrugged and grimaced. "Ah, they are silly, but they are fun. It is tomorrow. You might consider joining us."

The sneering guard shifted and looked from me to Saalim.

Why are you doing this? I wanted to ask, thinking of Dima. She was more beautiful. What would I provide that she couldn't? It did not matter, though, the hook had snagged. It was an offer I could not refuse. Any moment more with him I would take.

"If Altasa can spare me."

"I'll send Nika to work in your place."

He laughed when I told him Altasa would not be happy. The sound pleased me, and his laughter rang in my memory long after it had ceased.

"Why is he inviting a palace worker to the camel race?" Altasa spat from the kitchen.

I held my tongue as I changed into dry clothes. Had I not learned to expect her ill-mannered behavior when it came to the king, I would have been hurt. But it seemed that everything about Saalim and his palace displeased her. I once asked her why she stayed if working for the king vexed her so.

"Simple," she had explained. "Here I have a bed and coin. It would be unwise to leave."

Altasa continued. "Doesn't he have ahiran to take?" She did not care that Saalim could be out in the gardens hearing everything she shouted at me.

I thought of Dima as I slipped my arms through my fustan. It was fancier than anything I'd worn back in the settlement, but still nothing compared to what she wore.

The drawer beside my table was open. I curled my fingers around the edge and pulled it toward me, peering inside. The vessel was still filled with the sand I had scooped up when I first lost Saalim, trying to scrape him together from the dust he had left behind. As soon as I opened the vessel, I smelled him— moon jasmine and ocean and dust. He had smelled the same this afternoon. I closed my eyes, pretending he was beside me.

"You won't like it, you know!" The healer called.

Visions of Saalim dispersed like smoke in wind. "Why wouldn't I?" I closed the vessel, and went into the kitchen where Altasa was pressing her knuckles into a mixture.

"It's a mockery of our lives," she said, pushing harder now. "You'll see."

"What do you mean?" I took the bowl from her and continued the task as she scraped the sticky vestiges from her hand back into the bowl.

Ignoring my question, she asked, "What about that nice boy from the market you told me of?"

"Kas?"

"Yes, that one. I wish you'd go to the race with him."

I narrowed my eyes at her. "And tell the king what? I would rather be with an urchin from the baytahira than you?"

"An urchin?!" she laughed so hard I thought she'd collapse. After she calmed herself, she said, "Nika won't do. I have errands I will run on my own, since you'll be no use to me."

"I'm here now," I said. "What can I do for you?"

After promising Altasa I would send Nika away, I was sent to the spice souk.

Madinat Almulihi grew more familiar each day. The marketplace quickly became a second home. I knew how to navigate the shops, and more importantly, the people. My appearance misled many into thinking me another ignorant foreigner. But once I started dressing as they did and haggling more skillfully even than a local, they quickly abandoned the advantage they thought they would have.

Of the shops I frequented, the keepers knew my face and knew I came from the palace. At the spice souk, the proprietress flew up to me when I stepped under her canopy.

"What does she need?"

I listed off the spices Altasa had requested, and the woman listened closely before she collected my sacks and jars and hurried off.

At the back of the shop I saw a stack of salt bricks—gray, coarse, and stained with the ground from which they had been pulled. A man ran his fingers over them like they were the most fragile thing in the world. Much of the salt traded now was from Madinat Almulihi's shores and not my father's magic stores, so where was the mine that had birthed these bricks? The things that occupied me back home rarely crossed my mind anymore.

When was the last time I had seen Tavi? At our last meeting, she walked me through her neighborhood as if she'd lived there all her life, trying to show me things as though I wasn't living in the same city.

"Unground," I said. The shopkeeper nodded, scooping coriander seeds into a sack.

"She will do it herself?" the woman said with eyebrows raised.

"It's proper that way," Altasa had told me. "Masira prefers sacrifice."

The better Altasa felt, the busier she was. She was more frequently visiting peoples' homes to treat them, so I saw her less often than ever, and there was a constant knock on the door for requests from the palace staff—aching tooth, fever, cough, cramps. It never ended. The bustle of working for Altasa had taught me much about tonics and healing, but left me little time to do much save for the occasional evening when I would find Kas so we could sit and talk of nothing.

Walking through the narrow aisles in the souk, I inhaled the scents. This entire area of the market smelled like the spices and oils they sold, and the bazaar back home was the same. Glancing at the oils, I saw a vial of oud—twenty dha for maybe ten drops.

"You can sample," the keeper said beside me.

"No." I shook my head. "I was looking at the oud."

Without hesitation, she turned the vial until a drop was on her fingertip. Then, with a smile she placed it on my temples and behind my jaw. "What do you think, eh?"

"It smells . . ." I was unsure how to describe it.

"A bit strange? At least some think so. Some like to layer it with this." She picked up a vial of rose and smoothed the scent over the oud oil on my skin.

Suddenly I was back in the zafif, being prepared for a muhami. Then came thoughts of Dima. Was that the most I could hope to be? My gaze dropped back to the oils, and I saw frankincense.

Mama.

She wanted me to be free, and now I was.

Mama, I am here. I have Tavi with me, too.

I thought of Tavi's shrine—Wahir's gift that she gave to Mama and Sabra every day. Tavi did more for our family than I did.

I thanked the shopkeeper and left the souk in a hurry, suddenly eager to find Tavi. The bundle of bagged spices were tied together with a strong rope, and I slung them over my shoulder as I walked, leaving a scent trail behind me.

Glancing at the temple to Wahir as I passed by, I remembered Saalim saying that he thought it might be the most beautiful place in Almulihi. I had yet to go, knowing that there would be no place I was more unwelcome. Some days I missed the rama—pressing my brow to burning sand—but when I saw Tavi dip glistening stones into cool water . . . when I saw the temple, shaded from the sun, I wondered if perhaps that was not the kinder god?

It felt traitorous, thinking those thoughts.

"You can go in." The voice was familiar. I turned and saw Kahina leaving the temple.

"No, I . . ."

She swung out her arm. "They will not force you out. Wahir would be displeased. Have you read the Litab?"

"Only a little. When I can borrow it," I confessed. Wahir like the mother, Eiqab the father. "For Almulihi being a city of Wahir, its people do not always reflect the Son's ways."

Kahina smirked. "We are not far from my home. I will give you my Litab so you can read it all. Unless you will visit the temple?"

"The Litab?" I gasped, the temple a forgotten thought. "A book is too valuable to be given to a stranger."

"I have too much coin to be hoarding books from people who have not read them. Come."

Kahina sounded so sincere, I followed without much thought.

"Your friends seem to have settled right in," she said, leading me through narrow streets.

"My friends?" I asked, skirting around three goats.

"Firoz and Rashid."

I nodded. "You remember their names?"

"I remember everything." She waved at three children who sat on the street with a worn game of maha between them. "My husband told me my memory was my magic." When her arms fell to her side, I noticed the sleeves of her robe were wet from the temple rituals. "I disagreed. Told him my magic was enchanting children. Children love me, see."

We were walking along the baytahira now. Though it was midday, people were in and out of the food and drink shops, the Bura-dens, the jalsa tadhat.

"King Saalim, in particular," she went on. "He loved for me to tell his fortune. My husband told me I would anger the queen. But it was not my place to manage her children."

We were standing outside Kahina's home now, but I wanted to know about Saalim as a boy more than I wanted the Litab. "What was he like as a child?" I asked.

When she smiled, I could see she was very pretty. The lines on her face reminding me of Hadiyah. It was a face that smiled as much as the mouth did.

"Oh, that poor boy carries his history with him. Always something to prove. He would come to me, wondering if he would be a good king or did his brother really hate him or did his sister really know magic." She laughed again, looking past me down the street at the baytahira as if checking on a child.

"He was lazy, though. And entitled. He thought all would be handed to him. Especially as he got older. He grew ugly. He and his brother fought, and he spent less time with his sisters and parents."

I adjusted the sack on my shoulder, the weight starting to ache. Kahina saw this.

"I am talking too much. Come inside."

Her home was as small as Altasa's, which surprised me, given that she owned most of the baytahira. She shuffled around down the hall while I waited in the front room. Some of the most beautiful maps I had seen hung on the walls. They were inked like mine had been before I began filling it in myself. There was a detailed map of Madinat Almulihi—so careful were the illustrations, it seemed as if the streets were alive. There was another of the desert. I stepped up to it, peering at it carefully. Everything was there: oases, mines, settlements, and other cities. My heart pounded. It was everything I wanted my map to be, and I tried committing it all to memory.

"Here you are," Kahina said, handing me a book with thick pages.

"Thank you," I said, taking the soft, leather-bound book. I pointed at the maps and asked, "Where did you get these?"

"My husband made them."

"He did?" My eyes grew wide. I might finally finish my map! "I have a map that needs so much to be filled in. Would he help me?"

Kahina's eyes softened and she tilted her head. "Oh, no. He died." She blinked, and pressed her fingers lightly to the edge of the map. Did she touch it, knowing that his fingers had once been there?

"I am sorry," I whispered. "I did not realize."

"My husband loved people who were different. He said no matter where they came from, they loved the same things. Stories and music, family and friends. In Almulihi, many find it easy to think 'salt chasers' are something foreign because they look and act and sound different. But my husband knew better. They love their children the same, have chests that ache with grief, and . . ." She sighed. "He traveled all over, and through stories, taught people of a better life." Kahina looked again at the maps on her wall.

Hugging the Litab to my chest, I thanked her again. On the way out, Kahina called to me.

"Castor seed?" she asked.

I nodded, looking at the sack with mesh so fine the seeds could be seen through it.

"Why do you need that?"

"I collect ingredients for Altasa, the palace healer."

"Castor seed to heal?"

I shrugged. "The oil is used for many things."

11

EMEL

The day of the camel race, there wasn't a cloud in the sky. Summer was nearing, and the sun was hotter than I had yet felt in Madinat Almulihi. I did not know what to expect for the race, but I knew that we would watch from the palace steps. Apparently, it started at the desert and ended at the sea via the same road I had taken into the city. It happened once a year, Altasa told me.

I admired my new fustan once more before pulling my abaya over my head. Draping my scarf on my hair, I heard Altasa loudly grumbling still.

"Skip the race. It is for fools."

"I will not." I debated whether or not to tie my veil. Few wore veils in Madinat Almulihi, and I knew it might attract unwanted attention. But then, few wore abayas and covered their hair. What did it matter what others thought?

The feeling of the fabric against my face, over my hair, the abaya heavy against my shoulders . . . it was like rain in the desert. I nearly melted from the comfort. Home. This was who I was. When I stepped into the kitchen, Altasa dropped her hands onto the counter in a quiet clap.

"Oh, sweet," she said when she saw me. She sounded so sad.

"What?"

"Why are you wearing that?"

"I will be standing under the sun at midday!"

"Today of all days you choose to wear this? Take it off. Wear the sirwal I got you, with the tunic that has the palm fronds. Or that new dress Mariam brought."

Lifting my abaya, I showed her the dusk-blue dress. "I am wearing it."

Her shoulders fell, and she shook her head.

There was a knock at the door. "Well," I said to Altasa as I as left, "I will see you later then."

She did not turn. She did not reply. Instead, she looked down at the countertop where her hands were clenched into fists.

Nika's eyes swept over me when I opened the door, but she said nothing. Her lips pressed together. Then she commented, "So the king invited you to the race."

"He did."

When I told her that Altasa had no interest in an assistant today, Nika happily followed me out of the gardens.

"You have been meeting each other?"

"Only when I deliver his medicine," I said.

Nika grunted, somehow making even that sound skeptical.

When we entered the atrium, Mariam was passing through. "Oh!" she said, though it almost sounded like a question.

"Taking her to the king," Nika said.

Understanding washing over Mariam's face, and she smiled warmly. "I thought you said you hadn't been to the race before?"

"I haven't."

Mariam tutted and said, "The king is in the sitting room."

When we entered the room, Saalim rose. Before he approached he held back for the briefest moment. There was a pause, a question, but it was gone as quickly as it came.

He nodded to Nika, excusing her. She dipped her head slowly and asked if there was anything else we needed before he confirmed there was not. I saw her hesitate. She wanted to stay, wanted to see what we had between us.

"We will have sheltered viewing of the race's end," Saalim said. "There are others who will join us. Well-known families and guests."

"It will be lovely." My pulse quickened. What would people think when a palace worker joined the king?

"Some of my guests wait for us now, if you are ready to go. Unless you've changed your mind?"

Did he sound hopeful?

When I told him I had not, he gestured for me to follow. Something seemed untoward with Saalim. We met two of his guests in the palace, and he made quick introductions. The couple greeted us warmly—the woman was dressed like me! Apparently they were titled people from the east here for trade business but enjoying the city in their idle time. He introduced me as Emel, someone new to the city.

An odd introduction, I thought. Was it because he did not want to be seen with a palace worker? A poor woman? Or, I realized with a sudden flood of shame, did he not want to be seen with a salt chaser? Though clearly the people joining us were of the same blood.

We followed Saalim and several guards to a raised viewing box constructed just past the palace steps. It was painted prettily with golds and blues and was much larger than I had anticipated. There were already nearly a dozen people milling about inside. After more introductions—most of the guests were noteworthy families who owned ships or mills or workhouses—we sat down.

He was beside me, our arms just brushing against each other, our knees almost touching.

"Have you been down the canals yet?" Saalim asked, pointing to the waterway that circled behind the palace. A small boat glided by, ferrying two passengers.

The couple from the east had not, and neither had I. The man who stood at the prow of the boat used his long oar to move them along. Kas had been trying to convince me to join him on a boat ride. I could barely trust the wood and stone that made steps to carry me into the sky. Trust wood that floated on water and would drown me, should it have its chance? No. I told this to Saalim, and the couple in the carriage laughed. Saalim's smile appeared more like a grimace.

"But here you are floating above the ground!" the man said.

"My bravery is all a ruse."

"Convincing, indeed!" the woman said.

Saalim said, "That way can be found some of the most beautiful homes in the city."

As I looked out in the direction he pointed, I noticed all the people who sat along the street, waiting for the race.

The same soothing comfort that had filled me when I pulled my abaya over my head, when I tied my veil, returned now. Women lined the streets wearing the same clothes as me. Men alongside them wore long robes and guthras tied under their chins or across their faces.

People were waving at the king, and with a smile so wide it hurt, I waved back. We all did, the woman and I giggling at all the joy. Now I understood why Saalim had invited me. This was a beautiful reminder of my home.

A servant passed by with food, later another offered us a drink.

"Thank you for inviting me," I said, tearing the orange blossom sweet into a small piece before bringing it to my mouth. Saalim had been silent, sipping his drink and staring out at the crowd.

"The camel race has a long tradition here. The winner receives one hundred dha and a place in the Falsa Mawk." He looked down at his drink, swallowed the rest, then looked back to the road. "Most of the racers are traders, see, so it is an opportunity for them to tell of their wares."

Red-dyed sand was spilled in a line at the end of the road, dividing it from the plaza that led to the shore. I watched the sea, marveling that it could appear so smooth from afar when up close it was so tumultuous. I wanted to go back there, wanted Saalim to take me to that place again, where it was just us amongst ruins.

Three blares of a horn sounded in succession. People scattered to the periphery of the street, creating a wide, empty path for the racers.

"The race has begun," Saalim said flatly, echoing the cries of others.

Pitching forward, hands pressed to my knees, I stared down the road and waited. And waited, and waited.

Finally, I saw something. A horse, I realized, was tearing down the street, the man atop with a straight sword and flag of Madinat Almulihi fluttering behind. He had large sacks that bounced on the horse's flanks. The man was shouting, but it was not until he was near that I could make out his words.

"You can't have my salt! You won't catch me! The salt is mine!" Over and over he was saying it, laughing all the while. I gasped and looked around, wondering if anyone else was concerned.

Behind him, there was pandemonium as a mass of camels surged forward.

"Salt chasers!" the spectators shouted.

Salt chasers?

It was all shouts and grunts and the clatter of hooves as they approached. The camels were undisturbed by the clamor, their faces coated in thick, white saliva as they were whipped down the street. Men and woman atop the camels were dressed like me and most of the spectators. They waved their arms, yelled about Eiqab, screamed for the salt. And in the midst of it all, hysterical laughter.

Saalim shifted beside me, his arm tucking close so that we touched no longer. I barely had time to register all of this before the winner brushed across the red sand, kicking it into the plaza. The racers descended from the camels, and the chaos calmed.

Like dust settling, I began to understand. They were not wearing guthras and carrying scimitars like the men I'd known back home. They did not wear abayas and veils like mine. They were wearing costumes.

This was no celebration of the desert or the people that lived there.

It was a mockery.

At once, Saalim's behavior toward me made sense. He was embarrassed by me.

But then why had he invited me? Had he forgotten who I was? Hot shame rose to my cheeks, and I sat as still as I could, trying to stare anywhere but at the racers who laughed and threw their arms in the air dancing as the nomads do or pressing their foreheads to the ground in false prayers. The people who drank and ate with us laughed and smacked each other, pointing at the participants and retrieving their winnings from bets.

Saalim shifted beside me, his embarrassment growing as fast as my shame. "The winner will be announced soon."

I could barely breathe. My hands shook, my heart raced, my eyes watered. I wanted to leave, but feared that would draw more attention. Really, I wanted to be swallowed by the sea.

We waited until the very end. I sat through every painful mockery of my people. Of me. I hoped that Tavi had not come, hoped that she was too busy with Saira to see this.

She who walked into this city preparing to adopt it as her own, who prayed to a different god, who embraced her new life without blinking, could not see that the people whose approval she so desperately wanted laughed at her all the same.

Altasa had told me not to come. Why hadn't I listened?

When the winner was awarded his dha—the displeased camel decorated with the sham salt bags—Saalim rose. The people in the street saw him stand and dropped to one knee. I did the same, relishing the opportunity to hide my face. If the Saalim I knew was there, he was buried deep.

Perhaps it best he was to be married. Let me be done with this delusive hope.

When we arrived back at the palace, he hesitated before he said, "Thank you for joining me." It was the only thing he had said to me since the winner was announced.

I bobbed my head, unable to find words.

"I thought perhaps that you would join me for dinner, but . . ." He turned his palms up to the sky as if that explained everything. *You are a salt chaser* were the words he could not say.

"I have made other plans." Grinding seed with the pestle.

"Of course." He was not taking leave, and I did not think I could bear any longer the growing divide between us.

"I will go," I said.

"Of course," he said again.

With every step, the clothes I wore grew heavier.

When I entered the front room, Altasa was reading through her book of recipes. I cannot know what she saw when she looked up at me, but she closed the book, sighed, and stood swiftly. "Child," she whispered, coming toward me.

And then I cried.

Altasa called me at sundown. My eyelids were still heavy from my tears.

When I stepped into the kitchen, she pushed a bowl of soup toward me. "Here. I had Thali make it."

At the table, I stirred the soup with a piece of flat bread. It was my favorite. Chickpeas with thick chunks of lamb meat. I smiled weakly at Altasa and sipped at the broth.

She sat down across from me, her own bowl untouched in front of her as she watched me eat. "I wish I could say they have not always been like that, but they have."

I picked up a piece of lamb with my bread and waited.

"My sister, you know, fell in love with a man from this Eiqab-forsaken city. He left her like she was nothing."

"I am sorry."

"None of that. It is far behind me."

"That is why you are here?"

She nodded. "I wanted to find him."

Remembering what she had told me before, I said, "Revenge."

She tossed her long, silver braid over her shoulder and tutted.

"Did you find him?" I asked.

"Yes."

"What did you do?" I narrowed my eyes.

"I did very little. It is not hard to convince people to do something for you if you say the right things." Her eyes glinted wickedly.

I did not want to know the details. Some things were better left unsaid, unknown. "But still you are here. And still, you are angry."

"Madinat Almulihi is a constant reminder of what I lost, and who took it. This city is beautiful, but its people are vile."

Her words resonated with me. People had been cruel. Judgmental and prejudiced. It seemed only Altasa—in her crude way—along with Kahina and Kas, accepted me as I was. Even Saalim had disappointed me.

Altasa swallowed the rest of her soup in one tipping of her bowl. "If you find a gem, you stick with him." Her tongue circled her lips. "They are rare in this city of stone."

Kas was sitting in his usual spot at the drink house across from the jalsa tadhat. "To watch for Odham," he had told me the first time I met him there. He would not miss an opportunity to remind Odham that what he did was dangerous.

"Sons, you look like you've been beneath camel's hooves." Kas tilted his head back as I sat down. "What's happened?"

I debated whether or not it was worth telling him. He might be as blind as Saalim.

"Tell me you didn't go to the race today," he said when I did not respond.

My shoulders fell in and I nodded, unable to speak for fear that I would cry again, feeling the tears climb my throat.

"I am sorry you weren't warned."

"The worst part," I said, my neck tightening as it fought the sorrow. "Is that I was. I just didn't think . . ." Feeling the shame and embarrassment anew, tears fell. "I am sorry," I said, wiping at my eyes.

There was a scrape of wood against stone, and Kas was suddenly seated beside me, pulling me into his chest as he curled his arm around my back.

I stiffened for just a moment, before I let him comfort me.

"I'll be right back," he said when I had gathered myself.

I watched him go inside before I turned to the jalsa tadhat. Its door was closed, curtains pulled across the single window at its front. It was dark out, so I was sure an arwah was taking place inside.

Kas returned with a goblet and set it in front of me.

"Pomegranate wine," he said. "Have you had it before?"

"Yes. Once," I said, remembering the Haf Shata back home and drinking wine with a happy but drunk Firoz in the street. "I loved it."

Smiling, I took a drink and let myself remember what now seemed a happier time.

"Damn them all straight to Eiqab's sun," he said after he shifted his chair so that it was again across from me. The scar on his temple seemed deeper in the shadowed light.

I laughed weakly, watching him.

"Do you miss your home?" he asked quietly.

"Every day."

He nodded. "What do you miss the most?"

Everything, I thought. "That people did not stare at me like I was a goat dressed in woman's clothes." He laughed, and I continued. "That I knew where every street led. That I knew the changing of the seasons by the feel of the air. That . . ." Did I tell him of Saalim? "There was a man I loved."

Kas hid his surprise well. "Where is he now?"

"I don't know." I refused to cry again, already having embarrassed myself too many times that day. Pressing my lips together, I stared at the table.

"Do you love him still?"

My shoulders fell forward thinking of that afternoon. "I don't know."

"You don't know very much, do you," he said with a small smile. He folded his hands on the table, his bracelets softly clattering on the wood surface.

I opened my mouth to respond, but before I could, my name was called from across the street.

"Do you know him?" Kas asked, looking at Firoz as he waved frantically, heading in my direction.

"I do," I said as I stood. Seeing Firoz in that moment reminded me of everything I missed. He was as close to home as I could find. I ran to him.

The comfort of his arms was tainted only a bit by the reek of alcohol.

"Firo."

Suddenly, he stiffened and pushed away from me. "You know that man?" Firoz asked, nodding to someone behind me.

I turned. "Kas? Yes."

"I'd stay away from him. He's a rock in Odham's shoe. And mine."

"Shhh," I whispered.

"Oh, he knows it," Firoz said more loudly. I pressed my fingers to my temples. This was not at all how I envisioned our reunion.

"He means well," I said. "Come and meet him. He has been kind to me. We are friends."

"Friends?" He stepped back. "I haven't seen you in over a moon and you tell me you're friends with *him*?"

I sighed and looked up at the night—the moon a thin sliver. Had it been that long? Sons, I was tired. "If you are only here to fight with me, then go." I pointed at the jalsa tadhat where people were walking out, talking excitedly to each other. I saw the woman who worked there saying goodbye and reminding them that it is never too soon to be a part of another arwah.

"I don't want to fight," he said. His curly hair was longer than I had seen it before, and it fell in front of his eyes. I remember the turban his mother made him wear, and how he would take it off as soon as he was at the market. He hated it, he had told me. He had despised our home as much as I did when we lived there.

I am sure he did not miss it like I did.

"Will you sit with us?" I asked.

Firoz looked at Kas, then shrugged. "For you."

"Where is Rashid?" I asked as we walked back to the table.

"Working. He will be home soon."

"This is Firoz," I told Kas with narrowed eyes. "My friend from home. No talk of work, eh? You both must agree before I will sit between you."

Kas rolled his eyes. "Is she always like this?"

Firoz assured him I was. Then, Firoz was telling Kas all about "how I was." I sat back, not minding that my friends had found something in common, even at my own expense.

During their discussion, four people cloaked in black strode by. Kas watched them as closely as I did.

"They are everywhere," Firoz said once they had passed.

"Who?" I asked.

"Those people. Dressed in black. There is at least one at every night arwah."

"Who are they?"

"The Darkafa," Kas said, leaning back in his chair.

My attention turned from the four people to Kas, waiting for him to continue.

Firoz spoke. "They speak of the goddess and the Sons. Waiting on the 'second-born' Son."

"To do what?" I asked.

Firoz shook his head. "I can't make sense of it."

Kas said, "To replace the first-born." He buzzed with the pride one has when whispering rumors.

"At the arwahs, they claim to search for the goddess." Firoz shrugged.

Kas was concerned. "They don't mention her by name?"

"Masira? Ah . . . " Firoz squinted, attempting to search his hazy memory.

"This is an unexpected gathering," Rashid said, coming up from behind me. He smiled at Firoz, nodded to me, and hesitantly introduced himself to Kas.

"Come sit," Firoz said. "We were talking about those cloaked men. The Darkafa, according to him."

"You know of them, eh?" Rashid said, suddenly interested. He looked around, found an unused chair, and pulled it next to Firoz.

"Of course," Kas said, crossing his arms.

Rashid leaned forward. "These Darkafa have plans to dethrone the king."

"Ha!" Kas threw his hands up in the air, still talking to Rashid. "Them? They are not so strong."

Confused, I said, "I thought this was about the Sons."

Rashid scowled at Kas. "You seem to know them well."

Kas shrugged. "They speak loudly and are everywhere."

Rashid turned from Kas to me. "They have a child. The keeper, they call it. Say they've done everything the goddess has asked. Now, they wait for her here, because it is here that she will dethrone the king."

I waved my hands, demanding their attention. "Dethrone the king? I thought they waited for the second-born Son, not the goddess?"

Rashid shrugged. "The second-born Son will destroy the first-born. Wahir to be killed by Eiqab. The king of Madinat Almulihi is like a . . ." He cocked his head. "What is that word? Metaphor? For the Son."

"What does the child have to do with it?" I asked, sitting back again. This story sounded like a tale spun by those who took people's coin to conjure spirits.

It was Kas's turn to share. It felt like ghamar for gossip, each man wanting to out-tell the one before. He set his elbows on his knees and looked gravely from Firoz to Rashid to me. "This child possesses a jinni."

"Bah!" I waved at him. "I can assure you there is no such thing." *I freed him already*, I wanted to say. "This sounds just like the Dalmur, obsessed with fanciful tales that do nothing but stir distrust and worry." I narrowed my eyes at Rashid. "What are the Darkafa doing with a jinni, and why do they want to take the king from his throne? Let me guess . . ." Pressing a finger to my lip, I said, "To restore the desert? To return it to its better place?" *It's already restored!* I wanted to scream.

"The Dalmur?" Rashid asked, appearing perplexed. "What are you talking about?"

My mouth dropped open. Now it was my turn for confusion. "The Dalmur? The ones who carried the symbol of . . ." But of course. Masira had made certain none remembered. So had the Dalmur never existed? My gaze darted between the three men. Firoz looked vapidly confused. Rashid bewildered. And Kas looked . . . I could not describe his expression. Terrified? Disbelieving? Understanding?

Sons, he had wondered if I was a crazy salt chaser, and now I confirmed it to be true.

"Oh, never mind then," I said, standing up to leave.

Firoz pitched forward in an attempt to follow me, shouting about waiting and wanting me to explain what I had meant, but he stumbled onto his knees in a sloppy display.

"Emel, wait!" Kas hurried to reach me. "I will walk you home."

"Really, you don't need to." I didn't want him to. I should just tell him—

"Your day just seems to be getting worse, doesn't it?" He was at my side now, matching my pace.

"It does."

"You don't fear the Darkafa?"

"No."

"You live in the palace. What if there is an attack?"

"The king is prepared."

"What if they have a jinni?"

I glanced at him only briefly before I quickened my pace. This was absurd. Although we both respected magic and its consequences, he did not know that jinn did not worry me as the legends demanded. I knew jinn too well. Finally, I said, "Jinn are nothing to fear."

"Really?" He asked it with such incredulity I regretted saying it. "What *do* you fear?" he asked.

We reached the steps of the palace. I moved up several of the stairs, until our eyes were level.

"What I fear is already in my past," I said.

Kas did not move. He considered me with a furrowed brow, and from the way the torchlight hit his face, his eyes appeared almost silver.

12

SAALIM

The force of the blades shook my arm. I pushed forward, swinging to the left, jabbing to the right, faster than was safe. But Azim was a master swordsman and he would not hurt—

"Sons!" I shouted when his sword smacked my arm. Instantly there was pain and blood and panic, but it was gone just as quickly when remembering we used only training swords.

Azim smirked, and said, "Up. Again."

I rose.

"Slower, Saalim. This is a lecture, not war."

And so we went, Azim critiquing how I held my shoulders, placed my feet, rotated my wrist.

"Let us break," he said. "You've other things on your mind. Tell me."

It was Azim's rule: no conversation during lesson. "If you are talking, then you aren't paying attention."

"No," I told the head of my army. "There is nothing. We should continue." Should the Darkafa attack, I wanted to be ready. This time, I would fight in the streets beside my people.

"Saalim, sit." Azim pointed to one of the few chairs in the empty room. We were in a dirt-floored space beside the horse stalls, meant for working the horses should the weather forbid use of the arena outside. It was the best place to practice the sword.

My sparring sword grew heavy in my arm, and I let the dulled tip of it drag through the dirt as I walked to a creaking wooden chair.

Azim sat across from me, on an equally decrepit chair that sagged under his weight. He leaned back. The soft leather protecting his back and legs told of a man who lived a good life, and the lines on his face and the scars on his hands told of a man who had earned it.

He was like a second father to me, not in kindness nor understanding, but in his intolerance for weakness, for his relentless instruction, and his enduring patience. He had been there for Almulihi when I had not. He had been ready, when I had been arrogant and foolish.

"The Darkafa are being followed," Azim assured me. "None have been seen carrying weapons. Veiled threats are not enough of a reason to capture them. If we captured every person who challenged the throne—"

"I know."

"Questioning hasn't gotten us any further."

It was not as if these Darkafa were keeping secrets. They were open about their cause: Long ago, their ancestors had been tasked by the goddess with the protection of a treasure: a latched box. None were to open it except the goddess, and she would return only when the king crossed the desert.

Once she returned, they said, the second-born Son would destroy the first.

None knew how it would happen, and none admitted to having attacked Madinat Almulihi before. Nassar said most seemed appalled by the thought of killing. They were simply fever-crazed for the goddess.

But I did not trust them.

"They do not carry weapons," Azim said. "They are watched. The palace is watched. You are not left alone."

And perhaps that was part of the problem. "There is much we don't know about them. The role Masira and the Sons play in their plot confuses me even more."

Azim nodded. "They are not the first group of zealots to walk these sands."

"We can't let down our guard."

Azim shook his head. "I never do." He put his hand on the sword's hilt. "Now, is that all that worried you, or is there more we should discuss?" He said it as if talking to a little girl.

I laughed, standing, and raised my sword until I saw it shining before me.

My shoulders ached, and my brow was slick with sweat as I sought out Farasa at the stalls. I pressed my hand to her neck before promising I would take her out again soon. *Once it is safe for me to leave*, I thought.

Crossing the plaza back to the palace, I saw Altasa leaving in a rush.

"Where are you heading? Should I fetch a servant to help you?" Even if she had the strength to make the journey, the pickpockets and thieves worried me.

"No. I am only going to the market."

"It's nearly night." The marketplace would be closed by the time she got there.

"I know that." She rested her hand on her brow, shading her eyes. "It's always open for me."

I nodded to her, and she was gone.

Nassar was expecting me for dinner, but it was not yet sundown, so I had some time. I considered returning to my tower—addressing correspondences that had piled up. There was some dispute concerning the Hayali—when wasn't there?—and another trader was angered because he had not been paid his full price for his wares, saying the sandstorms had cost them more time. This was not an unusual request these days. There had been many storms lately. I had waited too long to address these things already, but knowing that Emel might be at Altasa's—alone—made my decision. Like those who waited for my responses concerning business, my apology to Emel was long overdue.

I had not seen her since the camel race, and that had been days ago.

Never had I felt like such a fool as that day. To have completely forgotten where she came from, what the race was . . . I closed my eyes, my fists clenching again. I had simply wanted to show her a tradition of Almulihi. I had not been thinking at all. My mother would have made me sleep out with the goats.

The servants in the gardens flew into a busy flurry when I passed. The need to trim the leaves just-so seemed suddenly pressing. Nadia loved the gardens. I would tease her for doing a servant's job, but now I understood that her trimming flowers was the same as my swinging the sword. Everyone needed something *else*.

Smoke rose from Altasa's home. If Emel was not inside, I would have Mariam once again talk to Altasa about leaving the fire unattended. Zahar had indulged in the same problem, and my mother had almost thrown her out for all the worrying she did about the palace catching fire. The door to Altasa's was open when I approached. Rustling came from inside.

Emel's back was to me; she was bent over the counter, working steadily at something.

My knuckles rapped against the open door.

Emel did not startle as Nadia would have, should I have crept up on her. When she saw it was me, though, she quickly put down her knife, wiped her hands, and bowed her head.

"I am sorry to disturb you."

"What do you need?" She hastily collected everything from the table, shuffling it to the counter where she worked and pulled out a chair.

She was dressed as any laborer in Almulihi would be. Those damn clothes were the reason I'd forgotten where she had come from.

Before I could answer, she gestured to the empty chair. "Can I get you some tea?" She seemed almost as nervous as I was, her hands fidgeting with her clothing.

My mother had taught me people wanted to provide, so when the offer was small, it was courtesy to accept.

"Tea would be welcome." I sat at the table and waited.

She pulled a kettle from the fire. I could not stop watching her move. She did not once look at me.

I took a drink of the tea. It was unexpectedly sweet.

"Do you dislike it?"

I shook my head. "I like it very much."

"What do you need?" Emel asked again, sitting down with a piece of flat wood and a charcoal stick. "I can start today; I am almost done with other orders."

I sat forward and pushed the wood aside, remnants of charcoal dust gritty against my fingertips. "Nothing. I have come to apologize."

My hand was near hers. Her fingers were dark where the charcoal stick had touched them. She pulled her hands to her lap.

"I had forgotten what the race was. What it would be to you."

Emel asked, "And what was it to me?"

"Cheap entertainment at the expense of you and your family, your neighbors, and friends. I am sorry that I invited you. But I am even more sorry that it is a custom in Almulihi to behave that way."

"People like me are not welcome here," she said, not sadly but as a matter of fact. "I did not expect a city who receives so many travelers to be so cruel." There was no question of where Emel was from. Her dark skin and face looked ancient and unyielding. She would not be able to hide in this city, even with a veil.

"There is little excuse." I knew where the prejudices originated—salt chasers took jobs and homes. They worshipped the angry brother. And if a salt chaser stole or was violent? Sons, it was a mark against the whole people. It was not fair, but it was the reality. They were watched more closely, especially after the attack.

"I want you to see a different part of Almulihi," I said finally, immediately feeling silly. Why was I continuing to foster this . . . *whatever* this was between us? My fingers, clasped together, clenched. Here I was, begging that she give me another chance.

"What do you want to show me?"

"The Falsa Mawk. The parade will pass in front of the palace. Watch it with us. It will be a better, truer show of Almulihi than the race. There are enormous feasts and parties—we host one, of course. And at night . . ." I smiled. The night was spectacular, and I did not want to spoil the surprise.

The corner of her mouth lifted. I tried not to stare too long.

I continued. "It is hard to describe. You will see regardless, but if you join us for the day, you will have the best view."

"I imagine you will have much to celebrate with the impending wedding."

My smile fell. "Indeed."

"I would be honored to celebrate with you," she said. Other than to bring the tea to her lips and back down again, she did not move in her chair. It seemed as if we danced with our stares—she looked at me, looked away, and I did the same. "We had a winter and summer festival, too."

"The Haf Shata and Haf Alsaf." The words came out almost before I could think of what I was saying. Why did I know that?

Emel stared at me as if she had just seen magic. "You remember?" she whispered. She sounded surprised, and . . . hopeful? I did not understand. Why did she say *remember*, as if it was something I had known? We must have talked about it on the journey from Alfaar's.

When I remained silent, Emel described the parties—the way the ground was covered with carpets, how fabric was spun from the frames to look like a cold winter wind or summer sunset, and how the guests wore robes of all colors and drank and ate the limitless drink and food supplied by Alfaar.

"And you," I said after a lull in her descriptions. "You and your sisters were the center of it all, weren't you?" I could feel a flickering of disgust, of fury. "Collecting coin from the wealthy to give to Alfaar?"

Her knee touched mine, and she pulled it away. I shifted, so that we touched again. I felt the heat of her skin through the layers of our clothes. Her hands, pressed firmly against the table, were a mere turn of my wrist away. I moved to turn my hand, but as if she suddenly remembered something, she stood and went to the shelves. There seemed to be no order to the jars and vials scattered there. And few had any indication of what they were inside.

Why had she left so suddenly? I sank back in my chair. She must think me no different than a man like Omar.

"What is the Falsa Mawk like?" She pulled a jar from up high, smelled it, then set it before her. She did this with a few more before she began taking pinches out and putting them on the work surface.

"Like the Haf Shata, it seems. Though the entire city is a part of it. The parade calls the largest crowd. Some have been working on their exhibitions since last year's Falsa Mawk, as you'll see. It's a celebration of the city, of the trade, and of the people here."

"Only locals may participate?"

I heard the accusation. "Not necessarily," I said. "Nassar chose the participants this year."

"And the years before?"

"My mother did."

"Oh."

"No," I said, "It is all right. My mother loved Falsa Mawk. I didn't know if we would continue the tradition this summer after . . . everything. But we decided it is what she would want. And, too, it is what the people want. So much has changed for them—a new king, more guards, stricter trade—it seems like the right thing to do to let them have this familiar joy."

Emel was at the table again, watching me with soft eyes and wiping her hands on her tunic. She had brought with her a small jar filled with a muddy liquid.

"You said you know about the Darkafa," she said finally.

"Yes."

"I heard mention of a jinni."

Once, I would have laughed. Instead, I remembered water that came as if from the wind. "A jinni," I repeated. Something in the way the word vibrated through my chest was familiar. And terrifying. "The Darkafa claim to have one?"

She clutched the edge of the table tightly. "Or *had* one? Protected one? I don't know."

The way her face bent under her words told me she carried more concern about this than she needed to. "We are diligent," I said by way of consolation. But then I remembered what the cloaked men in the temple said.

The child has it still.

"Soldiers can't stop a jinni," she pressed.

Rising from the chair, I said, "No, but if it was true that the Darkafa were using a jinni to remove me from the throne, wouldn't they have done it by now?" I rubbed my hands together and nudged my cup away from the edge. "Thank you for the tea. You will have to tell Thali how you get it just so."

Emel frowned, following me out. Then, "Oh! I nearly forgot." She took the small jar from the table. Handing it to me, she said, "It's a tonic. Like the salve. Altasa said it will serve you better, but that you never want it. Perhaps you should try it?"

The jar was cool in my palm. Emel was right, I would not take it from Altasa. I did not make it a habit to drink things others made for me. My father told me to be wary of gifts that might leave me poisoned or dead. But Emel, inexplicably, I trusted.

"I will. Thank you."

The hallway was empty as I returned to my tower, the scratch of my boots against the floor loud in the emptiness. Where were the guards? Probably off to the kitchens—or the pots—but they knew better than to leave so many posts empty.

The stairs all but disappeared under my feet as I ran up them.

When I was seated at my worktable, a shuffling sounded from behind me, rapidly moving closer.

I reached for the knife I kept on the tabletop, but the space was empty. I kicked the chair behind me in hopes of stalling whoever approached, and I spun around. A man ran toward me with my knife held clumsily in his fingers.

"He is here!" His shout echoed around us. The man stepped back from me with the knife in front of him, as if to protect himself.

There was no time to plan. Since I was unarmed, I, too, staggered back in the direction of my sword. Besides the shorn hair and the gloves on his fingers, the scars on the man's head identified him as one of the Darkafa.

He surged toward the stairs when he saw me retreat. Against a table holding a basin of water lay my sword, waiting for me. Easing toward the table, without looking away from the man, my fingers curled around the hilt, and I swung the blade out in front of me.

The man faltered, then skirted around, trying to retreat.

I leapt forward, sword gleaming.

Behind the man, there was another flash of black. I turned to defend against an ambush, but this person—holding his hood over his head—sped past my attacker and fled down the stairs.

The man and I circled around my desk until his back was to the stairs. I edged forward, hoping that he might slip and fall backward. But he arced his arm out to the side, grabbed hold of the basin sitting atop the table, and in one swift movement, swept it onto the ground. Water and ceramic exploded onto the floor, the wooden table toppling after it. The man turned and fled down the stairs.

Leaping over the wet debris, I sped after him down the hallway. "Stop!"

Where were the damn guards?

I chased him until he disappeared into the gardens and was gone.

I found guards stationed at the entrance, leaning against tiled walls with swords limp at their sides.

"Trespassers!" I screamed at them. "Darkafa! In the palace!"

They heard the hoarseness of my voice, the urgency, the call of their king, and their eyes widened with alarm. They rushed past me into the palace without a word, dispersing at once to secure the rooms.

I was standing alone—my chest heaving as I tried to understand what had just happened—for only a moment before two guards ran out of the palace to join me.

"King Saalim," Tamam called, chagrin clouding his typically stoic face. "We are searching. Stay out here."

I could tell by the way his eyes flitted back to the palace he would rather be inside looking for the Darkafa himself.

"Where were the guards? I saw not one when I came through before the attack." I was shouting now. The other guard took a step away from me.

"Azim has been calling meetings, I know—"

"This can't happen! Our guards cannot be idle, cannot be elsewhere." I ran my hands through my hair. "Our home—our liberties and life—is at stake should the throne be taken!" I could not lose the crown.

Bless Wahir Helena had not been here. What if something had happened to her? I thought of my mother falling to invaders' swords. I could not fail my people again.

It did not take long before the palace was secure. The Darkafa had fled. The only trace of an attack was the fractured basin, spilled water, and turned-over table.

Azim met me in the sitting room. The gauzy curtains that billowed alongside the windows were too gentle, too calm. My heart pounded, my fists were clenched so tightly they hurt. I wanted to rip the curtains from the wall.

"Your mother would be disappointed if you destroyed her home." He gestured to the curtains.

"My *mother* wouldn't care." I laughed mirthlessly.

Azim shook his head. "Don't walk down that path of thought, Saalim."

He was right, I was being immature. But I was furious.

"Where were the guards?"

Azim shook his head and stared at his hands. Remorse, heavy and holding fast, pulled him into the chair. "My oversight. I can't understand how I made such an error." He clasped and unclasped his fingers. He did not look at me except to admit fault. Then, back to his hands, his brow furrowed in confusion.

This negligence was not like him at all. "What were you thinking?"

"I . . ." He met my gaze. "Was not."

The flames of my anger diminished with his confession. Though it was unlike him to be so careless, I could see the same thoughts circling in his mind.

"The palace should be closed completely," I said finally. The palace was ordinarily open to the citizens of Almulihi who had business here. But now, even that was not safe. None could be trusted.

He nodded. "It will happen immediately."

I returned to my study once Azim had left, still rubbing his brow in confusion. The table had been restored and the broken basin swept away. My knife rested on my desk. I searched the room but found nothing to be missing. The same in my bedroom. Everything as if none but myself and the servants had been inside. In the bathing room, my mother's decanter, filled with water, sat on the shelf where I had left it. On the surface around it lay flakes of dried black paint from the Darkafa's gloves. What business had he in my bathing room? With the dregs of anger guiding me, I picked up the decanter and threw it against the wall. Another explosion of water and ceramic.

I regretted it as soon as I did it. Especially after I had to explain to the frantic guard that all was well. Another part of my mother now lost irretrievably.

Returning to my study, I scanned my shelves. The toy soldier from my childhood lay on its side behind a vase. The carved, wooden man stood tall with a long, straight sword by his side. Most men carried scimitars, but not the men of the palace. Not my father. Our swords were straight, just like this soldier's. I picked up the man but saw that only his legs remained. His sword was missing now, as were his torso and head. When had it broken?

Returning to my desk, I looked through the letters.

Salt mines, trading, invitations. Ibrahim requested I visit his court. I had no desire. Nassar would go in my stead. I tossed the letters into a pile for Nassar to address. The Hayali were being unfriendly traders again, as I had predicted. If not for my mother, I'm certain they'd have come for my throat themselves by now. I tossed it into Nassar's pile, as well. Oh, this one was rich. A woman writing because her husband had been killed at Alfaar's settlement—now, mine. She was grieving, she was angry, and her people had been left without a leader. It went into the pile for Mariam. She would smooth it over with salt and a gift. I would write to Usman to do better.

Picking up another letter, I exhaled. Sons, I had to return to the desert. There was much there that demanded my attention. I dropped my head into my palms. In truth, I would not be comfortable leaving this city anytime soon.

Finally, I held the last letter. It had no seal nor indication of when it was sent, as if delivered by person. For the briefest moment I thought of Emel, but when I opened the note the handwriting was far too elegant. It was written by someone who had been diligently trained—like my siblings and I had been.

Saalim,

If you have this letter in your hands, then she has done it. I weep with the thought of you returning to us, because I have missed you.

There is so much to tell you, but I fear there is not enough parchment in the world.

Beware of Zahar. She has not died. She seeks to take you from the throne. I did not know this when she mentored me. I wish I had, because I might have stopped it. Be wary of her, Saalim. She may not appear as she once did.

Lastly, she has something at her disposal to help her. Rumors say a jinni, but so many have seen a black-cloaked army. Be careful.

Should you need me, I am in the desert now. It is the only place where I feel, at last, home.

With so much love,
Edala

My hands shook as I stared at the words, trying to believe them to be lies. A cruel joke someone thought to play on me.

Because Edala could not be alive. It was impossible.

My sister, like the rest of my family, was dead.

13

EMEL

As I tied the twine around the fifth sack of herbs Altasa had tasked me with delivering that morning, I was reminded of the threads my sisters and I would weave together to pass the time. Tavi and I sitting side by side, pulling or folding.

"My sister would be good at this," I said to Altasa, who stuffed the bags much more quickly than I was tying them.

She looked up at me. "Why doesn't she come and help, if she'll be faster than you?"

"Too busy to see me, I'm sure."

"Well, I don't see you clawing out of here trying to see her."

I cinched the knot so tightly it rubbed raw my fingertips. "She doesn't care if I'm here or there."

"I doubt that is true. Do not underestimate the love one feels for family. It takes a grave transgression to fracture that relationship."

I thought of my father, whom I barely cared for. For whom I'd given no tears when he died.

Grave transgressions he had committed, indeed.

She paused her task. "My sister truly did not care if I was here or there."

I stopped, too, and looked at her, waiting.

"She was the beautiful one." Altasa patted her cheek. "I know this surprises you. She was supposed to marry a fine man. My father and mother put everything they had into her dowry, but then she goes and finds some man who isn't looking for a wife. Learns she is with child." Shaking her head, she began scooping the mixture into the bags again. "She ruined our entire family's chance for comfort. I don't know if she felt shame or anger. But I never gave up on her. Never let her believe she wasn't loved."

I remembered the soup we had shared after the camel race. Despite her disapproval with my choice, she did not give up on me, either. "It's why you followed her here?" I wished Tavi would follow me, want me, need me. "Where is she?"

"Left me here. Went home, I suspect. Not sure if she even still lives."

I let out a long breath. "Is this supposed to make me feel better?"

"Because although I no longer have her, I, too, have no regret."

***

Later that day, Kas led me down the shore, coaxing me along with promises that we were almost there.

The palace was well behind us now. This part of the shore was rockier, and only grew more so the farther along we walked.

"Here we are," Kas said, gesturing to what appeared to be a pile of rocks.

Looking back at the palace, now the size of my thumb, I groaned.

"All this way for rocks?"

He clucked at me the way Hadiyah used to when I spoke of the salt trade in the zafif. He moved toward the rocks, stepping behind one until he disappeared.

"Kas?" Quickly, I followed him. Dragging my hand along the rock's rough surface, I moved around it until I realized there was a small space—enough for one person to fit through. "Kas?" I called into the space. My question called back.

Nothing.

I walked into it and followed the opening into another turn that led me into a hole. Soon, the sun was only a weak light behind me.

With a shudder, I realized I was in a cave.

"Kas?" I said much more quietly. His name bounced alongside the sound of crashing waves. I heard the dripping of water and a small metallic clink.

At once, there was a whoosh, and Kas was standing an arm's length away from me, cast in the orange glow of a fire.

"Sons!" I screamed, too loudly.

Kas laughed just as loudly.

I smacked his arm. "What were you thinking, eh? I might've killed you."

"You?" He laughed harder. "Can you kill anything?"

"I wouldn't tell you if I could." I went farther into the cave, the shadows from the fire pulsing around me. "How'd you light that?"

"I came down earlier today so that it would be lit and ready. Carrying a lantern with us would have ruined the surprise, no?"

"But it was dark when I walked in. Then it was not." I glanced back to him. He was holding the lantern up to peer at the jagged walls and low ceiling.

"I had it covered, see?"

He held up a dark blanket in his other hand.

Looking around, I asked, "What is this place anyway? A si'la cave?"

"Si'la?" He sounded offended. "Why do the vilest spirits get all the fun? Why not simply a cave of wonders?" He waggled his fingers around like he was doing magic.

I reached the end of the cave—a dense pile of rocks—and began to walk back. It was long and narrow, not much to see, and I wondered why he had brought me here.

"It's an old salt mine," Kas said finally, pointing to the rock pile. "If it weren't for the collapse, they'd probably still use it."

"I've never been in a cave. Nor a mine for that matter." There was something comfortable about it. It was private, closed in. Secure.

"It's why I thought you would like it. It's the closest one to the city."

It reminded me of the fallen dome Saalim and I had found shelter in.

"We cannot stay too long, though," Kas said. "When the water rises, it fills in. We'll be up to our knees." His grin was discordant with the flash of terror I felt. I did not care how shallow the water would be. If it had a current, I didn't want it near me. He reassured me the tide would not rise for some time as he sat down against the wall.

"What would you wish for?" he asked.

"Wish?"

"If jinn were real?"

"This again?" I fanned out the blanket beside the lantern and sat. Now that we were out of the sun, I was growing cold.

His smile was as soft as the sand. There was a pause, and he asked again. "Your wish?"

Pulling my knees to my chest, I rubbed my legs to warm them. "I wouldn't wish for anything."

He narrowed his eyes. "You lie."

A warm wind found its way into the cave, and I closed my eyes against it. "I don't." And it was true. Magic no longer had a place in my life. "Should I want something, a wish seems the wrong way to go about getting it." Never mind the consequences.

"So be it. Tell me *one* thing you want. I bet I can find a way to give that to you without magic, eh?" It was very much like him to promise big things. Wasn't it just the other evening that he had sworn on Masira he could rally an army to steal a ship to sail with me across the sea?

But I didn't want to sail now, no matter how appealing the guitars and grapes were in the north. The thing I wanted now, Kas could not give. Life in Madinat Almulihi was good if I ignored the skeptical stares and questions about my home. The only thing that left me wanting was Saalim, and I was not even sure I wanted him anymore. Not only betrothed, but too, he was not the Saalim I had known. Did I still dream of walking hand in hand with him along the shore? I was not sure I did.

"Are you still thinking about it?" Kas asked. "Or have you forgotten I asked?" His head was tilted toward me, his scar deep in the shadows.

"Love," I said, uncaring if I sounded a fool. "Find me that."

He looked at his hands. "You want the love you had before." He sounded sure.

I sighed.

"You don't have to tell me." He closed his eyes and leaned his head against the stone. "It doesn't matter, not really. Except . . . sometimes I wonder if I'm a fool to chase you."

"Kas," I whispered.

"Sorry, is this too much? I wondered if I should . . . but then I thought if I did and maybe you felt the same . . ."

The same as what? What did he feel? We had seen so much of each other the past two moons, especially since the camel race. He seemed to understand me where Firoz, Tavi, and even Altasa could not. He knew my mind and my heart.

"Where are you from?" I asked him. Was he from the desert as I was? It would explain so much.

"What sort of question . . ."

I brought my face to his, his question slipping away with the waves. He didn't look like a salt chaser, but his parents might have been nomads. He never talked of his home. His eyes reflected the flames, his hands nervous as they moved against each other. He was vulnerable now, so unlike the Kas he showed the rest of the world—boastful and proud. That vulnerability softened me just a little.

What was I chasing now? Kas was kind. He was certainly handsome—although not rich. I thought of Pinar, my sister who always wanted someone rich over someone handsome. I grinned at the memory.

"You're laughing at me?" Kas asked, a small but shocked smile curving his lips.

"No!" I said, giggling more and waving my hands around us. "It's just everything."

Perhaps it was the tension breaking off piece by piece, but Kas began laughing, too. And together, we laughed even more, the glee circling us in the cave.

With love, life was amplified. Perhaps I could find that with Kas.

"Kas," I said, but then I stopped. What was I going to tell him? I did not want to lose my only friend. "It is not a no." Carefully, I placed my hand on his.

"I will take it." He wrapped his fingers around my palm. His hand was cool.

We stood, hand in hand. Like children, we looked anywhere but at each other.

Then, "Emel." His face was closer now, I knew what he was going to do. What did I care if a man kissed me? That had been my entire life so recently.

Turning my face up to his, I waited. So swiftly he pressed his lips to mine. There was no magic that sent warmth to my fingers, no scent of Madinat Almu-lihi that wrapped me from head to toe. It was only Kas.

And that was all right, I decided.

When I did not flinch or step away—whatever he had been expecting—his eyes met mine. The gray shimmered brightly in the dimness. They were not Saalim's eyes.

I closed mine.

Do not think of him.

The heat of Kas' body was near now, and I felt his lips press against mine again. This time I let myself feel it, feel him. They were not Saalim's, but—Sons, I could not keep comparing them.

He was warm, he was gentle. His mouth moved against mine, and I did the same, coaxing and inviting him to stay. See, Kas? This was not so bad. Perhaps we could make each other happy.

His fingers were on my shoulders now, slowly drifting across my neck, over the bones that slept there, and finally, down my breastbone.

He hesitated. The gesture perhaps too intimate? Why wasn't I hesitating? Kas stepped back from me, and when I mustered the courage to look at him, he was peering at me curiously.

"What is it?" I asked, feeling absurdly self-conscious in the cave.

"The tide is coming in." He pointed down to his feet, where, sure enough, water was just beginning to trickle in. Wordlessly, I followed him out, my eyes aching at the brightness of day.

We did not talk much during the walk back, save for Kas pointing at various buildings near the shore, telling of the families that lived there.

Had I done something wrong? Was I so unappealing? The years of suitors who rejected me flashed through my mind as if confirming that yes, I was not a woman of worth. But no, that was not true. Their rejections had been due to Saalim's magic.

Soon we were walking up the stone steps that led to the city's center. Near the large trading ships, I saw the tunnel, into which a small boat carrying two people and a net filled with writhing silver disappeared. Fishermen. I thought of Tavi. I had not seen her since my last visit.

"Where do you live?" I asked Kas, realizing I had no idea.

"Why, are you going to come find me in my bed?" The corner of his mouth twitched.

"And if I do?"

He didn't answer, and an uneasiness settled between us.

I said goodbye to Kas near the palace. He shifted from foot to foot, then said, "Will I see you at the Falsa Mawk?"

Altasa was counting down the days until the festival, so I knew it was a long way off. "But that is not for nearly a whole moon," I said. "Won't I see you before then?"

He recovered some, his unease dissipating when he smirked. "You want to?"

"Of course."

He crossed his arms and raised an eyebrow. "Good."

Glad he had returned to the Kas I knew, I said farewell. Unsure of how to say goodbye after our exchange in the cave, I wrapped my arms around him.

Walking away, I could not understand why he seemed so reluctant to hug me in return.

Saira told me that Tavi was out when I arrived at the house.

"With Yakub again." Though she sounded stern, there was a crooked smile on her lips. She did not know where they had gone, and so I left, disappointed.

A boat drifted by with a woman and two young children, whose curious faces turned to watch me as they passed. I imagined floating down the canal with Kas, him laughing and holding my hand as I gripped the boat's edge in terror as it swayed.

Maybe Kas was the answer to everything. Perhaps Masira marking me was not because she wanted me to be free and stay with Saalim as I had thought. Maybe she simply wanted me to find joy in my freedom and his. Perhaps it was her providence that Kas's path had crossed with mine. I was buoyed by the thought. Yes, maybe that was it.

"Emel?"

I turned in the direction of the voice and smiled at my sister coming down the canal. "Tavi!"

Yakub guided their narrow boat toward me, nodding with a shy smile. "I'll tie up the boat, then. You head back home."

Tavi swiftly kissed his cheek and hopped off the boat with remarkable ease. "What are you doing here?" she asked as we embraced.

"I came to see you. It has been far too long. I am sorry."

"You're sorry? We both have failed each other," she said. "Come on. Let's walk."

Tavi took me along the canal.

"Where does it go?" I pointed at the water.

"To more homes and shops. Yakub's family lives further down."

The canal widened out as it broke off in two directions.

I said, "I did not realize so much of the city could be reached by boat."

Tavi shook her head. "Not much can. The city is enormous, and the canals only reach small parts of it."

At the split of the canal, steps led down into the water. Tavi saw me survey the stairs and took me down them so we could sit with our feet just above the water.

After a pause, she said, "I heard the palace is closed completely now."

When I told her about the Darkafa, she grew concerned. "Is it safe? I am sure Saira will let you stay with us if needed."

"Right now it is the safest place to be, I suspect." Sitting so near the water, this felt particularly true.

"Can you believe people swim in here when the sun is hot?"

I gasped. "Why?" The water was so dark I could not see its floor.

"Yakub said people do it for enjoyment." She shrugged. "He said he would teach me."

"You wouldn't! If you can't feel the bottom with your feet, you don't belong in it."

She shook her head, the gold hoops from her ears hitting her neck. "I am a child of Eiqab! Wahir would drown me no matter how many times I have prayed to him."

"Good," I said. "Now tell me more about Yakub."

"He helps Josef at sea. His parents are very old, so he and his siblings take care of them. He has six brothers. Can you imagine?"

"I can. We lived with two dozen sisters."

"At least we were liberal with scented oils."

"But who is Yakub to you?" It was the question she was avoiding, I knew. I looked at her, and she smiled, her eyes falling to the water.

The way her face was turned, I could see a shadow of Sabra in the curve of her cheek. A new ache grew, remembering our older sister and how she was killed with my wish. How Tavi had grieved, then resolved that her life would be different. Even Sabra, I think, would have been pleased to see her now—happy and fulfilled.

"He is so patient. You're at ease here the way you navigate the city like a native, but I am still very scared."

I nearly laughed. Did I hide it that well?

She continued. "He has been considerate, showing me things, telling me what to do or what to avoid . . . like that camel race. Did you hear of it? I thought it would be fun. I was glad I did not go."

"I wish I had done the same."

Pity turned down her mouth. She placed her hand on my knee. She had new rings on her fingers, each shaped and twisted differently. I scooted closer so that our sides touched.

A man of Madinat Almulihi who did not carry the prejudice of his neighbors did not sound so bad.

"Do you love him, then?"

Tavi pressed her fingers between mine, separating my hands as I fussed with my nails.

"Something like that, yes."

Leaning my head against hers, I said, "Maybe you can take me to the temple one day. I heard it is beautiful."

"I would love that."

We sat on the steps together for some time. Sisters of the sand staring at the reined-in sea. When we first arrived in this city, we were homeless, threads ripped from a tapestry. But Tavi, at least, had found people to help weave her back into place.

It was time for me to do the same.

I lay beside Kas on the shore, watching the water slide up to the edge of the blanket before slipping back down the sand.

"I keep expecting Altasa to have words with me for how much I've been gone, but she doesn't seem to mind." I reached out and touched the foamy lip of the sea.

"It's like you said, she's feeling better."

"I suppose." I glanced at him, lying with his chest down, chin on his stacked hands, just like me. He stared off at the horizon, his eyes soft and peaceful, as if he might fall asleep.

The sun was setting, and I knew I should be returning soon or all the dinner would be gone from the kitchens. With more soldiers around the palace, there seemed to be less and less food to spare.

"What about you?" I asked, nudging him with my elbow. Our sides were next to each other, nearly touching.

"What about me?"

"Are you missed?" Never did Kas talk about his family, his work.

"Missed by whom?" he asked.

"Your family?"

"I live alone. I have no need for family."

"By your friends then? Where is your family?"

"Emel," he said as he rolled to his side to face me.

"What do you do when you're not with me?"

"You want to go down this path?" Now he sounded irritated. "What would impress you the most? If I said I was amassing that army to fetch you a boat? If I said I was at sea catching fish? If I said I was sitting on a throne? Or perhaps if I was a prisoner, escaped?"

"I only want to know more about you," I said, rolling into him, knowing that would soften him some.

"Do you?" He kissed the slope of my neck, and I curled into myself, feigning shy delight. No matter how hard I tried, being like this with him felt wrong. It was the only time I thanked my father for my training as an ahira. I do not think Kas knew I was insincere. In time, I could learn to love him.

When I finally straightened out, I rolled back toward him. Expecting to fall into his chest, I yelped when no one was there, and I collapsed onto my back. Scrambling up, I swiveled around.

Kas was gone.

I looked up and down the beach. I saw lovers, families, and wanderers who strolled alone, but I did not see Kas. There was a small crowd that ascended the stairs to the city. Was he among them?

The steps to the city were nearby. Had he run up those so quickly? My gaze followed their path, skimming past the white flowers whose petals were beginning to unfurl at the setting sun. The palace rose up over the steps, and I followed the walls up to the nearest tower. There, on the balcony, I saw the silhouette of someone who leaned against the rail.

Saalim.

I stared at him, wondering if he could see me. Then, a black-haired figure walked out beside him. A woman. Dima? She rested her hand on his shoulder, and the two of them walked back inside. I looked back at the beach, at my leather slippers, still stiff in their newness, at the cuffs of my pants embroidered with so many threads.

Furiously, I clawed sand into my fist and threw it at the sea.

14

EMEL

A few days before the Falsa Mawk, Tavi and I met early at the temple.
"I have never seen it so quiet," I said with a yawn, peering down
deserted streets. The sun had barely risen.

"The city sleeps late," Tavi said. "Josef usually leaves when it is still dark, so
I have gotten used to the city asleep. I like it best." Tavi pointed to the temple.
"Shall we go in?"

There were so many windows that I could nearly see through it. When we
entered, it did not feel as though we were inside. The water was loud, and the
wind that whipped through was cold. The entire room was cast in pale purple
from the dawn's light.

"The water is Wahir's gift," Tavi whispered, minding the few others kneeling in the shallow pool. "So here we honor him and show gratitude for the gift."

"Because of Eiqab, we have this." I trailed my fingers beneath the falling
water.

Tavi smiled. "You know this?"

"I am reading the Litab."

My sister whispered of her jealousy. I promised I would try to teach her
some time. Then, she dropped her voice, pointing to the people across the
temple that stared at us, evidently irritated by our chatter.

Ceasing our conversation, we continued walking around.

"You are not welcome here," a man said from across the pool. He had been kneeling there, ripples spreading fast across the water's surface when he stood. His anger was a lash, and its whip echoed through the room.

Tavi faltered, and I stood still, neither of us knowing what to say.

"Go burn your skin on the sand," he spat when we did not move.

"We will leave," Tavi said, pressing her hands at the air in front of her.

I did not want to leave. I wanted to refuse. This man was not the ruler of Madinat Almulihi; he could not tell me where I could stand.

But he was right. I did not belong there. Standing my ground was not so easy when the ground was not mine to stand upon.

As I turned to follow Tavi, footsteps—assertive and incongruous with the gentle surroundings—clattered into the temple. I spun to the source.

"Kas?" I gasped.

"You can't speak to them like that in Wahir's home," he said, striding in.

The man was untroubled by Kas. "Salt chasers don't belong in the temple."

"Anyone—salt chasers or spice-slingers," Kas looked the man up and down, "can pray here."

"I don't know what this city has become." Without another glance to Tavi and me, he left. The few others in the temple watched us only for a moment before they returned to their prayers, surely only counting their breaths until they deemed it appropriate to leave.

"What are you doing here?" I asked Kas, approaching him quickly. Seeing him there, chest heaving with anger on my behalf, made me feel like a young ahira again. Back when I cared what muhamis thought of me. My fingers flew to my hair, smoothing it down behind my ear, brushing out the folds in my tunic. I had not seen him since he'd fled from me. I thought I would not see him again. Nearly every day Altasa asked why I wasn't out with *that boy*. It was getting harder and harder to lie. "Where have you been?"

"I am sorry that happened," he said softly, reaching a hand out to me. I took it in mine cautiously, wondering if he apologized for the man in the temple or for his disappearance.

Kas led us back outside.

I gestured to my sister. "This is Tavi."

Tavi's wide eyes danced from me to Kas to our intertwined hands. Quickly, I let go.

"Where have you been?" I pressed. "What are you doing here? How did you find us?"

"I come here most mornings." He said it like a confession.

Tavi tilted her head. "You do? So do I. How have I not seen you before?"

Kas looked down, then said, "I have seen you many times."

Tavi turned away with her brow furrowed, drawing her finger to her mouth. Then: "I must have forgotten. Kas." She pressed her hands together, looking at the yellowing sky. "It is nice to meet you. I should be on my way. Emel, we'll see each other soon, eh? I want to have some of those sugared breads you told me about." She raised her eyebrows in a way that told me she really wanted to hear about Kas. I could tell by the way her mouth curved she liked the look of him.

"Mazha's?" Kas asked, suddenly excited.

"Ah, yes," Tavi answered, then politely listened to Kas explain how to get there and how much the bread cost and which flavor was the best—the lemon, apparently. Soon, Tavi was gone.

"I've missed you," I told him as he led me down the street, and I really had. The city was waking up now, horse-drawn wagons and carriages beginning to fill the streets as people left their homes to head to the markets.

"I am sorry," he said quietly. Kas waved down a man pushing his cart toward the marketplace. "All that talk about sweet breads," he said as he pulled me along, scurrying to keep up with him.

After passing coin, the man handed Kas a sack of something that he then gave to me. "The best in the city."

Inside were dates dusted with coarse sugar. A wide smile stretched across my face, and I quickly popped one in my mouth.

"I love these," I said. But with those words came an unwelcome ache. The last time I had eaten sugared dates, I'd been sitting in a magicked tent with Saalim, listening to the sounds of the bazaar around us.

My steps slowed.

"What is it?" Kas asked, wrapping his fingers in mine. His hand was so warm, so careful.

"Where did you go that day? You left." I quickly swallowed the date. A horse the color of a salt brick trotted alongside us.

He sighed and covered his face. "I had . . . matters . . . I needed to deal with that I'd forgotten. It is no excuse. I should not have left you like that."

"And then I heard nothing. Not even a message."

"If I am honest—"

"Please."

"I thought to reach out, but then I . . . You know how I feel about you, Emel. I don't know how you feel about me." He spoke quietly.

"You are very important to me," I began. I bit my lip, wondering what exactly I did feel.

"But you don't feel for me like you felt for him."

Him. Perhaps my acting had not been so faultless.

"That is not true." I rubbed my thumb over his knuckles. "I care deeply for you."

Kas said, "The Falsa Mawk is in three days, as I am sure you know."

Letting go of his hand, I plucked another date from the sack and slowly chewed the fruit from the seed, waiting.

"There is a good place to view the parade in the baytahira. Goes right by the drink house on the corner there. You remember?"

The one where we had first shared a drink. Before I knew him at all.

"They have a rooftop," he said. The one from which Kahina had watched the caravan's arrival. "It's the best place to see the day parade—well, besides the palace steps—and it will be a perfect place to see the firepaint at night."

"Firepaint?" I turned to him, my confusion apparent.

An enormous grin spread across his face and he rubbed his hands together. "That is right! You wouldn't know. Well, I won't ruin the surprise."

"Don't do that! Saalim wouldn't tell me either," I said before I could stop myself.

"Saalim? The king?" Kas's eyes darkened like storm clouds.

"He had mentioned it in passing," I said quickly. "When I was delivering his medicine."

"To call him by his name is very informal. You speak often, then?" How much he had gleaned from one slip of the tongue.

"No, almost never." I'd eaten nearly the entire bag of dates. I offered it to Kas. He shook his head. He hadn't had a single one.

We were silent for some time. I watched the streets grow busier, the people leaving their homes with calls of goodbye.

"Will you join me then? I would like it."

I had planned to join Saalim but could not say that now. But then, why meet Saalim and his royal friends? The camel race still made me shiver, and Saalim's invitation had been out of apology. But could I refuse him? Every day telling myself to leave the king behind got a little easier. Even if there were threads of that life that snagged, continuing to pull me back.

I should cut them free once and for all.

"Where should I meet you?" I asked, leaning into him, my face upturned. He grinned and kissed me, smacking his lips when he tasted the sugar on mine.

After finding peace with Tavi, I wanted the same with Firoz and Rashid. I still had some time to myself before Altasa awoke, so I went to invite them to join Kas and me at the festival. Smiling, I envisioned us all sharing food and drink, me tucked under Kas' arm, Firoz and Rashid hand in hand.

The baytahira was nearly deserted, but in front of the jalsa tadhat, a man lay curled on the street, eyes closed as if asleep.

"Firoz?!" I ran to him. Pushing him from his side to his back, I said his name again.

"Mmmemmeh." His face was puffy, eyes swollen. His lips were dry and his hair was stuck to his brow as if he had been there all night.

"What are you doing out here?" I asked him. A man sweeping the street in front of his Bura-den cast us a quick glance before looking back to the ground. As though a half-dead man in the street was of little concern. "Wake up," I hissed, slapping his cheek. His eyes parted slightly, cloudy in focus, before closing again.

I went to the jalsa tadhat, but the door was locked. Had they barred him from his home? Where was Rashid?

"Sir!" I called to the sweeping man. "Have you any water or tea?"

He looked at me, pausing his task only briefly, before looking back to the ground. "I won't waste what I have on him."

"I will pay." Fishing out my purse, I flashed a fid at him.

The man set down the broom and went inside. He returned quickly with tepid tea inside a chipped ceramic cup. I handed him the silver coin.

I dipped my finger in to feel its temperature before I dumped the tea on Firoz's face.

His eyes opened and he sputtered, wiping his face with his sleeve. Finally, he saw me.

"What—why are you here?" he asked as I helped him sit up. Slowly, he looked around us, considering the sky and the location of the sun. "What am I doing here?"

"I thought maybe you would know the answer to that question."

He dropped his head into his hands, staring between his knees.

"Do you remember anything?"

He blinked. "I am not sure."

Sighing, I waited.

"There was an arwah last night . . ."

I resisted the urge to stomp away.

He said, "We summoned . . . a spirit . . . I think." He took heaving breaths, as though he had just run a footrace. "Yes, we did." His voice was sharper now. "One of the Darkafa, I think? He said something about the jinni . . . he said he wanted to know where the goddess was, wanted proof that she was here and that the jinni was real. That he would help take down the first-born Son." Firoz wiped the hair from his brow. "The man was not convinced of her powers. He doubted aloud . . ." The heels of his hands dug at his eyes. "It is so cloudy. I can't remember if anything happened after that."

"Where is Rashid?" I asked, looking back to the locked door. Was he in there, sleeping comfortably while Firoz lay in the street?

"I can't remember. It was so sudden. Like some hand, some force . . . I don't know. It . . . it pushed us all, or took us. It was so angry. I . . . don't understand. A man came? And now . . ." He held his hands out, looking around with apparent confusion.

"You're here," I said, anger rising.

Slowly, he nodded.

"Sons, Firoz! What happened to you? You don't even know! Do you value your life so little?" I stood, clenching my fists and pacing around him. "I told you to stop tampering with magic. You could have died! Rashid could be dead!" I shouted the words. Each like a lashing.

"He wasn't there," he cried. He sounded defeated. Pathetic and sad. "Well, I don't think he was there. He was upstairs, I am sure of it."

"What of Odham and the others?"

Firoz simply shook his head. "Your friend was there. I think."

"My friend?" At first, I did not know who he meant. But then, "Kas?"

He nodded.

"No, he wasn't. He despises the arwahs even more than me."

He nodded. "He was there arguing with Odham. I remember hearing him in the hall."

"Well," I spat. "He is fine. I saw him this morning."

Why hadn't he mentioned what had happened? That my friend lay on the street? But then. Maybe he had not been aware of the magic. The rift created by Masira could have made him oblivious to the change.

Firoz stared at his hands opening and closing. Then, something pulled his attention to what was in front of him. His eyes brightened with relief. I followed his gaze and saw Rashid walking toward us, treading hesitantly, as though his legs had been under camel's feet.

Firoz scrambled to get up. Reluctantly, I helped him. "Let's go see what he has to say about last night, eh?"

"Are you all right?" Firoz breathed when he met Rashid.

"I am. Are you? What happened?"

I spoke before Firoz could give his clumsy recount again, my patience dispersing like smoke. "No, you answer first. Where did you come from now?"

Rashid looked as dazed as Firoz, running his hands through his hair, squinting at nothing in an attempt to remember.

I could not bear it any longer. "This," I said pointing at the both of them, "is what happens when you meddle with things you don't understand. This is what happens when you meddle with magic. It's for fools. I hope that you have learned something."

They both blinked at me.

"But I can see that you have not."

Without looking back, I stomped away, vowing I would never see them again. Never would I associate with someone who dallied with their life. The risk of Masira's ill-will was not one that I wanted to take. Her magic, her providence—whatever it was to be called—was better off stripped completely from the desert.

When I returned to the palace, smoke rose from Altasa's chimney. So she was awake. I could hear her rummaging about in the back. Following the sounds, I was surprised to find they came from my room.

My door was open, Altasa's back to me when I walked in. "He said he . . . can't believe," she mumbled.

"Awake finally, eh?" I asked.

She jumped and there was a loud clatter. The familiar rattle of glass and metal.

"Oh!" Altasa slammed the drawer at my bedside table closed.

I turned hard as stone. "What are you doing?"

"Looking for another pissing pot. Thought I'd left a spare in here."

"Those are my things."

"Fancy things you have there. Careful," Altasa said with a new hardness to her words. "The king might think you stole them." Her eyes dropped from my face to my chest as though she were searching for other stolen treasures.

She walked past me and back in the hall, grumbling about never having a damn pissing pot when she needed one. "Oh, and Emel?" She called from the kitchen, "I think it's time for you to start a new lesson."

15

SAALIM

I wanted to tell Mariam I would give her one hundred salt bricks to never speak of the Falsa Mawk and the wedding ever again. It all could not come at a worse time.

Each day I searched for clues of Edala, sending letters to monarchs and tribal leaders asking if they had seen her, questioning traders who had arrived from the desert, sending Nassar to different parts of the city, requesting that people report any information they might have. Tomorrow would be an entire day wasted watching displays roll by on wagons, pretending that all was not amiss.

The wedding would follow the day after. I dropped my head into my hands, not wanting to think of the days that came after, when I'd have to be a doting husband at a time when there was so much else to do.

Helena was a crown-bearer, the binding of two arms, the bringer of peace. My father's marriage to my mother had been arranged, of course, but he had always talked of how much he loved her. My mother was the heartbeat of the palace, of Almulihi. Did he love her because she had done so much for him, forgiven him for so much? Or was it because he was fortunate, and she was truly his other half? Perhaps it was both. Though I appreciated Helena's breeding, I could not see myself loving her as my father had loved my mother. It was my duty, though. A royal marries for power, not love.

Helena and her family had arrived five days ago. There had been feast after feast to welcome the new queen, my court receiving her with lavish attention and gifts. Bless Wahir for my people, since I barely managed to receive her myself. Each meal, my attention was divided between my guests and Nassar coming with messages. Whenever she and I had the opportunity to be alone, I promptly excused myself to see what news there was.

Helena was not blind. She could see something troubled me, but she played her part well. I could not tell her that my city was threatened, nor that I had only recently learned that my entire family was not dead, as I had believed them to be.

Edala was alive.

It had been years since I had seen her, so long ago had she left us to live in the desert. She might know the people who attacked Almulihi. Perhaps she knew more about Zahar, and where she was hiding. That damned woman. My mother had never liked the healer. Edala had clung to her, though, desperate to learn magic. I had thought Edala a fool for believing Zahar's tales, but now I wondered if I was the fool all along?

A memory pulled, something trying to drag itself to the forefront of my mind. Something about Zahar and magic—

Footsteps approached. I placed my hand on the hilt of my sword, waiting.

Nassar's head appeared as he ascended the stairs. My grip on my sword released.

"Saalim," he panted. One would never guess that this man had crossed the desert with us. "More soldiers have been sent."

"Good."

"I do not think it wise to send more."

"Azim will have the final say."

He was in front of my desk now, taking a seat in one of the heavy wooden chairs.

I said, "None have returned, I assume?"

My advisor shook his head. "Maybe tomorrow, but I would not expect it."

"We have to find her."

"I know, but we cannot lose sight of the Darkafa's warning—"

"We haven't!" I slammed my fist onto the surface. "They are being sought out, questioned!"

"They are." He leaned onto his knees now. "I have said this before—"

"You think them sand with salt."

"I do."

Staring at Nassar's shoulders, his small frame and sinewy neck, I wanted to send him back to Alfaar's and demand Usman come in return. How many times he had told me he thought that the Darkafa were no real threat. Nothing masquerading as something, a mask behind which the real threat stood, salt spoiled with sand. They did not have the will, he had said. They wanted their goddess, not the throne.

"They worship Eiqab," I reminded him. "They plan to take down Wahir."

"There is a distinction you forget that is important. They are unfurling the rug for Masira to send Eiqab. I've dealt with the type of people you think the Darkafa are. People that come in and unsettle, warning of attacks." He stared at nothing as he remembered. "Those do not wait in the open like the Darkafa. They are insidious."

"What do you mean you've dealt with people like this? I remember nothing like this happening to my father."

He looked at me, gaze glassy and unfocused. He was tired, and I think, too, he was scared.

<hr />

Passing Altasa's home, I stared at the curtained windows, the door ajar. Voices came from inside. I paused. A man was speaking with Altasa.

I kept walking, thinking of Emel. When she joined me tomorrow, it would be the last time I could gaze at her untethered.

The birds began chirping and cooing, rustling their feathers as I approached the aviary. Lazy things all hoping I'd toss them meat rather than take them out to hunt on their own. I fed scraps of meat to all of them, except Anisa.

Though she wanted to stay for her easy meal, I wanted at least one thing I could depend on. Nassar had demanded I leave the palace. *I can write letters, Saalim! It is why your father kept me around.* He was right. Sitting and waiting was doing me no good, so, with guards at my flanks, I went to the hunting grounds.

I stood with the golden eagle, her jesses tied to keep her on the glove, and let my shoulder tire from holding her. Let myself feel something other than worry. Anisa was agitated as she waited for my shoulder to burn.

Finally, I untied her and watched her fly. I remembered her soaring around Alfaar's tent, capturing another bird in her talons, and flying to the goddess in my challenge for the throne. How long ago that now seemed. My futile attempt at finding the people who killed my family, finding instead only trunks of stolen salt. And Emel.

I had never been able to make sense of the quantities of salt Alfaar possessed. There was something impossible about it.

Never had I believed jinn to be real. But the day our water stores were filled, many of the soldiers swore they remembered a group of nomads stopping to fill our barrels enough to reach to the next oasis. I *know* that did not happen. Unless I was going mad. Now the Darkafa claimed to have a magical jinn that would somehow unseat me from the throne, and my thought-to-be-dead sister had written me a letter saying the same.

It could not all be a coincidence.

Anisa vanished into the blinding sun. The desert unrolled before me, the sea to my back. Edala was out there, and something told me she would be able to answer my questions.

Anisa appeared first as a speck in the sky and grew into a bobbing bird as she neared. Finally, she spread her wings and landed on my arm, searching my hand for the dead rat.

She had nothing in her beak for me in return.

"You lazy thing," I hissed at her, as she took the carcass and ate.

"Someone approaches," Kofi said from behind me. "It looks like Hassas."

A glossy, brown horse galloped toward us, holding Tamam and kicking up dust behind her like the cause of a sandstorm.

"Find out what he wants," I said to Amir. Anisa was not yet done with her meal and would not be pleased with the interruption. I watched Amir approach Tamam. Their horses shook their heads against the reins as the men spoke. Before the beasts had even settled, Amir was returning.

"They have a child of the Darkafa!"

Anisa could finish her meal later.

⁓ ౿ ⟩⟨ ౿ ⟋

The child was so repulsive that I could barely recognize it was human.

"And you found it?" I asked the pair of women who stood beside the child.

One, dressed in the red-stained browns of a spice-slinger, wiped at her cheeks and with a shaky voice said, "She was in a cage."

With her was a heavyset woman who looked as though she had raised children her entire life by the way she softly traced her hand over the creature's brow. "On the docks. The cage was covered with a cloak." Her eyes misted. "We heard her bang that—" the woman eyed the metal box in the child's hands "—on the bars. There were so many people around. None paid her any attention."

I could understand why they kept her covered. Her skin was as pale as the full moon. Her eyes the same. She turned her head at our voices yet stared at nothing. She could not see. Her mouth opened as if to speak, but only garbled sounds came out. I saw no tongue.

A heavy surge of nausea came over me.

The woman was still speaking. "—must be done. They must be punished."

"And this box?" I asked, nodding to that which the child clutched tightly. A chain attached the box to a silver cuff on her wrist. It appeared like a puzzle box that children kept. My brother had had one to keep his frivolous children's treasures in.

The spice-slinger said, "She won't let us have it for long. But even if she did—"

"It is locked," the heavyset one interjected, kneeling beside the girl and whispering that she was safe, she was well, none would take her box. The girl leaned into the woman, who seemed soft and warm. Like Mariam had been to us when we were young.

"We will keep the child here," I told them. "She will be cared for until we can find a place for her." I was not sure if even the orphans' home would take her.

"My king," the large woman said. "I will keep the child. I have—"

"It is not safe. There are those who may search for her and do whatever it takes to get her back."

She nodded gravely, the red-eyed spice-slinger reaching down and pressing her hand against the woman's shoulder.

When they left, I called for Mariam, who seemed as distraught about the state of the child as the other two women.

"Your heart is soft, Mariam," I said quietly as she coaxed the child—who struggled with her large black robes—up from the floor.

"My granddaughter would have been her age now." Mariam did not look at me.

I did not know she'd had a child, let alone a grandchild.

"Would Nadia and Edala's tower suit?" I asked. "The child might like seeing the garden." Most importantly, it was opposite mine.

Mariam gave me a tired look and tapped her temple.

The child was blind. She would not see anything, let alone the garden. I stood in a rush. "Look after her. You can stay there, too."

Mariam spoke warmly to the girl and then smiled widely at me. Never had I seen her so happy.

I said, "We will break the chain that attaches it to her. If she'll give you the box, bring it to us immediately." Though we had far more important things to do than investigate a child's trinket.

When they had gone, the throne room was quiet. The guards lining the room were both silent and still.

My father's throne—my throne—was firm against my back, soft under my thighs. So the back never bends, my father had said. The throne to my left was empty. Helena would be seated there in two days. I remembered Alfaar's throne—twisting metal that poked and prodded and insisted that none sit in it for prolonged lengths. It was the chair of someone who did not address his people. And there was no chair for a queen in that tent they called a palace. His wives held less importance than the piles of stolen salt that had a seat beside him.

Shaking my head, I tried to rid myself of thoughts of that so-called king. I could not understand my fascination with Alfaar. I thought of him too often.

When I rose, the guards bowed their heads. I used to dream of being king. Now, I dreamed of anything but. Maybe a life where I could be a seaman. Where I could take a wife like . . . Emel . . . or someone who boasted no high breeding.

"Send Nika," I said to the guards. She had not yet finished telling me of the schedule for the Falsa Mawk. "I will be in the atrium."

She did not take long to arrive. I had barely begun to pick apart the pomegranate the servant had brought. The highest victory if no seed was destroyed. Had Emel ever had a pomegranate? When I saw her at the festival, I would ask.

Nika talked through where I would need to be and when. The places the people expected me to be seen, where I would need to sit to greet them, how the seats would be arranged. Drivel, compared to my thoughts of Edala and the Darkafa.

"You've coordinated these things with Azim?"

"Of course. There will be a full guard with you."

"Inconspicuous?"

She nodded. "Half will be in plain dress."

"Good." It would not do to have the king swarmed by guards. The people would question why I felt unsafe around them. "I've invited one more guest."

She folded her hands in front of her. "Who should I prepare for?"

"Emel."

"Altasa's apprentice?"

"Yes."

She pressed her lips together as her eyebrows flicked upwards.

"Is there anything else?" I asked.

"No, sir."

"Very well. Tomorrow we will be ready at midday. Oh, and Nika?"

"Yes?"

"Make sure there are pomegranates."

"Pomegranates?"

"Halved."

She bowed her head.

"Actually," I said. "Some seeds in a bowl." In case Emel wore something light in color. I remember Nadia had hated the stains.

Through the windows, the city was still, the sea at its side appeared to be frozen, too, as though this magic had reached out its wayward hands and sunk its fingers in to calm it. But a sea without waves, without current, would be no sea at all.

Magic would bring ruin.

16

EMEL

I n the limpid light of morning, I sat up, heart pounding with anticipation. Today was the Falsa Mawk, and I was to meet Kas to watch the parade. I would tell him that perhaps he and I might find a place to live together. I was choosing him, leaving the palace behind, leaving Altasa behind.

Leaving Saalim.

As I rushed to dress, splashing my face with water and rubbing jasmine oil into my skin, I heard a commotion in the kitchen.

Altasa was at the counter, pulling jars down with a fervor I had never seen.

"An urgent request?" I asked. She had promised me we weren't working today.

"I want you to make something." The tip of her tongue pressed her upper lip as she stared at the wall of ingredients. "Yes." She pulled two more jars down then patted the counter by way of invitation.

I went to her. "Now?"

She tapped a page in her book. "Follow the recipe."

"But the Falsa Mawk . . ." My eyes drifted to the page. The recipe was called Haraki. "Cricket?" I clarified, not understanding. "Altasa," I glanced out the window, the pale purple light quickly turning blue. "My sister and I plan to meet."

"And you'll miss your meeting if you keep talking. I need you to do this. Now. Before . . . I need to know . . ." She mumbled incoherently and pushed the ingredients to the edge of the counter toward me.

Sighing, I looked down at the recipe. It was unusual, prompting me to turn the mixture several times in one direction or the other. To use a specific water source that Altasa provided to me. Once mixed, the instructions stated to turn it onto the counter surface. I hesitated, looking to Altasa. It would spill everywhere and be a horrendous mess to clean.

She nodded excitedly. "Do what it says."

So I did.

Turning the bowl upside down onto the counter, I tapped the bottom several times, then removed it. When I saw what lay on the counter, I screamed, flying into the table behind me.

There was no slopping wet mixture. Instead, there was a single cricket that leapt off of the counter and onto the ground. Within a moment, it was gone completely. Lost in the labyrinth of furniture.

"What?! What happened?" I said, out of breath and terrified at what I had just done. I remembered the first time I had released Saalim from his vessel—the impossibility of what I saw.

This felt the same.

Fatigue washed over me, as though I'd just climbed up the palace tower three times its height. Altasa sat me down at the table, a strange spark in her eyes. She had a vibrancy that made her seem even younger, especially with her silver hair hidden beneath her scarf.

"Magic, child," Altasa whispered. "You did it. You can do it."

"Magic?" I leaned away from her. "But how?"

"With my ingredients." She fluttered her fingers at the items on the counter. "I could teach you the preparation of such ingredients. How to wield her providence."

I was barely listening, my mind racing to catch up with what had just happened. What she was telling me now. "You know magic." It was a question, but it wasn't.

"Yes. I want teach you."

"I don't want to learn," I said, thinking of Sabra, the scars on my back, my father's empire.

"Lies!" She slapped her hand on the table, the other holding a single finger in the air. "To use Masira's gifts to speak with her? To wield her power as your own? You would not want that?"

"It is not so simple—"

She laughed then, a loud and musical laugh I had never heard from her. Chills crept down my back.

I continued, determined. "It leaves traces of confusion and ugliness behind. It has consequences."

"But see here," she hissed, "the more important question is how do *you* know that?"

Hesitating, I interlocked my fingers and squeezed.

"Twin golden cuffs. A vessel of sand. That necklace you wear." She pointed at my neck, where my mother's golden necklace hung behind my clothes. "Where did those come from, hmm?"

"Tavi is waiting for me." I stood.

Her hand softly held me back. "Where did you get them? Tell me," she pleaded, her voice gentle. "The truth could change everything."

I opened my mouth, then closed it again.

"Did you steal them?"

"No."

"Did you get them from *him*?"

Him? "Altasa, I—"

"I have gone about this all wrong," she said to herself. Then she looked at me again. "We seem dusty and worn in this city of lives built atop salt bricks, but we are more. You are marked by Masira." How had she known? "You can wield Masira's will. You can be more powerful than them all. And that is without even *knowing* what you were doing." Her eyes were alight with excitement and . . . almost a crazed jealousy. "These people think they know us, think they can ridicule us because we are 'salt chasers.' They are wrong, we are sun-seekers, and we can show them that we are not something to mock but something to celebrate. Something to fear."

Her words stoked a small pride.

"You can do amazing things," she pressed. "We could do them together."

Together. That did not sound so bad.

"I could teach you to rein hate, craft a fountain of endless magic, to hold sway over love."

Love. Kas flashed in my mind. Then Saalim.

The healer's hands clasped tightly together as she waited for my answer. There were thoughts running behind the words she said aloud. Things she would not say.

Power thrummed through me. That which I held the potential for, that which I wielded now.

"I need time," I said. It was not a decision I could take back.

"Good," she said. "Tonight, we will talk. Enjoy your evening on the rooftop with that boy."

My mind reeled with what had just happened.

Then I realized I had never told Altasa that I had chosen to meet with Kas instead of Saalim that night. More curiously, I had never told her where.

───────

There was a huddle of women dressed in bright colors in the front room of Saira's, and I could see Tavi seated in the middle of them all.

Saira was in the kitchen smiling to herself as she prepared a sweet breaded something that she turned out of the sizzling pot and into a basket. Her children fought with one another as they reached up to grab the hot bread.

"Well," Tavi said. "It was often worn like this."

As I moved to the cluster of women, I saw Tavi placing an embellished veil over her brow. The strangeness of my morning with Altasa washed away as I cringed, unable to look at the faces of the women that watched Tavi, fearing they mocked her.

"Emel! Come here!" Tavi exclaimed when she saw me. The women parted when they saw me. "This is my sister. She can show you even better perhaps than me."

Reluctantly, I knelt beside Tavi. In front of her were two long dresses dyed a vivid blue; the hems, a pale purple the color of dawn. They were colors we would have worn as ahiran. In her hands Tavi held two veils decorated the same as our mothers' back home, glinting discs hanging from the fabric.

"What is this?" I said, touching the bronze discs, distracted from my unease by the familiarity. It was not dha that decorated the fabric, as our mothers' would have been.

"Old bronze Yakub found for me." Tavi smiled shyly.

"Saira showed us. They are so beautiful," a women said, bright yellow flowers woven in her hair.

I smiled at the genuine praise.

"You should have seen the ones our mothers wore," Tavi said, handing the veil to another woman, whose eyes sparkled as she touched the fabric. Tavi described how they looked, how our mothers wore them.

"How many threads for the embroidery?" a woman asked, peering at the veil being passed to her. When Tavi explained, she nodded and said, "I am sure Jameelah could do something like that for me."

The women's attention broke off, and they began discussing the veils amongst themselves.

"You made me one, too?" I said to Tavi, looking at the second veil still lying with the dress. I could not take my eyes from it—the lines had been embroidered on the veil just as Mama's would have been, the obvious work Tavi had gone through to recreate something that was of both Madinat Almulihi and our home.

Nika said that the city would be dressed in its finest today, and the people would be, too. On the way to Tavi's, I had seen that the streets—the cleanest I'd ever seen them—were thickly lined with potted, strung, and arranged flowers. Stray petals blew along the stone. Now, at Saira's, I was beginning to understand what Nika had meant.

When I saw how these women—dressed so beautifully—peered at our veils, I felt a stirring of pride.

"You can use beads, too," I said. "To decorate them." Picking up the fabric, I showed them how.

Hearing the activity from outside, others came into the house. Saira doled out food to those who came through with wishes for a bright Falsa Mawk, and as they chewed their sweet bread, they learned from Tavi and I how to wear the abaya, the veil.

"And this is how all women dress where you're from?" one asked as she peered into a mirror with the veil draped over her head. She pulled her shoulders back just so, admiring herself.

"Not all this elaborately, but yes," I said.

The morning was spent with people I did not know, celebrating the traditions of Madinat Almulihi while showing the traditions of my home. Had Tavi told me of this prior to my coming—that I would walk into a room of people who examined something of our lives with scrutiny—I would not have come. But there was no mockery here, no fun at our expense. These people seemed as envious of me as I was of them. One even exclaimed she would like to wear something like it next year.

It felt as though I had barely arrived when Saira was clucking at everyone to leave. "They need to get ready, too! The parade starts soon."

"Soon?" I gasped, looking outside. Sure enough, midday was fast approaching. I had to meet Kas soon! My breath caught. It was time to find him. Time to tell him.

Tavi and I rapidly dressed.

"Will you be with Yakub today?" I asked.

She nodded, adjusting the bronze discs in the mirror so that they lay exactly right. "He told me he'd go early to find us a good spot on the street. Where will the king's party watch it?"

"I don't think I am going to join them . . ."

She spun to me. "But you'll have the best view!"

"Kas knows where we can watch from the roof in the baytahira."

"That sounds nice, too." She sounded disappointed, but I did not want to argue with her. Instead, we said our goodbyes.

Even the smaller streets were decorated. Some homes had flower wreaths as bright as the sun hanging from their doors; others had strung cloth in vivid colors from ropes to flap in the wind. Petals sprinkled the paths to some front doors; very few were left undecorated. Almost everyone I saw was dressed as the women in Saira's home, and many carried food to and from their neighbors' homes.

The air was sticky sweet with excitement, and with every step, my smile grew.

This was why I had come to Madinat Almulihi. This was the life I'd dreamed of, the life I'd hoped Tavi would share. My smile widened as I made resolutions that stuffed away my pride. There was no need for grandness, for big dreams.

Here I was living in a beautiful city with my sister and friends. That was enough. I didn't need magic if I had Kas and Tavi . . . if I had everything else. With newfound joy, I nearly ran to find Kas.

Never before had I approached the baytahira from the neighborhoods that bordered it. The homes were small, cramped. They were not as decorated as the homes near the canals. The smell of sweets had drifted away, and lingering in their place was the smell of Bura-dens and drink houses. Babies cried, people shouted, goats bleated.

"Lost?" a man asked, staring at my festival clothes, garish in the shadowed alley.

"Salt chaser, eh?" I heard another man whisper to a woman.

When I turned the corner, three cloaked people huddled together in a doorway. Chills swept down my back, my arms. With gloved, black hands, one pulled the hood over his face.

The Darkafa. If I hurried, I could run back to the palace to alert a guard.

A door opened into the alley, and someone stepped out.

I stared at the ground as I passed.

"Are we all ready?" a voice asked.

No.

Anything but that voice.

Turning my head slightly, praying I was wrong, I saw Kas standing amongst them.

We, he had said.

My vision blurred, roaring filled my ears. My feet carried me from the alley and back toward the palace. People lined the streets in droves. I stepped on petals and over pots mindlessly. Finally, I was on the steps of the palace, trying to squeeze between guards to get to Altasa's.

Suddenly her offer of magic was the most appealing thing in the world. I would accept it, and the first thing I would do was curse Kas to a life of—

"Emel!"

Saalim stood outside of the viewing box by himself, only a pair of guards at his back. He fidgeted for just a moment before he approached me.

"I worried you weren't going to make it," he said as he gestured to the crowded street.

He had been waiting for me.

17

EMEL

T he viewing box—the same one as the camel race—was filled with guests. My shoulders fell. I wanted to be anywhere but in there.

A figure separated from the crowd. A woman moved to the edge, watching her soon-to-be husband.

Helena.

In the way she placed her hand on the smooth wood railing, I knew she was born to be a queen. Her pallor, the almost-straw color of her hair, and eyes so bright blue I could see them from where I stood, gave her the appearance of someone conjured by a storyteller. She stood like a closed door, a reminder that I was unwelcome.

My gaze darted between Helena and Saalim, then back to the palace. A split in the path. The healer or the king.

Saalim's clothes were resplendent with swirls of summer, golden threads as luminous as the crown on his head. His hands were in front of him like an unsure admirer confessing love, looking at me for only a moment before he looked away. Like a man staring at the sun.

He appeared exactly as he had that night on the beach when he conjured a fire and told me he had fallen in love with an ahira who was forbidden to love him in return. Standing there now, I saw not the king, but the jinni, and

I nearly collapsed with longing. Confusion, heartache, and grief rolled in like storm clouds. Now, more than ever, I needed my companion, my friend, my lover back.

"I hope you haven't been waiting long," I said, stepping toward him.

"Not long," he said as he followed me up the stairs. "Your robes are befitting for the festival. Please make yourself comfortable, I must see to my guests." Then he was lost in the crowd and I was again alone.

Music sounded from far away, starting very softly. Voices around me buzzed excitedly. Soon, a trio of musicians walked down the center of the street. Behind them, I could see the beginnings of the parade: waves of color, dancers and props flowing like a river of splendor. The musicians moved rhythmically, leading people who carried thick boughs of flowers and flags that flapped in the air. It was captivating, so much grander than anything I'd ever seen.

The first exhibition rolled by, pulled by two black horses with red flowers decorating their empty saddles. I heard a man murmur, "The winner of the camel race."

A man and a woman stood on the rolling platform, silk on display between them. They had arranged the fabric so that it flapped with the wind. They had large baskets at their feet, and as they passed, they reached down, grabbed fistfuls of petals, and tossed them toward us. Soft pink and white and orange floated down.

"There will be much more of this," a woman said to no one in particular as she brushed the few petals from the rail.

Beyond her, Saalim was seated beside Helena, both smiling politely to the people on display. I chewed the inside of my cheek, wishing I could sit beside him. Just as I considered that it may have been foolish of me to come, Saalim's eyes met mine. With the slightest twitch of his lip, he nodded and turned back to the parade.

Blushing, I spun and stared at the parade, seeing nothing but his shy smile.

The woman was right about the flowers. Every display tossed petals in our direction. From fanciful exhibitions or synchronized dancers that swayed to the music, there were more and more flowers. Soon they were piled on the ground around us, trailing down the street. Near the end of the parade, an enormous wagon pulled by four horses and strung with bright flower chains rolled by. Men and women stood atop it, some holding decanters and laughing as they raised their vessels to the spectators. Another held a pipe. Some sat on the edge of the wagon, dressed to lure, smiling and waving in a way that suggested it was more than a plain greeting. On the ground around the wagon, dancers waved gauzy fabric that almost resembled smoke.

Everything about the display, about the way the people moved, was dreamlike. At the center of the wagon, Kahina stood on a small platform, her arms outstretched. Golden hoops hung from her ears and thick chains from her neck. Beside her stood a young man who seemed less comfortable but waved all the same.

"The baytahira." Saalim was by my side, and I startled, not realizing he had risen from his chair.

Helena was on the other side of him. She nodded to me when our eyes met. I hoped the smile I offered was believable.

Kahina waved to me and gave a knowing grin to Saalim. Leaning toward me, Saalim said, "Before Kahina's husband died, they would share his mapmaking during the parade. Now, it's this." His words were flat.

"You know Kahina well?" I asked.

"I used to. Visited her often as a child, asking her to tell my fortune." He laughed. Helena watched him politely. Saalim continued. "I did not know her husband, since he was often gone. But I loved his maps."

A mapmaker . . . The familiar young man beside Kahina . . .

"When did he die?" I asked Saalim, my voice shaking.

"For certain, I don't know. Sometime in the past year. On a route, I believe."

"What was his name?" I held my breath.

"I can't remember. Why do you ask?"

"A man named Rafal came to my village with his maps."

Saalim frowned. "That would be a long journey."

I wondered.

The end of the parade came too soon. The final display was a tribute to the royal family. Saalim stiffened when he saw it: a tapestry carried on a long rod resting on the shoulders of young men. A family of six was woven against a blue background. There were no features, only the silhouettes in various shades of purples and reds. The pair at the center each had a golden crown atop their heads. When they were in front of Saalim, they turned so that he would see the tapestry fully and kneeled.

"A gift from your people," one of the men called, his eyes to the ground.

"Your gift is acknowledged and is appreciated. Thank you," Saalim said. Those who did not know him would not have heard it, but I could not miss the tightness in his voice. The slight tremor when he thanked them. And perhaps it was only me who saw the slight quiver of his hand at his side. He gave a signal, and those who had kneeled were on their feet again.

"It is beautiful," Helena said.

Slowly, he nodded. I wanted to take his hand, but instead stood beside him and watched his clasped hands on his lap.

"Where will it be placed?" Helena asked.

"They will bring it to the palace. It was customary to conclude with a gift for the queen. I did not expect they would do anything . . ." He stopped.

Following his gaze, I saw what had caught his attention. My breath hitched when I saw.

The tapestry was two-sided. On its back were two silhouettes with crowns. The second, a woman, was a pale pink and had long straight hair. *Helena.* The silhouettes were in front of a crescent and moon-jasmine.

"Ah," he whispered, then dutifully turned to his betrothed. Helena saw the tapestry, too. She bobbed her head with a smile as formal as the gift.

The depiction was as regal and elegant as one could hope. It was even more stunning than the family on its other side. I could barely stand to look at it.

People funneled into the streets, waving to the king, uniting with neighbors and families. Saalim's guests buzzed around, the chatter growing louder. Saalim and Helena were quickly lost amongst them.

It was time to return to the palace.

No matter how much I wished it, my place was not here.

As I descended the steps, Amir stopped me. "You're not leaving are you?"

"I am."

Amir appeared wildly offended. "You can't! It's your first Falsa Mawk, and you plan to skip the best part?" He told me to wait for the guests to disperse and then we would travel to the party.

I felt like I had little choice, and I agreed to stay. As I waited, I relived the day. From Altasa's offer of magic to finding Kas in the alley with the Darkafa. I tried to convince myself that it wasn't him, that it could have been someone who looked like him. But I knew better. I had seen his face. Seen the scar. And I knew his voice.

Like I'd been splashed with cold water, I turned to Amir. "I saw the Darkafa before the parade," I said urgently. People trickled down the stairs, moving slowly to their carriages.

He nodded. "We know they are here. Azim has guards stationed on every corner of the city today."

"But I heard them talk. They spoke of being ready."

Now he was interested. "For what?"

"That was all I heard." I pursed my lips, feeling a little foolish.

"Thank you for telling me. You are very loyal."

Saalim and Helena finally came down the stairs. When Amir proudly told Saalim that he'd convinced me to join them, Saalim said, "We'll go to the docks now. Would you prefer riding or walking?"

"Riding? On a horse?" I asked, wide-eyed. Docks?

"Not in the saddle," he said, laughing. The guests beside him laughed, too.

A guard stepped up to him and said, "The carriage is here."

"That settles it then."

As the group of us moved toward the carriage, Helena dropped back to me. "I do not ride horses either," she whispered, her accent the strangest I'd ever heard. "They terrify me."

And despite wanting nothing less, I found that I liked her. Being so near, I was able to watch her closely. She smelled of faraway, unfamiliar places and things. She was shorter than me, her frame smaller. I thought of what Hadiyah would say. "A man wants flesh in his hands." But a royal title mattered more than wide hips.

It took longer to reach the dock by carriage than it would have on foot. The sea of people so dense, the horses could barely nudge their way through. If there was a break in the crowd, it mattered little, as so many wanted to speak to their king and tomorrow-queen. Whether it was simply to greet them or to thank Saalim for one thing or another, we were continually being stopped.

Helena, seated across from me, leaned forward and lightly touched the veil around my face. "This is so beautiful; I have been unable to look away."

Thanking her, I felt compelled to return a compliment, but her dress was so formal, so dull by comparison, that I felt it would have come out flat on my tongue. Helena preempted my trouble, asking me about my home. The other people with us stopped their conversations to listen. She coaxed me with questions, seeming so enamored with my life that my pride for my home grew.

The horses picked up speed as we moved off the main street and the crowds dispersed. "Almost there now," Saalim said.

"Where are we going?" I wondered aloud as we were led down the empty dock bordered with enormous ships. Nearly all the ships were tucked in, with ropes pulled tightly over their sleeping sails, silently swaying with the waves. At the end of the dock, a single ship had its bright sails bent against the wind, the ship lurching with the force.

Amir pointed at it. "There."

I hated walking on the docks, and now I was supposed to step onto a ship?

Laughter spilled into the air before us, and I looked up to see that there were many already aboard.

"This is the party," Amir said with a grin, nudging me with his elbow

"On the ship?" I swallowed the nausea that rose.

"You'll see!"

The walkway that led to the ship was no more than a thick piece of wood. The people walked up the path with only mild uneasiness, the women squawking and laughing when the men bounced on the platform to shake it. Helena ascended with an ease that spoke of her comfort on the sea. Saalim moved aside to wait for me. It was only us and the guards now.

"I can't," I whispered.

"Emel," Saalim urged. "It is steady, see?" He pressed his foot into the center of the path, and I swear I saw the planks give.

The ship rocked with the enormous waves, coming closer to the dock, then falling away, stretching the ropes that held it fast. Should I fall between the boat and the dock, I would be crushed.

"Please," Saalim tried again. "With me?" He offered his hand.

It would be the last time I touched him.

Slowly, I placed my hand in his. It was like fire, like cool water, like a bed of feathers. Everything that comforted, spilling down my arm at his touch. *Don't let me go.* Did he feel it, too? The way he looked at me then, as though he didn't want to let go either. Everything told me to fall into his chest, to hold him, to tell him everything.

His fingers closed around mine, and all I saw was him. The blur of the ship and guests behind us, the guards around us, was just that. A blur. A background. Unimportant. Following him, I stepped onto the path.

When the wind blew, I gripped his hand tighter and paused. Feeling my fear, he adjusted his hold so that his other hand was on my shoulder.

"I won't let you fall," he said quietly. "Nearly there." His thumb brushed against my knuckles. The smallest movement, but it felt like it could have moved a dune.

And then we were there. My feet were on the solid ship, my knees buckling with relief.

Everything fell into focus. I was aboard something completely ungrounded. The ship rocked, and I lurched with it. Saalim still had not removed his hold, and he tightened his grip, holding me steady.

"You will get used to it. Just give it a few moments. Here." He walked me to a bench laden with cushions. Other women gathered on the bench smiled politely at me. "Sit here. Let me find you something to drink."

It was from the low bench that I was finally able to see what surrounded me.

People of wealth, spun with silk and coated in decadent oils, glided around laughing and talking and leaning against the rails that protected them from spilling into the sea. It was, indeed, a king's party.

When I straightened my spine, I could see the jagged edges of Madinat Almulihi peaking just over the boat. The palace's domes, brilliant in the sunlight, required no stretching. They reached into the sky, taller than my father's palace ever had been.

"Are you a king's ahira, then?" one of the women asked eagerly. She was very young, maybe Raheemah's age.

"I am not," I said, stiffening.

Surprise flashed on her face, but she recovered quickly.

"Are you?" I asked.

The woman shook her head as though she was disappointed she was not and took a sip from her drink. A shadow passed over her, and the corners of her lip lifted just a little.

"Drink this," Saalim said, suddenly in front of me.

I stood quickly, eager to command more of his attention. But when I stood, I stumbled again with the movement of the ship and Saalim encouraged me to stay seated.

"When we depart, I will find you. There's a rhythm to it." He looked at the deck and spread his feet as though to demonstrate.

"Depart?" I asked. "We are going out there?" My voice was low.

He nodded once before he left me.

When the ship finally left the dock, I sat with my hands gripping the bench, the tea Saalim had gotten me long since forgotten. I could almost understand the appeal—the freedom that came with the whip of the wind and slap of the sails as the boat moved out into deeper waters—but the further out we moved, the more terrified I became.

Should the boat sink, we were doomed.

"You have been here since high sun," a man said. I felt the cushions depress beside me. "Care for a companion?"

Omar.

Sons, would I ever escape him? He still smelled the same—liquor and sweat and whatever cloying scent he insisted on smearing on his skin. The aroma carried with it memories of those awful nights when he had requested me as his ahira. How was it possible that despite the magic that has transformed the desert, this man was unchanged?

"I prefer to be alone," I told him quietly.

Most of the people—much braver than I—were at the edge of the ship, watching Madinat Almulihi grow smaller as we ventured further into the horizon's mouth. "I am here with the king. He will be coming for me."

"The king?" he laughed. "I don't think he will be tending to you anytime soon." Omar nodded toward a cluster of people at the bow of the ship, Saalim amongst him. The setting sun set him and Helena alight.

My shoulders fell.

"Don't worry, dove," he said.

Dove. It is what my father called me. It is what he had called me on those horrid nights. "There are plenty of men with wealth that might take a liking to you. Men like that need women of royal lineage." He leaned toward me. "Us men of the desert, we are not so picky, eh? We like our women to be of the same cloth."

Seeing nothing but the rocking horizon, I stood. I had no obligation to this man. No Salt King dictated my behavior tonight. Willing myself to remain steady, I strode toward the rail.

"Have I upset you? My apologies," Omar said, following me.

"You have." I turned to him, letting my anger give me strength. "By your condescension now. By your behavior when I met you in the palace. By your very presence in my father's court those moons ago. By the bruises you left on my arms."

I did not know if in this changed desert Omar had come to my father's court, had bed me carelessly and violently. Had he the memories? I still did, and I refused to continue to live with them alone.

"Omar," I said, leaning into him. He arched away from me. "Did you know I was almost given to your father to serve as your whore?" The boat dipped down, and my knees sank into it. But I did not fall. He opened his mouth and closed it again. *Do you have these memories, Omar? Let me give them back to you.*

And so I did. In glistening detail.

"There was nothing I wanted less than to be the plaything of an animal. My lineage," I spat the word, "is royal. I am the daughter of a king. And even if I wasn't, I do not rely on men like you to tell me my worth."

I did not give him the opportunity to reply.

Wheeling around, I saw a woman descending below the deck. Swiftly, I fell in line behind her, my steps calm and light despite the hammering of my heart in my ears.

Omar, thankfully, did not follow.

Below deck, everything was darker, hazier. One inhalation told me people here were smoking the Buraq rose. A servant whose eyes appeared as glazed as some of the guests' sauntered by with silver bowls filled with the petals of the flower. Seeing me, he tipped the tray in offering. I shook my head.

Another walked by with full goblets, and I took one. Sitting against a tall-backed chair beside a window was Dima. The fading light outside cast her in a purple-gray glow. She looked more beautiful than ever.

"It is a fine party, no?" she said staring out the window as I seated myself beside her.

"Improved only if it were it not on a ship."

She turned to me with eyebrows raised. Her face softened. "You are the one who assists Altasa."

When I confirmed I was, she relaxed.

"I have seen you with Saalim a few times," she told me, not unhappily. The way she said his name made it clear with whom she spent her nights. Like Helena, I wanted to find her unlikeable, but I could not. "He seems interested in you, no?"

I shook my head and explained the superficial nature of our relationship. Why I was on this boat in the first place. "Had I known this is what it was like, I'm not sure I would have agreed."

Dima smiled but quickly grew serious.

"Better to be here, I think, than on land tonight. The Darkafa will search for Saalim. Thinking him easy prey if celebrating."

"But aren't we easier prey on a boat?"

Her soft eyes fell on mine before they flicked toward the window, the sea spray nearly reaching us. "You don't have to worry. The guard is very strong. They are aware of all of these things. Even here," she tipped her goblet toward the people inside, "we are surrounded."

Searching each person for some sign that they were Saalim's soldier proved useless. Too many thick robes and long tunics hiding weapons.

I leaned back and curled my legs under me. Dima seemed a safe companion.

My head buzzed, my limbs grew light. The Buraq smoke was slowly sending me up and up and up.

Dima said, "There are those who will always be eager to pry Saalim from the throne." She echoed my movements and curled into the chair, her slippers left on the ground in front of her. Soft, jeweled, and looking as though they had not been worn once.

I replied, "To be expected, I imagine."

Her mouth, normally so soft, pressed into a thin line. "Many never wanted him there in the first place. If it weren't for his father's wishes, he never would have sat on the throne."

It was a strange thing to say. "But why not?" It was customary that the first-born son was heir to the crown.

Dima cocked her head. "You don't know?" Her voice was not lowered. Should anyone at the party want to listen to our conversation, they easily could.

"Know?"

"Where Saalim comes from?"

I opened my mouth but closed it again. Did she know he was once a jinni?

Dima leaned forward. "His blood is 'impure.'" The corners of her lips lifted as though she found the idea comical.

"Impure?"

She sighed. "He was the king's son, but he was not from the womb of the queen."

"I don't understand. How would you know who his mother—"

"Oh, everyone in Madinat Almulihi knew. No one speaks much of it any-more. It does not matter now. But see, a baby can't be born to a woman who had no swell." She gestured to her belly. "The queen had never been pregnant when Saalim was born. In fact, they had not been married long." She flicked her hand and muttered, "Not like that matters."

My thirst for understanding burned. Saalim had never told me this. How could I have been so close to someone and yet not know everything about him? How many secrets did he keep?

"Then who was his mother?"

Dima leaned her elbow onto the sill of the window, uncaring of the wave that sent a spray of water against her skin and hair. "That was where all the trouble began. She was a salt chaser."

18

SAALIM

N assar told me the prince's name, but already it had slipped my mind. He was talking about our camel's wool, but I heard nothing. Too distracted after seeing Emel and Omar beside each other. The sun was setting. I had left Emel for much longer than I'd planned. I wanted to go to her but scanning the crowd now, I could not find her. Where had she gone?

The prince asked me a question. As I turned with a request for him to repeat it, Nassar answered. Praise Wahir for that man.

The guests kept talking of this and that, exchanging compliments and gratitude for the invitation. Over and over, raising my glass again and again. I only took enough to taste—for the drop to disperse on my tongue—not to swallow. Despite sip and sip after sip, I had yet to be on my second glass. The ground was still steady, and my mind was still clear.

"Your guests seem happy," Helena said coming up beside me.

"Tomorrow they will be your guests, too."

She nodded, brushing back her hair. She smelled so different from the women here. She smelled like the plant houses—floral and warm. I stared at the curves of her cheek and brow, the subtle lift of her lips. I imagined her with my mother's crown. Life would be very different with her.

"When do we take our place?" She gestured to the stern. A private area where we would view the firepaint.

"Whenever you like. There are no rules."

"I think I will go now," she said, relieved. I understood. Entertaining was exhausting, especially when everyone scrutinized each word as it was spoken.

"I will join you once I've spoken with a few more guests." Feeling only a slight guilt, I left Helena to find Emel. I searched through the faces and robes and scarves for one that glinted bronze, but I did not find her. I imagined her fallen from the ship, terrified and unable to swim. Excusing myself hastily from a pair of young women that approached me, I went to the stairs that led below deck.

Thick smoke drifted up the stairs. How much Buraq would these people smoke tonight?

"You are not just buying them leisure and food," Nassar had said when I complained of the cost. "You are buying their loyalty. Their diplomacy."

Below deck, few had the mental clarity to nod or bow, but most glanced my way, then stared back at the sea through the wide windows.

My mother hated those windows, complaining they let in too much spray. But Ekram had shaken his head. If the boat was to be used for gatherings or short trips, the windows were necessary to prevent the rocking sickness guests often experienced. I remembered going into closed ship rooms as a child only to sprint back to the deck to purge my meal.

Dima leaned against the sill of a window, looking like a queen herself in her shimmering dress. Her face was soft, but her eyes were sharp. I knew that face. Conspiring, I could tell. Edala would love Dima if she met her, respect her assertiveness. Nadia, dovish by comparison, would disapprove.

Dima's eyes met mine, and her lips curled into a smile, her eyebrow raising just enough to tell me she found something most amusing.

Then I saw with whom she spoke. Her scarf sparkled as though in greeting.

"Dima. Emel," I said. Emel looked at me with a new expression on her face. Not displeasure, nor eagerness. I said, "I am sorry it has taken me so long to return to you."

"No apology needed," she said, shifting herself so that she was not folded so casually on the cushions. Her back straightened. "Dima has been quite entertaining."

Sons, what trouble was Dima stirring? "Ah, well then . . ." Feeling a fool for my stuttering words, I took a gulp of my wine.

Dima smiled. "I have helped mortar the stone, as I think the builders say?"

"I should not like to think with what." Then to Emel: "It is nearly dark."

Like Dima's, Emel's eyes were still bright. She had not smoked the Buraq. She tilted her head in question. How could this woman who stared so assuredly and asked questions with the press of her lips alone make me feel like a boy stumbling through his lessons? Like everything I said should be re-said, like everything I wanted should be reconsidered. "The firepaint will be soon. You'll want to be on deck"

I held my hand out to her. "Let me help," I said aloud, hoping that everyone who saw would understand it was simply to help her get her footing. Dima, who missed nothing, watched Emel's hand curl into mine. It seemed she had a greater understanding than even I possessed.

I again did not want to let Emel go. It was not like Helena, whose fingers pressed against my arm with formality. It was the hand of someone who wanted me to hold it. I clasped her hand more tightly and led her up the stairs, back to the deck. Inhaling deeply, willing the scent of the Buraq from my nose.

People looked our way, and I let her hand go. "Steady?" I asked.

She nodded, peering around nervously. When Dima came up behind us, Emel relaxed and moved toward her.

"Enjoy the rest of the evening," I said, disappointed that I had no reason to stay, and went to the stern, where Helena was waiting.

A short stairway led me up to where two guards protected the area from guests. Helena was sitting atop cushions scattered around a low table. I remembered how, as children, my siblings and I would sit here, peering down at the guests spinning on the deck. Our parents forbade us to leave the area. Knew we would find trouble. So the guards would keep us confined here, watching us play our silly games until our mother and father would finally join us to watch the fire splash through the sky. Now I had no family to join me. I had Helena, who would be my family tomorrow. Maybe next year Edala could be here. If I found her.

I had to find her.

"Drinks," I called to the guard, who wordlessly beckoned a servant. "Do you need anything?" I asked Helena as I seated myself beside her, gaze skittering over the guests to ensure all was well.

"You should relax," Helena said as she took the wine from the servant. "I thought the ship was well-guarded?"

"It is. But people can always slip in . . . ." I had considered canceling this party, fearing that someone from the Darkafa would make their way aboard, aiming to sink both the ship and me. The guards had promised security, and so far the day and evening had gone smoothly.

"This will pass," Helena said confidently. "My father receives threats like this monthly."

Monthly. I still had no understanding of the unusual calendar she referenced.

"It changes when your family is killed."

"They would be proud of you, I am sure. Your guard is reinforced, stationed appropriately. Even my father was impressed. And he is impressed by very little."

Scanning the people on the deck, I looked for her father. Apparently his approval ended there, because he had had much to say about my ships earlier that day. I was grateful for the wedding to be done, so her family could finally return to their home. Emel and Dima had found places near the center of the ship, their heads bent together in talk.

"How many women do you keep?" Helena asked, staring at the pair. She must have followed my gaze.

It was a forward question about a usually tacit agreement between husband and wife. Many kings had ahiran.

"Just one," I said finally, and most of the time that was true. Dima was my favorite lover.

"Not the other?"

"The other?"

"The . . . what do you call them? The salt chaser?" The name sounded odd with her accent.

"No." I set my empty wine on the table and the servant hustled to re-fill it before I waved him off. I tried to think of anything other than Emel without clothes.

"Men don't keep women other than their wives, where I am from."

I shut my eyes. This was not a conversation I wanted to be having tonight.

A flash of light burned across my closed eyelids. And not even a breath later, an enormous boom echoed through the night. My eyes flew open. Red, so hot it was nearly white, curved up toward the night and was falling slowly back down. Helena gasped, arcing her neck to stare at the sky. She smiled widely, watching the fire.

Immediately, I searched for Emel. Her posture mirrored Helena's, though her hand seemed to be held in front of her mouth. Beside her, Dima laughed. I wished I could stand in Dima's place.

As the show went on, the wind around us picked up. The waves grew taller, the ship lurching dramatically. By the time the firepaint ended, most people were sitting on the benches or the deck floor itself. Few were below deck, the waves so tall they were spraying us.

Climbing down to the cockpit, I found Ekram barking at the seamen. "Luff with the gusts. We're not steady! Prepare to reef and clear the deck. If this keeps up, we're going to heave-to!"

"How did you miss this squall?" I asked him, shouting above the loud gust. There had been no indication a storm was brewing. I knew Ekram and his crew were the best in Almulihi, but still, I felt a spike of terror. The ship should be fine, we weren't too far from shore. But I kept imagining drunk guests falling into the sea with each drop, a swinging boom taking more unexpecting souls with it.

"There were no clouds," Ekram said curtly, then went back to barking orders.

Rain soon fell, and guests ran below deck. I helped to usher people down the stairs. I couldn't find Emel anywhere, and with a touch of sea spray to my wrists, I prayed she had found a safe place to wait out the storm. A massive wave crashed into the stern, the water slipping under my feet and bringing me to my knees. A guard ran to help but fell just as I had. We were back up as quickly as we'd fallen.

"This storm is picking up!" I shouted to him. "Get below deck."

"You too, king!"

I grunted, using benches and rope to hold myself steady as Ekram and his crew took us to shore. Lightning flashed, and above me, I saw sailors scrambling along the masts, ropes in hand, acting on Ekram's orders.

The ship lurched again, and one of the men slipped from the mast, held only by his rope. Unable to run to him in the turmoil, we only could watch the poor man swing until he was able to grab hold of a beam.

In my ears, my breath was as loud as the storm. Despite us nearing the shore, the wind grew more violent. It was as if the storm was intentionally pushing us away, forcing our ship to sink. We were not going to make it.

But then, it was as if we passed some divine test, Masira's anger could not best Ekram's sailing, and as we neared the dock, everything quieted. Before long, the crew was flinging ropes to the dock, cinching the boat tightly. As the knots were pulled, the storm receded completely, leaving only a light wind in its wake. Unsteadily, guests went ashore.

I found Helena still at the stern where I had left her.

"Did you not go below?" I asked, seeing her drenched clothes.

She shook her head and shrugged sleepily. "I always thought storms at sea to be calming. To be floating so easily over so much turbulence? It feels like magic."

A shout came from behind me.

I turned and saw a man in seamen's clothes sprinting toward the stern. In one blink he had a scimitar raised. Helena screamed. Guards shouted and gave chase, but it was too late. He was too close. I found the hilt of my sword at my hip and clasped it tightly. Just as I was to draw it from the sheath, he swung his scimitar at me. I ducked and spun away in time, and the man tripped forward, landing on hands and knees.

Helena was on her feet behind me. *No!* Nothing could happen to her on my ship, under my care. Stepping back, I pressed her further behind me.

"Keep your distance! Stay behind me!" I shouted at her. More might come.

"Saalim, leave this fight for the soldiers!" Helena cried. My guards filed up the stairs from below deck. They were behind the man, who was scrambling to his feet.

This was *my* fight, *my* city I defended. I would not stop just because Helena had asked.

Securely between her and the assailant, I took lunging steps toward him, bringing my sword overhead. The man's scimitar flashed in the light of the moon as he held it in front of him. My sword fell into his with a sharp clang. My soldiers stood back, waiting for my command. Tamam called for me to back away so that he could take my place. I would not. Our swords hit over and over. He tried to turn me so my soldiers were not at his back, but I would not leave Helena.

Finally, Tamam approached carefully from behind. The man leapt away from his reach, and he lost his footing. He slipped on the wet deck, falling to his knee.

And that was all it took. I was there in a rush, my sword through the man's neck.

<hr />

It was silent as the carriage took us back to the palace.

My heart still raced when I considered the storm and the subsequent attack, and my hand did not leave my sword the entire ride home, expecting someone to come running from the shadows at any moment. The evening had gone without difficulty for so long. How had it changed so suddenly and ended so poorly?

My bed did not feel so welcoming when I finally undressed and lay down for the night. A heightened alertness buzzed through me, and I was unable to sleep.

Emel had not ridden with us. Had she made it home? I had not seen her since the firepaint.

Closing my eyes, I thought of the day and what lay ahead tomorrow. A wedding seemed impossible after the attack, with all that was happening. But was that really the only reason I wanted to stall the event?

Eventually, sleep found me. I dreamed of Edala, black-robed villains, Anisa with a broken wing, and Emel in glinting red clothes with swirls of gold. We were in a tent. She was pushing me away.

"There can be nothing between us," she said. "There can be no future."

The urgency of the voice that called to me was so intense, I rose without the weight of sleep. I was pulling on my robe before I was even fully awake.

It was a night guard.

"What is it, Cadoc?" But even as I asked, I knew. I could smell it.

"A fire," he said in a rush. "The healer's."

Sons! That woman always leaving her damned fire burning. She never listened and now—Emel!

I pushed past the guard, whose steps were loud behind me as we flew down the stairs. "They are trying to contain it now," Cadoc panted behind me.

In the atrium the smoke was denser. I could taste it on my tongue.

"It is not safe," a soldier said as he saw me approach. "You should remain in the tower in case this is a diversion."

He was right. The tower was easily guarded from intruders with only one entrance. A servant pushed an empty wagon toward the front of the palace, while another rushed in with his wagon full of sand. But if the fire moved to the palace, the tower was the last place I wanted to be. Ignoring the guard, I followed the servant out to the gardens.

The snap of burning wood and the roar of the flames was so loud, I could hear it before I saw it. The heat rolled into me like waves. Altasa's garden, her home, was being devoured by the fire. With relief, I saw the flames had not yet reached the palace. People were everywhere: running furiously around each other, some scooping water from the fountains, others using the sand to douse flames or create barriers. Everyone coughed while they ran, some holding their tunics over their mouths. Others had scarves tied around their faces.

The ash was slippery under my feet as I strode toward the chaos. Nika stood off to the side, her eyes wide as she watched the flurry, her own scarf tight across her nose and mouth.

When she saw me approach, her eyes widened more before she averted them. A king with bared feet and a bed robe was not a proper sight.

"No one knows what happened," Nika said when I asked, her eyes fixed on the people who gathered the water. "When she comes to, she might." Nika pointed off to the side where a man knelt over a woman.

"Where is Altasa?" I asked. And where was Emel?

Nika shrugged. "No one has seen her. We fear she was lost . . ." Nika stopped. "But it is not safe to check." She looked at the burning building with terror. I shuddered at the thought of Altasa caught in the flames.

I left Nika and ran to the man and woman. Maybe they would know where—

"Emel!" I cried when I saw her. Her eyes were closed, her face dark with soot.

"Is she all right?" I asked, sinking to my knees in the grass.

He shrugged. "She breathes still." He carefully wiped her brow.

"Who are you?" I asked the man. He was familiar, but I could not quite place why.

"Firoz," he said.

"How did you get in here?"

"I walked in."

"Into the palace?" I was aghast.

"There was no one to stop me." He did not look at me. He brushed Emel's cheeks softly with his fingers.

My fury clamored nearly louder than the flames. The guard was supposed to be impenetrable.

Especially tonight!

Firoz continued. "I was just in time. Reached her before the flames did."

I bent over Emel, peering at her quiet face. I reached out my hand to replace Firoz's, but stopped myself. Not here, in front of so many.

I went to the fountain and cupped water into my palms like a foolish, desperate child. Most bled through my fingers by the time I reached Emel, but there was enough to splash onto her face. Firoz pressed it to her cheeks and brow, gently rocking her shoulders.

She stirred, her legs shifting, fingers twitching. I allowed myself a glance at the rest of her. She wore a sleeping dress that was dark from the smoke. By divine fortune, her hands and feet did not appear burned.

"How did the fire start?" I asked Firoz.

"I don't know. It seemed to have started in the front room. She was in her bedroom, I found her trying to crawl out the window, but I think she had already breathed in too much smoke. She was not making sense."

"You went through the fire to reach her?" Finally, I tore my gaze from Emel and looked to the man. The sleeves of his tunic were black and burned. Patches of his arm, the backs of his hands, were shining and red, even blistered. He had not been as lucky as Emel. I exhaled. "Thank you for saving her."

He finally looked at me. Did he know I was king? He did not seem to care if he did.

"Emel," I pleaded. Her head fell to the side.

"Why did you come here?" I asked him.

"I heard a man boasting of lighting the palace on fire tonight. He knew there would be no palace guards. He spoke of a storm and an attack . . . it was all confusing. But I knew Emel lived here and—"

"The Darkafa."

He nodded. In the way he watched her, like a sister or old friend, I understood why he had been familiar. "You are from Alfaar's settlement? You journeyed with us?"

"The Salt King? Yes."

"You are a good friend," I said, patting his shoulder. "Do you need someone to tend to your burns? We will take care of Emel."

Firoz watched me like a bird guarding its nest, but I was much larger than him, and I was the king. He bowed his head. "No, I will be fine. Tell her I was here."

Lifting Emel from the ground, I pulled her to me, wishing she was awake and could wrap her arms around my neck. Even still, her skin against my hands was soft, her body so warm. I called to Nika. Together, we took her to my sisters' tower. It was furthest from the fire, so the air was cleaner here, though the scent of smoke was still strong, clawing my throat. The smoke was my excuse when Nika asked why I walked so slowly. I could not tell her it was because I did not want to let go of the woman in my arms.

Once Emel was lying on a cushioned bench, Nika said, "I'll fetch tea, and some cloth for her brow." She spoke quietly, aware that Mariam and the child slept just up the stairs.

"Emel," I whispered over and over. We were alone in the room. Glancing at her hand, I imagined brushing her knuckles against my lips.

Nika was back too soon with a basin of water in one arm, towels in her other. A servant shuffled behind her with tea, and four guards trailed them. I sent them to guard the tower entrance.

"Here," Nika said with uncharacteristic softness, wiping Emel's brow. I resisted taking the towel from her hands to do it myself. Nika wiped her cheeks, her hands, her legs and feet.

I sat on the chair beside them, watching Nika care for Emel. Then I heard the relief in Nika's voice. "Emel."

There was mumbling, and I dropped to my knees beside her. A haze of confusion clouded Emel's eyes, but she was awake.

"Saalim," she breathed and reached over, placing her hand across my forearm. "You are all right." There was the familiarity again. In the way she said my name, in the way she touched me.

"Me?" I asked, confused,

Nika backed away, a portrait of curious surprise.

"There was the storm . . . and then I heard there was an attack. I did not see you . . . I was sent home. I worried . . ."

She blinked a few times, her brows colliding with the effort of remembering.

"I am all right. No one was hurt," I assured her, incredulous that she would be worried of my safety when she had just nearly died. "Now, tell me what happened."

"I had just fallen asleep, I think. There was a commotion at the door. I thought it to be Altasa. She still hadn't returned home." She rubbed at her eyes with her finger and thumb. Her fingers smudging ash on her face. "It wasn't her. It was Kas. And . . ." Now, she sat up, curling her legs under her. Nika proffered the tea and Emel took it, taking a long drink. "It was Kas." She said the name like she couldn't believe it, was still trying to make sense of it all.

I wanted her to hurry and finish, but I bit my tongue. Now that her well-being was assured, there was an urgency to determine who had done this and where they had gone. Before they destroyed more of the city.

She sucked in a breath, then said, "It was like magic. He was there, talking to me, and then—"

"What did he say?" I asked.

"A lot of nonsense." She began rubbing her curled fingers with her thumb. "But he was angry. Said it was all my fault and it didn't have to happen like this. He pointed to the ground. When I looked down, the door had caught fire.

"It moved so quickly. I did not even have time to ask Kas for help before the entire doorway was aflame. The kettle didn't hold enough water. I tried." She looked at me then. "I'm sorry."

"And . . . Kas?"

"He was gone. The house was consumed all at once—more quickly even than tents would catch back home. The smoke was everywhere. I could barely see. I thought I'd go through my window . . ."

"Here," Nika said, handing her the towel. Emel had been staring at her hands, wiping them against her night dress.

"How did I get here?" Emel asked. As if seeing me for the first time, her gaze dropped to my robe and then to my feet and hands. She did not look at me like she was embarrassed. Desire, ill-timed and stubborn, moved through me as swift as the fire. I shifted, pulling the robe so I was more covered.

"Some man found you," Nika said when I didn't respond.

Clearing my throat, I said, "Firoz."

"Firo?" Her feet were back on the ground, she began to push herself up. "Where did he go?"

"He left here."

She settled back.

"Who is Kas?" I asked her.

"My . . . friend," she stumbled on the word.

Like an itch, something in the deepest part of my mind began to tingle. "What does he look like?"

She described his height, his hair, his eyes. "And he has a scar, right here." She pointed to her temple. She said it so offhand, so casually, that she could have no idea what that scar, what that name meant to me. Like a rug had been pulled from under my feet, I fell into a pit of confusion, of disbelief and fear.

It couldn't be possible. "The one with the scar was named Kas?"

"Yes."

No. It was as impossible as magic.

"A scar that looked like this?" With the nail of my thumb I drew a line down my temple.

Emel stilled. I already knew her answer.

"Yes," she whispered. "Why?"

"Because my brother, Kassim, had one that appeared the same."

III.

STRUGGLE

QAWIL

. . . appear as a box. Keep it locked and pass it from death to birth until she comes again. None should open it, but if one does, be wary of its influence. If one has a tongue to speak or eyes to see, it will control all the person. The recipe to mute the tongue and blind the eyes of the unborn is written below.

We have been chosen to protect it for her. As we search, keep it secret from others. None would believe what it contains and may try to take it, failing to understand its deadly power. If there is no sign of the goddess in a settlement, leave the mark behind.

Remember that she will come for it, as she is the only one strong enough to wield it. This has been our task for generations. It has made us outcasts amongst all others, but care not for heretics and nonbelievers. We are chosen. They are swine.

—Torn correspondence found amongst cave ruins and human remains

19

EMEL

While I waited for someone to fetch me, I peered around the room. I hadn't been in the daughters' tower before. After Saalim left, Nika quickly retreated back downstairs with a harried demand that I not move. How long had it been since she left?

The chairs around me had a swirling pattern both embroidered on the fabric and carved into the wood. The table held a single metal basin with decorative petals that rendered the lip jagged. The water inside was rose-scented, and five smooth stones sat at its base.

Now there should be only four.

With Saalim's declaration still ringing in my ears, everything began to make sense. Why Kas had been strangely familiar, why he had known so much of the palace, of Saalim, why he had taken so much interest in Saalim and me, why he was colluding with the Darkafa: He was Saalim's brother. He was the king's second-born son, but he was the first of the king *and* queen.

I clutched at my chest. *The second-born Son will put the first-born to death.* It was not about Eiqab and Wahir at all. Kassim planned to kill Saalim, because he believed he was the rightful heir to the throne.

Could Kassim, then, be responsible for the attack on Madinat Almulihi that had resulted in the deaths of his family? I remember Saalim telling me how

Zahar had turned him into a jinni. Was she involved with Kas? Had he some-how recruited Zahar to his cause?

It seemed impossible, yet how many times had Kas boasted to me about the ease of rallying an army?

A garbled sound came from behind me. More than one set of footsteps clapped down the stairs from the room overhead.

"Don't rush," a soft voice said. "That is how we fall."

I turned just as Mariam and a small person—a child?—arrived in the sitting room.

"Oh!" Mariam exclaimed when she saw me. The child, who I quickly re-alized was blind, startled at Mariam's cry and pulled a metal box to her chest.

"It's nothing to fear," Mariam said to the child, her voice calm. "A friend is here to see us. Emel is her name."

The child made a strangled sound.

"Yes, Emel," Mariam nodded as she led the girl to a chair.

I pressed my back into my own seat, watching this child as I would a predator.

"This is Bilara." When Mariam said her name, the little girl's face morphed into the most beautiful joy. Her eyes, despite being as white as the healer's back home, glowed with happiness.

Her mouth opened in a wide smile.

And then I saw that her tongue was not whole.

I had to look away.

Mariam must have seen the change in my face. "I don't know how I guessed it; it was like a bird whispered it to me. But her response confirms it." So the girl could not speak.

"Hello," I squeaked. She seemed uninterested in me, staring only in the direction of Mariam.

"Are you well?" Mariam glanced at my blackened night dress. "I smelled the fire." She put her hand on Bilara's back.

"I am uninjured," I confirmed. I still did not understand how I was so lucky. Nodding to Bilara, I asked, "Is this . . . family of yours?" Her fustan was too big on her, and its dark color made her pale skin even paler. The way she held her head, the way she curled her shoulders in . . . the box . . . there was something eerie about her that felt too familiar.

Mariam shook her head. "Someone the Darkafa kept. They left her unwatched. Two women found her at the docks. At first I thought they had taken her from her mother, but she has been so happy here. I cannot think a child well-tended would be this glad away from her family."

The girl dug in her pocket and pulled out a sack. From it she retrieved sugar-coated dates similar to those I had with Kas what felt so long ago. Though those memories were happier, too, they were drenched with ignorance and lies.

"You had those with you all night?" Mariam flapped her hands and tried to take the sack away. "I swear this sack is always full, and I can't figure out where she is getting them." The girl popped a date into her mouth with a gleeful smile that even I could not resist returning with a smile of my own as she pulled both sack and box tighter to her chest.

"What is that?" I asked, gesturing at the box.

Mariam shrugged. "We found it chained to her, and she carries it with her always. I don't know what is inside."

Standing, I said, "Can I see your box? I will give it right back."

Bilara swiveled her head toward me and hesitated, at first holding the silver box close to her. Then she slowly held it out.

Mariam's mouth fell open in disbelief.

The box was warm in my hands, and I turned it carefully, looking at the tarnished swells and depressions. There was some kind of pattern to it. An ocean, I realized, set in front of a city. Madinat Almulihi?

A broken chain was attached to one end. The rings, imperfect circles.

I tried to open the box, but it did not shift. The metal rang with my effort. Bilara began wailing at the sound. She pocketed her sweets and reached in my direction.

"Give it back to her," Mariam said, concern clouding her eyes. She shushed the child and cooed calming words. As soon as the box was back in Bilara's hands, she soothed.

"It happens every time," Mariam said as the child buried into her chest. "I'm sure we could find a way to get it open, but . . ." She petted the girl's head, short wisps of hair as it grew back in. "It is hers. What good would it do us to upset her so?" I could tell this was not the first time she was discussing this. If the Darkafa kept a child who kept a silver box, I would also want to know what was inside.

Walking around the circular room, I could make sense of Edala and Nadia living here—the tapestries on the wall, the books on the shelves, the small trinkets. I glanced up the stairs, but that room belonged to Mariam and Bilara now. A pang of grief struck with the realization there were lives that had once walked this floor as I did. Lives that were snuffed out by . . . I prayed not by a jealous brother.

On one shelf was a small portrait. I had never seen anything like it. Two faces were framed in wood. The man's face was familiar.

"Nadia or Edala?" I asked Mariam, pointing at the woman's portrait.

"Edala. They're unusual, aren't they?"

There were likenesses of the royal family all over the city, but they were often similar to the tapestry presented at the parade. I had seen nothing so realistic before in my life.

"Oh!" Mariam said. "We were going down for morning meal, and I had completely forgotten. Bilara, no more dates. Let's go to the kitchen." Together, they left the tower.

Morning meal? Was it morning already? The sky through the windows dotting the room was indeed a deep blue. My eyelids were heavy, and hunger gnawed at my insides, but I had promised Nika I would stay.

As I lay on the bench, my mind whirled with all that had happened the day before: Kas with the Darkafa, the parade, the firepaint, the storm, Kas at my door, the fire.

Jerking upright, I remembered my things hidden by my bedside at Altasa's.

"No!" I cried. "They could not be burned. They could not be missing. It was all I had." "No, no, no." I ran down the stairs. When I didn't stop at the guard's request, he followed me out to the gardens, where there were far fewer people now. The fire, it seemed, had died. I swerved around the people sweeping and shoveling.

A man tried to stop me when I ran through the burned remains of Altasa's gardens.

"It is hot!" he called.

The man was right, the ground still smoldered. But I did not care of my feet; I wanted my things. Smoke was still heavy around Altasa's home when I climbed into the ruins. I prayed to Eiqab, to Wahir, that my memories of Saalim, my life, were whole.

"Please," I begged aloud.

When I turned into my room, black smudges marked the walls. I coughed from the smoke as I took in the surroundings. My bed was whole. My side table, too. Dropping to my knees before it, I slid open the drawer.

It was there.

It was all there.

I nearly cried in relief, pulling everything out one by one, uncaring of the smoke. I had to see it all, account for everything. Saalim's gold-petaled cuffs—one of the first things I had noticed on him—which had once wrapped his wrists. Decorative bracelets, I had thought they were. I had been wrong. They were manacles.

My focus blurred. I now saw Kas, sitting across the table from me at the restaurant. His fingers laced through one another, the chains on his wrists hanging down on the tabletop.

I never saw him without those chains.

Twin bracelets, they seemed.

"What would you wish for?" he had asked me, eyes flashing silver.

Suddenly it was all there: the cowrie on the nose of the snake, the empty table in the crowded drink house, the impossible light in the cave, the fire that sparked in Altasa's home.

They weren't bracelets on his wrists. They were manacles.

The brothers shared a common fate.

Kas—Kassim—was a jinni.

Nika found me in the gardens.

"The king and his men request your presence."

"Why me?" I could not think of a place I belonged less than at the royal table with men speaking of war plans.

Her face was pinched in annoyance as she dragged me to the dining room, where Saalim and the others were already seated.

"Emel," Saalim said. The chair scraped across the floor when he stood. He gestured to an empty seat, and I sat quickly. "She saw him, confirmed that it is my brother. That he started the fire."

"Ah," I said. "About that, Saalim—"

"How could she know it was Kassim?" Azim asked, with a mixture of relief and pain.

Saalim explained. "The name, the scar." He hesitated. "The motive. We know he is colluding with the Darkafa. We need to find out how they know Kassim, and too," he took a deep breath, "we need to find out if he is connected to the attack on the city."

I nodded.

"He would never!" Azim stood, outraged. "He is your brother! King Malek's son!"

Saalim was taller than Azim, and in the way the fury rolled off of him, he seemed stronger, too. "He was not here when Almulihi was attacked. Where was he? I refuse to believe the timing was pure coincidence. We know he disagreed with my father's decision to make me his successor."

There was silence now. Only the occasional swallow of wine or clunk of a shoe against the floor as legs shifted.

"I will go with you," Saalim said at last, looking at Tamam.

"You cannot leave the throne empty again," Azim said.

"And what of the wedding today?" Nassar said, exhausted.

The wedding.

I had forgotten that was today. Where was Helena?

Saalim looked at Azim. "I *can* leave the throne. I will join the search for Kassim and Edala until they are found. I am their brother; it must be me who confronts them about their disappearance while our city was attacked and our family killed."

Edala?

Then to Nassar he said, "This is no time for a wedding. I have spoken already with Helena."

Nassar pressed his chin to his knuckles. "Saalim . . . the entire family is here. The arrangements, the guests that have traveled . . ." I heard the worry building as he considered how he was going to restore the celebration that had been so long in the making.

There was only small guilt for the relief I felt at hearing that the wedding was canceled.

Saalim looked at Nassar like he was a fool. "Our home was attacked by *my brother*. And somewhere out there, my sister is alive. Right now we face more pressing matters. Her family has a ship prepared. They depart today, and will wait until things have settled to return. You cannot be naïve to the possibility that they, too, do not wish to involve themselves in such affairs."

"I will see that their departure is smooth," Nassar said with saccharine obedience.

There was no amount of tacit begging I could do to make Saalim understand I wanted to speak with him. In fact, none of the guards seemed to pay me any attention. The only one who noticed the head-tilting and widening of eyes that I kept using to command Saalim's attention was Nika, and she appeared as curious as ever.

"We will leave tonight," Tamam said. "He cannot be allowed to travel far."

Kassim had been seen leaving the city with a woman no one knew.

"We will continue to search for the Darkafa here," Azim said, leaning his elbows on the table.

They were all sitting around that table, the great room draped elegantly as though it were a stage for this dramatic play. There was food in front of them all—a prop none touched.

"Emel," Saalim said. Our eyes met, then his gaze dropped to the sack in my hands. A question passed across his face like a shadow, but it was gone as quickly. "I want you to come with us."

There was murmuring. My mouth dropped open, and I clutched the sack more tightly.

Why?

"Is it wise?" Kofi asked, gaze flitting to me before looking back to Saalim.

"She has spent the most time with Kassim, was attacked by him. And," he continued, holding out his hand as though it were obvious, "she knows the desert best of all of us."

Nassar frowned, and for once, I agreed with him. I wanted to shake my head. I knew nothing of the desert, nor of Kassim.

But I was sure that I knew the most about jinn.

20

EMEL

By the time evening fell, I still had not had an opportunity to tell Saalim what I suspected about Kassim. I wanted to find him alone, fearing others would think me mad, but it proved impossible. Too, I had not yet seen Altasa. I wanted to tell her my decision, tell her goodbye. People said she had died in the fire, but I know she had not been home, and her room was untouched by flames.

It would be Saalim, Tamam, Nassar, and Amir I traveled with. I was pleased Amir would join us. Of Saalim's men, I liked him best.

"I hate camels," Saalim said to me as he held the reins of the camel carrying our water.

"They are not all so bad," Amir said, leading his out of the pen at the city's edge.

We arrived here under the disguise of traders, so that none would realize that their king had left. Most, anyway, were catching up on the sleep they hadn't gotten the night before. The Falsa Mawk seemed so long ago.

"Where will we go?" I asked. Tamam walked on my other side. He eyed me carefully. Earlier, he and Saalim had exchanged stern words with each other while Amir happily showed me his map. Distracting me, I assumed, from the conversation.

"To the closest settlement," Saalim said, pointing in a vague direction. "The Hayali are just a few nights away."

"You expect to find Kassim there?"

"No. I hope to find someone who has seen them, if they are even willing to share this information." His voice was strained. What was it about the Hayali that he did not like? "We will follow the common trade route. It's likely the route he took."

"Better than the one from your home," Amir explained to me. "With this route, there's only a day or two of travel between oases and settlements. I think you'll find the journeying easier."

"I hope," I murmured.

Saalim glanced to me. "I hope so, too."

The journey that night was anything but easy.

I hadn't slept the night before, barely slept during the day, and now we had traveled nearly the entire night without sleep. My eyelids were heavy as iron, my feet the same.

When dawn came, I nearly collapsed beneath the olive tree where we were to rest for the day. It had been a long time now since I had traveled across the sands, and I had already forgotten the exhaustion that comes from staying awake until sunrise. Saalim and Nassar themselves were already lying back onto the sand. Tamam and Amir topped off the water stores at the shallow pool a ways off.

"Saalim," I whispered, seeing that his eyes were closed. He needed to know about Kas.

"Hmmm?" Saalim hummed, not moving.

He was nearly asleep. I watched his hands, linked across his chest, rise and fall with each breath. I wanted to reach out and lay my hand atop them. Glancing toward Nassar, I saw his eyelids had cracked just enough to watch me.

I curled into my mat. I would tell Saalim about his brother later.

"Get some rest."

Days later, and still with no opportunities to separate Saalim from his overly watchful guards and Nassar, we descended into a shallow canyon just before sunrise. Within the valley, little orange flames dotted along the cliff faces around us.

"The Hayali can be hostile," Amir said to me as he took the lead of our small caravan. We fell into line behind him, our camels carrying us slowly.

"Someone approaches," Nassar said, resting his free hand on the hilt of his sword. Saalim mirrored his movement. Tamam was behind me, but his hand was never away from his sword. I suspected this news instilled in him no new sense of vigilance.

Before long, I could hear the clank of tack and chuff of breath as a man arrived on horseback.

"Why have you come?" he asked.

Amir said, "We are of Almulihi, on the king's orders."

"Answer the question, sea citizen."

Saalim stiffened as Tamam settled his camel between him and the stranger. Saalim glanced back to me.

Still here! None have taken me yet. I was glad he could not hear my pounding heart. The men had said little about these people other than that their preference was to kill first, talk later. They could afford it, Saalim had explained. They lived amid a salt mine.

"We search for two people," Amir said, voice level. He was undisturbed by the violence in the man's voice. Amir described Kassim. He was with a woman who was not old—in the middle of life—and suspected to be of the desert.

"Not sickly, like you," the Hayali man laughed.

Amir did not pause. He proceeded to describe Edala.

The Hayali man grunted and led us deeper into the valley, each step pulling tautness through the men like they were attached to string.

As the sun crested, I finally understood what I was seeing around me.

When Saalim had said they lived amid a salt mine, I had not realized it meant that they lived *within* one. I did not know a mine could be so deep. These were not cliffs that towered around us.

They were walls of salt. Carved into them were what looked like homes.

Stairs led up the sides of the mine, breaking off at different levels to lead into dwellings or onto platforms with burning cookfires.

We passed piles of salt bricks—men beside them eyed us carefully as they held curved metal picks in their palms.

More and more Hayali came out to see us, some watching from their ledges while others moved down to the mine floor to view us up close. As we arrived at the center of their village, so many crowded around us that the man leading the way was soon lost amongst them.

These people felt feral in the way they gazed at us with bright eyes and hungry sneers, gripping their sharp metal tools tightly. They wore little clothing and had dark ink painted in complicated stripes down their arms, backs, and legs.

Most stared at me.

There was a shifting in the crowd as a woman came toward us. Her sleeveless robe was belted at her waist with ivory. The bone-white crown on her head was of the same. Her robe was so thin, it covered little.

"Descend," she said, fluttering her hand. The ink on her arms was intricate and fastidiously painted. This woman was their leader.

Amir and Tamam did, the latter helping his king down, the former assisting me.

"You did not tell me the king was among them," she snapped at someone behind her.

So she knew him by face.

"I was sorry to hear the news of my sister," she said, dipping her head.

Sister? I glanced to the men. They appeared unsurprised.

Saalim said, "Her death was swift and honorable."

"How does the throne treat you in her absence?" she approached Saalim and offered her hand. He pressed his lips to her knuckles.

"Well, I am here."

She laughed. "Kena said to give you a chance."

Kena. This woman was the queen's sister? The queen of Almulihi had been of the Hayali?

The woman dropped her hand to her side. "Now, Sul told me of your questions. What do you offer?"

Amir pulled two large bottles from the pack slung across the camel's back. "From our sea," he said.

Her smile was broad and greedy as she took them from Amir. She curled the bottles into her chest and with a fan of her fingers, invited us to follow.

We walked into the dark mouth of the mine—much like the cave Kassim had taken me to—and arrived in a wide audience room. Striations of salt lined the walls, lit by the several torches. The woman seated herself on a narrow chair and poured the bottled sea into a goblet. She took a small sip and sighed.

"Please sit," she said. "I can't imagine you've changed your opinions of this?" she asked Saalim, holding her goblet aloft.

"I have not."

She gestured to all of us, and we declined. "Good. More for me. Did Kena enjoy it to the end?"

Saalim shook his head. "She lost her taste for it."

"A shame. Just a little keeps the body strong." She swirled her goblet as her gaze flashed to mine. "This is unexpected," she whispered, smiling again. "Sul did not tell me about you, either." In the firelight, I could see that she was older than I first realized. Though her body appeared young, there were lines through her brow, around her mouth. Her hair, too, had gray twisting through it. "Did you bring her here for your protection, then?"

Protection?

Saalim set his heel on his opposite knee and leaned back into his chair. "She knows much of the desert, so she travels with us, Liika." The use of her name snapped her attention back to him, away from me.

This woman—Liika—was clearly a well-respected ruler. But Saalim met her and rose above.

"Will you stay here for the day?" Liika asked.

"It is best we return to our site." Saalim gestured at the room around us. "But I am grateful for your generosity."

"Your soft skin," she chided.

It is true that already I felt my skin to be drying from the salt walls.

"If that is what you want to call it." Saalim shifted again, seeming to relax further despite the conflict.

Liika and Saalim countered each other's remarks like they had a world of history behind them, and if Queen Kena was Liika's sister, then clearly they had. It was nearly hostile, almost toppling into conflict. Although Amir and Nassar appeared at ease, Tamam and I sat rigidly.

Liika's eyes met mine again. There was more talk of nothing, and Saalim grew frustrated with the drivel. Finally, Liika said, "Your brother, my people have not seen. Your sister, I could not say. I would know her face if I saw it myself, so much does she look like Kena."

Saalim exhaled. The hope that held his shoulders back was gone. "She does."

Liika went on. "There is magic that lingers out there, though. Sometimes disguised as a nomad or a hatif. Sometimes as a woman. It has been impossible to lure it here, to pry the magic away and learn of it." She looked at me. "But then you bring me this, and I feel satisfied."

I stiffened.

Liika's gaze drifted up and down me. "What else does she do? I can't place it."

"She is my companion and brings her knowledge of the desert," Saalim said, but I saw the silent question when he looked at me.

"My people will delight in her presence. The goddess follows her."

"If you have no other information for us," Saalim said sharply, rising from the chair, "then we will take leave."

Liika waved her hand. "Kena would be displeased. Stay for the day."

⁘

Being outside the cave was a relief—I felt like my body could breathe, that my mouth was not so dry. To endure that, the salt-born must be a different people entirely.

We were taken to an area beneath the shade of the cliff that Liika demand-ed be kept quiet for us. So instead of people crowding near to peer at our pecu-liarities, they stood a stone's throw away.

When the man who brought us water—nothing had ever tasted so fresh—left, and it was just us, I could wait no longer. I turned to Saalim.

"There is something I must tell you," I said.

They all turned to me. Saying it aloud would sound absurd, but Liika had mentioned magic in the desert. They all needed to know what it was.

"Kassim is, well, I think . . ."

Saalim waited.

"A jinni."

He tilted his head in the same way he used to when I asked him something about the Dalmur or jinni magic or the salt trade. The question of *why do you know this*, and *why do you want to know this?*

Nassar tipped his head back. "Ah."

Saalim ignored him. "If you had told me on our journey from your settle-ment, I would have denied its possibility and claimed you a fool." He pulled the fabric of his tunic into his fist, then let it ago. "But I received a letter."

Tamam and Amir had their eyes trained on the people who watched from afar, but Nassar watched Saalim.

Saalim went on, "From my sister, Edala. She told me that if I was reading the letter—well, wait." He reached into the sack that he carried and pulled out a letter. He handed it to me, then hesitated. "You can read?"

Nodding, I took the note and opened it. The writing was curving and fluid, so I had a harder time with it than Altasa's recipe book or the Litab. For a mo-ment, my mind took me back to Altasa's home, to sitting at her table and going through the words on the pages. She would lean over when she heard a pause in my whispered words and ask which I struggled with. My chest tightened when I thought of her home, of how she would feel when she finally returned and saw that her gardens, her whole life, was gone.

Slowly, I read the letter. When I finished, my hand trembled.

Edala knew everything.

"I wonder," Saalim whispered so only I could hear, "if you perhaps understand more of what is in that letter than I do."

If you have this letter in your hands, then she has done it. How did Edala know? I searched around us, expecting his sister to be a face in the crowd.

Saalim said, "So when you tell me that Kassim might be a jinni, I cannot understand how nor why, but I believe it."

"I think he is the jinni that Zahar keeps."

Saalim nodded. "The woman he left Almulihi with."

Hiding behind her jinni, just as my father was able to do. Still, it did not all make sense. "I can explain why Kassim would want the throne, but what does Zahar have to do with it? What is it she would gain?"

Nassar broke in. "Perhaps Kassim promised her power. It's why anyone would seek to take the throne, or aid someone in doing so."

Saalim said, "She and I always were at odds. Edala loved her for her supposed magic, but I never believed it possible." He let out a breath that sounded like an attempt at a laugh. "I do not understand how this came to be, though. Has he willingly become a jinni?"

Nassar nodded. "If it gave him unlimited power, it seems it would be worthwhile."

I shook my head. "Being a jinni does not offer unlimited power." I explained how they were limited by their master, tethered to that person. Free will with many, many limitations. "But I would be surprised if he was changed by force." I conveyed what I understood of jinni-forging.

"How do you know all this?" Saalim asked. Behind him, Nassar's eyes were narrowed. Even Amir had turned to listen. I could not tell them it was from stories Saalim had once told me.

I opened my mouth, then closed it.

Saalim looked at the crowd of people. Quietly, for only me to hear, he said, "There are so many questions I have, and you will not answer them."

"It is an impossible truth."

"Like Edala, Kassim." Amidst the silence, he reached into his pocket. He removed two smooth stones and rolled them in his hand. The same two were sitting in the basin in his sisters' tower. Like Tavi's shrine to Wahir that celebrated my mother and sister, it had been a memorial for his lost family.

Except he had removed two of the stones. The two that lived.

"Sometimes," he said staring at the stones, "I wonder if the *she* that Edala refers to is you."

21

SAALIM

Though I had no interest in keeping any part of our party—least of all Emel—amongst the Hayali for a moment longer, we were now seated around a fire waiting for some kind of lizard to finish cooking. Were these people not so prone to violence, I would have left the moment my aunt told us she knew nothing. Though she promised we were safe, her guard had also told Tamam how leathers made from humans were the strongest as they patted that which they wore across their hips and shoulders

They served the meal to Emel first, a young man showing her how to avoid the claws on the leg he handed her. He bent so close to her, I nearly launched forward to push him away, but a face flashed in my direction—Amir, shaking his head in warning.

A child brought Emel a drink that she peered at skeptically before thanking her. Then, the child pressed her hand above Emel's chest, eyes wide and curious.

"Dyah!" A woman called from the fire, where she turned blackened lizards with a long stick. "Don't!"

"But Mama, the goddess!"

There was a strangeness in how these people conducted themselves toward Emel. In many ways, they behaved with more respect, more reverence, with her than they ever had with me or my parents. Catering to her like she was royal herself.

The goddess. I thought of the Darkafa and their obsession. That question still had not been answered. *When the king crosses the desert, the goddess will return. She will unleash the second-born son to put the first-born to death.* Unleash Kassim, because he *was* a jinni, and he had been sent to kill me. But the goddess? Emel was not who they spoke of, was she? No, that made no sense. So where was this "goddess," and where was she returning from?

"Yes, child," the woman said. "And the goddess might strike you down if you linger."

Dyah ran away giggling. Emel watched her with kind eyes.

Nassar leaned toward the woman. "What does the girl refer to?"

"Nassar," I warned.

The woman was unbothered. She pointed to Emel and said, "She is protected by Masira."

Emel asked, "Protected?"

"From magic," the woman clarified.

No one said anything for a few moments, then the young girl stepped forward, inching closer again to Emel. "And the things you care about, too."

"I care very much about you." Emel smiled pulling Dyah to her side.

The woman's smile was even wider than Dyah's.

After the meal, Liika walked us to the edge of her valley as we left the Hayali. The high walls of the salt mine rose up around her.

"I hope you find what you are looking for," Liika said to me. "And that you are wrong about Kena's son." Because I was not Kena's son. Not by blood, at least. Liika called to a man behind her. He ushered forward a small package wrapped in linen. She took it carefully and held it out to me. With knowing eyes, she said, "For Kena. Do not get it wet."

I unwrapped the oddly-shaped package, and when I saw what lay inside, my throat tightened. Swallowing my grief, I thanked her.

Liika offered me her hand once more. Her skin was coarse, almost desiccated. The salt mine did that to the Hayali.

I often wondered if that lack of moisture made them erratic and crazed, too.

"Find peace," she said.

"In the shadow of Eiqab's sun," Emel whispered.

The corner of Liika's mouth lifted. "If there is magic out there as we suspect," she said, then tipped her head toward Emel, "it will find her."

~~~~~~~~~~~~~~~

"That went better than expected," Nassar said once we were well away from the shadows of the mine. "I think you should be pleased."

That these people could offer such minimal comforts to their guests and be so highly praised grated at me. "They are more trouble than they are worth."

Amir laughed. "They are family."

"That is the problem," I said.

Nassar chuffed and said, "Did you see that mine? You know—and they know—they are worth everything."

We left later than I had planned, and our trek to the nearest oasis was long and hot in the sun. Tamam was ill at ease despite the fact that we were far too close to Almulihi for there to be violent nomads. He did not relent, his sword always at the ready.

"Do you think it could be true," he asked me. "That Kassim is out there? That Edala is?"

"I have to believe it possible," I said.

"They are," Emel said, her eyes clinging to the dunes as if they were water for a dry throat. Though his guthra covered most of his face, I could have sworn Tamam smiled.

When the home of the Hayali had become nothing more than a curve of land against the sky, I dropped back to Emel.

"Do you know what the Hayali meant when they spoke of the goddess protecting you?"

She shrugged. "I'm not sure."

There it was again. The way she said it, I knew she was not being honest with me. I felt the answer humming through me, but I couldn't decipher it. "Why is it that magic and talk of it seems to follow you?"

"I am not the one who has a healer with a jinni at my heels."

I smiled despite her forwardness, her blatant disregard for my station relative to hers. I rubbed at my wrists, unease flowing out through restless hands. There was no time now for subtleties and innuendoes. "Why do you speak to me like that? No one else in your place would dare." Would she tell me the truth? Or would she keep the secrets bottled? The ones that moved through her like smoke.

"My father was a king. I am not so easily intimidated."

My father was a king, and still I was intimidated by him. "There is something more." My men were far enough ahead I knew my words would be lost to them.

"There is so much more," she whispered. She sounded sad.

"Tell me," I begged. When Emel did not respond, I said, "I will speak honestly and hope that perhaps you can do the same."

My father's advice rang loudly in my ears: Love has no place in the life of royalty. But I did not love Emel, I reminded myself. I was simply drawn to her. A current pulling me closer, closer, closer without doing anything at all.

I said, "I fear this will sound improper, or even a bit mad, but there is something . . ." I looked at my hands now tightly gripping the reins. "Something that draws me toward you." Well, I had said it. There was no taking back the words now. Beside me, she stiffened. "Since the day I saw you, Emel. What is it? You have looked at me like you know me. I feel with you something that settles me, like I've known you for a long time. Like an old friend . . ." *Like a lover*, I did not say. I hoped she did not hear the tremor in my voice.

"Oh, Saalim," she said. I could barely hear it through the hiss of wind, but I heard it. I heard the way she said it.

Like she understood completely.

My pulse raced. *Tell me!* I wanted to shout.

"You would not believe me." She sounded so tired. "Or, maybe you would."

"Please."

"I did know you. I knew you . . . so well." She looked at me, her eyes wet. We rocked with the camels beneath us, the beasts dutifully following our small caravan.

"How?"

She said nothing.

"You won't tell me?"

Emel shook her head. "There is nothing that will make sense. If I could, I would have told you the moment I saw you in my home." She wiped her eyes.

Just knowing there was something between us, something that happened even if I couldn't remember it, filled that yawning void. It drew me closer to her with comfort, rather than uncertainty.

Yes, *this* made sense. Whatever *this* was.

At the oasis, we yoked the camels and unrolled our mats. Emel set herself up between me and a nearby bush. Though I missed the raised bed of my home, sleeping within reach of her, so close I could hear the sighs of her sleep, was a solace I did not expect. That, I would give my bed for.

"The south!" Tamam said suddenly, his words spilling out around us.

I saw them immediately. Four—no, five—people moved over a dune. Had they seen us?

At once, we re-packed our things, hurling them behind the bushes near the camels.

"Keep this one near," I told Emel, handing her my pack. "If you must flee, it has the most food and my bawsal. Almulihi is northeast of here."

She took it in her hands, and flung her own pack over her shoulder. She carried that with her everywhere, but never did she open it.

Tamam, Amir, and Nassar gathered together as we waited for the group to approach.

When they were closer, I could see they were nomads—dressed smartly against the sun. That they traveled by day told me they were desert-born. Amir stepped forward when they neared us, and I moved to stand in line with my men. Emel, I hoped, would stay behind.

"We've no ill will," one of the men said, their hands open showing no blade in their palms. "Eiqab take my water." His guthra—orange as the sand—revealed only his eyes.

"We have already made camp," Amir told them. He held one hand over his brow, the other near the hilt of his sword.

"We did not arrive soon enough, it seems," a different man said, descending from his camel. They moved slowly. "We will just refill our stores."

"There is a fifth," a man in the brown said. "A . . . woman?"

"You've hidden her from us," another said, his words rough with anger. "What else are you hiding from us?"

My hand moved to my sword. Tamam had already begun to pull his free. Amir cracked his fingers at us in warning, and Nassar stepped forward. "A woman is an easy hostage. It would be foolish not to hide her from those who travel."

They nodded. It was true. It was why I wanted these men gone. Suddenly the Hayali did not seem such dangerous companions.

"Have you far to travel?" I asked. "We do not. Should you need to camp, we can leave."

Amir glanced back with ill-concealed irritation. I was his king, but he and Nassar were my diplomats in the desert. Were I not desperate to find Edala—to find Kassim and wrap my hands around his neck—I would turn home now. This place belonged to Eiqab. Let him have it.

"There is no reason we cannot all share, eh?" a tall man said, his shoulders broader than Tamam's. He had twin scimitars at his hips. He gestured to the shade. "We can all sit, talk of our travels."

He played his hand well. To refuse would put us in the position of conflict. To agree, we would risk exposure and weakness. Suddenly, Emel was beside me. I withheld my groan.

"A desert dweller?" the man in brown said. "Did you steal her?" The accusation like a stone dropped on my foot. Now, I was angry.

I snapped. "She is nothing to be stolen. She comes on her own." Beside me, Emel drew back her shoulders like an arrow in a bow. I pressed my hand to her back. Now was not the time to show defiance.

It was too late.

They sprang forward, their scimitars unsheathed a moment faster than our swords. I freed my blade and met the silver arcing toward me. The man in brown faced me, pressing his advance. Defending his swings was easy compared to Azim. He was a sloppy, poorly trained swordsman.

"Stand down!" I called to the nomads. "We will kill!" The man was faltering against my blows, and I soon was able to push toward him. Quickly, he retreated to his camel, barking to his comrades to do the same.

"It is not worth it!" he yelled, and they backed away.

It was a battle easily won. The victory buzzed through me as I watched them make to leave, taking the reins of their camels and pulling them to follow.

Then, I realized, there were only four men.

Where was the fifth?

Spinning around, I saw him.

"Emel!" I sprinted toward the man dragging her away. His hand was tight around her mouth, muffling her cries with her veil. Her arms were cinched behind her. Now I understood why they had so easily surrendered. They had something more valuable than our supplies.

"Give us your packs, and she goes free!" he shouted.

Tamam circled me, sword at the ready. He murmured to Amir and Nassar and moved forward slowly. Too slowly for my comfort. I lunged forward, my blade aloft.

Emel shifted, freeing her arms. She began clawing at the arm wrapped around her neck and face when suddenly, she stopped. A glint drew my gaze down.

The point of the man's scimitar arced toward her abdomen.

"Stop," the man said. "Or I will push."

I froze, staring at the scimitar. He had not harmed her yet.

Terror pinned Emel to the man. Her eyes locked on mine, and I could see the pleading, the fear. I was unable to protect my people despite the soldiers at our sides. Shame fueled my fury. I should be better.

"You can have the packs when you let her go," I said, edging closer.

The man shook his head, pressing the blade harder. In my periphery, Tamam waited. The other nomads circled behind their companion with their camels.

"Packs first," the man said. "Then I let her go."

Damn this desert and its lawless men! I opened my mouth to respond when Emel spoke.

"He will do as he says," she said around his loosened hand. "Eiqab heard his words."

The man's eyes shifted when she spoke, his guthra billowing with his heaving breaths.

Sheathing my sword, I nodded. Amir pushed through the small bushes and grabbed the packs, heavy from our water stores and large food supply. Valuable loot for these men. Dropping the packs at the man's feet, Amir stepped away.

The ease with which they commanded us was too great a reminder of the soldiers taking my family from the palace, taking the peace from Almulihi.

I could not be weak again.

"No," I said once the man pushed Emel toward us. She was safe. I knew I should be satisfied. But suddenly I was standing in the palace, watching soldiers die. Listening to my mother shout at me to run. Feeling pathetic in my inability to fight.

Again.

With a hiss, my blade was unsheathed, and this time, it would taste blood.

Emel screamed, "Saalim, no!"

The desperate panic in her plea made me hesitate only a moment. But it was a moment I could not afford.

The nomad spun away from me, and called, "Masira guide my sword!"

Blinding pain seared across my thigh. And a line of deep red followed.

A shadow passed before me, and the man slumped in the sand, his blade, marked with my blood, falling with him. Tamam pulled his sword from the man's neck as I dropped to the ground.

"Saalim! Why did you do that?" Emel was at my side. "They would have left!" She sounded so angry. "Now look at you."

Blood welled between my fingers as I pressed the wound on my thigh. Pulsing, burning pain ripped through me again and again. I fell to the ground.

There were men's voices, angry and barking.

Then, Emel whispered, "We are safe. Move your hands." She pressed against my skin, murmuring things I could not hear. Closing my eyes on the spinning world, I clenched my fists against the pain and waited.

"Leave them here," Emel said.

Someone—Tamam?—responded.

"A loose camel raises suspicion. Five even more so," she said.

"She is right," Nassar said as he passed by. "Others will think our company twice as large. They won't come so quickly."

I sat up, unable to comprehend the conversations that happened around me.

Emel was still at my side. We were under the shade of a small tree now. The sharpness of the pain had dulled to a tremendous ache, an awful throb.

"What should I ask for?" Amir said, rifling through a pack.

Emel said, "Aliyba, if they have it. Or cypress or las. And more dressing, if possible." She was leaning over me, her scarf around her neck so I could see her mouth. "How do you feel?"

"Like a fool," I said, staring at her lips.

"As you should."

The corners of my mouth turned up. Emel smiled, too, but it held no strength and was gone just as fast.

"It is a very deep wound," she said.

Dark linen, damp with blood, was wound tightly around my thigh. I asked, "Are you hurt?"

She shook her head. "I am unharmed."

Remembering how she had no burns after the fire, I said, "Masira does protect you, doesn't she?"

Emel met my gaze. Then: "Amir and Nassar have gone back to the Hayali to see what they have that might help you."

"They will not give freely."

A. S. Thornton

Emel shrugged.

"Tamam?" I asked.

"Dealing with the bodies."

"Bodies." Of the nomads.

"They killed the others."

Tamam moved behind me. I could hear the whisper of bodies being dragged through sand. "What is he doing?"

"Sky burial."

"They did not deserve—"

"Those men were a product of the desert that raised them. They were dishonest, yes. They stole, yes. But they would not have hurt me. They were killed dishonorably."

I bit my tongue. It would do no good to argue with her now. Dishonesty, stealing what did not belong to them, and bargaining for people as though they were objects—that was dishonorable.

Emel continued. "So the birds will take them to Masira, where she can decide."

Stretching my fingers, I found her hand and took it in mine.

"Wahir takes bodies in his waves."

"That is how you return your dead to the goddess?" she asked, making a face.

"What is wrong with that?" I asked.

"They offer nothing to the desert."

"I have never understood the worship of Eiqab. He is cruel."

"Not cruel. Unlikeable, yes, but he must be harsh. The desert does not yield or allow leniencies for its people. Why should Eiqab?"

"But should not the one who offers the shelter from the hardships be the one who is worshipped? Wahir's water allows us life. We would not need his water were it not for Eiqab."

"Maybe," she said slowly, staring at my leg. "But I think we need to save praise for the one who has taught us how to endure."

Quietly, I said, "Your father was cruel. He deserves no praise."

She did not look at me, blinking away the mist in her eyes, swallowing hard.

"What is this?" I touched a wet trail on her cheek. "I would not have expected this from the woman who stared at me without sorrow when her father was slain in front of her."

She rubbed her face with the back of her hand, the stains from Altasa's work long gone. "It has all been so lonely. Being there."

"Almulihi?"

She nodded. "I have missed home, and I have missed . . ." She didn't finish her thought.

Tamam dragged another body out to the sand behind me. Emel did not once look in his direction.

"My mother would tell me that was a failing on my part."

She met my gaze. "What do you mean?"

"No one in Almulihi should miss their home. Least of all miss it so much they wish for horrors to be relived. I am sorry that I have hosted you so poorly."

"No," she began. "It is—"

"You have felt unwelcome. I know I have played a part in it. And, too, my people are not welcoming to salt . . . to those from the desert."

"Salt chasers." Her eyebrows raised for just a moment.

"It is my fault. I have allowed it to go on. The camel race should not be continued."

She watched the horizon. "At the heart of mockery is shame."

"I don't know what you—"

I did not finish, because I did know.

The question, though, was how did she?

Then, as if testing the words, she finished, "Son of the salt chaser."

22

EMEL

Tamam swept away the silence. "It is done." He walked toward us, sweat shining on his brow. "We should leave soon. The vultures will attract attention when they come."

Saalim groaned as he looked out at the desert—already rippling like water with the sun barely overhead—but he nodded.

"We can't leave so soon," I said, pointing at his leg. "The bleeding must stop for some time. Moving will make it bleed again. We have time. It is said 'a man not home by moonrise won't be coming home.'"

Tamam nodded. "So we have until night before they are missed. We leave no later than dusk." He seemed restless, agitated. Sitting and waiting did not suit him.

At midday, Tamam retrieved his pack and divided the dried meats and fruits between us. My sack was sitting at my side again. I resolved never to remove it from my body.

Sickness ebbed and flowed as I thought of the nomads. Blinded by his anger, Saalim had not seen that the man would not have hurt me, would not have hurt him.

He only wanted our packs, not another mouth to feed. Only when Saalim attacked did the man defend himself.

The swing of the nomad's scimitar . . . I thanked Masira that it had just missed Saalim's gut to hit his leg. It was as though Masira's hand pressed away the blade.

While Saalim attempted sleep, I watched for signs of Nassar and Amir. Tamam had told me to rest, but I could not. I did not think I would sleep again until we were far away from the vultures that circled and dove on the corpses behind us. I remembered my mother's sky burial, watching the vultures return her to Masira.

"They approach," Tamam said. Saalim stirred from his restless sleep, his eyes opening, then closing again.

Amir dropped quickly down from his camel. "They had only las, but they gave it freely," he said with some surprise.

"Freely?" Saalim asked groggily.

Amir nodded. "They gave these, too." In his hands were folds of thick linens, more than I hoped we would need. "Liika said it was for Emel. For the goddess that protects her."

Saalim stared at me.

"Give me the las," I said, reaching out my hand. Amir passed a small vial to me. Eiqab—Wahir—whomever, be praised. They had given us the oil! With Amir's help, we undressed Saalim's wound.

The wound was a dangerously clean slice. The skin would close too quickly. I remembered Altasa telling me that an open wound was better—that it allows for dressing, cleaning, and air. If a wound closed too soon, there was a high chance of it festering.

With Saalim clenching his fists and jaw, I gently separated the skin for Amir to pour water into the wound. Saalim bucked under our attention, but he was silent. He did not pull his leg away. I dripped the oil into the wound. *Sons, let this help.* My mind kept barreling toward a future in which the wound became foul, in which Saalim could not continue the journey, could not survive it.

The linen was folded beside me, and I took the first strip in my hands.

"Bend your knee."

With the greatest reluctance, Saalim did.

"I can do this," he said, sitting up. He sent the men away, saying he felt like a child with them all tending to him. "Really, you don't . . ."

I pushed his hands away. "Let me," I said, and began to wrap the linen around his thigh, my gaze following his leg under the blanket. My palms brushed against his skin, reminding me of when his body was mine to touch. In the pool of the oasis, in the tent of the bazaar, in the fractured piece of Madinat Almulihi's palace on the shore.

My fingers trailed across his leg, and Saalim groaned under my touch. I picked up another piece of linen, drifting my hands across his skin as I tied it in place.

"Emel," he said so quietly I barely heard.

"Hmm?" I hummed, glancing at Tamam and Nassar, both of whom reclined on mats. Amir was sitting at the water's edge, his back turned to us, moving his arms in prayer.

Carefully, I wound the last bandage around his thigh.

"Emel," he said again, his hand reaching toward me.

He did not take his eyes from my face as I secured the cloth on his leg. "What is it?" I asked, leaning my ear closer to his lips. The heat of him touched my temple.

"Come here," he whispered, his voice tremored. He opened up his arm as if to invite me to curl up beside him. "Please."

My skin tingled, my body ached with longing. There was nothing I wanted more. Shaking my head, I sat up and collected the clean linens. "If only there were fewer eyes to see us," I said. Then slowly, I pressed my lips to his brow. With my lips against his skin, he was again the Saalim from my past. I held the kiss for just a moment. His breath hitched. "And you were less of a fool."

By the time we had arrived at the next settlement, I was desperate. The las was not enough. The edges of the wound were swollen. The fluid that seeped from it was a sticky, pale yellow. Festering had begun, and with it, fever had set in.

"We need to find a healer," I urged Amir as we waited for someone who would guide us to the leader of their village.

"I know," Amir said, haggard with worry, before he and Nassar were led into the settlement. "We will find one before anything else."

Though Saalim insisted he was fine, we all saw the sweat—even under the cool moon—that dripped from his brow, his arms, his neck. He was hunched on the camel as we traveled. He was not well, and he was getting worse quickly.

This settlement was not unlike the one I had come from—tents for homes, organized based on the direction the wind blew that day—and I wondered if this community was still nomadic or if, like my father's people, they had decided to lay shallow roots in this part of the desert.

Amir and Nassar soon returned with two men who promised they would take us to their healer.

"You are lucky," one of the men said. "He is one of the best."

∼⸎⸏⸎∼

"It will not heal," the man said, peering at Saalim's uncovered wound with nose upturned. "He will die."

We gaped at the healer, Saalim included. Death was not an option.

"No," I said at the same time as Amir.

Tamam and Nassar waited outside.

"What can you do?" Amir asked. "We can pay—coin, salt. We have food—"

"I will not waste my supply on this," the healer said. He pointed at the dark red lines that traced up Saalim's thigh. "It is too late. It spreads to the heart." He rose, smoothing down his tunic.

Muffling my whimper, I watched the man. How could he turn down Amir's offer? Saalim could not die!

Finally, Saalim spoke. "I am the king of Madinat Almulihi. Whatever you can spare us will be returned to you in three times the quantity."

"You are nothing but ill," the healer said. "And my answer is no."

I forced myself to look at Saalim, though I did not want to see him. I did not want to see the face of someone who had been told they were to die. I did not want to see the man I loved look . . .

Scared. His eyes, dulled from the fever, did not meet mine. They stared at the healer's back.

The shelf holding the man's ingredients and salves was not far from us. Only the healer stood between. I considered stealing the supplies from the shelf, running past him to stuff them in my pack.

Instead, we left, Saalim leaning heavily on Amir. Nassar was gone.

"He went to ask about Kassim and Edala," Tamam said.

"Good," Saalim grunted.

One of the guides led us through the tents until we came into a large clearing with an enormous fire burning at its center. Beyond it were several large tents—their entrances tied open with thick rope.

Nassar emerged from one and approached us. Three woman flapped their arms behind him, rushing toward us in a hurry, eager to host.

"He's heard nothing," Nassar said. "But he said we may stay here as long as we need to, until you are healed."

Saalim chuffed a laugh. "I'll die here, then," he said as, with the help of Amir, he followed the clucking women.

Confused, Nassar glanced at me as I followed them into an unoccupied tent.

"Tell Pedu he shows more hospitality than his healer," Saalim said as he was eased onto a chair. There was a raised mat lying in the center, and the way the women were ushering Saalim to it, I suspected that this was a space for him.

"I'll tell him," I said, desperate and angry. My fists were still clenched from the healer's unwillingness to help.

"No, Emel," Nassar said. "It would not be well-received." Nassar shooed the women away who were telling him about the bed for Saalim. "Yes, I see it, thank you." With his attention returned to me, he said, "Stay here."

Nassar was right. It would do us no good for me to cause trouble when they offered us a safe place to sleep. Nassar asked me to stay with the king, so I did.

I went to the chair beside Saalim. He watched me as I moved, his face still clouded with fever. Water was sent for and brought to him quickly. A bath was prepared—slowly, with two trips to the oasis and two completely filled barrels. Saalim was given privacy to soak, and when I made to leave he stopped me.

"If you go, I will have no company." He sounded unexpectedly sad.

As if the emotion were strings, I followed their tug. Closing the tent to the people outside, ignoring the way Tamam watched me with questioning eyes, I asked, "Do you need help stepping in?"

Small grunts and groans. Then, "Yes."

I went to him, taking his forearm in my hands as he removed his clothes slowly, carefully.

Saalim naked, stepping into a bath. Me at his side. It was more than I had dreamed, yet it was my nightmare. He winced as his wound was submerged.

"You will not die from this," I said tightly, infusing my words with urgent anger. He was giving up, caring less.

"Do you know, I keep thinking of mountains. Higher than any I've ever seen in my life. And there is ice—frozen water. I've never seen it before, you know. But I can see it when I close my eyes. I can feel it. And I'm taking it into my hands. It is like powder, see, and I am pressing it on my leg, on my neck. It is so cold." His words came out in slow, tired breaths.

I stilled, listening to him. "That sounds impossible," I said tightly, drawing the chair to sit beside him. He could not know that he *had* visited a mountain before. At least, when he was a jinni he had told me such stories. There was that imperfect magic, its tattered shroud.

"Here," Saalim said, resting his elbow on the edge of the basin so that his hand was stretched out toward me. "Fewer eyes."

I took his hand and pressed it to my lips. Leaning my cheek into his palm. His fingers twitched, caressing my face. I closed my eyes against the tears.

He would not die. He would not die. He would not die. Not when I was this close.

Not when *we* were this close.

Water sloshed up the sides of the basin.

"Will you tell me now?" he asked as he reclined further into the bath. His head was against the basin's edge, his face turned toward me.

"Tell you?"

"About us."

I hesitated. What would it do to someone to learn of a past they remembered nothing of? I remembered hearing about the mad woman who lived in my village. She knew nothing about the world we lived in, always living twenty years prior. The children loved to tease her when she asked after her husband. "He's dead!" they'd shriek, and she would mourn him anew.

"When my day was hard, or I needed to be distracted," I began. "I had a friend who would tell me the most amazing stories."

Saalim opened his mouth as if to protest, but the energy was not there, and he closed it.

"My favorite was the one about the jinni and the ahira." If anyone listened through these cloth walls they would only hear a story. They would not understand it was an impossible truth.

"An ahira, eh?" Then he frowned. "And a jinni."

"This jinni is good," I whispered, running my lips across his fingers. Slowly, careful that I said everything just right, I told Saalim the story of us.

"Where did he go?" he asked after I told him of the ahira's wish that split them.

"Home," I said as I helped him stand from the bath. Carefully, we moved to his bed. When he finally lay down, his breath came in heavy, fast gasps.

After his breathing slowed, he asked, "And then what happens?" His brow furrowed when I shrugged. "I do not like that it ends there."

"Neither do I."

"That story has far too much romance. Not enough battles or swordfights. What did this jinni do all of the time? Swoon over this ahira?"

Unable to stop myself, I grinned. "He did."

"You must finish the story. How does it end?"

"Happily," I promised.

And when he closed his eyes, I cried.

"We need to return to Almulihi," Nassar said at dawn.

"Almulihi?" Amir asked. "And take Saalim where? To Altasa? We've already discussed this. Her supplies have burned. We have Emel."

I balked. "Oh, no—"

"The bazaar will have what he needs! There are other healers," Nassar said, angry now. He spoke loudly, and I turned, expecting Saalim to awake at the commotion. The knot in my chest tightened. He was still asleep. When we'd first taken the journey to Madinat Almulihi, it had seemed he never slept. Always awake, always preparing.

"There are other settlements we can travel to," Amir said. "Ones that are closer, that perhaps are more easily bought."

"It will take us further from Almulihi. We can't take that risk."

"There is a settlement a night's journey southwest of here. Almulihi is ten—probably thirteen with our current pace—nights away. We don't have that kind of time." Amir looked at me then.

I knew he was right. "We don't."

At dusk, Tamam and Amir helped Saalim onto his camel. Saalim swore he would be fine, that he was strong enough, but his glazed eyes and shaking hands belied his words. Nassar looked as wary as I felt.

Though I was tired, sleep did not threaten me as I thought it would, worried as I was for Saalim. He attempted stoicism, but I saw the slump in his shoulders, the way the camel's sway sent his body rocking.

When the moon was high, he lurched to the side and fell to the ground.

"Saalim!" I cried, leaping from my camel.

Tamam was already there, kneeling beside Saalim.

"Are you hurt?" I asked, skidding to the ground beside him. His cheek was hot under my hand.

I spun around, looking desperately—foolishly—for anything around us that could help him. Sons, why did this have to happen *here*? The helplessness was suffocating. I could barely think.

"It is fine," Saalim said with thready breaths. "Just tired. Fell . . . asleep."

"We will rest," Tamam said.

Amir was beside us now, Nassar behind him with camels' reins in his hands. He looked out at the night with a stony gaze.

"We can't stay!" Amir said, pulling his map from his pack and pointing to it violently. "We still have half a night's journey to the next settlement. We can't wait until sun-up to resume. It will be too hot. He will . . ." His voice trailed off as he stared at the map beneath the moonlight, his eyes darting around it as though he was trying to grasp at any alternative. When I looked back to Saalim, his eyes were closed, his breathing rapid.

No, no, no. I couldn't bear it. I could not stay here and watch Saalim sputter and die like a lamp out of oil. I walked away from them, from the camels. I went straight into the night, remembering what felt like so long ago when I was at the Haf Shata, feeling trapped as my father's ahira. How I stared at the desert, wishing to run into it.

Desperate to be free from the cage of my father's palace.

Now I was more trapped than before. I rubbed the heels of my hands into my eyes, digging through memories for a solution. Trying to remember recipes in Altasa's book, anything that might help us. Was it too late to return to the settlement we had left? I could find the ingredients I needed in the marketplace or steal them from the healer.

My hands swung down at my sides, and I stared at the horizon, the sun just rising above.

Sons, was it dawn already? It couldn't be. The moon was still high overhead—still bright.

I looked back to the horizon, to the sun.

No, it wasn't the sun.

It was a flame.

"A traveler!" I hissed as I approached the men. They looked where I pointed. "I will go and meet him."

"No!" Tamam said, his urgency taking me by surprise. "You will stay. We will all stay."

I pressed my hands to my hips. "He might have something that can help us. Maybe there is a closer place with a healer. Maybe Amir's map is wrong." Amir scowled at the suggestion but said nothing.

"Tamam is right," Nassar said, shaking his head. "A traveler who walks with a flame wants to be seen. Wants to be approached. No one with sense would waste oil like that."

"Where there is no sense, there is motive," Tamam said.

We had little to lose. Without waiting for them to protest, I strode away.

The risk of what I was doing caught up with me once I was near the traveler. My steps grew smaller, and I looked back from where I had come. I could not see the men anywhere. My breath caught, my chest pulled tight. *Of course.* It was too dark. Why did I think I could approach this person and return without issue? Shouting would not help. Voices carried across the desert even more poorly than sea-born people travelled across it. My heart slammed against my chest as I peered through the dark.

The traveler was close to me now. Squinting, I saw it was a woman—unremarkable in every way except that she was holding the lamp low to the ground, examining the sand as though looking for something.

I pressed my shaking hands to my brow, closing my eyes and mustering the courage to approach her. When I opened my eyes, the woman was standing within arm's reach of me, staring at me with question.

"Sons!" I screamed, my hands pressed against my chest.

The woman was on the precipice of age. She was older than me, but not yet so old that she belonged best in a settlement.

"You sneak up on me; I sneak up on you," she said, voice smooth as oil. Then she looked down. "No scorpions here, eh?"

"I—no," I confirmed after peering at the ground.

She dropped the lantern from our faces and waved it over the sand above us. "They hide well."

"Do you live here?" I asked, growing hopeful.

"Here? Yes." She did not look up at me, but I heard amusement bending her words.

"Nearby?" I hoped.

"Right there." She pointed over her shoulder, my gaze following as if tied to her finger.

I faltered. There was a home—lit like her lantern—sitting not far from us. How had I not seen it before? I rubbed my eyes, trying to make sense of it. When I looked back to the woman, she was gone.

I turned, and let out a relieved sigh when I saw that she had just moved on, searching for more scorpions.

"My friend needs help," I said. I could not lose her. Glancing back to the home, I was reassured to see it was still there.

"Help? From me?"

"My friend. He is sick, dy—dying." I closed my mouth tightly, stopping the sadness from leaving me.

"You need no help from me, then. Masira will take him here."

"No," I begged. "I need to save him."

"A lover, eh? You'll find more."

"He is a king," I whispered. If I saw the men again, they would not be pleased that I told this to a stranger. "Of Madinat Almulihi."

The woman smiled now. "Well, why didn't you say? I would love to see this king of Madinat Almulihi. Take me to him."

"I, ah . . . I am not sure where they are. I ran here so quickly."

Her eyes were like a lash as she whipped toward me. "You ran on foot to a traveler by yourself, without means of return?"

"If he dies, then I would face troubles far greater than that. I have nothing left I can lose."

"Lucky for you, I am not so foolish. And your men are loud."

As if she followed a path made from my footsteps—and perhaps she was, though I saw nothing—we found them.

"Who is this?" Nassar said with biting anger.

The woman ignored him.

Her stare lingered on Tamam for just a moment before she set the lamp beside Saalim and kneeled.

I watched her face, but aside from a quick pinch of her brow, she gave nothing away.

"Fever?" she asked.

"Yes, from a wound."

"We will take him back to my home." She looked at the three men. "You can come, but you must stay outside."

"We are not goats," Nassar said.

"But you smell like them, eh?" she said, rising. She did not tear her gaze from Saalim until she turned toward her home. "It is just there. Come with me."

Despite Saalim and the camels slowing us, the walk to her home felt quick.

The woman was already inside when we arrived. "Come in today, tomorrow, whenever you are ready. I will wait."

Wait, indeed. We all stared at the home. An enormous skull—bigger than the tents back home—jutted from the sand. Tusks longer than the canal boats in Madinat Almulihi dipped under the sand before emerging again. Rope was strung across them, clothes hanging from the line. Lanterns were hung from the tips of the tusks. Atop the skull was a large piece of oiled camel fur. The skull was the most inexplicable home I had ever seen.

"What . . . ?" Amir whispered. I heard Nassar grunt in echo of his question. Tamam was silent.

I stepped forward, walking under the upper jaw to enter. "Where is the king?" the woman called when I came in alone. Her back was to me, allowing me the opportunity to stare at the bizarre room.

There was almost nothing in the space. A single mat lay on the ground beside the lantern the woman had been carrying.

There were no food stores, no shelves with pitchers or goatskins of water. There was not even a puzzle board or game with dice. We must have been closer to a settlement than Amir realized; otherwise, what did she do with her days? Sleep? And hunt for scorpions?

As I stared at the austerity, it occurred to me that in the bleakness of the room, there was no medicine. Nothing that would help Saalim. I was unsure how to voice my concern.

She did not give me the chance, "Do you want help, or have you changed your mind? Bring in the king."

Slowly, Amir helped Saalim inside.

"Out," the woman said to Amir as soon as Saalim was lying on the mat. Amir glowered at her, then glanced to me. I nodded. It would be okay. I hoped.

"May I see your wound?" she asked Saalim. Her voice was quiet, gentle. Like a mother's. Suddenly I, too, was calm.

Saalim nodded. Had he even heard her question? Did he even know that it was a stranger who spoke to him? I sat beside him, taking his hand. The woman glanced at us as she removed the bandage, but she said nothing.

"I can heal this," she said as she stared at the wound—thick, milky fluid, sticky along its edges.

"You can?" I rocked forward on my knees. My heart was thunderous, although now not from fear, but from joy, hope. "How?" I looked around. Beside the woman was a thin book, not unlike Altasa's recipe book for tonics. Did this woman keep the same? "Where are your ingredients?"

"Ingredients? For what?" She laughed, her smile spreading across her face, revealing strong rows of teeth.

Saalim stirred at the sound and I leaned into his ear. "She said she will help you. I promised, eh?"

"You love this man?" the woman asked. Her voice was low, as though she did not want the men outside to hear.

Hesitating only a moment and sparing a furtive glance to Saalim to confirm he was without awareness, I said just as quietly, "He is the reason for my life." His knuckles were coarse against my lips. I counted them: one, two, three, four. Little dunes making up my world.

"I see," she said. She softly pressed her hands on his thigh beside his wound. "Can you lend me your cloak?" she asked after a pause.

Unthinking, I pulled it off and handed it to her. She took the cloak and watched me as I straightened the tunic over my shoulders.

Just then, Saalim's voice broke the strained silence. "Have you seen . . ." He exhaled, his eyes closing again. "Brother, sister. Emel?"

"We are searching for two people," I said, and told her of Edala and Kassim. "The man travels with someone we can't well describe. It is a woman, younger I think than you."

The woman nodded slowly, then stood and went to the edge of the room where she had a leather sack I had not noticed before. Feeling around inside the bag, she pulled from it a jar of salve and carried it back.

"This is saha. It will help," she said. Taking a goatskin from beneath her dusty cloak, she unstopped it and poured water over his wound. When she had determined it to be clean enough, she lathered the salve over it. Saalim winced, but when the salve was placed, he visibly calmed. I could have sworn that even his face looked cooler. She took my cloak and draped it over Saalim. I pulled at the edges, helping to ensure it covered him.

"I can dress the wound," I said.

"No. It has been trapped too long. It needs air." The woman stared at Saalim's face, something inexplicable in her gaze. As if she sensed my wondering, she whispered, "A king."

She stood.

"There is a settlement nearby. I will go tonight and see what they know of these people."

"Oh no—" I began, but she was already tightening her cloak and walking outside. Her face was taut, holding back some emotion I could not decipher.

"Don't you dare enter!" I heard her warn to the men outside. "I will be back and will know if you've been inside. He needs rest and care. Emel can help with the second bit. Doesn't need ninnies like you fussing over him."

Saalim's lip twitched, but he did not open his eyes.

"Emel?" Amir was at the entrance, the fabric closed in front of him.

"I am fine," I said. "He looks . . . better already." I tried not to let my hopes soar too freely. Tried not to stare at his face and see the dampness disappear, or the strain ease.

"She just walked off." Nassar was not talking to me now, but I could hear the surprise in his voice all the same. He mumbled something about salt chasers, but it was not without respect.

"I am not convinced we can trust her." It was Amir.

"What choice do we have?" Tamam said.

Indeed, what choice did we have? Saalim's breathing was hushed, gentler, quieter. He rested easily now.

Seated beside him, I pulled my knees into my chest, watching him heal before my eyes. Relief was settling on me like a blanket in a cool night. It took away the fear, the anxiety, the desperate, aching sadness. But as it washed it away, I felt there was still something that lingered. Something nagging. What was it?

I sorted through my memories, the things that had happened and were happening. The woman, her home, the strangeness of it all.

Then, I found it.

Emel.

She had known my name. Just like Saalim once did.

I know I had not told her my name.

23

EMEL

S omething nudged me back and forth and back and forth. I was on a ship
again, watching fire paint the sky. Back and forth. Light was bleeding in,
water seeping into a poorly oiled tent. Slowly, then faster. It flooded me
until my eyes fluttered open.

An empty room. The woman's home.

With the realization of where I was came my fear for Saalim. How had I let
myself fall asleep? I sat up gasping.

"Oh," Saalim said quietly, quickly.

I twisted to face him.

He was there. *There* right in front of me. He was sitting up, and though he
looked tired, he looked . . . *well*.

"Saalim?!" My voice fractured on his name, my hands moving to my mouth.

He held his finger to his lips and nodded toward the entrance. They were
sleeping outside.

"How long have you been awake?" I scooted closer, my greedy eyes flitting
over him, checking to see how he moved and breathed. The color of his skin,
the strength in his hands, and finally his wound. It was covered still, but the
way he held his leg made me wonder . . . no, it could not have healed that
quickly.

"Since dawn." He told me I was sleeping so heavily, he had not the heart to wake me. His men told him what happened. Apparently he remembered little.

"The woman has not returned?"

He shook his head, leaning back onto his hands and stretching out his legs.

"Your wound?" I asked. "Is it better?"

His smile was a better answer than anything he could have spoken aloud. As he tugged at his pant leg, I marveled at the ease in which he moved. No wincing or groaning or stilted movements.

He rolled the fabric above his thigh. Were it not for the shining strip of skin that lay across his leg, I would have thought he had never been injured.

Sucking in a breath, I crawled near to peer at it more closely. It had healed so quickly.

"How long have I been sleeping?" I asked. Days? An entire moon?

"It is unbelievable. I wondered the same when I awoke this morning."

It *was* unbelievable. It was impossible. I brought my fingers together, worry spinning a tight web. "This was no simple healing salve."

The way he stared at his leg, I knew he suspected the same.

I said, "This was Masira. This was magic."

He rubbed at his wrists. "Why would the woman heal me with magic?"

"Because you are a king."

He frowned. "You told her." It was not a question.

I said, "It is why you are healed now."

"Does she know where we are from?"

I shrugged. I could not remember telling her specifically, but there were many things she had asked me at high moon. My name not being one of them. Nor had I asked hers. Who was she?

Saalim leapt up, and I was too distracted by his effortless movement to care about his frustration. "We cannot stay here." His voice was loud, intending to wake the others. I could hear them stirring already.

He continued. "She has left us to wait for her to return like sea-washed clams. The Darkafa might be heading straight here."

He was right. I stood up, rapidly shaking off the sand and slipping on my sandals.

Saalim strode out of the makeshift tent. I spared the boney cavern only a moment's more consideration before I was outside with him.

Nassar and Amir were rolling their mats, folding their cloaks and stuffing them into their packs. The sound of rapid breaths came from behind the woman's house. We waited, and Tamam rounded the corner.

"She comes," he said, surprise dusting his face when he saw Saalim standing in front of him with both feet firmly planted on the ground.

"Alone?" Saalim asked as he tucked his guthra around his neck.

Tamam nodded. "On foot."

Amir unrolled his map and squinted at the ink. Edging closer, I followed his finger as he traced our path to where he thought we might be. He pointed to a settlement south of where we were on the map.

"Hmm." He pulled his bawsal from his pocket and confirmed something. "She comes from the west, yet the closest settlement I have is a few nights south."

Before long, the woman rounded the corner. When she saw Saalim, she nodded once, the most subtle softening of her face revealing relief. "You have recovered."

"I have. I owe you more than gratitude. How can I repay my debt?" He said it politely, but I heard the strain at the back of the voice that said, *please let this be quick, we want to leave.*

"I would like to join you on your journey," she said. There was something strange about her request. I could almost feel it in the air.

Saalim straightened, discomfited by the thought of a stranger among us. I, too, thought it a bad idea, but Amir nodded slowly. Nassar and Tamam appeared to be considering it.

Saalim glared at the three of them, and as he did so, the woman looked at me with eyebrows raised. Did she also see the horror on my face?

"I cannot allow that," Saalim said when he turned back to her. "Is there something else I can do? If nothing now, I will send whatever you request when I return home."

She shook her head. "No, I think you should have me join you."

Tamam said, "It is a good idea." The woman smiled as she looked at Tamam. Nassar and Amir mumbled agreements.

Saalim's mouth dropped open. To disagree with their king before a stranger? Never mind to think it wise that she join us? Though I could not forget how easily she healed Saalim, it was risky.

"I will not have you," Saalim said. His words were final.

The woman chuckled and looked at me again. "I am impressed," she said. I did not understand.

"Because I am generous," she said without waiting for a response. "I will take you at least to the village nearby. They have information that you will find helpful." Then she gave me a knowing look. "You will like it there, too."

It was agreed, mostly because she would not accept another answer. We finished dressing for the one-day journey, securing our things on our camels, and headed toward the village.

"It is not far," the woman promised after we had left.

I turned back to look at her home, sure I would never again see anything like it. But it was gone. Had we already walked so far?

"See, it is just there." I followed the direction of the woman's finger. There, like a blanket atop the sand, was a band of green that split the ground from the sky.

<hr />

Trees, as dense as Altasa's gardens—no, even denser!—stood like a wall before us. The woman led us straight into them.

First, it was the ground that changed. The sand grew wetter, less grainy, reminding me of the dirt in the gardens. There were leafy bushes. Then small trees, then taller ones.

The woman said, "There is a river just beyond. Soon, you'll hear it."

And soon, we did. As we stepped under the canopy of trees—shaded almost completely by their branches—not only did I hear the water, I could feel it.

Though it felt cooler away from the sun, the wetness in the air made our coverings intolerable. Saalim stripped his surface layers.

We all did.

"It is so wet here," Nassar said. He was right. Sweat was no stranger, but this was different. I'd wipe my face, and immediately there was more.

Amir began murmuring again about how he had not realized that this was so close.

His disappointment in his navigation spilled through the words.

"No one expects you to know the entire desert, Amir," I said as I stepped over tree roots twisting out from the ground.

"I do," Saalim said. The woman glanced at him and matched his crooked smile.

Right where the trees were the thickest, the sound of rushing water grew.

We had come to the river. I gawked, the water snaking rapidly in front of me. I looked from side to side, watching branches and leaves rush past.

"This is a river?" I asked. I had heard of rivers before, but I had not expected this. In many ways, it was more terrifying than the sea. A branch floating down swiftly along the surface was suddenly swallowed by the water. I took a step back. The lazy canals in Almulihi were nothing like this.

"It is," the woman said when none of the men responded. I wondered if they had ever seen one. She continued. "It travels far to the south, taking its green along with it. You would not know a desert so dry lay on the other side, eh?" She turned down the river's shore and walked along it, careful not to tread through the mud. My feet were not used to this—wetness and sticks and sharp leaves. My sandals served little purpose.

"This way," she said as we followed.

Before long, I saw a bridge made of rope and wooden planks. It was suspended just above the water.

"This is safe?" Nassar asked as we approached.

"It held earlier today," she said with a raise of her shoulders, then strode across it. I watched as it bobbed up and down with her weight. Amir followed without fear, then Nassar and Tamam, all trailing the woman like hungry goats.

Envisioning the bridge collapsing, me tumbling into the water and flowing away as fast as the river could take me, I hesitated. Saalim stepped onto the bridge, then turned toward me with his hand extended. "Together?"

I grasped Saalim's hand, and let him lead me across. At first he walked cautiously, to minimize the bobbing of the bridge.

"Faster," I begged when the bridge sagged under Saalim's step.

He pulled me along so quickly I was nearly running, frantic until solid ground was beneath my feet again. I nearly dropped to my knees in relief, but the curious faces of our companions—who had watched us run hand in hand across the bridge—stopped me.

Ahead, there were structures and movement through the trees. Finally, we had arrived.

Everywhere I looked was something foreign and fascinating. I could not take in my surroundings quickly enough. The first home we saw had walls of mud and thick sticks, roofs of branches and fronds. The people watched us as we passed. I imagined we were as interesting to them as they were to us. Women wore brightly colored, sleeveless tunics that fell to their thighs and were cinched around their waists. Men wore coverings around only their hips, their chests left uncovered. Some women and men wore snug-fitting turbans and bright jewelry made with shells and beads.

A woman waved to us as we stepped onto the well-worn dirt path. Her wrist was layered with bright blue beads so familiar I nearly stopped to gawk at them. *Slave beads* we had called them. We used them as betting currency back home when we played cards—ghamar. Is this where they came from? These people appeared to be the opposite of slaves.

The woman who brought us here seemed to know everyone. They greeted her like an old friend.

"Jawar is just this way," she told us after greeting an older man with a kiss to his cheek. We moved into a clearing, and my eyes immediately traveled up into the trees.

A sturdy ladder led to a wooden platform jutting off of a tree. Atop the platform, there was a home not unlike the ones we passed on the way in, though this one had been fastidiously built and decorated with etchings carved around the door and windows. Rugs like the ones that lined my father's palace were set across the platform, the edges hanging off revealing their patterns. There were two other homes like this one, tucked behind, and they all were connected via rope bridges.

"Jawar, they are here!" the woman called.

The sight simultaneously excited and terrified me as I watched a man cross one of the bridges. Then, he exited the home and descended the ladder.

There was something familiar about Jawar—the way he walked over to us, gentle but confident, the way he bowed to the men, grasping Saalim's forearm, and the way he welcomed me with equal warmth.

"If you are comfortable," Jawar said, "you may come up. I have tea and yassa prepared by my wife."

"Thank you. Nassar will join us." Saalim gestured to me. "Amir and Tamam will stay here."

Jawar nodded and gestured for us to follow.

The woman said, "I have things I need here. I will return before you are finished." Then, she was gone. I watched her disappear between the trees. There was something about her, about this, about Jawar, that was not quite right. I could not yet fit together the hazy puzzle my mind was sorting.

Though I had no interest in climbing the ladder, I very much wanted to see inside the tree home. I scrambled up after the men. The platform was, indeed, covered in rugs. I couldn't help but smile. They reminded me so much of my home.

The decorations inside were no different. Rugs covered the wooden planks. A low table with cushions around it was at the center of the room. Frankincense scented the space and with each breath I was reminded of my mother. It felt just like the harem, but better, because up here, I could hear the leaves rustling with every breath of the wind. The birds were loud and nearly ebullient with their songs.

And perhaps even more importantly—and surprisingly—it felt like the safest place I had ever been aside from the palace in Almulihi.

"Your home is beautiful," I said, peering at the things on shelves. I ached with the memory of my life with my sisters.

"Thank you. It is due to my wife. When we wed, it was the first thing she did." He gestured to the rugs and the cushions. "I did not want her to mourn for her home."

I smiled, touching the tapestry that hung on a windowless wall. "It is so much like where I am from."

"So then you must find great comfort here, too."

A small deck of cards sat on a nearby table. "My sisters and I loved that game."

Jawar laughed. "Don't mention it to my wife! She will keep you playing all through the night." Then, turning to Saalim, he said, "Before we discuss the matters that have brought you to me, let us first have a drink and talk of something idle. The Sons do not like work before joy, and I must agree."

I could not take my eyes from him as he spoke. Was it simply the home around him that made him feel so familiar? No, there was something in his manner. The softness of his words, the nodding of his head and the movement in his hands as he spoke.

A woman came bustling in from a back door. She was the brightest thing in the room with her ruby fustan and scarf draped over her hair, and we all stared at her as she set a full tray at the center of the table.

She looked up at us and Jawar clapped his hands together and said, "Excellent! I would like to introduce you all to my wife, Rah—"

I gasped. "Emah?"

SAALIM

E mel pushed herself onto her feet and stumbled to Jawar's wife.

"Emel!" the woman cried. Her hands shook over her mouth, and at first, I could not understand if she was horrified or ecstatic. Maybe both. "You are here?" She looked at all of us, then back to Emel.

Emel pulled her into her chest. "Raheemah, it *is* you!"

"You promised me you'd come, and you are here!"

They hugged each other like reunited family, and we watched them speechlessly.

"Jawar," the girl said. "It is my sister! The one I've told you about!" She blinked away tears, and I could see it then, the slight familiarity.

Jawar smiled broadly at his wife. He waved his hand. "I am happy for you. Go talk to her. Spend time. Maybe I can convince our guests to stay an evening." He raised his eyebrows as Raheemah and Emel left. Rotating on his cushion, he faced us around the table.

He had no weapons, I noticed. It was a disarming gesture. I feigned to scratch my side, my gaze skirting around the room, through the windows, and beyond. There were no guards. It took much trust to allow strangers into your home without guards or weapons readied. Though it made little sense, I knew Jawar was trustworthy.

I had an understanding of him that I could not pin down. Raheemah, too.

"Raheemah has said many things to me about Emel," Jawar said. "When she went back home, she looked for her. Was distraught when she heard she'd left. She needs this happiness." Jawar looked at his hands, his mouth pulling into a grimace.

After we had finished our yassa and our frivolous talk had dwindled, Nassar said, "Our guide has said you know something of the people we seek."

Jawar nodded as he nudged aside his empty plate. He rested his elbows on the tabletop.

"Three days ago, a group of four came through. Dressed in black, skin pale. They lingered in our village, asking after a goddess and her servant. They were not violent," Jawar said. "But they were crazed, leaving black hand marks on our trees. Talked of the rightful Son. That the desert needed its true heir.

"The group left us, and the next day," Jawar continued, touching his fingertips together and resting his chin against them, "a man and a woman came. The woman in the middle of her life, the man perhaps the same as you." Jawar gestured to me. "They spoke to none about their business, but they asked if any others had come through. I told them of the crazed people, but that did not interest them. They seemed relieved when I told them there was no one else."

The man he described sounded like Kassim. When I told Jawar how my throne was threatened, his eyes darkened with worry.

"That man seeks to take the throne from me. We must find him." Then, I described Edala. He shook his head, knew of no one who looked like her. Jawar detailed for us the timing of Kassim and the woman's departure and the direction they went. Amir marked a wide area on his map in front of him.

Finding two people in the desert was like trying to find salt grains in sand. What had I been thinking when I insisted we take this journey?

"Saalim?" Amir asked.

I looked up from the tabletop.

Amir continued, "It is your choice."

"What is?"

Jawar hummed for a moment then repeated his question. "If you will stay? We have lodgings for guests. Plenty of space for five." He pointed somewhere behind him.

If we stayed, it was more time lost in finding Kassim. Finding Edala. But then perhaps it was time to give up the chase.

It seemed impossible, after all.

Tomorrow evening we would begin the journey home. Almulihi needed me more than I needed to find my sister and my Wahir-forsaken brother. If he returned for me, I would be there waiting.

"We will stay," I said. "You have my gratitude."

⌇⌇⌇

Jawar led us to three more houses buttressed in trees. A single ladder led up to the complex, and like Jawar's, these homes were connected by bridges.

"The ladder can be pulled up, so that you might all sleep at ease," Jawar said, placing his hand on a rung.

"They are clever, these homes." I stared up at them, wondering how I might be able to devise something as easily defended back home.

"Yes. My grandfather conceived of them. But they are not easily made, otherwise our entire village would be up in trees."

Unlike Almulihi, which sat on the ground waiting for invaders. For Kassim.

Dusk was fast approaching, the darkness arriving more quickly in the shade of the forest. Emel and her sister were still in Jawar's home.

I thought to wait for her, but with our sleep getting turned around each day and night, I was ebbing and flowing like I'd had one too many drinks of wine. And surely Emel would wish to remain close to her sister.

"I will take first watch," Tamam said.

I shook my head. "We can all sleep. We'll bring up the ladder."

The idea made him uncomfortable.

"We shouldn't sleep the whole night anyway," I conceded. "At least sleep for some."

Though I still braced for the pierce of my wound, each step up the ladder was painless. What had that woman done to me? It was impossible my leg could be healed in the span of a day.

My room was well-prepared. Oil clusters were burning, filling the room with scents from a souk. The carpet on the floor was thick and comfortable, the cushions of similar quality. There was a fine mesh over the windows and doors—I had noted the same at Jawar's home. For insects, I presumed. That, at least, was not a problem we had in Almulihi.

Lying back, I closed my eyes. Through the din of the life in the forest, I could hear the scrape of skin against parchment as Amir fussed over his map, Nassar confirming the direction of his bawsal. Beyond them, the river hissed.

The slap of shoes against wood roused me from sleep, the house swaying just a bit as someone crossed the bridge.

A silhouette appeared in the doorway. "Who is there?" I asked.

Emel started. "Sorry. I thought this one was empty," Emel said. She began to leave, the net falling back in front of the doorway.

"No, please come in," I said in a rush, standing up to light the lantern. My exhaustion fled as soon as she came inside. The room flared orange. I turned. "You're wet."

Emel smiled and gathered the dripping strands of hair over her shoulder.

"Raheemah took me to the baths. A waterfall, it's called. Do you hear it?" She tilted her head and pointed outside. "Sounds like the sea."

"It does." I searched the shelves for a reason for her to stay, not ready to lose this opportunity to be alone with her. *Tell me more about our shared past.* A silver kettle sat on a tray. Warmth radiated from its side. Praise Wahir!

"Please sit," I said, preparing the tea.

She gathered a few of the cushions and leaned against them.

As I set the steeping cup in front of her, she said, "You pour tea like a woman."

"My mother made us learn so we wouldn't always rely on servants. For times like this, I suspect."

"Dutiful host." She sipped the tea.

"It is not sweet, though."

She grinned. "Did your mother make you remember that, too?"

"No."

There was silence. Emel traced the rim of her cup with her finger. Such a delicate gesture for someone so resilient. She looked up at me. "Did you know your birth mother?"

"No. She did not want to be a part of my life." Not wanting to talk of my past, I asked her about Raheemah.

"I was terrified when he chose Raheemah. I was so worried he would be wrong for her, but you—" And the cadence of her words skipped just a beat. "You have to trust that Eiqab will not do wrong."

Each *you* was different. The second could have been anyone. The first was for me.

It reminded me of my fevered dreams, where there was an *us* in a hazy past. I was not the same *me*—it was someone restrained, held by powerful hands—but it was undoubtedly Emel. There was an easiness in these dreams, a freedom between us. She had been mine to hold and touch as I pleased. When I awoke from those dreams, I was delirious with pain and heat. At first, I thought I wanted to return to them to escape the suffering. But now, I suffered no longer, and still I wanted to return.

Helena's pale face flashed in my mind, so I looked to Emel's to wash it away.

"What are you thinking of?"

"Helena."

She picked at the threads of the rug. "When will the wedding be?"

"When everything is settled, I suspect." I leaned back on my hands, looking out the window at the night. The buzzing, hissing, and croaking creatures were cacophonous.

"Do you want to marry her?"

I hesitated, unsure even if I knew the answer to that question. "For my father, I did." I filled our cups again. The water was dark, the leaves steeped far too long.

"Your father?"

"He made a mistake." I pointed at myself. "I am not to err in the same manner. It is the responsibility of the king to marry for power. My father ended up loving my mother. He was very lucky."

"The Hayali queen."

Nodding, I said, "It was a valuable match. She was nothing like her sister. All soft where Liika was coarse."

Emel was both.

"Did he love the salt chaser who carried you?"

"He regretted what harm he had caused her and me."

"And you will not make the same mistake." Her words were flat, final.

"He made a mistake, yes. He and I would disagree on what the mistake was." I met Emel's gaze. Her eyes were even darker in the shadows, beckoning me. "The decision to marry Helena was so easy . . ." I took a breath. I should not do this, but the table had already been set. Damn me if I did not sit down at it. "Before you."

She pressed her mouth together. "Me."

The need to tell her everything spilled from me like water. "If I can burden you with another confession . . ."

"Of course."

"There are things I feel when I am around you—things that are good, things that make me feel whole. And what is more . . ." I searched around, trying to find some way to explain how I felt. "Layered beneath all that is something old. An echo, a foundation—I don't know how to describe it—that tells me, yes, this is right. Like a palimpsest. Do you know what that is?" I was blathering now. "I feel happy, Emel. It terrifies me, because I fear I shouldn't feel this way."

"Because it would be a mistake?" Her voice was softer than my bed back home.

"No. I know it would not be a mistake. It is the same fear I have when my eagle hunts. Each time I let her fly, I do not know if she will return to me."

"You fear that I do not feel the same."

Stomping from outside grew louder.

"Saalim!" We sat upright as Tamam stumbled into the room. "Emel has," he looked down at us as he said, "not returned."

She stood in a rush, turning up the cup to finish her tea. "I was just leaving." And before either of us could utter a word, she had slipped past him and was gone.

"My apologies for interrupting," Tamam said as he fidgeted at my doorway.

Falling back into cushions, I said, "Don't you ever sleep?"

When I opened my eyes, the torch had burned through all its oil and left behind a suffocating darkness. Feeling my way around the dark room, I found the door.

Moonlight barely filtered in through the leaves, and I could not at first find the ladder. I dropped to my hands and knees, searching in front of me until I felt it. It had already been lowered. I descended the ladder to find who else was out of bed.

When my feet hit the soft ground, there was a voice. "Couldn't sleep either?"

Tamam.

He leaned against one of the trees holding up the homes, finding a way to keep guard even when there was no threat of an attack.

I moved to the bushes to relieve myself. "No, I suppose not."

"I am not blind," he said.

"Say what you mean, Tamam."

"You and Emel."

"Ah."

"You will not regret it?"

"No," I said, certain.

He sighed, but it did not sound weary. Instead, it sounded . . . relieved? He said, "A warrior will kill for the love of a woman. But for the right woman, he will stay his hand."

When I was back on the path, our eyes met. What did Tamam know of women? I'd never seen that man anywhere but the palace.

"When she asked with the nomad, you stayed your hand," Tamam said. "Foolish though it was."

"I am going for a walk."

"I will stay here." His gaze was trained on a large fire at the end of the path.

"Yes. Sit down. I will not be far."

Beside the fire, the woman who had healed me sat with half of a large fruit in her lap. She was not surprised to see me.

"This is the best spot to avoid insects," she said as the smoke collected around her. She spat a cluster of black seeds onto the ground.

"May I?" I asked, gesturing to a tree stump out of the path of the smoke. She nodded.

"Where did you go when we arrived?" I asked as I sat.

"To find you all lodgings. Though I see Jawar provided his own. He regards you very highly, to allow you to sleep in the trees."

"He has been very kind to us. It helps that his wife is Emel's sister."

The woman smiled now, her mouth glistening like that of a child who had been indulging in sweets. "I thought as much." She was occupied suddenly with her fingers, wiping them carefully one by one as she tossed the carcass of the fruit into the fire. "Did Jawar tell you what you needed to know?" she asked.

I stretched out my legs, again preparing for the pain and instead feeling relief.

"He knew some, but not enough. We will begin our return to Almulihi tonight. Tomorrow night?" I looked up. "I cannot see the damned moon."

The woman smiled. "Tonight. Sunrise is closer than sunset." She drank from her goatskin. "You will give up?"

"If you want to call it that. But," I took a deep breath, feeling that just as Emel decided she could trust this woman, I could do the same. "My city is without its king. I cannot leave it long. I was being foolishly hopeful, I think, wanting to find my family."

"Wanting your family does not make you a fool."

"No, but abandoning your duties to find them does. My brother poses a risk, and it was not wise to seek him out here. If he wants me gone, he'll come to me. If he hears of my absence in Almulihi, I worry what he will do."

"I have heard of that brother. The second to the throne. Of course he poses risk. People talk of both seaside sons. Spoiled, entitled."

"Ah, yes." I had heard it hundreds of times. Before, I did not care. Let them think what they want. Now, I wanted them to know I was not the same man I was before. I was changed.

The woman folded her hands together and leaned on her knees. "But I can see they were wrong about at least one."

The pleasure that resulted from her compliment was indulgent. I did not need the approval of a stranger. Yet here I was, unable to meet her eyes.

She said, "And the woman you sought?"

"My sister. I want her to be alive." I took a deep breath, uncaring of my candor. "Desperately. She might be, but I do not know how to find her."

"What made you think she was alive?"

"I received a letter from her that made me think it true."

"A letter."

"Arrived without address, without seal. No way to find her. Almost like magic." I met her stare then. My conviction hung in the air.

"Magic?" she said, taking my bait. Her brow creased as she leaned away. "This is something you believe?"

"Only when things go unexplained. Like an impossibly-healed wound."

The woman frowned at the accusation. "And what of the girl you are with?"

"Emel?" It was a strange change in topic.

"Where does she come into this? Why is she here with you?"

"Her life was threatened." By my brother, I could not bring myself to say. Too much shame. It is one thing to have a brother want your throne. Another entirely for that brother to attempt to kill an innocent.

"Why?"

Why? It was a strange question, and one I realized I could not answer. I had not asked her why Kassim had tried to kill her. Did Emel know?

"So that is the only reason you have brought her. For protection?"

I was silent.

"I thought so," the woman said. "The way she watched you when you were ill . . ." She turned her hands, knuckles to palms, palms to knuckles. "Like she owed you everything. Like she would give anything in return." She leaned forward. "Saalim, do you know when she left you and your men that night she found me? She came to me, running, wild-eyed. She could have been lost. She would have lost you all in the dark like that. It was a fool's move. Do you know what she said when I told her so? That she had nothing more she could lose."

The flames were tall in front of me, illuminating the branches above, creating shadowed movement though there was nothing there.

"Have you considered," she asked, "what *you* might owe *her*?"

The question was strange. Something in her words struck cords of thought I had been holding taut. Something was there, but I did not understand what she knew about it.

She grew stern. "Tell her now if you plan to refuse her. While she can still return to her home."

"I won't tell her . . ." I stopped myself. This woman had no business discussing this with me.

"Look at you, fidgeting with your hands, staring at the ground, unable to finish your words. A boy in love, indeed." Though she chided me, it was done gently, and I did not take offense. "So this is how the king of Almulihi feels about a salt chaser?" I heard the surprise in her words.

"I am betrothed." Elbows resting on my knees, I watched the fire.

Who was this woman who called me Saalim and called my home Almulihi as if she had been born there? The flames were reaching, reaching, reaching up high. Reaching for air, for something they could not grasp. I felt like this woman and I were reaching for the same thing.

"Have you figured it out?" she asked, and her voice was changed. It was naggingly familiar. I turned to her, and the woman sitting there was no longer the stranger who had healed me. She was changed. She was someone else entirely . . .

She said, "Never did I think I would see the day my brother turned soft for a woman of the sand."

I barely heard the words, barely registered their meaning.

"Edala?" I stood up in a swift movement, both wanting to move toward her and away from her. She smiled, and I knew she could be no one else. I went to her, desperate for my family. She was all there: the impatience, the slyness, the self-satisfaction. "How?" I asked as I drew her to me. She felt the same as I remembered her. All bones and sinew.

When we sat back down, I stared at her, unable to turn away from the sister I thought I would never see again.

"That same magic you speak of," she said.

"But . . . *how?*" I pressed. "It was you this whole time?"

She nodded.

"Why did you not reveal yourself sooner?"

"I had to be sure of who you were." She waved her hands to stop me before I even started. "I knew you were my brother. But *who* you were, eh? Had you changed as the legends promised?" She smiled, then nodded. "You have."

I stiffened. "Legends?"

"The lost prince who is a slave until he—" Seeing my face, she stopped. "Do you know of what I speak?"

I shook my head, feeling a little sick. Something about what she said felt both right and wrong. There were no legends about me. But then, why did I crave hearing the words like a lost nomad craves water?

"Don't you have . . . ? Do you know . . . ?" She could not frame her question, chewing so much on her words. "Tell me: After Almulihi was attacked, what happened?"

I told her about how our father was so weak—had grown sick, did she know this?—that our mother had to kill him lest he be killed by the invaders. I told her how so many of the people died trying to fend off the army from the palace, how so many soldiers died, how Nadia was killed.

Edala looked away, holding her hand to her mouth, when I mentioned Nadia.

Our army defended the palace enough that eventually they retreated. I thought Kassim dead, Edala dead, because neither ever returned home. It seemed the news of what happened in Almulihi spread through the desert like wind, so many correspondences did I receive from people across the desert, across the sea, sending their condolences and mourning gifts. How could Kassim and Edala be alive and not have returned home immediately?

As I told this to Edala, the anger I had harbored toward her and my brother surfaced anew. That they left us, left our father sick. And to know that they were both alive. Gripping my knees, I thought of how I had grieved for them, for the loss of my entire family. They had been alive this whole time, selfishly biding their time until whenever they decided it was right to return.

And for Kassim, apparently, it was to steal the throne.

I wanted to lash Edala with my words, but her expression made me hold my tongue. Her cheeks were wet when she looked at me again, horror pulling her eyes and lips down. Her hands came up over her brow and she groaned.

"The worst part was that I could not return home. I could not return to you."

"It was selfish of you to stay away," I said.

"Masira," she murmured, "is so cruel. Oh, Saalim." She looked up at me, pleading. "There is so much that you are missing, so much that has happened. Does Emel know?"

"Know what?" I snapped, growing impatient.

"She must," Edala whispered to herself. "That would explain everything. Of course, I thought she would have told you, but then perhaps not." She looked at me again. "Let me start at the beginning." She took a deep breath, then began.

The palace had never felt like home for Edala. Maybe it was because there was always tension—between Kassim and myself, between my mother and father, between Edala and my mother—or maybe it was because life as a royal was not what she had ever wanted.

"Being a princess, to smile and be dressed in beautiful gowns to receive gifts, never did attract me as it did Nadia. And I fell in love, Saalim," she said quietly. Never would I have thought Edala and I confessing our secret loves to each other. She stared in the direction of the tree homes as she spoke. "Father forbade it, see, because he was not royal." So Edala went to Zahar.

Zahar let Edala spend days and nights at her home, allowing Edala the escape from the life she resented. Hidden in the palace gardens, Zahar taught her magic.

"She saw my unhappiness and was so kind to me that I couldn't see that she was driving the wedge further. I couldn't know what she planned . . ." Remorse made thick her words.

Zahar was a very capable enchantress. She was powerful. But Edala saw what it took to get that power, and knew she could have more. She went into the desert. "Father wouldn't allow me the life I wanted with the man I loved, so I would leave. I went to study, not to visit settlements, as I had said."

She learned about sacrifice and what was needed to take what she wanted from Masira.

"When I thought I could give no more and still had not achieved the connection to the goddess I wanted, I decided I would try once more. I would give her my soul."

Edala left her tent at high sun and journeyed well away from shade or shelter. She lay on her back, letting the sand burn her skin, letting the sun burn her body. It was painful, torturous, as the heat sucked her dry. If she died, she would die trying to have more magic than any enchanter could ever have. Finally, when she thought she could bear it no longer, she pretended she was a scorpion with a hard shell that protected her from the sun. She closed her eyes and believed it.

When she opened her eyes again, she had become exactly that.

"Masira took my soul," Edala said. "But she did not keep it. She gave it back and with it, she gave me everything. I am not at her mercy like an enchantress, who is fatigued by her use of magic. Or like jinn, who are bound by the ropes of their master and Masira. I am a si'la. I am free."

I was silent. I had only heard of si'la from legends. A shape-shifting, all-powerful spirit often described as evil. I told her what I knew, and she laughed.

"Yes, well they say that about jinn, and I can tell you that is not always true." She looked at me with a knowing glance that I did not understand.

"So you are magic." I exhaled. "That does not yet explain everything."

"No," she agreed. "It explains nothing. Saalim, have you heard the legend of the jinni and the ahira?"

Puzzled, I stared at her. "No, but Emel told me something . . ." It was when I was ill. I did not remember it well.

Edala nodded. "She does remember." Then she told me the story again.

A prince was trapped in a vessel after he begged an enchantress to save his home. He was forced to serve the wishes of others while his city crumbled to ruins, transformed into a place only of legends. His home would only be able to be restored when the prince was freed. He was a slave to one man after another until one day, an unusual master found him. She was an ahira, bound to her father's court. A slave like the jinni.

They fell in love, and when she was threatened to be sent away from her home—from the jinni—she made a final wish of freedom. The wish made the jinni human again so that he could become the king of his restored home.

"And what of the ahira?" I asked, heart racing.

"It seems she followed him home," Edala whispered. "Madinat Almulihi was his home. The enchantress was Zahar. You were the prince."

Chills swept down my neck. I clenched my fists tightly, willing this story to be false. "It is impossible." But even as I said it, I knew it was not.

"I can prove it."

"How?" The word was barely audible over my pounding heart.

"I can give you back the memories Masira has kept from you."

My eyes flashed to hers. "What do you mean?"

"When Emel wished for freedom, Masira gave her what she wished. But the goddess covers her tracks. Those who would be affected by the change—by the resurrection of Almulihi when before it did not exist, by the change in the salt trades, by the presence of a king who had been absent for hundreds of years—had their memories smudged away. That includes you, Saalim. But you feel that emptiness, don't you? That press of something that isn't quite what it seems. That lingering feeling that there is something more. You feel it with Emel, don't you?"

Searching through my mind for these memories felt like swimming in the canal. Open water, freedom, and then a wall of stone. Now that she said it, I felt it. The traces of what Masira had done.

"You can give me my memories back?"

"I can uncover Masira's tracks. If you want me to," she said. And I saw it again in her face: deep-seated pleasure that she had power, had out-smarted even a goddess.

It was not a question. I wanted all of what was rightfully mine back in hand. I looked up at the trees, the shadows still dancing above us, and saw the sky brightening from black into a deep blue.

What would those memories show? What would the ground reveal, turning up all that was buried? Was I ready to face that unknown and finally understand what had happened between Emel and me?

No.

Not yet.

First, I must finish with the past I knew.

25

EMEL

T he next morning, my skin was sticky from the air, my hair still damp from the night before. Remembering the evening—my time with Raheemah, Saalim's confession—I smiled and curled into myself.

On the day before, when Raheemah and I had left the men, she took me back to her living quarters. I followed her across the suspended bridge, each step making me grip the ropes more tightly as I bounced. How strange it was to be hosted by my young sister. We were close to the treetops here, and each brightly colored bird and flower pulled my attention.

"It is so different from home, eh?" Raheemah said, watching me as we crossed the bridge. "I love it," she continued as I nodded at her. "But I missed home, and still do sometimes."

Why did she sound so sad?

"It is why Jawar let me bring so much of our home here. Now if only I could share some of the wetness with the rest of the desert. We'd all fare better." She smiled, wiping away the hair stuck to her temple.

"The air is so thick, I can barely breathe," I said once I'd reached the end of the bridge.

"You get used to it." Raheemah led me inside, and I was surprised to see we were not alone.

Leaning forward, embroidering a long swath of linen, was Raheemah's mother.

"Sasha!" I cried. When she heard my voice she tore her gaze from her work and beamed at me.

"Emel!" She stood slowly, wincing as she straightened her knees, and wrapped me in a long hug.

"Once the stories of Father's death reached me, I begged Jawar to let us return home to get her." Raheemah said it so pragmatically. Did anyone mourn him?

Sasha caressed my face, cooing about how much I looked like Isra, how much she missed me. My chest squeezed with longing for my own mother, for the soft embraces of the harem.

Over tea, we told each other stories of our lives.

"Traveling with the king of Madinat Almulihi?" Raheemah was surprised, understandably. I told her a story of coincidence. I worked with the healer at the palace so, of course, I encountered him frequently. No jinni found his way into the tale.

"I am useful to him on this journey," I lied. "Because I know something of the desert." She did not need to know the bit about Kassim. She did not need to worry.

Raheemah and her mother told me about their village, how they had acclimated. There was an undercurrent of tension, though, which I could not understand.

"Jawar is a good man," Raheemah said after a long pause. She stared out a net-covered window. "I . . ." She paused and sipped her tea. She left it lingering there, never picking up the rest of her thought.

"What is it, Emah?" I looked from her to her mother, waiting for an explanation.

"He will be marrying another soon."

That did not suffice as explanation.

"Mama and I will be moved to the guest lodgings. His new wife will stay with him. Three moons and it will be a year since we were wed. I have not yet carried a child." Her eyes met mine meaningfully, and I understood then what she was telling me.

Now I began to understand the hurt.

Was the pregnancy all that time ago her last? Had the tonic she had taken from the healer harmed her womb? I thought about that choice she had made. Her life was beautiful and happy now, but she could not have a child to share it with. Had she known this would be the result of the tonic, would she have taken it? Or would being isolated from the palace—for she surely would have been cast out by our father, alone with an infant—have been any better? Unseen consequences lingered like shadows around every choice made.

Sasha said, "Jawar has been kind, but he needs children." She caressed Raheemah's hair with tears in her eyes.

"I am so sorry," I said to them both. Raheemah would still be his wife, but she would carry with her a lifelong burden of feeling as though she had failed.

After seeing her mother, she took me to bathe under the cool water, and we found ways to laugh despite her harbored sadness. We reminisced about our life before, comparing it to our lives now. How different things were.

Now, in the guest-house bed, I rolled onto my side, thinking of Saalim. What would have happened last night, had Tamam not come in?

Sitting up, I looked around the empty room. My gaze lingered on the vivid wall hangings and smooth wooden cups and bowls sitting on the nearby table. These things were so much like home, yet so different. I rose, wanting to find Saalim. I needed to tell him how I felt.

When I reached the clearing, Tamam, Amir, Nassar, Saalim, and an unfamiliar woman all glanced toward me as I approached. My eyes were fixed on Saalim, feeling like an ahira at dawn, wondering if the muhami would want to relive the night. Tentatively smiling, I moved toward him. He smiled in return, but his eagerness did not match mine. My pace slowed. There was something else in his eyes. Something had changed.

Saalim gestured to the woman. "Emel, this is Edala, my sister. She is ah . . . the one who helped us, who helped me."

Much had changed, indeed.

Her smile was genuine. "It is nice to meet you without disguise."

Amir scooped gruel into a bowl and handed to me. Then, he turned back to Edala. By the way he looked at her, I understood that I had interrupted something.

"Let me see your map, and I can show you," Edala said, taking the map from Amir. "The cave is here." Edala pointed to a blank space.

"And you think Kassim will be there?" Tamam asked. He stared at Edala, watching her hands, her face, the cross of her legs.

"If he is anywhere in this desert, it is there. Zahar spent much time in this cave. I suspect it is where the Darkafa live."

"Do you think it possible the woman he is with is Zahar?" Tamam asked.

"I do." She looked at him swiftly before she turned away, brushing back her hair.

I had missed so much. The gruel sat uneaten in my palms, and I stared at Edala nearly as intently as Tamam, as Nassar and Amir.

I remembered the drawing of Edala in her room. Though this woman was older, she looked the same. Clearly bred from royal blood, she had the high angles of face just as Saalim had, except her coloring was darker, like the Hayali.

"Emel," Edala said as Saalim and Amir discussed the suggested route to the cave. "Might we talk alone?"

Following Edala off the path, we walked through the trees, passing mud-crafted homes with families inside preparing for the day.

"I can change my form," she said when I asked her to explain her appearance. When we were away from listening ears, she added, "I am a si'la."

A si'la? I had not believed such things existed.

"Do you know what *you* are?" she asked me.

"I don't understand."

"The magic you carry, do you know of it?"

Though I stared at the ground, careful to step over every stick and bush and root, I still managed to catch my foot. "Masira's mark?" I asked as I gathered myself.

"Yes. It is much more than a change to your skin, though. The goddess herself has chosen you—for what exactly, I don't know. But because you carry that mark, you can do anything you desire with magic, should you choose to. You could become a si'la, like me. Maybe even more." Her eyes glittered like Altasa's had when she tried to sway me.

I would not let this illusion that I had any interest in magic go on longer than needed.

"I have no desire to be a conduit for Masira's volatility."

"A si'la does not pull the reins of Masira's fickle desires." She seemed smug. "The magic is mine to do with as I please. Do you see the difference? It is nothing like jinni magic."

She said *jinni magic* like she knew I was familiar. "You sound like Altasa. She tried to coax me to do the same."

"Altasa?"

"The healer of Almulihi."

"She knew magic?" she sounded doubtful.

I told her about the cricket.

Edala hummed to herself, running her fingers through her hair. "Do you know what else Masira's mark has done for you?"

A lizard sashayed up a nearby tree. In the canopy above, two bright red birds perched side by side.

Edala said, "Magic cannot affect you—or the things you care about—directly. I have seen it myself." She sounded so excited, I looked away from the birds back to her.

"Many times I tried to make you all do something. You and Saalim were untouchable."

"Saalim?"

She nodded, smiling warmly. "Because he is protected by you, I suspect. It must be the reason Zahar and Kassim have been unable to remove him from the throne."

I recalled all the occasions Saalim had nearly lost his life: the attacker on the ship who had taken him by surprise, the storm that ravaged the boat and yet left all the passengers alive, the night the guards went suspiciously missing from the palace and the Darkafa slipped in. Was it all me who had saved him?

Out loud, my thoughts continued. "But there was water on the journey, when our stores were depleted. I could not have done that . . ."

"Well, no. You aren't the only one who cares for Saalim." There was a glint in her eye. "Emel, have you not wondered why a jinni could not simply magic Saalim away?"

I had wondered that on our many nights of journeying.

"Magic cannot affect him, not if you don't want what it is asking. That tells me so much more about how you feel for him than words ever could." She placed her hand on my back. "For that, Emel, you have my gratitude and my promise that I will do whatever I can to help you. You have saved my brother twice now."

Twice.

"Because you loved him, he lives and Almulihi stands." When I finally met her eyes, I saw that there were tears. How did she know? "Anything you want. Anything you need. I feel it my duty to fulfill it."

I said finally, "You, too, saved Saalim. And I am just as grateful, if not more—"

"I could not find my brother only to lose him again."

"If I want anything," I said, taking a deep breath, "it is that I want nothing more to do with magic. I don't want it happening to me nor around me. I don't want it in my life."

She looked at me suspiciously. "You fear it?"

"I fear the shroud Masira covers us with when it's used." I thought of Saalim, a history he knew nothing of. Of Firoz and Rashid, living as though they had committed crimes they could not remember. Of all the ways peoples' lives were changed without them having any say at all. Thinking of my life as an ahira—a life I had no control over, a life I never chose. Magic did to people what my father did to me.

It took away choice.

It was wrong.

The rest of that day I spent with Raheemah. Each moment with her a little harder than the last, knowing our time together was dwindling. During our midday meal, we pulled out my map.

"I'm so embarrassed," she laughed, pointing at the R she had drawn almost a year ago. "My hand is much steadier now." She looked behind her. "Oh, where is Jawar? He will think this hilarious." She took the map from me and ran it across the bridge.

"Look at this!" I heard her cry. Though I could not make out his words, I heard the teasing in his tone and then their laughter.

I was still smiling when Raheemah tumbled back in.

"He said we are not even close. It's here." She pointed to an empty spot north.

"Yes, Amir has told me," I said, pulling the map away from her.

Later, we walked back to the waterfall. The villagers we passed smiled to Raheemah, waving, and bowing to her. *Akama* they called her.

"What does it mean?" I asked.

"It is what I am here. It means 'parent of the adult.' It is like a queen, but . . . Jawar explained that here they do not have kings and queens. Instead, he is their guide, their ears, their tongue should they need help. He is the one they seek should something need resolution, but otherwise he lets the villagers do as they see fit."

"I like that," I said.

"Me, too. Though it feels strange to be an Akama to women three times my age."

When we reached the fall, those who sat at the river's edge moved aside for Raheemah and me to lay down our things.

"I cannot believe you can bathe somewhere like this every day. I have never felt so clean," I said, untying the wrap Raheemah had provided for me.

Raheemah stripped off her clothes without pause, just as she had the evening before. Wading into the river, I let myself enjoy the pull of the current on my legs, the soft bed of mud beneath my feet. When I stood beneath the fall of water, it pounded my skin so hard it stung. I could hear nothing around us.

"Emel, come," Raheemah called into my ear. She tugged hard on my wrist and led me into a very narrow space between the rocks and the water that fell. The splash of water was so loud around us I tensed, squinting as the spray of water reached my face.

"What is it?"

"Your friends." She tilted her head to our left.

Though it was blurred through the water, I saw figures moving slowly down the river's edge. They were with two brightly-dressed figures. From what I could tell, none of the women bathing seemed bothered by their presence.

"What is it like, traveling with all of them?" Raheemah asked. "I know it is unfair of me to say, but something about Nassar makes me shiver. He is kind to you?"

My laugh was muffled by the splashing water. "He is very loyal to Saalim and Madinat Almulihi. He would do me no harm unless he thought me a traitor." The rocks scraped my back as I leaned against them. "They are all good men."

"And what of Saalim? Are you going to tell me about him or continue to lie?"

Her arms were crossed, one eyebrow raised.

"There is nothing—"

"You're lying to me. I know he did not take you on this journey because you 'know the desert.'" She leaned out from the water. "Come, they've left."

We passed through the wall of water.

"Edala said you are a pair."

My gaze snapped toward her. She called her *Edala* like she had known her forever. The same magic Edala used to disguise herself now blended the past and present, brushing away incompatible memories. None in the village were surprised to see a new woman with us. In their minds, it was always Edala.

"Fine," Raheemah said, misunderstanding my scowl. She looked up at the break in the trees. It was growing dark. "Don't tell me anything. I don't want our last moments together to be . . . whatever this is." She folded her wrap around her and tied it closed. Slipping on her sandals—the same ones we wore back home, I saw—she took my hand.

"I don't want to say goodbye to you again."

"This time," I said, "we know it won't be goodbye. I will come back."

"Promise me one thing."

"Hmm?"

"That you will be as happy as I am."

"But what about . . . ?" I pressed my hand to my stomach.

"Look at my life," she said quietly, trailing her fingers under the waterfall. "It does not serve me to dwell on that which I do not have when I have so much."

"Since when has my baby sister become so wise?"

We left Raheemah and Jawar that evening with warm goodbyes and packs stuffed with fresh fruit. More than we could eat, I told Raheemah. But she did not care, she said she felt better knowing I had something.

We found our camels still tied near the river crossing, just as Edala had promised.

"See," Edala said as we took their reins in hand. She claimed someone from the village came to care for travelers' camels several times a day, but now I wondered if it was all lies, and she had simply magicked their well-being.

With Edala leading the way, we began our journey to the cave of the Dark-afa. If they weren't there, if Kassim couldn't be found, we would return to Madinat Almulihi and wait for him to find us.

26

SAALIM

"Look here," Edala said to Amir, pointing at his map when we had stopped at an oasis. These two were always back and forth about the damn map. "This is where it is. We are right here," she said, leaning back onto her hands. Beside Edala was Tamam, whose gaze followed her hands as they slid near him.

I would have thought nothing of it had Emel not mentioned it to me—the way Tamam looked at Edala, acted around her. Emel was right. Now I could not unsee how they seemed to orient around each other. Never had I seen him like this.

Could he be the man Edala referred to—the man she once loved? I remembered nothing of them before Edala fled into the desert. Then again, I had thought of little except the crown that would one day sit upon my brow.

Following the line of heads bent over the map, my gaze settled on Emel, her mouth curving into a half smile at something Amir said. My blood thrummed, pumping swiftly through me, and I looked away, thinking of Edala's tale to distract me from Emel's mouth.

I was a jinni. Emel had freed me. How could I possess no memories of such wild stories? It was well into the morning as we sat under the shade, deciding on the best time to arrive at the Darkafa's cave. We were surprisingly close to

Emel's home, I realized, when I glanced down at the map. Saying as much aloud, Emel looked puzzled.

"How can we be so close? It took us nearly forty days to get to Almulihi. We have been traveling half that time."

She was right.

Edala smiled. "I don't take small steps."

Darkness crossed Emel's face.

Amir gasped. "What do you mean?"

"The desert bends beneath my feet so we can travel more swiftly. Each step might be twenty."

Amir appeared wildly delighted.

"You use magic," Emel said bluntly. Even I recoiled from her tone. Tamam scowled as he turned to Emel.

Edala was unapologetic. "Time is not an unlimited resource."

Without another word, Emel rose and went to find shade under the furthest tree. I followed.

"What is it?" I asked, watching her unroll her mat with the methodical movements of someone in prayer.

"I don't want to be around it."

Magic. It was like she had said this one thousand times. She seemed so tired.

She went on, "It might seem harmless, warping the desert beneath her feet, but that is what Zahar thought when she made you a jinni. Who lies in the folds of the desert? What happens to them?"

"She said with her magic there is no change to the people affected by it. There is no loss of memories," I said feebly, trying to tear down the wall growing fast between them.

"Still, it should not be used so carelessly. It is not the way for a human to live—with divine gifts, without real work."

Understanding, I sat next to her as she brushed sand off the mat's surface. After a long stretch of silence, I said, "Anisa still flies."

Emel stilled. "Your eagle?"

Lowering my voice, I said, "Tamam interrupted us at Jawar's. I have been left without an answer." I waited, but she continued to brush the mat. "Edala told me of our past."

Her mouth fell open. "Everything?"

"No, not everything. Some."

Though her face was drawn in exhaustion, when her eyes met mine, they were wide and awake. "Then you have your answer already."

"Dare I believe it?" I held out my hand.

"Yes," she whispered as she took it. "There is so much I want to tell you."

"But?"

"Fewer eyes," she said, gently squeezing my hand.

Behind us, I could hear our companions talking back and forth about the journey, Edala and Nassar arguing about his opinion of the people who lived in the nearby settlement.

I asked, "May I share your shade?"

She helped me unroll my mat, dusting it just as carefully with the palm of her hand.

When everyone had quieted down and found places to sleep, I rolled to my side.

"Would you want to see your sisters again?" I thought of her with Raheemah, how happy it made her. "We can visit your home."

"You would delay our return so I could go to my village?"

For her, I would do anything.

Before I could answer, she said, "I do not want to. Not yet."

Her eyes were as dark as night. I studied them as if there were stars I might find in their depths, trying to understand what she could not yet face at home. "You will travel into a desert you've never traveled to before, and you will see the Hayali and go into hostile caves, but you will not return home."

"It is easier to face that which you don't know."

Returning to a city I'd failed where people knew my father's secret. My secret. Yes, I understood. "We will travel to the cave just after midday, so try to sleep."

A long pause. She turned to me. "Why do you hate the desert so much?"
I could not meet her eyes. Instead, I stared at the sky. "I don't hate—"
"You do." She sighed.

"It can be a hostile place with people who match it in inhospitality."

"I see beautiful bleakness with strong people who have learned to thrive in it."

"Taking another's life because of this or that minor offense, trading people like something to be sold. Never mind the incessant heat and the scarcity of water and food."

"But with every bad there is good should you choose to see it. What of the night so dark the moon is the lantern? And the fox that hunts by its light? Or Masira's birds that take water and meat from the dead? Or the sand that is smoothed by wind, the same wind that moves dunes like they are nothing. And the people who live here make it even better. We've been shaped by the hands of the desert—by the sun and sand. Think of Raheemah, of Edala. Think of me. Of your mother."

I winced, hoping Emel did not see my face. "I did not know her."

"But you are half of her, and since I know you, I know that she was good."

What I knew of the woman that gave birth to me was that it was a mistake. Right before my father was to be wed to my mother, he visited a band of eastern nomads so prominent in the desert, they often sent correspondence to the larger settlements and cities letting them know where they headed next. There he met a woman who captivated him, he said. He was drawn to her like no other. They lay together, and he thought he would make her his queen.

But, of course, that was not to be. His father forbade it, and the pieces had already been placed for a wedding to the daughter of the Hayali king.

It was not until I was born that my father—married to Kena now—learned of my existence. He sent for me and my birth mother, and took me in as his firstborn.

The timing was such that most could be fooled into believing the queen had a son. It is not often that the people saw their queen, especially when carrying a child. Of course, though, the palace staff knew, and word spread.

But I was accepted and raised as one of their own. Queen Kena's tolerance for my presence was boundless. She treated me like one of her own, and as she grew to love me, she found many ways to forgive my father for what he had done. My birth mother was brought to Almulihi to watch me grow, I learned much later in life. She stayed for years before she finally left the city to return to her family. There was still a bitterness—an acrid over-steeped tea that dried my tongue—when I thought of how she could leave her child behind.

"Where did you go?" Emel whispered when I did not respond to her.

I said nothing, sorting the angry thoughts.

"Are you thinking of her?"

I nodded. "Just as you cannot face your home because it has left wounds, it is hard for me to face the thought that the woman who gave birth to me was good." I told her what I knew of her, of how she left.

"It is unfair, isn't it? Our expectations of mothers?"

"How do you mean?"

"We want them to lay down their lives for us. Stop everything they want or plan to do so that they can be there for us. As if they have no life of their own. Many mothers do that, even *want* to do that. So we take it for granted."

Her fingers stretched toward my neck, and she rested them there. Her touch was comforting and familiar, but I could still remember a time where it was foreign and exciting. Two worlds collided in my mind, creating clouds of dust that cleared only to obscure and confuse something else.

"My mother tried to flee our settlement and was killed," she said. "I was angry and jealous." Her voice softened. "I hated her for what she did—leaving her children. But I envied that she was strong enough to do it. Even as her selfish child, I could see that she had to take care of herself." Her fingers were soft on my cheek. "So maybe that is why *your* mother left. She had to do the same."

It was hard to hear Emel defend the woman I had grown up despising.

"Maybe," I said, no longer wanting to think of her.

After some time, Emel fell asleep. My eyelids grew heavy, the heat of the day lulling me into lethargy despite the urgency of my thoughts, the planning and preparing for what lay next.

Still, sleep did not come. I sat up. The sand was smooth as Emel said, with watery heat, moving like a spirited wind, rising up from it. The sun was white-hot against blue sky. A breeze, the faintest that could be felt, nudged the leaves and I could hear their whisper. I had vague memories of admiring oases. Of a life where I had learned to love the desert.

Was this something contained in the memories Edala could return to me? Perhaps I could take those memories, take the words from Emel's lips, and learn how to do so again.

"If we don't leave now, we will arrive when it's dark," Edala said, her voice a rope tugging me awake.

Slowly, I roused, rolling the stiffness from my shoulders. I jumped up when I saw the sun had begun its descent. We should have already been on our way.

Emel sat with Amir sharing strips of dried meat.

Edala said, "If it wasn't clear, that meant that we all need to leave now."

We were packed and on our camels before Edala could chide us again.

We traveled toward a cluster of dunes that hid the cave where the Darkafa were believed to be. Edala reminded us repeatedly that they were not a people prone to violence and to behave as such. Still, I feared what we were walking into. I was glad Edala would be with us. It would be foolish to seek out Kassim and Zahar without her, as they could easily overpower us. And even if they weren't there and it was just the Darkafa, we would be greatly outnumbered if she was wrong about their peacefulness.

"What do you know of this goddess they search for?" I asked.

"The goddess!" Edala laughed mirthlessly. "It took me a while to piece together *that* story. Luckily, the Darkafa have been all over the desert, searching for hundreds of years now. Sorry, I know the warping of time is confusing." She looked at me with a small shrug, then back at the dunes we approached. "Over time I learned the Darkafa were much more than a strange cult. It did not take much to convince them to tell me their mission." She rubbed her finger against her lip. "See, when Zahar made you a jinni, she was depleted of strength. It took all she had left to do the same to Kassim."

"But why turn Kassim?" I asked.

"I still don't know the answer to that question." She chewed her lip, lost in thought.

She did not speak for some time, the silence stretching as we waited.

"Please continue your tale," I begged.

"Where was I?" Edala asked. Then, "Ah. She lost your vessel during the attack on the palace. I wish I could have seen how angry she was to have lost you." She chuckled to herself. "She did not want to lose Kassim, too. She needed someone to protect his vessel while she recovered.

"She showed small magic to aimless nomads who thirsted for a purpose, convincing them she was a goddess. They promised to protect Kassim until she was strong enough to return to him. Did they know he was a jinni, or did they think his vessel treasure? I don't know, but I do know they were devoted to their task like zealots. After so many generations, they transformed into their own sect, really, idolizing the goddess Zahar." She rolled her eyes and then looked at me. "They knew 'when the king crossed the desert,' Zahar would return. See, she had set the rule that when Saalim was freed, he'd return as king. She rightfully assumed he would be long gone from Almulihi by the time he was freed—taken away from the ruins to wherever his masters lived.

"The Darkafa were diligent stewards of the vessel—always leaving a maimed child as his master so they could not—"

"Wait." I stilled, a chill spreading across my back. "The child is his master?"

"Do you know the current keeper?"

I explained the girl Bilara. "She has no eyes to see, no tongue to speak."

Edala nodded. "I imagine she was the keeper. Of course, now that you have returned to Almulihi, Zahar had to retrieve Kassim. She is his master now, I am sure."

Mostly to himself, Nassar said, "So that is the reason for the black hands they leave behind. Their way of telling others they'd already searched that settlement for the goddess. I've never seen anything like it . . ."

I asked, "So she was waiting in the cave for me to return? Playing a goddess?"

"No. After Kassim, she had to heal. She changed her form." Edala shook her head. "Unlike how I change, she required ingredients and mixtures to become something less of what she was to save her energy and heal. From what I've heard, she was first a cricket."

Emel's inhalation was sharp. "How do you know all this?" She was finding fewer reasons to speak with my sister after Edala confessed to using magic to speed our travels. So even though the question was layered in accusation, I was glad she spoke to her at all.

Edala held up her hands. "Whether I want to or not, I feel the magic in this desert. Like strings attached to me, I feel their vibrations when magic is used. And, too," she glared at Emel, "people are always talking. It's their constant storytelling of unusual events that get me most of my information. I don't *magic* the information from them, I use my ears." She took the camel's reins in her hands again. "I suspect that when Zahar grew strong in that form, she changed to the griffon, still requiring less energy to heal than a human, eh? I can't tell you how many people have reported odd behaviors of a griffon over the past sixty years or so."

Amir's eyes were glazed as he shook his head slowly back and forth. I felt the same as him. This was all too much.

Edala went on excitedly. It was very much like her to enjoy an audience. "Being a griffon allowed her more easily to search for Saalim, I think. When she was strong enough, she finally was human again. I imagine a very weak one, because I have not seen her nor felt much in the way of her magic."

Amir said, "This is the wildest thing I have ever heard."

Edala continued. "People have told of impossible things: crickets that jumped into a bird's nest, a griffon that dove into waves and never returned to air. When those impossible things coincided with tugs of magic, I put it together." Her smugness made me smile. My sister had, indeed, returned.

The sand grew coarser as we neared the cave, and I could see these dunes were more like mountains than hills of sand—they were jagged and sturdy.

Emel was beside me. "We are moving too fast, Edala." Her words were so taut, I thought she might snap in front of me. The sun seemed to have barely moved, yet we had traveled a day's journey. Still, we had far to go.

"We'd otherwise arrive in the middle of night," Edala said.

Emel tugged the reins of her camel. "It was the one thing I asked." She twisted her body so she faced my sister.

"I live and breathe magic. You asked of me something impossible." At once the camels stopped moving. My eyes shot to Edala. The pull of her fingers, tucked into her palms, told me anger—and magic—drove her decisions. She was fury and bone beneath her traveler's robes.

Emel did not back down.

"You cannot deny the drain the magic causes, the misery and ache that it can leave behind. Every time you do something even small, there are ripples that turn to waves, and the desert suffers. Even if you claim your magic leaves no traces, it is inevitable that it will!"

Now was not the time for this. Magic, I agreed, had fouled us, but right then, we needed what it was giving us. "Emel—"

Both Edala and Emel stared at me. I closed my mouth.

My sister turned to Emel. "You overstate."

"I don't!" Emel clenched the reins in her fists. "I lived through it. So did he!" She pointed at me. "So did Nassar!"

Confusion creased Nassar's face. He opened his mouth to protest, but Emel did not let him.

"See? He doesn't even remember a past he's lived. But you feel it there, don't you?" Emel asked Nassar. "You don't remember handing my father the whip that gave me the scars on my back."

My mouth dropped open. Nassar recoiled from her words, and looked at me apologetically. "I . . . I did not . . . I don't know what . . ."

"It is all right," I whispered to him. Sons, what was happening?

My sister leapt off her camel and went toward Emel. "Magic can never be cleared from this sand."

"Edala," Tamam said, a warning of caution.

She acted as though she didn't hear him. "So grow used to it."

Emel said, "Leave Masira to her own doings. Cut her off from this world. It belongs to her Sons. I'd do it myself if I could."

"You would have to kill every single one of us."

Emel leaned down off her camel, staring into Edala's eyes like an eagle peering at prey. For a breath, I admired her bravery, but then she said, "If you won't stop on your own, it would be for the best."

Leaping off my camel at the same time as Tamam, I moved toward them. "Stop this." I turned to Edala and said, "We can move more slowly, arrive tomorrow at dusk. Let us travel without your help right now." I was putting too much pressure on everyone in our party. Stress was adding tension where it didn't need to be.

Edala pinned her gaze on me. "Clearly, I am not wanted here. It matters not to me. I can live happily whether Almulihi is standing or rubble." She turned away from me as she wiped her cheek.

A violent wind whipped up around us, the sand pelleting my face and hands. When the wind passed, she was gone.

"Edala?!!" Tamam called. He spun on his heels, calling her name again and again.

"She's left," Emel said, almost as smug as Edala. She wouldn't look at me.

Tamam continued to call her name, pleading with her to come back, his voice splintered with longing. I could not stand it.

I said, "Let's continue."

Amir gasped. "To the cave? But we will be outmatched, outnumbered." That we would have no magic on our side was left unsaid.

"We go." I nearly shouted as I went back to my camel, trying to coax the beast down so I could mount it. It wouldn't listen. As if it sensed my willingness to kill it with my naked hands, it finally lowered to the ground, and I was able to seat myself upon the saddle. When we were all ready to continue the journey, I noticed Edala's camel was gone.

Silently, we traveled on. The journey took much longer than we expected. Bleary-eyed and quiet, we arrived at the cave just after dawn.

"What if they attack?" Nassar whispered to me as we dismounted.

Handing my camel's reins to Amir, I said just as quietly, "We are trained soldiers. We fight." My tone implying more confidence than I felt. Should they attack, should Kassim or Zahar be there, we would be easy prey without my sister.

"And if Kassim is a jinni?"

I exhaled away my doubt. A leader must feign confidence if he does not feel it. "We are brothers. I refuse to believe he won't at least talk with me first."

"But if his master commands otherwise?"

He was right. But what choice did I have? "You can stay with Amir if you wish."

Nassar followed us, and we left Amir with the camels. The cave was tucked into a rocky dune, and as we moved near its mouth, sand dripped down its entrance like the falling water in Jawar's village.

Emel looked up uneasily, apparently more worried about sand blocking our way than walking into a cave of madmen.

The cave darkened quickly. Slowly, voices trickled down the tunnel, and as the light dimmed behind us, a bright glow grew before us.

"We should let them know we approach," I said. "I do not want them to think it an attack."

"But brother," a voice said from behind us. "We already know you are here."

Kassim.

At the same time I felt my belt lighten, the sound of my own blade leaving its sheath rang in the air.

I had not removed it.

Everything happened so fast. My wrists were grabbed, pulled behind me. I could hear the huff of Emel's breath as she struggled. Darkness and tugging hands kept me from comprehending what was happening to Tamam and Nassar. "Careful with them. It will be no fun if they die," Kassim said. "Hello, dove. Sorry about the fire . . ."

"Don't touch me," Emel spat.

I struggled hard against my restraint to no avail. "Leave her!" I shouted. Kassim sighed.

Tamam was still fighting, I could hear his effort, feel the jostling as they bumped into whomever restrained me. Pulling my hands was of no use. The man had them locked behind my back.

"Why are you doing this?" I could only see my brother's silhouette, but his voice was unmistakable.

"You mean to say you don't know?" Kassim asked, drawing near.

Silence fell as Tamam was finally overcome. Relieved when I heard his ragged breaths, I said to Kassim, "All this to be king? We are family."

Kassim just laughed.

A sharp pressure hit my back, driving me deeper into the cave toward the orange light.

We entered a cavern taller than it was wide. People gathered at the periphery. Behind them, I could see more tunnels that led to places I did not want to know. Were it not for their pale skin and scarred scalps, I would have thought them travelers by their dress. But even without their black cloaks or dark gloves, I knew it was the Darkafa. Just as Edala had predicted, this was where they lived.

We were pushed to the center of the room. "Secure them," Kassim said. And then, impossibly, he reached into the sand and with his fingers coaxed a stone rod from the ground. The Darkafa cheered at the magical display. It was then that I saw the ropes and short knives they clutched in their hands. Bile burned my throat.

"Let them go," I said when they shoved me to the pillar. "If you want to be a king, you only need me dead." Emel was still unharmed. Nassar, too. Tamam's fight left him with swellings on his cheeks and bleeding from his brow and lip, one eye closed tight.

Kassim approached me as the others were bound. Nearly my height exactly, our eyes level. Our mother had always said we were as opposite as our eyes. Mine like the sun, his a storm. Now, his eyes glittered like polished silver.

"Actually," he said, "that is not quite true. It seems as if we might do better without her." He nodded to Emel.

She did not miss it. "What of our friendship?" She paused. "Was I only a means to reach Saalim?" I heard it loudly: her sadness, real and undulating.

Kassim looked at her with a flash of regret, but he said nothing.

The Darkafa watched us. What were they planning? Women were clustered behind the crowd; I saw babes in their arms. Did they really live here? Disgusted, I looked to my companions. We all were still standing, though the hang of Tamam's head worried me. There was a press of another's hand against my own. Emel.

"I am sorry," she whispered, and I felt her breath against my ear. "This is my fault."

Pressing my fingers against her palm, I said to Kassim. "If you are so powerful, be done with me. Why this show? What are you waiting for?"

"I am unimpressed," Emel said, her voice hardening. "I've seen a jinni work his magic. He needs no display, no show. You must not be as powerful as Saalim was, eh? Is that where your anger lies? Are you jealous?"

The ground shook, sand fell from above us like rain. The people in the cave screamed and dropped to the ground, glee etched on the faces of most despite their fear. The knives that slipped from their palms in their panic told me Edala may not have been wrong. They carried weapons, but they did not know how to use them. Violence was not of their nature.

Emel whispered, "Still, it isn't enough, is it?" Kassim's chest heaved like he'd pulled an anchor by himself.

The ground shook harder. Tamam fell forward, his arms taut behind him like a sail in wind. Emel knocked into me, and I dropped onto my knees. The shaking stilled, but the sand cascading from crevasses above did not stop.

A rolling whisper rushed through the people, and they rippled apart. Words slipped through the susurrus: goddess, presence, here.

I stiffened.

"Kassim was waiting for me," a voice said from the parting swarm. I knew that voice. I remembered that voice. I felt sick at the sound, as if I had drunk some foul tonic.

Zahar.

She came forward, just as I remembered her: small as a sparrow but face as sharp as a griffon's, mouth pulled down with perpetual displeasure.

Forgetting I was tied, I lunged forward, fury for all she had done driving me. I snapped back hard, my skin burning from the tight ropes. "What have you done?" I cried.

She sighed. "What have *I* done? Me? What about you? What about your father?"

My father?

"This is all more complicated than it needed to be." She sounded bored. "Were it not for that girl, we would have been done with this already, see? I had hoped I could change her mind about you, but it was not to be."

My thoughts reeled. Zahar and Emel? I could not make sense of anything.

Zahar came close enough that I could see the creases around her eyes. She was not much younger than my mother. Facing Emel, she said, "We could have been something together—salt chasers, eh? You have the ability, but you shun it. Squandering your gift. You betray the sand in your blood by choosing him." She spat onto the ground.

The people around us trembled, staring at the spit muddied with sand like it was salt.

"Altasa?" Emel asked quietly. I heard the confusion and the certainty tearing each other apart as she sorted through them.

Altasa? I stared at the healer. She looked nothing like the frail old woman who had traipsed through the palace. But then, hadn't Mariam mentioned Altasa looked well? Hadn't Nika said the same, that Emel had been good for her? I had not seen the old woman for . . . how long had it been? Two moons? If she had magic at her disposal, what could she have done in that time?

Zahar laughed. "I've always thought Altasa was a nice name . . . But we are not here to talk of me." She grew serious and stepped in front of me, just out of reach. Even with my arms bound, she was not strong enough to risk getting close. "We are here for Saalim. And Emel, of course. We have tried our magic. Imagine my disappointment—and Kassim's!—when he found that even he could not sway Masira to act for him. Curious how she placed you in my keeping. Purely accidental, you know. I was happy to take on an apprentice while I healed. Even grinding seeds put me out for too long. And when I learned you were marked? When I learned that it was *you* who freed Saalim and forced me back to this form!" She gestured to herself. "Ah, Masira . . ." She laughed. "If we had swayed your opinions, if you had cared less about Saalim, we might finally have brought about his death through magic. But you were stubborn as my sister." She shook her head and looked at the sand. "How could we kill him if Masira's chosen wanted otherwise?"

Chills pulled taut my skin. It was *only* Emel who protected me from death? I stepped ever so slightly in front of her—as much as the ropes would allow.

"Ah!" Zahar barked, missing nothing. "It is too late, Saalim. We have to do things more *traditionally*. We did not expect you to walk right into our nest. So now, my king, your protector has to die. Then, we can kill you."

Zahar spun and faced the Darkafa. "My children!"

They dropped to their knees, mumbling about the goddess and her voice and her power.

The same healer who had cured my fevers, aches, and wounds when I was a boy, now gestured to us. "They are here, and they are ready to be sacrificed. Kill the girl first. Then, the king. Unless . . ." She held up a hand in question to Kassim. "The brother would like the honors? It is your throne, after all."

A gust of wind pushed the torch flames into a frenzy, but I did not blink.

I watched Kassim, and prepared to be killed by my brother.

IV.

Reborn

———◆———

Wilajad

I t was in those days that Eiqab came to the desert to walk amongst the People, for he grew greedy for the praise of Man. Disguised as a human, he wandered for many moons. He was pleased by the strength his cruelty wrought, but angered to find his worshippers living beside Wahir's oases and dancing beneath Wahir's pale light.

Eiqab hung his head and returned to his brother in shame, saying, Even in the deep vastness of the desert Man worships me by name only, for in their hearts they praise the gifts of Wahir.

Wahir confessed then, The men who live upon my great waters and worship me grow weak and resentful, so I made the oceans as a desert, poison to drink, that Man might face adversity and grow in strength and virtue.

In this way, the Brothers understood one another and recognized Life was best when balanced between desert and ocean, sun and moon.

Masira once again saw wisdom in her sons and said: I am not desert nor ocean, sun nor moon, but I am all things and unfit for such Life. I will leave here and ask only that you give to me the Dead, so all things that are mine return to me.

In this way the vultures of the sands and the waves of the sea carried the Dead back to Masira.

—Excerpt from the Litab Almuq

27

EMEL

The Darkafa were restless, waiting for Kassim's response to Zahar's question: Would he kill us, or would he let them do it? There was an ethereal stiffness to Kassim's posture. He looked just like a jinni. How had I missed it before?

My mouth grew dry, and my heart thudded. I silently pleaded that he look at me, just once. Then, his eyes met mine. Silver and bright, with magic brimming in their depths.

I had hoped to goad him into something foolish: trying to make him use his magic to bring chaos to the cave and secure us time to escape. But those efforts had failed. Now, all I had was our short past together.

"Please," I mouthed to him.

For a moment his face softened, the menace gone. Then, he turned away from me, gestured to us, and said to the Darkafa, "Let the devoted culminate their life's work."

Slowly, they pushed toward us, and Kassim was gone.

No.

Edala had said they were not a violent people, and though there were many things she had been wrong about, I did not think she would have been wrong about this. She had lived lifetimes in this desert. She knew its people.

But my lifetime in the desert was not nothing, and the craze in these peoples' eyes reminded me of the craze of my father's people. Those who had worshipped him like a god. The Darkafa were *not* violent, but they would be, if their god asked it of them.

"You will kill for this woman who claims to be a goddess?" I called, desperate now. "What goddess needs you to kill for her? The true goddess—Masira—can do it herself."

"Masira has done nothing," a man hissed as he approached me, a short knife clutched at his chest like someone who has only used it to skin a carcass.

"Have you seen the si'la on the sand?" I pressed. "The one who sleeps in the skull of the beast, who bends the desert to lengthen her steps?" Others stopped and listened now. It felt like a game of ghamar. I held two cards in my hand: the healer, the si'la. "What goddess cannot even wield her pet?" I could not see Kassim nor Zahar as the Darkafa drew closer. "Zahar is not a goddess. She is a healer who has learned to use Masira's gifts. Her magic is limited. Weak as the ingredients she uses! The si'la uses nothing but her will. And the si'la is out there. You can find her. I can take you to her."

"Lies!" a man shouted.

"All has happened as the goddess said it would," another said.

They were not of a mind to be persuaded, and like a ship with a fractured hull, I felt myself sinking.

A man with rope in hand rushed to Saalim's feet, binding them fast. I thrust my heel down hard on his arm. Kicking, kicking, kicking. With a grunt, he grabbed my feet as another bound them. The rope burned.

A man brought his knife to my face, showing me the blade.

"The child!" Saalim said suddenly. "I know where she is."

None seemed to hear.

"Bilara!" I shrieked over the din. "We know where Bilara is!"

There was a noticeable drop in the chatter. The man dropped his knife to his side.

"My daughter?" A woman said from a cluster of bodies. "You know where she is? They took her from me. They took her to that place."

"The keeper," some whispered.

The man with the knife said, "The goddess said she knows where she is. That she will take us to her." He turned to his people. "We don't need them."

"Why hasn't she taken you to her yet?" I said, looking at the mother. "It's because she doesn't know where she is. I've met Bilara myself. She carries a locked silver box with her, and she loves dates sweetened with sugar."

The mother's eyes filled with tears as she made her way through the crowd. Her palms pressed together as she neared me, desperate to hear more of the daughter she missed. The more I spoke, the calmer the Darkafa grew. We had found a way out.

Suddenly, a great crack shot through the cave, loud like thunder, shaking the ground as Kassim's magic had done. Then, the darkness was gone in a flash as sunlight broke in. Blinking, I saw an entire wall of the cave fall away as if torn open by an enormous hand.

Wind cleared the dust, and at the entrance was Edala, striding forward silently.

"Fools," she said to us as our bindings fell away. "Why would you think it safe to come here without me? You should have gone home." She ushered us away from the Darkafa, suppliants on their knees as they watched Edala. More a goddess than anything I had ever seen. Magic undulated off of her like heat from the ground, her eyes bright as flame and her movements strong as iron.

Saalim nudged me toward the cave's exit. "Hurry. Go to Amir. He should have the camels ready." Nassar was already sprinting in that direction. I glanced behind me and saw Tamam had fallen to the ground. He was on his back, his eyes closed. "Saalim—" I pointed to his best soldier.

Edala saw him, too. "Tamam!" Never have I heard such a broken cry.

A great force struck my back, stopping my breath and dropping me onto my knees.

Clutching my chest, I sat up. Everyone in the cavern had been pushed away. Then I saw Edala bent over Tamam, her cheeks wet. He hadn't moved.

No.

I curled away from the scene.

Edala pressed her hands to his face, her lips to his brow. Saalim tried to rise, to approach them, but he was met by an unseen barrier. None could move near them.

Another shudder rocked us, and stones dropped from the ceiling, sand spilling more rapidly this time. "It will collapse!" someone called from the mass of people.

The Darkafa scrambled to their feet, trying to flee the cave, but were caught against the same invisible wall. They were blocked from coming near us. From escaping. Another crack of splintering stone sounded from above us. As I jumped to my feet, silence fell like a thick blanket muffling everything around us. I knew that silence.

It was the quiet of stilled time.

At the peak of the cave, a stone, broken off from the fragile ceiling, was suspended in the air. Edala's magic was the only thing keeping the cave from complete collapse. I gaped at the scene for only a moment before I realized that Saalim, Nassar, and Edala were all still moving. Then, motion on the ground caught my attention.

Praise Eiqab, it was Tamam! He was alive! He shifted his head, bent his knee. He reached up and covered Edala's hand resting on his face. She cooed his name before she yelled at us to get out.

Saalim lunged to me. "Are you injured?" He grabbed my hand, leading us out of the cavern.

"No," I huffed.

Never had being under the sun felt so liberating. I slowed to a walk. The stillness of the desert, of dust in the air, hurled me back to when Saalim would stop time so we could move freely through a world with its breath held. Only now it did not stop life from moving forward. It stopped death.

The maw of the cave was jagged and gaping, pieces of it scattered all around. We wove between boulders as we went to Amir, who waited with our camels. Had he seen Edala arrive?

Saalim slowed. His grip on my arm tightening. I followed his gaze.

No.

Amir was lying on the ground, unmoving. Praying it was only Edala's magic, I followed Saalim as he ran to his soldier.

Saalim dropped to his knees by his side. When I saw Amir's slack face, the pallor of a body without a beating heart, I knew there was no magic at play. His soul waited for Masira's birds.

"Amir!" Saalim shouted, grabbing his friend's shoulders and shaking him roughly.

Nassar was beside Saalim, shouting to his friend to wake up. Nassar's eyes were wet, lip trembling. My vision blurred, and I wiped at my cheeks with my fists.

"He is already gone, so stop this," Edala said from behind us. The bow in her words revealed the sadness she felt. Tamam walked beside her, face healed like the wounds had only been painted on and were washed away. When he saw Amir, he dropped to his knee beside his king and bowed his head.

Wind brushed its fingers against my cheek—soft and soothing—and the sound of rock crumbling split the air—sharp and sore. Time, with all the beautiful and horrific things it carried, moved again.

The dune above the cave collapsed into itself like quicksand, the rocks at its core crumbling beneath it. The loudest sound I had ever heard, and the greatest destruction I had ever seen. With trembling fingers, my hand covered my mouth as I watched the cloud that rose from the wreckage. The cave was gone, and with it all those people, all those children.

"I'll hear none of it," Edala said, gaze pivoting between us. "They could have killed you." She held her eyes open wide as if waiting for a response. Saalim turned to watch the cave, his face blank. Torn between his friend, the destruction, and whatever regal duties still pinned him down.

Though Edala, too, held a brave face, even a si'la could feel guilt, pain. She blinked two, three times, and the moisture was gone.

Amir's sword lay unsheathed beside him. Saalim went to retrieve it. "Who did this?" His voice shook with fury.

Edala lifted her chin. "It was foolish to try to stay Zahar and Kassim with sword alone." Then, her voice softened. "He was no match for magic."

Amir's body was unscathed. Kassim had killed Amir in his attempt to stop them from fleeing?

My fingers trembled as I covered my mouth.

"Where are they?" Saalim asked slowly, seething.

"That way." Edala pointed her thin finger in some direction.

I looked for Amir to explain, but grief struck me anew realizing he was gone. Biting my cheek, I looked anywhere but at him.

Saalim heaved a noisy breath. "To Almulihi."

His sister stared off in that direction, her hand clutching Tamam's. "Yes."

"Tonight, Edala, our steps will be long." Saalim said it with such finality, one would not dare disagree.

His sister glanced once to me, the smallest, satisfied smile on her lips, then said, "Of course."

Nassar helped me pull Amir away from the wreckage for his sky burial. I uncovered him carefully, then we waited. I do not know if Edala magicked them or if they came because Masira wanted Amir's kind soul, but the vultures circled swiftly.

"It feels wrong for him," Saalim said beside me. "He should be in the sea."

"He returns to that which gave his life purpose." Amir loved the desert, loved the study of it.

When the birds descended, Saalim winced. I held his hand and after a few breaths, the tension in his grip eased. I knew well how he hid his sorrow, I saw it there hollowing him out, pulling him down.

Softly, I sang a plea for Masira to take Amir to her side, to keep him well. Saalim said nothing—his lips pressed tight together to keep in all that he hid. When I finished, he stood.

"Wait," I said, the guilt clawing its way out. "I was wrong to fight with your sister. It was selfish. Had I held my tongue, she would not have left, and Amir would not have died. I could have killed us all."

He watched the birds. "But I made the decision to go to the cave without Edala." He took a deep breath. "We cannot always predict the consequences of what we do, but we have to live with them all the same. We were both wrong, but it is done. And now we live with it forever. Remembering our past is the burdensome rite of living."

Our eyes met, and I knew he spoke of magic as much as he spoke of us.

"If she hated the palace so much, why did she stay?" Saalim asked of Zahar as we journeyed through the night.

Edala shrugged. "Why not? It paid good coin and was secure."

With magic, Edala promised us it would take only two nights to return to Madinat Almulihi.

"I did not realize the extent of Kassim's jealousy," Edala admitted, and even sounded ashamed. Magic, as it turned out, was the draw for them all, though none of us could fathom how Zahar had convinced Kassim to become a jinni—a slave.

"Power?" Nassar asked.

"But shackled power?" I said, looking at him. He avoided my gaze. He had not looked at me the same since I told of the atrocity he had committed in a past he did not remember.

"It was an easy decision for you, of course," Edala said to Saalim. "You would have done anything to save Almulihi. But Kassim?"

When the unanswered questions piled too high, silence covered them. There would be no solving our problems this night.

We stopped at a large oasis before sunrise. The trees lining the perimeter were so thick, Tamam and Saalim walked through them several times before they decided we were alone and safe.

After sitting down to a quiet meal, Edala stood, claiming if she was not left alone until sundown, a sand wind would ruin everyone's sleep. As she walked away, she called behind her, "Tamam, that excludes you."

With the smallest smile, and deepening of color on his tanned cheeks, Saalim's most stoic soldier rushed after her. She took his hand in hers and together, they found a hidden space to make their bed across the pool.

I watched them go, longing for the same intimacy and privacy. Saalim's fingers found mine in the sand, as if sensing my thoughts. He said, "Nassar, can you take the first watch?"

After noticing our joined hands, he seemed eager to leave and collected his things rapidly.

"There is a nice place," Saalim said as he helped me to my feet, "just over there."

He took me beneath a large tree with low hanging branches. The leaves were so dense, almost no sunlight marred its shade. Under the tree were oleander bushes that bordered a small pool fed by the larger one. "After being so spoiled by daily baths at Jawar's, I thought you might like to bathe here." He watched me carefully, hiding his emotions well. But I heard the slight tremor in his voice.

"I would love that," I whispered, gazing at the luxurious privacy created by the bushes and tree.

Dropping my things, I knelt at the pool's edge and submerged my hands into the water. It was perfect.

I was suspended between delicate moments in my life: my recent past where Saalim was both a perfect memory and a desperate hope, and my very near future when we were in Madinat Almulihi and Saalim belonged forever to only Helena. Perhaps it was my awareness of this that made me bold. Still kneeling beside the pool, I pulled my cloak from my shoulders.

"There are fewer eyes," I said, heart racing. It had to be now, or it would never be.

Saalim made a strangled sound, and I did not have to see him to know it was desire that choked him. It was all I needed.

Like the best-trained ahira, I removed the rest of my clothes. Only, unlike an ahira, I cared very much of the man's opinion who watched me.

"Emel," Saalim muttered from behind me.

I pulled my hair over my shoulder as I looked over my shoulder at him, brazen in my nudity, the uncovering of my scars. He must see all of me.

He was fixed as a statue, his knees bent ever so slightly as if they threatened to collapse beneath him. His eyes traveled hungrily down my back, my hips, my legs.

He dropped to his knees, his pack falling to his side. In three kneeling steps, he was at my back, the heat of him melting over me like fire's warmth.

His hand hovered above my shoulder, uncertain.

I nodded, and he placed it on the slope of my neck, his thumb tracing over my skin. He was so careful, so reverential in his touch, I nearly cried.

"Saalim," I breathed.

His fingertips slid along my scars as they once had so long ago, and though this time there was no magic, heat still trailed in their wake. Then his lips were pressed against my shoulder, his beard the only rough part of his touch.

"Do you know," he said between unhurried, cautious kisses, "how often I have thought of you like this?"

"This?" I asked, leaning into his chest. His tunic was coarse against my skin.

His fingers moved away from my back, over my arms, across my chest. Holding me to him, he said, "It is better than I imagined." His voice was rough and thready, need pulling his words apart.

His hands moved down my front, stopping to feel and worship. Like I was a rare jewel for a beggar, a god for the supplicant. My eyes closed, head dropping back against his chest as he touched me.

At once the warmth on my back was gone and I heard the crashing of water. I opened my eyes, and he was in front of me, kneeling, uncaring that his clothes were soaked. "I want to see you," he said, laying me down on the sand.

And see me he did.

First with his eyes, then with his hands, then with his mouth.

"We have all day," I reminded him, as I reached for the edge of his tunic.

"It is not enough."

When he, too, was unclothed, he lay atop me. The weight of him crushed me into the soft sand, his thigh pressed between my legs as I wound myself around him. He groaned, and I could not get him close enough to satisfy me. I wanted him closer, closer, closer still. The silken heat of his skin pressed against me, his heart thundering even faster than mine against my chest . . . a dizzying euphoria.

His mouth met mine with measured urgency, and at last, we reunited in the way that only two lovers who have been parted for so long could meet. We were joined, in love, sharing breath and life and all that was vulnerable between us. We were slick with sweat, while the cool water of the oasis lapped at our tangled legs. Sand covered my hair and his, my skin and his. It was fragile and coarse and terrible and beautiful. It was everything it should be as we clutched at each other, fingers curled into each other's skin, shaking with love so dazzling, it crippled with its scarcity.

When all was quiet, Saalim lay at my side, peering at me as though studying a tapestry.

"What is it?" I asked.

"You have all of these memories," his finger swept across my brow, resting at my temple, "of us. Of me."

I nodded.

"I am envious. I have only this." At first he looked toward the horizon, as if there was something more he wanted to say. Then, his eyes dropped from mine, and again, he looked at my body, bared beside him. "I am greedy." As if he could not help himself, his mouth again trailed down me, kissing my neck, my chest, my belly. "I want so much more," he murmured against my skin. As he moved, he dusted the sand from my skin like I was the most sacred thing in the world. Then, he took a fistful of sand, and said, "If this is what the desert offers, perhaps it is not such a bad place."

Grinning, I wrapped my hands around his neck and pulled him to me.

My bath was forgotten completely.

The next day, we arrived in Madinat Almulihi.

Edala hesitated on the steps of the palace, and Saalim stood beside her while our packs were taken inside. I still held mine tightly.

"It is different without them, isn't it?" he asked his sister.

Not wanting to intrude on their privacy, I went inside. In the atrium I stopped, realizing I had nowhere to go. Altasa's—Zahar's—house was half-burned. Even if my room was still standing, safety would not be found sleeping in the home of the woman who had betrayed me.

Still, after so long away from green, the gardens beckoned me. The waxy leaves of manicured trees and flowering bushes glistened beneath the sun as I moved passed them. A pair of familiar servants walked by, nodding to me in welcome. It was strange, being back in the palace and feeling that, in many ways, I had returned home.

At the edge of the garden, the faintest scent of char lingered. Gray smudged the stone path that led to Zahar's door. Standing under the trees' shadows, I marveled at how my life had changed since I first came to Madinat Almulihi with Saalim. It seemed not long ago that I stood in this very place with ruined palace walls and shattered tiles at my feet, a lover at my side. Now, I had smooth walls and lush gardens surrounding me, yet I was alone.

At Zahar's, I stepped under the blackened arch into the kitchen. Most ingredients were destroyed, the shelves burned, but a few were still preserved in their jars. Some of the ingredients I knew were valuable. As I sifted through the wreckage, the edges of a book caught my eye. Zahar's recipe book.

After wiping off the cover, I flipped through it. Unbelievably, it had been unharmed in the fire. I paused on a page that was marked with the feather of a griffon. *Dhitah.* I remembered seeing this before—a tonic for death. Reading through the ingredients was easier this time. I paused at castor seeds.

Zahar had on numerous occasions had me collect them for her at the market. My head buzzed as I recalled the times Zahar had lamented that Saalim did not take her tonic.

Sons, all that time . . .

Footsteps approached from behind, and Saalim came toward me.

"I thought I would find you here."

Standing in a rush, I held up the book. "She was trying to poison you." This tonic *would* have worked, since it did not require magic. I served as no protection when Masira could not interfere. "Why didn't you get sick?"

He took the book from me and turned through the thick pages, seemingly undisturbed by this information. "I won't drink things from people I don't trust. My mother taught me that. Said my father was too generous with his trust, could've been poisoned by any merchant in the market."

I remembered the many evenings I spent grinding ingredients into a paste for Saalim's salves. "You drank the pain tonic I made you."

He said, "I trusted you."

"Even then?"

"Even then." He rested his hand on my shoulder, and I softened beneath it.

"You don't plan to stay here?" he asked, gesturing to Zahar's burned home.

"I do not." My pulse sped, imagining the privacy of sharing his tower.

"I hope it was not presumptive, but I had Nika make ready the guest tower for you."

I swallowed my hope. "Of course."

"Emel," Saalim said as I took Zahar's book from him. "Every part of me wants to take you to mine. But with Helena . . . I need—"

"I understand."

"No, you don't." He turned me to face him, pressing his hands to my shoulders. "I will not have you being perceived as an ahira." He hesitated. "And, too, my father's voice is still loud in my memory."

His father telling him to wed Helena. My chest cinched tight, my breathing stuttered.

"But lately I have wondered if I should just do what *I* want." Slowly, he swept his finger down my cheek, leaving my skin tingling.

I said, "A friend once told me that the right choice is the one that feels right for you."

"Was I that friend?"

I smiled. "You were."

"And what did you choose?"

I considered his question. "First, I chose me." I wished for freedom from the Salt King for myself.

He cocked his head.

"Then, I chose you."

Saalim led me back into the palace. As we walked up the spiraling stairs of the guest tower, I asked him about Kassim and Zahar.

Edala said they were heading toward us, but had not yet arrived. I wondered why Kassim did not magic them to Almulihi as Edala had done for us? Did they think to catch us by surprise?

"She can feel the magic everywhere in this desert," Saalim said with awe. He was proud of his sister, I could tell. The white walls of the sitting room were bright as the morning sun spilled in through the arching windows. "She said there are three people left who can use magic. Once, there were four." He met my gaze.

"You were one of the four?"

He nodded.

"And now it's Edala, Zahar, and Kassim?"

"As far as she can tell."

"No other jinn?"

"If there are, she believes they are caged, for she has felt the existence of no one else. They would have to be well-hidden somewhere."

Nika had left a tray of tea and a bowl of dates. The fire was crackling, recently brought to life with fresh kindling. Taking a cup of tea Saalim had poured, I said, "So we wait for them to come, and then what?"

He sat next to me on the cushioned bench, his thigh against mine. He took a deep breath, opened his mouth, and closed it again.

Silence confirmed my suspicions: They must be destroyed. They were determined to kill Saalim and put Kassim on the throne. Death was the only choice we had.

"Where are you going?" Saalim asked when I stood.

"To Edala." How would we kill a jinni?

I flew down the stairs, nearly running through the halls until I was on the other side of the palace climbing up Edala and Nadia's tower. Out of breath, I entered the strangest scene. Edala sat across from Mariam, whose arms curled around Bilara protectively.

All but Bilara turned to me when I stumbled in.

Edala stood, "What has happened?"

Shaking my head, I said, "Nothing. I was coming up to talk about . . ." My eyes darted to the girl who clutched the metal box tightly to her chest. Kassim's vessel. Now that I understood what it was, I felt as though I could see the magic spilling from it. We could get rid of Kassim right now, if we could open it.

"We will leave," Mariam said quickly, grabbing Bilara's hand and guiding her past me. I wanted to stop them, to rip the vessel from the child's arms. But Mariam helped her down the stairs slowly, Bilara trusting Mariam as she would her own mother. It left me with no heart to take that vessel from the girl. Not yet.

When they were out of sight, I rushed to Edala. "How do you kill a jinni?"

She raised her eyebrows and collapsed against the cushioned bench. "You kill the master and burn the vessel with the jinni inside. Or, if the master wants him dead, you burn the vessel." She had already come to the same conclusion as Saalim, apparently.

"Is this what we have to—"

"Yes." Her eyes shone wetly. She closed them.

Pointing in the direction Bilara went, I said, "And we are sure she is not Kassim's master? Why would Bilara still carry the box?" I nearly panted, the words pouring out of my mouth.

What if we have to kill a child?

Edala rubbed her eyes. Her disgust confirmed my suspicions. "Did you know they made a poison? Had the mother drink it so the child was born like that. A perfect keeper of a jinni. Be glad you did not see the babies in that cave. They bred for keepers." Her face hardened. "Now, they can't." Leaning forward, she pressed her hands together. Hands so small, to possess so much power.

"If we don't know who his master is, how can we destroy the jinni," even I could not bear to say her brother's name aloud as we talked of his death, "without harming Bilara?"

"Kassim needs a new master." Edala stared at the shelves behind me. Did she look at the portrait of her and a young Tamam? "I can take the vessel easily enough when we are ready, but the box is sealed. I can't open it."

"Sealed?"

"It does not open like a traditional box. It is more complicated."

There were footsteps, and when I turned to the stairs, I was surprised to see Tamam. He seemed as uncomfortable seeing me as I him.

"We have time," Edala said to me, ushering me out. "Do not worry today. We will worry when they are here."

When I turned back, I saw Edala slide her arms around Tamam's waist.

In the dining hall, the trays and bowls containing the midday meal had been laid out on the table. My stomach grumbled, so I lingered.

As I popped a piece of flatbread into my mouth, a shadow of movement crossed the balcony. Saalim stood by himself.

"What are you doing out here?" I asked.

His elbows were locked on the rail, his gaze trained on the sea.

He looked at the bread in my hand. "Same as you, I suspect." The corner of his mouth turned up as he watched me tiptoe near the balcony's edge. No matter how long I lived in the palace, I would not get used to floating in the sky. Below, I could see people going to and from buildings, walking along the streets. A few pointed up toward Saalim, one even waved. Saalim did not see it, or if he did, he ignored them.

"What is it like to live like this?" I pointed down at the people.

He thought for a while, then said, "It is mostly lonely."

I gasped. "But you have so many people around you. So many friends . . ." I thought of my life in my father's palace. Never would I have called it lonely.

"They are not my friends. They are paid by the palace coin, by the people of Almulihi, to be here." He crossed his arms and leaned his hip against the rail. "There are few I can trust, few that I know are not here only because I am a king."

I wanted to uncross his arms, and wrap them around me, repeating what Edala said. *Do not worry today.*

"You can trust me."

He laughed. "Yes. If you cared about my being king, you would not have had such impudence all this time."

I wanted his eyes to always shine that brightly. *Choose me, and they will.*

"Maybe it is all a part of my plan. I am an expert at capturing the attention of a man, after all." I swished my hips and strode away from him.

"You are cruel," he said, coming up from behind me. His hands clasped onto my shoulders as he leaned into me, whispering, "Even crueler now that I know how those hips feel in my hands."

Inside, a few servants turned in our direction. Discreet as ever, they showed nothing that indicated surprise.

"I want to snatch you up and throw you over my shoulder when you're like this." He nearly growled.

I giggled like an ahira, only this time the lust—the love—was real.

28

SAALIM

W hen the sky finally darkened that night, we took our seats around a table laden with food. Though I entertained my guests as I had been trained—as though nothing was amiss—I could see Emel watching me silently from across the table. People asked after her, wondering who this salt chaser was at the king's table. A king's daughter we were hosting, I explained. They looked between us with curiosity, whispering loud enough for me to hear.

"But what of Helena?"

"When will she return?"

"When is the wedding?"

Guests lingered long after the meal was over. Emel stayed, too, as if waiting for something. Sons, these people wanted to stay and talk deep into the night.

Emel stood and mumbled about a walk outside before she retired. As if she was the signal they needed, the others left, and I found her in the gardens, sleepy-eyed and smiling.

"It seemed to never end," she said. "You do this every night?"

I nodded, drawing near, breathing her in, wanting to have all of her. My hands never left my sides, though they yearned to touch her hair, her neck, her hand. We walked together beside the fountains, following a path through the grass and stone that felt as if it had been made for us alone. Helena flashed in my mind as I wondered about the answers to the guests' questions, but I brushed her away. *Think of her later.*

Next to Emel, I was anchored. I was home. It was there already, on this path that led me to her, I realized. In Alfaar's settlement, on our journey to Almulihi, when I saw her in the palace as the healer's apprentice. But it was Edala's words that had cleared the way, made me see it was there all along.

Emel and I talked of nothing that night, standing a fist's distance apart. Proper in case of watchful eyes. None could think her anything but a woman of court. But oh, how I thought of that day in the oasis. I longed to go back to that spot of sand, to live a lifetime with her there. We could string a hammock, dance under the shadows of leaves.

"I should sleep. So should you," Emel said after we had taken many steps in silence.

"Tomorrow night?" I held out my hand.

She took it, our fingers slipping through each other's until our hands were at our sides again. "I will be here."

It was not enough.

When I lay in bed, I imagined she slept beside me. Sleep did not find me that night, lost as I was in thoughts of my father and his choice. Was the woman who birthed me the one who, like Emel, uncovered the better part of him? Did he miss that part of his life by marrying my mother? Or was my mother his proper half?

How strange it was to shift into the place of your parents, and to realize that they, too, were humans who had secret thoughts and unmet desires. That they had lives separate from those of their children. I had thought my father infallible, but now I understood how his actions had led to Edala's unhappiness, Kassim's anger. Would his choice lead me to a life of satisfaction or unhappiness?

I held onto that question like a talisman until the sun rose and the day started anew. But with the day came duty. Rising, I pushed away thoughts of Emel and awaited Kassim and Zahar.

I returned to my role as king.

Our second day home, I found Edala in the atrium lifting the wilted leaves, her touch imbuing life. "Who cares for these now?" she asked me when I went up to inspect the vine's leaves, now shining and green.

"Ah . . ."

"That is your problem. You don't even know." She turned to me. "They are doing a poor job. You're paying someone to do nothing."

That she felt she could leave me in Almulihi by myself thinking my entire family dead, when she ran wild in the desert, then come here and tell me how to manage my staff was intolerable. I curled my fingers into my palms. The instant irritation, the venom that pooled on my tongue was familiar. That generous anger only reserved for a family member. Someone you think you can abuse because they are permanent and won't leave you. I took several breaths. Edala was anything but permanent. And I was a child no longer. I should not hurl my frustration with my own inadequacies at her. She was my sister.

"You are right."

Satisfied, she looked down at the polished floor. "I miss them more than I expected."

"I know."

"I saw the gardens. Nadia would have wept to see them charred so. I am glad she will not."

"They will regrow."

She eyed me and swept the vines aside. "Not with the same attention whomever is giving these."

"Fair."

She took my elbow, and we walked past the bubbling fountain down the hall. Past the dining rooms, the sitting rooms, the entertaining halls. All these empty spaces for people to come and be seen in the palace. I never filled them like my mother had.

Pointing down the tiled hall, Edala said, "I remember running through here during the parties late at night, trying not to be seen."

"And if a guard caught us, we'd run to our hideaways." I always hid in the alcove behind the roped curtains.

"We thought if they only caught one of us, the rest wouldn't get in trouble. As if they didn't see us all huddled together, whispering about this and that." Edala laughed.

"You and Kassim always led the group."

Edala scoffed. "That was because you always tried, and we hated how pushy you were."

"I was rather imperious, wasn't I?" Constantly, I had tried to control my siblings. Kassim and I had argued the most. He drove me mad with his stubbornness. Always thinking of himself, never stopping to help our father with the palace duties—especially as he got older. But then, I was not much different.

Edala said, "Truthfully, I had the best ideas."

"Ah yes, like the time you decided to steal the sweet cakes from the kitchens."

"How was I supposed to know those were to be thrown out?!"

"They were the saltiest things I'd ever tasted." My tongue burned at the memory.

"Kassim fetched us all water while Nadia sobbed her apologies to Mariam, remember?"

I smiled. "She hated disobeying the rules. Not Kassim. He was always on your side and ready to do whatever you thought of next. You two were very close."

She slowed some and gripped my elbow more tightly. "I think because our hearts ached the same. We felt like outsiders. I belonged out of the palace. He felt he belonged in your place."

Our footsteps were the only sounds in the hallway despite the guards standing by. I feared for them all when Kassim arrived. How easily they would fall to a magical sword.

"I can't understand how he has become this," she said quietly. "I wish I could talk to him, take him from Zahar. But he is a jinni. Every fiber of him bends to his master, to Masira."

"Emel said I had some control. Maybe Kassim has some, too."

"Perhaps if I talk to him, we won't have to . . ."

I did not have the heart to tell her what Emel had wondered aloud last night on our walk, when we spoke of castor seeds and poisons, the tonic I was meant to drink. It was enough to have a brother try to kill his sibling. Edala did not need to know there may have been more. I was not sure I even could believe it . . .

Kassim *needed* to die. No matter how we considered other options, nothing else was safe. A family forced to kill one of their own. Anger steeped in heartache.

Three days. That was the only peace we had together before the world shifted one final time.

Three days of planning and sending and arranging and warning and ordering. Guards sent here and there through Azim, Ekram monitoring the docks, pausing exports and meeting imports armed. Civilians were warned of strangers who might approach with odd requests. Letters were sent to settlements and tribes, warning that if a new king were to assume the throne in Almulihi, it was done through treachery.

Three nights of sitting with my sister, watching her radiate warmth as she took Tamam's hand. He grinned like a fool, a new man without his stoic soldier's mask. The quiet evening walks with Emel both settling and buoying me.

The nights made worthy the draining day. The rhythm of it was quite calming. So, of course, it could not last.

Helena had insisted we keep coffee in the palace. I was still not sure of its taste, but it grew on me. Emel refused it outright, saying it looked like sickness. The sun rose as I sipped it, flipping through the letters piled on my desk.

A woman's voice met my ears. Footsteps thundered up the stairs.

I held my breath, hoping I was mistaken.

It could not be time. Not yet. Sons, please not yet.

Edala rushed into the room. "They are here." Her cheeks were flushed, her eyes dark, hiding something.

"Where?" I said, standing up from my desk.

"In the west city. Kassim has done something. The pull was enormous." The sight of Edala looking out the windows, seeing something I could not see, was the most inhuman I had ever seen her. The soul she had given up to become this si'la had never been more absent. "I will go to meet them."

A low horn sounded. The signal of a threat. So the sentinels had seen something, too. Fastening my scabbard, I said, "Where in the west?"

Her gaze whipped to me, and she held out her hand. "You must stay."

"I won't let my sister go and kill our brother alone."

Her throat tightened, and I knew I had stumbled on the problem. But then she was gone. Damn that woman. I adjusted my belt and ran back to my wardrobe to finish dressing.

Emel needed to know. I ran to the guest tower and found her sitting up in the bed. Naked and as distracting as a pool in the desert. She pulled the bedding around her when she saw me.

"They're here?" she asked. The horns blared on. Everywhere in Almulihi people were either cowering or crowding. I hoped they all heeded our warning: Stay home.

"Yes. Edala has gone to meet them."

She scrambled out of bed and dressed quickly.

"Wait in Edala's tower or mine. Guards will be the heaviest there," I said.

She did not respond. She wrapped her hair in a long scarf, and pulled a dagger from a shelf, turning it in her hand a bit before tucking it into her waist band. She did not know how to wield a blade.

"You won't need that," I said, turning toward the stairs. The horns made me anxious. Though I wanted to stay with her and be the blade she felt she needed, I knew I must go.

"I will."

"You're not coming."

Again she said nothing.

"Emel," I said.

"Cover your face," she said like a mother.

Exhaling, I wound my guthra across my face. It was best if I went unnoticed in the city. No regiment of guards would be permitted to follow me—they would die too easily should Kassim desire it—and I did not need bitter opportunists taking advantage of a lone king.

"Come on, then," she said, slipping on her sandals and running down the steps out of the tower. Without another word, I followed her.

We found Azim in the weapon stores by the stables pointing this way and that as the guards were lined along the palace border. "She went that way," he said to us and nodded in the direction of the river.

"On foot?"

He nodded.

With Emel at my back, I ran to the stables, barking at a stable boy to ready a horse. Farasa did not appreciate being rushed, so I was given a black mare. In a hurry, she was dressed—straps tightened, reins pulled—and I helped Emel onto her back before jumping on behind her.

The horns soon were a hum behind us. The shouts of people and the thundering of hooves overpowering them. Emel gripped the pommel tightly, head bent down, fearless as she squeezed her legs against the horse's side.

As we neared the city's edge, I understood what the palace sentinels must have seen, because I could smell it.

It brought back the horrors from what felt like so long ago—the palace on fire. Now, it was Almulihi. The street was hazy up ahead. Pulling Emel tight against me, I hurried the mare on.

Turning onto the smokey street—completely engulfed in flames—I pulled the reins. Orange blazes licked up the sides of shops and homes. People were fleeing or were being dragged away by others, unable to collect their possessions. The mare was picking up her feet at the sight of the chaos. We dismounted, and I found a young woman who watched the destruction with fascinated horror.

Handing her the reins, I said, "Take her to the palace, and you will receive six dha."

She looked between me and Emel, then beyond us at the fire, deciding if the coin was worth missing the spectacle. With a nod, she took the mare away.

The canal was behind us, and the people were already hauling water to throw onto the flames.

Emel edged toward the fiery street.

"Where are you going?"

"Firoz," she said. "And Kahina. All her maps . . ."

Kahina? I looked at the street again.

We were in the baytahira, I realized. It looked different coming from this direction. It looked different without people crowding the streets. It looked different aflame.

Following her, I said. "Where is he?"

Before she could answer, water rushed down the street from behind us, nearly costing me my balance. It was at my feet, then ankles, then shins. Sons, what was happening?

"It is rising!" Emel said, terror ringing loud in her voice.

Behind us, the canal overflowed and surged down the street. *Only* the street of the baytahira. Several of those who had not gotten out of the water's path fell to the ground, sliding along with the current.

Emel clasped my arm as we waded through the flood.

"Stay away!" a voice boomed, and understanding flooded me just as the water did the street.

Edala.

Magic.

She had come from the same direction we had, with a retinue of guards at her back who helped to disperse and guide the people away from the bizarre scene. With invisible, impossibly powerful hands, she guided the water to the flames.

"Kassim!" she called out through the smoke and steam. "Stop hiding."

"I am not hiding," he said.

I could see him nowhere, but he sounded as if he was right beside us.

Then, a shadow blossomed like ink in water, and Kassim was in front of us. I edged in front of Emel.

"Why, brother?" Edala asked quietly, stepping toward him.

"If you have to ask, then you deserve death as much as he." He nodded to me.

"Where is Zahar?" she asked.

"She doesn't matter."

"She does," Edala said. "Does she hide somewhere safe while you risk yourself? I thought you were to be made king. Why should you die for her?"

"I have no intention of dying," Kassim said.

"She should be here with you."

"She is human. She would fall too easily."

"Or does she simply want you to risk yourself, because she has plans of her own?"

I glanced at Edala, who crackled with pent up magic. Emel moved around me. It was bold of us to be there, and I regretted allowing her to come with me. We were like Zahar—too human, too easily felled.

Did Emel hope Masira would protect us? It was not a gamble I wanted to make. Carefully, I picked up the water on my fingertips, pressing it against my skin in silent prayer.

"Kassim, you will not survive this," Edala said, now an arm's length from him. "I can free you. Make you human again. You can atone for what you have done."

"Atone? Tell me all that I have I done, Edala. There is so much even you don't see. Too far I've gone for atonement." His voice cracked. Was it rage or regret?

"Don't you want your freedom?"

His eyes narrowed, fury pinning his gaze to Edala.

"You're *imprisoned*," she said.

"I am freer than I was before. I know you feel the same. We aren't squashed under the thumb of some man who thinks he can control us because he fathered us."

Some man. I bristled, listening to him disparage our father. The water was at my thighs now.

Kassim continued, sounding almost manic. "Must we all suffer for his mistake?"

"Suffer?" I asked, unable to stop myself. "Because you are not to be king, you think you suffer? None of us have suffered. Is being caged and tied to the will of another better? Sitting on the throne is not all drinks and dinners and comfortable chairs. It is exactly what you are. I am tied to the will of everyone else, constantly at their mercy. One hundred scimitars hang by threads above my head. Do you see nothing?"

He came toward me, the water slowing his steps. "You can only act brave with Emel at your side." He searched behind me.

"Leave her out of this," I said.

"You are weak. We both know you failed to protect Almulihi from my army. You had to beg an old woman to save it. To save *you*."

His army? The people who attacked our home, who killed our entire family, who threw me into a vessel as a jinni, who made me the king of Almulihi . . . it was all Kassim.

Spots clouded my vision, dizzy with sickness and grief. Of course it was Kassim. That had always been a possibility, I knew, and yet here was the terrible truth. He wanted the throne, and he knew exactly how weak it had become. Father ill, soldiers complacent. Shame poured into me, sudden and suffocating. My family had destroyed my family. I turned to Emel to tell her to get far away from here.

But she was gone. I looked back to Kassim and Edala. My sister's eyes were wide, her head reared back in horror as she understood that our family was gone because of Kassim. "You didn't," she whispered.

Kassim smiled, boastful and proud. "It was not hard to gather people to our cause."

It was just the three of us standing in this strange, flooded street. Thank the Sons Nadia was not alive to see this. Never would I have thought being killed a mercy, but for her—to escape this—it was.

"There are those who felt like Almulihi should share its wealth, that the salt trade is unfair," Kassim went on. "People who don't want to work hard, prefer to steal what others worked for. They're everywhere, it turns out. They came in droves to kill the weakened king, take the stone city." He held his hands out with false shame. "It isn't how I wanted it to happen, of course. Father never seemed to die, you know. I tried to wait, let it happen on its own—"

I stepped forward. No, no. Emel couldn't have been right. "Let what happen?"

Edala raised a hand to her mouth, understanding.

The recipe for death in Zahar's book. Emel had wondered if the healer had not only tried to get me to drink it, but my father, too. An inappropriate dose of the poison would explain his disease if he didn't drink enough of it to die. If he had grown cautious after feeling ill from her tonic . . .

Kassim crossed his arms, the water at our hips. "If he had simply died, I could have taken you by sword and had the throne. But . . ." He shrugged, then nearly smiled.

Edala slammed her hands down to her sides, the water pushing away from us with a hot wind, and at once we were on dry ground. "She convinced you to kill your own father?" she shouted.

"She didn't have to convince me! You knew it was unfair, said it yourself." He waved his hands at her. "Even you said I would be best on the throne."

I looked at Edala. She had thought so? Had all of my siblings thought of me as an imposter?

"No," Edala began, her fingers sliding along her cheek. "Not like this, Kassim." She hardened to stone. "So you killed father to become a king, and as your reward Zahar made you a slave."

He shook his head. "Zahar will free me when he's gone." He nodded to me. "And then I'll wear the crown."

Edala said, "When will she free you? When she's done using you?"

Where was Zahar?

Surely she was not far. A wall of water spun around us as though Wahir himself guided the waves. The height of it grew until the maelstrom was nearly at my shoulders.

With fists still clenched, Edala said, "Because you were jealous, you killed our family. You are a monster, Kassim." Her voice broke on his name, the sorrow slipping through. "You deserve to be put down as such."

Kassim backed away, chains of fire forming in his hands. He flung the chain at me, but the heat dissipated before it touched, Edala deflecting it as if swatting a mosquito. The whole display so peculiar that I nearly forgot my own life, my home, was at risk.

"You wouldn't kill me," Kassim spat at her. "Your favorite brother."

"I would kill a jinni who threatens my home."

A flash of movement came from a rooftop.

Bent over the edge, watching us with a vicious grin on her face, was Zahar.

29

EMEL

The resemblance was obvious when I saw Kas beside his brother. So were the differences, especially as Kassim's anger boiled over. How could I have thought I could share a life with him? His exterior was just a carefully crafted mask to cover that which was broken on the inside.

Movement atop Kahina's roof drew my attention. I slipped away from the chaos on the street and moved toward her home.

In the front room, so much had already been destroyed by the fire and flood. Water soaked her beautiful cushions and smeared the ink of the maps that hung low on the wall. The stairs creaked as I ran up them, water dripping in my trail. The door to the back balcony was left open, the ladder ready against the wall that led to the roof. Curling my fingers around the rungs, I climbed.

At the top, I stilled. It was not Kahina. It was the same woman I had seen in the cave. The same face—just younger and more vibrant—of the woman who had comforted me when I cried after the camel race. The one who had made Madinat Almulihi feel like home.

"Zahar? What are you doing here?" I asked.

"Emel," she said, spinning away from the edge. Zahar's hair was nearly as black as mine—no longer white and coarse. Her face was now as smooth as my mother's had been. She had aged in reverse.

Stepping onto the roof, I said, "It seems cowardly to wait up here while Kassim does your bidding."

"Cowardly?" She laughed. "I have no need to be brave. I am not interested in losing my life."

I gestured around us to the baytahira. "Why have you come here?"

"I thought I'd serve revenge to several people at once, but alas, the one I thought to sweep away quickly is not here."

"Kahina?" I frowned. "What does she have to do with this?"

"That beast sent my sister away. The only family I had!"

Crossing my arms, I said, "Kahina would never—"

"You don't know her at all," Zahar spat. "She said being here did my sister no good. I was left alone!"

For just a moment, I thought I understood what Zahar felt. I remembered saying goodbye to Raheemah, living apart from Tavi, mourning Sabra, my sisters back home. My family. "Zahar, you could have gone after your sister, instead of turning your anger to the people in this city—"

"No, it had to begin with them, because this was all their fault." Zahar snapped, and thoughts of my own sisters disappeared. She went on, as if an afterthought, "I will find Kahina later."

"And when will you search for her? After Saalim dies? Edala?" Everything in the way she hid herself in shadows, in secret, revealed that she wanted nothing to do with the conflict on the street below. "After Kassim is dead, too? What are you waiting for?" I nudged closer, and she stepped back. For Kahina, the woven rug and low table on the roof would have served an intimate setting, a pleasant one at dusk—the breeze from the sea blowing in as the clouds rolled across the purple sky—but now, for me, they were merely an obstacle that separated us.

Zahar peered at the street again, satisfied with whatever she saw, then scowled at me. "Saalim never should have been able to break free. A privileged, rotten boy would never love his chains. I took you for a salt chaser, a daughter of Eiqab, not a soft child of Wahir. You have caused more trouble than Kahina."

Saalim could only be freed when he desired his freedom the least.

When we fell in love, his remaining a jinni had been the only assurance that we could remain together.

With a loud sigh, she said, "It was bad enough that I had to see Saalim take the throne, but now I am burdened with his idiot brother, useful though he may be at times."

"Kassim," I said, trying to piece it together. There was so much missing. "Why have you created this monster of him?" I moved toward the edge of the roof where she watched the street below.

"Me?" She was appalled. "I oiled a fire that had already been burning. He was an angry boy, so jealous of Saalim. Desperate to take the throne. So desperate, he was willing to kill his father and brother. What I didn't expect was having to use magic on Saalim."

I grimaced. "You encouraged Kassim to destroy his family."

As if she did not hear me, she went on. "See, Kassim I had planned to stuff in a vessel after Malek and Saalim were dead. I didn't actually *want* Kassim to be king." She flicked her hand toward me. "Can you imagine someone so erratic on the throne?

"But desperate people turn to desperate things, and when you think you're about to lose everything, you choose the impossible. When the army failed to kill him, Saalim showed up on my doorstep, begging me to save his home with the same magic he had denied existed. I was a weak old woman and wouldn't kill him myself. My sister's soul would find a way to destroy me if I did. So I put him away. At least then I would never have to see her face again."

Her face? Zahar was undeniably crazed. I took a step away from her.

She said, "I used the magic I intended for Kassim. Of course, with the final swallow of the tonic, Madinat Almulihi fell to ruins and Saalim was bound to Masira."

"So you gave Saalim the potion simply to do away with him?"

Zahar nodded as though I had asked her whether crushing leaves was preferable to chopping them. "Saalim locked away and Almulihi in ruins would have been enough for me. It was Kassim who wanted him dead." Zahar exhaled and waved her hand.

"But *why*, Zahar? Why destroy Saalim's life, his family, his home?"

"Malek destroyed mine." She spat the words.

Saalim's father?

There was something about all this that nagged at me, a cord tugging my spine and feet and hands away from her. Why was she divulging all of this to me now? What did she have planned that made her feel safe to tell me? I needed to warn Saalim. Edala.

But Zahar went on, and I was unable to tear myself from her flurry of words. "Those people Kassim recruited to destroy Almulihi? Barbarians. They did not discriminate and would have killed me. The magic that destroyed the city didn't stop them. I had hoped so desperately I would finally be left alone.

"But Kassim found me as I fled the palace. Impossibly. I think it was Masira's little fun. He was furious, of course. I'd ruined his city, and Saalim wasn't dead. The palace he was set to rule was destroyed."

"So you locked him away, too? To be mastered by a child?" I almost felt sorry for Kassim, his strings getting pulled by this woman.

Understanding flashed in Zahar's eyes. Then, she said, "He annoyed me, so I had to lock him away, too." She muttered something about being barely able to find enough ingredients to make a second tonic as she peered down at the street. Looking back to me, she said, "I pretended it was a part of my plan to imbue him with power. He, too, would become a jinni. Told him once Saalim was freed, I'd free him, too, so he could finally take the throne. It was *so easy* convincing him. He even found a little trinket from his childhood amidst the ruins to serve as his vessel. Soon he, too, was bound by Masira's chains." She batted her eyes apologetically. Finding a comfortable seat on a cushion, she rested her elbows against the table.

Pressing my hands together, I said, "But why do all this?"

"Because of him." She pointed to the palace. "Because of a man who cared too much of his legacy to make a salt chaser his wife."

I gasped. Was *Zahar* Saalim's mother?

Looking up, she smiled, her shoulders falling back and away. So relaxed amidst so much chaos. "Those brothers are sand in my shoes. Let them destroy each other. My job is done. Malek has suffered for his choice. Now I want all that reminds me of him gone. And because you stand in my way, I want you gone, too."

In a rush, Zahar pushed past the table and leapt at me. So surprised by the speed in which she moved, I failed to react. She grabbed one of my wrists and I turned, trying to pull away from her. With a violent wrench, she dragged me back toward her and caught my other wrist, and pinned my arms behind me.

She was unbelievably strong, her grip like an iron cuff, and I was helpless to fight. There was no trace of the old woman Altasa. With ease, she pushed me toward the edge of the roof.

"I *am* sorry I have to do it this way. I like you, Emel." Zahar seemed to be less apologetic as the reality that I would be thrown, that I would fall, became more certain. "But Edala's flood has made it so easy for me, and your damn curiosity will be the death of you." She laughed. "Go to Masira. Salt chasers don't swim."

Stone dug into my side, my legs tangled on the edge, and then there was nothing at all beneath me. I was floating. I was falling. Water came closer and closer and then swallowed me whole. Slick hands slipped down my throat and took hold.

I flailed my arms, my legs, coughing and spasming. I would taste air for brief moments then fall back into the flood.

I was going to drown in an impossibly flooded street.

My need to breathe fought with my insistence to keep my mouth closed. My desperation for air won, and I took a breath, the water choking me anew. Violent coughs snapped through me, and as the light dimmed, my attempts to swim faltered.

Something grabbed me. A hand. It pulled me up and up. Then, there was air and warmth and arms around me as I was jostled. A hard, dry street met my back.

"Emel!" Saalim cried from above me. "Emel!"

My eyes fluttered open. I saw him for only a moment before I rolled onto my stomach and coughed up water.

When I had settled, Saalim carried me across the canal bridge until we were surrounded by people who watched the flood with both terror and glee. The sound of water rushing and falling pulled my attention away from the crowd.

Water was rushing away from the baytahira. Straight toward us.

Panicked, I held my head and knees together, waiting for the water to take me again. But it never came, and when it quieted to a trickle, I saw that it had all poured back into the canal.

The crowd whispered about what had happened, lamenting the ruin of the baytahira, and praising Wahir that their homes hadn't been flooded.

Kassim and Edala stood in front of each other, bodies rigid as if each locked in some invisible effort, neither wanting to make the first move.

It would be Kassim's undoing, I knew.

I said, "Zahar's on the roof—she threw me."

"I saw her. It was how I found you."

There was an agonized scream, and Kassim fell to his knees. But almost as suddenly, he was standing again, flames rushing toward Edala from behind. She must have sensed it, and they were gone as quickly as they appeared.

"Look," Saalim said, pointing at the side of the street.

Zahar was leaving Kahina's home. She slipped between two homes and was gone.

"Emel." Saalim gripped my shoulders. "Go somewhere far away from this place, somewhere safe. Find Tavi and stay with her. Anything, please. I am going to find Zahar." With a wave of his hand, four guards came from within the crowd.

But I would not flee. I belonged to this fight as much as he did.

Once Saalim and the men were gone, I crossed the canal again, nearing Kassim and Edala.

This all was pointless. It would serve better to retrieve the vessel and put Kassim away, find Zahar, and be done with them both. And if Bilara was Kassim's master still? I shook my head. The child could not die. I had to find Bilara and take the vessel myself.

Zahar fleeing into the baytahira flashed in my mind again, and I clasped my hands together as I realized my mistake. Zahar knew that I had seen the child. I lived in the palace, where else would I have seen the girl? Zahar would never have known she was in the palace; she hated going inside. How often had she praised Eiqab that she had me, so that she did not have to step foot in *that place?*

Now Zahar had gone to find her. To take the vessel so we couldn't have it.

"Kassim, stop it!" I cried. "You would kill your sister?" I shouted, trying to distract him from my attempt to capture Edala's attention.

"As she would kill me," he snapped.

Edala stepped back, watching Kassim closely. "You are my brother no longer. I would not wish death upon him." She said the last part softly.

"You'd help me to become king, then?" He was petulant as a child.

"Stop this," she said. "It was father's choice to make."

I stepped closer. "A father whose death is on your hands."

Kassim looked unapologetic.

I shook my head. "You are only a tool for the revenge Zahar so desperately wanted to take against your father. She said herself she doesn't care who sits on the throne; she only wants to destroy your family. And you've done that for her, you fool." I turned to Edala. "It is where Zahar goes now—to take *it*." I hoped that would be enough. That Edala would understand without sending Kassim on our trail.

"It is locked," she whispered.

"Perhaps not for her," I said.

Kassim peered around, fury pouring from his hands as the stone of the street cracked and exploded into smaller pieces. A building to his left shook and fell.

Another beside it did the same.

The baytahira crumbled beneath his wrath.

I moved to run forward, to grab his hands and stop him from destroying his home, but I found I couldn't move.

"Don't, Emel," Edala said, coming toward me.

When her hands touched my shoulders, we were not standing in the middle of the baytahira any longer.

The silence of Edala's tower was so thick, it deafened. I fell to my knees when my feet hit the plush carpets of the sitting room.

"Where is Kassim?" I asked, looking up at her from the ground.

"I do not know if my control of time works on him."

"Could he follow you?"

She pressed her hand to her brow. "I don't know." She took deep breaths, lost in thought. "I can't kill him." Edala's confession snapped through the silence.

I frowned. "You don't have to, Edala. We can find another way."

"No," she said shaking her head. "I cannot kill him. It is impossible. He defends everything I do." She turned to me with heart-sick eyes.

Like dust clearing, I understood. "But of course. He couldn't die—even at your hands—unless his master wills it. Or unless the master is dead. First, he needs a new master."

She sat on a chair and dropped her face into her hands. "Sons, you're right."

"Zahar said the vessel is from Kassim's childhood. Something he chose?"

Clarity washed away her shame and she stared at me, amazed. "His puzzle box. I don't know how I didn't realize it before."

"You know it?"

"He kept the smallest things in there, something to keep secret from everyone. None could open it unless you had the key and knew how to move the pieces. Of course, none had the key but him." Her gaze grew distant as she remembered. "There is a small metal rod that . . ." She paused, gasping. "It is soldered to the chain." Edala spun, then ran up the stairs saying, "I know how to open it."

I followed her to the top of the tower that opened up into a large circular room. Bilara sat upon one of the two large beds, frozen as she clutched the metal box. Mariam's mouth was open wide, as if speaking loudly to her, surely to distract her from the incessant horn's blare.

Without any gentleness, Edala tore the box from the girl's hands.

I couldn't help but ask, "Why did you not take the vessel sooner?"

"I did." Her voice was low. "But I could not open it. I did not realize what it was, and a jinni's vessel can only be opened how it is intended, see? I could not magic nor force it open." She shook her head, holding the box carefully in front of her. "Now that you've said it, I see it. This is Kassim's puzzle box, indeed." Peering at the remnants of the chain that had been broken, she nodded, and took a small vestige of metal into her fingers. Working it slowly, the chain fell off and left only a thin silver rod.

"What do you plan to do?" I asked.

"You were not wrong about magic, Emel. It always has a price." She held the box reverentially, mournfully. "I will become his master. Then I will put him to death."

"You?" I asked. "But in order for the jinni to die, the master must want it. Or the master, too, must . . ."

"I know. He needs to die." She did not seem convinced as she cradled the box in her arms, her eyes wet.

"Edala," I said softly. "You don't have to do it. I can be his master." I wanted him dead.

"No." She shook her head. "I will do it. It is like you said. Magic is better stripped from the desert. Look at all the trouble it has caused . . ."

Chills swept down my spine. What was she implying? "We should talk to the others."

"So they can tell us what, Emel? Waiting will do nothing but make it harder." She stood.

"You will do it now?" It was happening so quickly.

"Now." Sliding the key into the lock, the smallest click sounded. With her thumbs, Edala slid the pieces apart one by one, until finally, the top opened up.

"Return to your vessel," she whispered needlessly. He would return whether she asked it or not.

Almost instantly, the box snapped closed, the pieces sliding and pulling rapidly back together. By the way Edala held it close, I knew that Kassim was inside.

"And now?" I asked.

Swallowing hard, she turned and walked down the steps. Bilara and Mariam remained, locked in stillness behind us.

Edala led us to Saalim's tower. We passed Tamam, face stoic and watchful as ever. Edala's gaze lingered on him for a moment before she hurried up the stairs.

We did not stop in Saalim's rooms, though. We climbed higher.

"It seems only fitting he . . ." Her throat made a constricted sound and she did not finish.

We arrived in what I could only presume was Kassim's room. Untouched, preserved like a shrine. For having insisted so vehemently on hatred, I was shocked that Saalim had left it intact.

The room was decorated with dark curtains and bedding. A simple tapestry hung on the wall depicting the royal family—not unlike the one that was gifted to Saalim. There was a large, empty desk I suspected had seldom been used. Had Kassim sat at the table imagining he was corresponding with kings?

Edala coaxed flames to life in the fireplace across from his vast bed. I remembered thinking of sharing Kassim's bed. How far would he have let me fall for him simply to sway me from Saalim, the more easily to kill his brother? I chewed my cheek, the bitter taste of betrayal on my tongue.

Edala began fussing with the lock again. It took her one too many tries to insert the rod into the box, her shaking hands making it difficult.

Backing away as she slid the pieces of the box apart, I held my breath. I did not know what it would be like to release an angry jinni.

Horns blared, and I nearly fell to the ground in fright. But I felt the brush of wind against my face, and the curtains began shifting again. Time moved forward, I realized. Edala paused her disassembly of the box and looked out the window. The horns stopped, but the wind still blew. Satisfied, she slowly opened Kassim's vessel.

Just as I remembered Saalim appearing, Kassim did the same. It was a silver smoke, nearly liquid in its iridescence that spilled from the box, first up and up, then back down onto itself as Kassim's kneeling form appeared.

"Yes, master?" he said. Just as Saalim had done. I felt as if I'd been dropped in cold water all over again.

When the smoke had cleared, and only Kassim remained, I saw he was wholly a jinni: skin glinting almost silver, eyes brighter still. The silver cuffs I mistook for bracelets appeared to melt into his skin as Saalim's once had.

Kassim took in his surroundings. His shoulders fell, just a little. His confidence flagging in the home of his childhood.

"Why have you brought me here?" he said, rising. Under the constraints of Edala's desires, appeared a reined horse. Limited, finally.

I exhaled, relieved Zahar could no longer control the jinni. Even if she could not get far with my protection, there were still many ways to wreak havoc that did not involve me or Saalim. I was relieved, too, that the girl no longer possessed his vessel, even if in her room she was inconsolable at the sudden loss of her silver box. There was too much power at risk.

Edala sighed, and brushed a hand through her black hair as she gathered it over her shoulder. "So you might remember us. This life." She seemed like a child then. A hopeful, naïve child.

Oh, Edala. Even I could see this life was not one Kassim wanted to remember.

"You don't have to destroy me," Kassim said, so vulnerably that I felt an intruder in their lives. He did not look at me, though. Only his sister.

Edala nodded. "I could free you."

No. If he could not be trusted before, he surely could not be trusted now. Not when he had so much fuel for his anger.

"Edala," I said. "Don't."

Kassim finally looked at me. In spite of the silver, his eyes and skin now seemed almost corpse-like in their pallor. I knew he could feel, just slightly, the desire with which I wanted him gone. Did it hurt to know that someone distrusted him, despised him, so greatly?

I tried again. "Think of what he did to your father, your mother, Nadia, Saalim."

Kassim's gaze flashed back to Edala, having felt whatever changed in her.

"Edala," he began. "You and I, we could go somewhere, find something else. We could fly across this ocean, explore those places we heard about in court." He was still kneeling.

A begging slave, tongue as silver as his eyes.

Edala nodded once, and I nearly pulled the box from her hands myself. Then she said, "The path you are on now is of your own doing."

Without looking at him, she began to open the vessel.

"Wait," he said, his voice telling us the fight was lost. In his hands a large sack appeared; it reminded me of the salt-filled bags Saalim gave me. "For Bilara." He tossed the sack at my feet. "She was a kind master. Tell her Kas will miss her."

When I looked into the sack I saw sugar-dusted dates.

"Kas," Edala hesitated. "I . . ." She stopped herself. She opened the vessel, and he was gone.

This scene was too familiar, remembering how my wish for freedom had torn Saalim from me. Rigid, I stood beside Edala expecting something to go horribly wrong. Expecting for everything to happen as it did for me. But there had been no wish, so nothing could go awry.

Saalim's sister knelt by the fire. The bones of her knuckles shone as she tightly clutched Kassim's vessel. Then, she threw the silver box into the flames. The fire roared around the box as if to consume it, and we both watched with delicate stillness. Waiting, breathing.

The silver box did not bend at the flame's hands, it did not change. Nothing happened at all.

Edala gasped and sobbed, her face falling into her hands. The sound of anguish, of relief. But of course, no matter how much she believed she did, Edala did not want to lose him. No matter how evil, how wicked. He was her brother. How strange family was that we made so many allowances, accepted the unacceptable, only so they would stay ours.

I searched for something to pull the vessel from the flames.

"What has happened?" Tamam strode into the room, worry creased his face. "I heard your cries," he said, voice lifting in question. "And then I felt something . . ." He searched for the word.

The stilling of time. Something perhaps everyone felt when it happened, attributed to an ache of the head or a cramp in the gut. But Tamam was intimate with magic now, and he could discern the feel of it.

Wordlessly, lip trembling, eyes red and wet, Edala took Kassim's vessel from the flames. The fire did not burn her. She held it out for Tamam so carefully in her palms. It showed me the depth of their love, of their trust, more clearly than anything I had seen yet. She was offering him everything.

Tamam stepped closer to her, reaching his hand not for the vessel but for her. "Kassim," he said.

She nodded as he knelt beside her. This side of Tamam was so different from the man I knew, I could not look away.

"I am sorry," Tamam said, then pulled her to him. She cried in his lap, curling the vessel to her chest.

Through sobs, Edala said, "He can't die." Tamam's face darkened.

"Why?" He looked at me.

I began. "I am not—"

"I don't want him to," Edala whispered.

So there it was.

"Let me," I said through her cries of guilt, relief, fear.

Edala shook her head. Would she refuse to kill Kassim? Would she be his master and promise to keep him at bay? Until, of course, she decided that he was right and went after Saalim herself.

Edala said, "What if there is some small part of you who wants a jinni? I thought I would be untouched by greed, but here we are."

"It is not greed," Tamam said. "He is your brother."

Edala took a deep breath. "Emel is right."

I stared at her, remembering what she had told me: *You were not wrong about magic . . . It always has a price. It is like you said. Magic is better stripped from the desert.* Understanding washed over me. No.

"We do not belong here," she said, sounding so defeated. She tapped the pads of her fingers on the box. Beyond her, the fire quieted down, disappointed by its lost feast. "Magic, I mean."

Tamam bent toward her, stroking her hair away from her temple. "You belong here, Edala. You belong . . ." He glanced out at the day. What did he want to say that he withheld because I was there with them?

She shook her head. "We shouldn't have meddled. Zahar, me. Look what it's done. Pulling strings that should have been left to fate. It was wrong, and I see it now." She looked at me, eyes shining in the dying firelight. "We have allowed Masira to step into this world. It is not hers but her Sons'. We must destroy the path."

I said, "There must be another way."

She shook her head. "We must die."

My skin pricked with chills.

Tamam went rigid and shook his head, grabbing at her arm. "Don't be absurd." I looked away, his sadness so apparent, I had to swallow my tears. "Can't you undo what you've done? Become human? Like Saalim." He waved his hand at me.

So he knew, too. Had Edala told him?

I was sure Saalim had not.

What was it like for Tamam? A loyal soldier, a devoted friend. To find the woman he loved, the king he served, had a history thick with magic, with legend and myth.

She bowed her head, her eyes dropping to the vessel. "I can free Kassim, but Zahar and I cannot undo what we've done."

"Edala," I begged. "There must be another way. Can't you stop using magic?" I continued in a whisper. "You cannot die . . . you cannot leave Saalim, Tamam. Me."

She laughed. "You care little for me; I respect that. I know how you feel about what I've done and what I do. That is why—" she turned to me, pleading with the vessel between her palms. "I know you will do it. When I am gone, feed Kassim to the flames."

I shook my head. "I can't."

"You must."

Tamam rose. "I won't allow this."

She stood and placed her hand on his cheek. "My love, our story will not be tiled into a mosaic." She pressed her hand to his chest. "But it will be here. The first time you mourned me should have been the last."

Tamam spun away from her. "You are upset. Let's take time to consider all options. First we talk to Saalim, we find Zahar." Then he went back to her, taking her hands and pressing them together. "Please." The desperation he tried to keep hidden spilled over.

Something about what Edala said hummed through me like a plucked sitar string. It nagged at a memory, at my feelings when I left my village, when I declared that magic—though it had done wonderful things—was no boon. It sowed fear and questions and hardship. Edala was right. I was right. Magic needed to be gone from here.

Is that why Masira chose me, why I carried her mark? Did she know that I would rid her of this obligation to humans?

"All right." Rubbing at my wet cheeks, I asked, "How?"

Tamam cried her name in warning.

"Tamam," Edala said, "you will either come willingly and kiss me goodbye as I hope, or I will bind you with magic and leave you here."

Tamam stormed away. I heard his steps clatter down the stairs. Edala stared in the direction he went until we could hear his steps no longer. Her lip trembled, and she looked at me.

"I want the waves to take me. Go to Wahir."

"Now?"

"Now."

"And Saalim?"

From the folds of her robes, Edala pulled a neatly folded piece of parchment, sealed closed with wax. No mark. Just a smooth slick of red. "His response will be worse than Tamam's, I suspect. Give him this."

He would be devastated. He had been relieved to have found his family, to not be alone.

My legs were weak and shaky when I rose from the ground. My heart pounded, breath shallow.

I reached for the vessel, but Edala did not give it to me. "I want to be with him."

Nodding, I followed her out. Tamam waited for us at the base of the stairs, eyes trained only on Edala.

I could not look at him long, understanding how he drank her in, noting every detail as I had once done to Saalim. I heard his steps behind us, slow and heavy with remorse.

When we were out of the palace, Tamam passed me and took Edala's hand in his.

Together, we walked to the sea.

30

EMEL

H ad the weather changed, or had Edala's choice stirred the sky? The
sun was gone, and dark, gray clouds blanketed the blue. Were I
home in the desert, I would be celebrating, waiting for rain. Now,
it felt wrong. It felt, somehow, sad. The wind whipped around us as we walked
down the dock. It was in disrepair, used only by lone fishermen and lovers who
wanted to stand above the sea. Today, none were out. Was it the impending
rain? Was it magic?

Madinat Almulihi was quiet behind us. Had Saalim found Zahar? Was he
unharmed?

Tamam and Edala reached the end of the dock. I stayed behind, feeling
like an intruder already. Their backs were toward me as they stared out to the
horizon. The wind gusting so hard the waves were flecked in white.

Tamam edged closer and wrapped his arms around her, their heads bent
together. I saw his mouth move, whispering into her ear. She nodded her head,
then pressed her face into his neck. Her shoulders shook, and he pulled her to
him more tightly.

My throat clenched so hard it ached. I remembered myself in the oasis,
grasping at the sand where Saalim had disappeared, remembering too well the
pain of a forever goodbye. The gutting, scraping, emptying out of one's soul.

I could not look away.

Their lips pressed together, soft, delicate, then harder, desperate. Tamam's face twisted into grief.

Finally, Edala called. "Emel."

When I reached them, she turned to me, pressing her lips to the small puzzle box that a young boy's hands had once pulled apart to hide his treasures. That boy would die with his box of secrets. That man, too. With infinite tenderness, she gave Kassim's vessel to me.

Edala's gaze met mine. "Thank you, sister. My brother has found his life's fortune in you." She pressed her lips to my brow.

Bending over, she crafted a small brass basin from nothing. It was filled with wooden pellets soaked in oil. It roared aflame. "When it is done, place him here," Edala said, her fingers caressing the edges of the basin like a baby's cradle. She went to Tamam and wrapped her arms around his neck. Like she weighed nothing, he lifted her into his arms. One last time, she whispered into his ear. He curled her into his chest, eyes shut tight as he pressed his cheek against her, kissing her temple, her neck, her mouth.

Suddenly, her head fell back, her arm dropped away from her.

"What?!" I rushed toward them.

"She sleeps," Tamam said quietly, his voice trembling. "She will feel nothing but the waves."

Moving as if the world had been stilled, Tamam went to his knees, then seated himself on the edge of the dock. I heard the rumble of his whispers as he held her to him. Was it a prayer or a goodbye? Then, he dropped Edala into the sea. The splash too small, like a stone had fallen.

Edala's eyes were closed, her hair flowing out beside her, the robes billowing at the surface of the sea as if trying to stay afloat.

Tamam flinched as if to jump in and grab her. I put a hand on his shoulder, squeezing gently.

When the fabric could buoy her weight no longer, Edala sank into the green sea. I was not sure if I imagined it, but her mouth seemed to lift into the smallest smile.

When I could see her no more, I went to the flames, fearing they would die with their creator. There were things I thought to say to Kassim, thought to whisper to the vessel about how he could have chosen differently. Could have chosen joy over jealousy, satisfaction over pride. But in many ways he was as broken as Sabra had been. He had made the wrong choices, and it was not my place to punish him in his final moments.

"Go to the goddess," I whispered, then tossed the box into the flames. It clanked loudly against the bronze basin.

Nothing happened. What if Edala had been wrong?

But then I saw the edges of the vessel bend, the carvings melting into something smooth, the sharp corners dulling. The entire thing collapsed into itself, glowing orange like metal poured for forging. It spread through the wooden pellets, the flames reaching higher and higher as it burned.

Perhaps I thought that there would be some final cry, something dramatic and frightening as Kassim was killed, as a conduit of Masira was cut from the goddess. But there was no epic end, no final signal that it was done.

The fire died away as the metal was melted completely. When no flames were left, when there was only smoke and charred wood with tendrils of silver between them, I reached for the basin. It was cold, despite the flames just having died. I poured the contents into the water, the waves of the sea carrying him back to Masira. Tamam glanced only briefly at the ash and silver as they spread over the ocean's surface before looking back to where Edala had disappeared. I left him there, watching the waves that took his lover, and returned to the city.

As I stepped across the dock, I considered how so much life could be lost with so little fanfare. No bang of a drum, no explosion of firepaint. Only the whisper of the wind, the snuff of a flame. No one knew, except those who had witnessed it. How could two lives so big end so small?

~~~~~~

A guard rushed up to me as I ascended the steps of the palace. "The king waits for you in the throne room." Light rain speckled his shoulders with dark drops.

As soon as I entered the room, I stopped. At least one hundred people were crammed in front of Saalim on his throne.

At first I could not hear his address. I could think of nothing except that he was whole and unharmed in front of me. I wanted to run and cling to him. Make him promise me that we would never part.

Slowly, his words seeped in. Without using his name, he told them of Kassim—what he looked like, what he might do. He advised that they should not approach him and to report to the guard if they saw him. Then he described Edala, told them her name. She was a friend and could be approached if help was needed. He had no notion of all that had transpired. Edging around the room, I tried to catch his attention. Finally, he saw me.

His speech paused for a moment—none would have noticed—and his shoulders eased ever so slightly. Then he said, "If there are questions, Nassar will answer them." Not concerned by the confusion left in his wake, he stepped away and through a heavily guarded hallway. I followed his trail of soldiers and servants into the atrium.

Saalim broke through the tangle of people and was in front of me.

"Saalim!" I cried, running to him, uncaring of who watched.

Tamam's farewell to Edala was burned in my mind. It brought with it the memory of feeling I had lost Saalim forever.

Saalim, too, was surprised by my urgency as I went to him, and when he saw my face he went rigid.

"What has happened?"

I shook my head. "Not here."

"A moment," Saalim said to his retinue of staff, taking me to the vacant hall adjacent.

He pulled me to a stone column of the balcony archway, stopping just before we were under the rain.

"Where is Edala? Kassim?" he asked quickly.

I stared off at the city, smudged by the rain. I could just make out the sea, docks tapering off into the haze. Squinting, I tried to see if Tamam was still there, but I saw nothing.

Saalim said, "Tell me, Emel." His urgency told me he was beginning to understand, beginning to fear.

"Kassim is dead," I said.

"How?"

I told him. How Edala and I magicked here to take the vessel before Zahar could, how Edala became his master, how at first he would not burn. I talked and talked, telling more details than necessary, I realized. Anything so that I did not have to tell him *why* Kassim was able to be killed.

"Emel," Saalim said as if he understood my sorrow. "I am sorry that you had to see that." I heard the tightness in his words, the bend as he fought sadness.

I dropped my eyes to the ground. He thought me sad because his brother had died.

Oh, Saalim.

He continued. "There was no other choice. His anger was the death of him." Anger fueled by the healer. "Where is Zahar?" I asked.

He gave a small smile, his eyes glinting like his crown. "We found her on her way here. She's in the prison now."

"What will you do with her?"

"I thought to ask you."

"Ah." What would be a fitting punishment for the woman who had dismantled Saalim's family, was the cause of death for so many? Weighing death with imprisonment, exile with isolation, it seemed a decision too great to allow for my opinion.

Saalim remembered suddenly. "Where is Edala?"

I opened my mouth, but no words came out. I cursed Edala for making me do this, for not being brave enough to face him herself. Finding the letter I had tucked away, I handed it to him with a shaking hand.

The shadows on his face darkened as he took the letter. The parchment crumpled in his hand. He did not bother to open it.

"Damnit!" he shouted, the word splitting as he spoke it. "Damnit," he said again, striding back and forth. He sucked a breath in. There was a muffled cry, and he threw the letter to the ground.

After several long moments of pacing, he said tightly, "She is gone."

"Yes," I said, wanting so much to turn away from the grief in his voice.

"She will not return."

"She said it was the only way."

He put his arms against the wet stone column, and hung his head between them.

Silently, I retrieved the letter and again stuffed it away. When he was ready, I would have it for him. "I am sorry," I said finally, pressing my hand to his back.

Wordlessly, he turned to me and pulled me to him, clinging to me as we hid from the others behind the stone.

<hr />

That night, after the city had been reassured that the threat was gone, while the guards were sent through the streets to find any lingering members of the Darkafa and people set to work clearing the street of the baytahira, I found my way to the prison.

The cells were beneath the palace, a place I had not yet gone. It grew cold as I took the steps down, and I could not pull my cloak any more tightly around me. The sounds and scents from below hit me simultaneously. Unwashed bodies, excrement and urine. Clamor of metal, demanding shouts. I nearly turned back, feeling dinner rise.

Though the narrow hallway was poorly lit, I could see servants carrying meals to and fro. Guards stood by, watching the fluttering servants, unlocking and locking doors for them.

Another wave of foulness hit me like a wall. A door paneled with interlocking wood and metal stood to my left, and inside I could just make out the shape of a figure on the ground, bent over what I assumed was his meal. Another chamber had two women inside, screeching at each other. A guard ran up to the door and banged the flat of his sword against it, startling me as much as the prisoners. Perhaps it would be better to return when Saalim could spare a guard to escort me. Or maybe—

"Emel?" a woman asked, pausing in front of me with a tarnished silver bowl filled with stew. I recognized her from the kitchens and felt ashamed I did not know her name.

The smell of yeast and spices wafting off of her was like shade on a summer's day. "I hoped to speak with a prisoner," I said, moving close.

"Ask him." The woman pointed behind her with her heel, then carefully moved past me.

The guard was facing a cell door, speaking quietly to someone. As I neared, I could tell he was soft-spoken, mild-mannered. Certainly not someone I would expect to manage prisoners.

He stopped his conversation when I was beside him. He was surprisingly young for his station.

"It is not often that a woman like you finds herself in this part of the palace."

Like me? He obviously had no idea who I was. Living the past few days inside the palace, wearing the fine clothes and rich oils, conveyed more than I realized.

"I need to meet with one of your prisoners."

"I might be able to arrange that. Who?" The way his eyes creased, the shape of his nose, the cut of his beard all nagged me with familiarity.

"Zahar, the healer."

He nodded. Though his face was shadowed in the dim hallway, I could see that his expression softened. "I wondered. She is this way."

He held out his arm, directing me down the hall, but I didn't move. I couldn't help staring at him. Where had I seen him before? "What is your name?"

"Rafal."

I paused. It was impossible that he was a younger version of the storyteller. "I knew a Rafal."

A little sadly he said, "My father?"

"Your father?"

"Mapmaker. We used to travel all over together to create his maps."

"The storyteller?"

"Yes!" He smiled so broadly that I forgot we were in a prison with stale air and unfriendly faces. "I played the drums."

"Yes!" I laughed. "I saw you! I thought you were familiar. But why are you . . ." I looked around.

Rafal's smile fell. "After my father died, I needed work. So many from my mother's neighborhood wound up here. Many unjustly, I think."

"Your mother."

"Kahina? You might have heard of her. Some might say her reputation is soiled. I think otherwise."

"The proprietress of the baytahira?" I gasped. "Rafal *was* her husband?" Saalim had not been sure. My head spun, thinking of the maps on her walls, the strange and beautiful illustrations I saw in her home.

"I chose to work here," his son continued, "to see if I might make it better for the prisoners. Those that perhaps don't deserve . . . this." He spoke quietly so none could hear him over the clamor. "Does that make sense?"

I remembered when I was imprisoned by my father for the whole cycle of a moon.

How unjust it felt. If it had not been for my brother—and Saalim—my imprisonment might have killed me.

"I understand completely," I said, smiling. Stepping in the direction he had indicated, Rafal followed behind.

Toward the end of the hall, he began muttering about new prisoners over here, then peered through a gap in the door.

"She's here," he said. "Zahar, would you allow a visitor?" Holding his ear against the door, he nodded, then inserted a key into the lock. With an easy push, the door swung in, and he gestured inside.

"I'll wait here. The door will be unlocked, so come out when you're finished."

Rafal swung the door closed behind me and what little light had bled in was gone. It was nearly dark, but as my eyes adjusted, I saw Zahar sitting on a mat in the corner, the same woman with smooth skin and black hair who had tried to take my life the same day.

"I imagine it gives you great pleasure to find me here," Zahar said once the door was closed.

"It does," I said after I had surveyed the space. There was no window, so was it always this dark?

Zahar was quiet.

"Did you expect me to deny it?" I asked.

"What do you want?"

"To understand."

"Explain yourself." Zahar spoke slowly. I imagined that even if she had no interest in seeing me, talking with me provided at least something by way of entertainment for her.

"They know what I can do," she said. "The food they've given me, the things in this room. Nothing I can use."

For magic.

"Saalim has asked me what I am to do with you."

"What have you planned?"

"I haven't decided. It is why I came. I still don't understand everything. Tell me the whole story, Zahar."

"Since I've nothing better to do." She stretched out her legs. "My mother only had two children. Daughters, of course. I was the youngest, so it was Tahira who was to ensure our parents could live comfortably until death. We were not poor, but we were not wealthy either.

"They pulled together a fine gift for any man of high status to consider. But then the sea royals came through, and my sister captured the attention of their king. We thought nothing of it—just another man looking for an evening companion—but two moons later she confessed she had not bled.

"My mother knew that if she ended the pregnancy, she could still be wed. Tahira would hear nothing of it. She wanted the baby. She loved the king."

Anger simmered beneath her words.

"So she left to find him. My family looked to me to take on the burden, but you have seen my hips—narrow as a boy's. My feet are big . . . it doesn't matter. I would never serve in my sister's place.

"I followed her to Almulihi. I planned to bring her back."

When Zahar finally found her, she was nearly ready to have the child, and King Malek had already wed the Hayali princess Kena. The king had known of Tahira's pregnancy by the time Zahar arrived. He promised he would raise the child as if it were the queen's, and Tahira could see the child grow happily and comfortably. She only could not meddle in the upbringing. Tahira agreed.

On the fall equinox, Saalim was born.

Zahar tried to bring her sister home. Her son would be fine, she said, there was nothing more she could do. But her sister would not leave. She wished to live and serve at the palace, but the king refused, worried that it placed her too close to Saalim.

"The king did not know how good my sister was." Each word, Zahar spat like poison. "She would never have said a word to Saalim that gave her away. She just wanted to see her boy."

The separation from her son consumed her, and she would spend nights sitting on the palace steps, staring at the windows instead of sleeping. There was nothing Zahar could do to convince her to leave, so Zahar worked to become the palace healer. If Tahira could not watch Saalim grow, at least Zahar could. She thought it would please her sister.

At first, it worked. Tahira was thrilled with every word of news, every token of Saalim's that Zahar gave her. Tahira carved wood into little soldiers that Zahar would give to Saalim. Stories of his joy delighted Tahira. Saalim was raised well, and this, too, pleased Tahira. But it could not last, and soon, she grew jealous. Zahar tried to temper it, tried to bring her more things, lead Saalim out with errands, but it was no use. In her despondence, Tahira grew distant.

"I lost the only sister I had. The only family that remained." She did not know where her parents had gone, only that they had long ago left their caravan.

"One morning, Tahira was not at the palace steps. I searched everywhere and could not find her. Kahina was a friend of Tahira's, see, so I went to her. She had housed her and provided her with small work. Kahina told me she sent her away. Away! Kahina said Tahira suffered watching her son from a distance.

Unable to share in his life. She said Tahira needed to leave for her health, her sanity. And my sister listened to her! She did not even say goodbye to me." Zahar's voice broke. "Here I was, in this city I cared nothing for, serving people I despised for family who had gone." There was a long silence.

Finally, Zahar said, "The king got what he deserved."

"Do you realize that you still have family? That Saalim is your family?"

She spat. "He is no family of mine."

"You hate him because of the king's blood he carries? But he is also your sister. He, too, is a salt chaser. You and he share blood, but instead of cherishing all the ways he was like you, you focused on the ways he was not. You destroyed everything." Were Tahira's eyes the same gold color? Did she have high cheekbones, too?

"I did only what Malek deserved!" Desperate, she clawed at the past.

"When did you realize that most of the mistakes were not your sister's, but your own?" I asked. Zahar had never needed to leave her family to force Tahira to do something she did not want. She had never needed to destroy the possibility for a friendship with her sister's son.

There was a long silence. Then, "Have you decided how you will be rid of me?"

"I have not."

She scoffed. "It matters not." She leaned against the wall, staring up at the ceiling. "I flew as a bird all over this desert. If I could, I would live that life again and again." She was far away now. "Do you know what the sea looks like from above? Flat, almost smooth but for the finest wrinkles in the surface. Do you know what your village looked like from above?"

I could not see her eyes, but I felt as if they bored into me.

"A faceted gem."

My breath hitched.

"Yes," she said, nodding. "I watched you. When I realized Saalim was there, I followed him.

"I thought I would stay there forever, watching ahiran traipse to the healer to make the decision my sister should have made. But it was better than being a pathetic cricket. It was better than this. I am so tired . . ."

Edala had been right about everything. I was reeling. Zahar had seen me? I tried to remember that day Raheemah and I had gone to the healer's. Two birds were posted on the entrance to his home. One, a brown griffon.

"I worried when the healer said you were marked," she said. "Still, I could not believe that one would free a jinni."

"I thought I would be stronger when I returned to my human form, but he was freed so soon. And then you landed in my home as my apprentice as though Masira herself had placed you there. I wonder if perhaps she did."

"You hoped to turn me against Saalim."

"I hoped you would see that he was a spoiled brat. That you would feel less *protective* over him."

"He changed because of you." Everything he was now came of who he had been as a jinni. Even if he remembered none of it, the hardships of being a slave to another had been carried with him into this life. Unwillingly, Zahar had made him a better king.

"He slept on a salt mine and appreciated none of it."

Unable to listen to her vehemence any longer, I stood.

"What will you do with me?" she asked.

"Return you home."

31

SAALIM

The palace was enormous, vacant. A sham of a home. And I was, once again, a puppet forced to live there forever. Only the swish of fabric and smack of stone were my companions as I walked through the halls. I lived through this before. How cruel to mourn a family twice.

I stopped mid-step. "Where is Tamam?" A slack-faced soldier was standing in front of my tower where Tamam should have been.

"I cannot say. Azim posted me here. It was empty."

Did Tamam know about Edala?

On the landing, I glanced up the stairs to Kassim's quarters. I would have the servants destroy everything that remained inside.

Turning into my room, I let out a breath of relief. Finally alone to think.

Since the death of my parents, I had spent much of my time remembering how I had failed and acting so that I would not repeat the same mistakes. Because of this, I had not behaved as king of this city. I was a blundering idiot, considering most that which would be perceived as right, not what *was* right for my city and the people that lived in it. It was not behavior of a leader.

Now, I needed to lead.

Pushing away from the window ledge, I went to the basin of water by my doorway. Three stones lay at the bottom: Father, Mother, and Nadia. Outside of the basin was the linen-wrapped package given to me by Liika. Peeling away the cloth, I peered at the jagged, white stone. Salt in rock form—halite, I think they called it. It would dissolve if left in the water.

It preferred the dry air, the sun.

It was my mother completely.

I pulled her stone from the basin and set it aside. I carried the salt rock to the window's edge so that it could spend its days in the sun. There my mother could rest. With Eiqab.

Kassim and Edala's stones were still in my pack. They clinked together as I tightened my fist around them. I hesitated after placing Edala with the others. Did Kassim belong with them?

It was not my decision to make. His fate was with Masira. Everything he was, everything he did, must remain behind me now. I set his stone—smooth and gray—in the bottom of the basin with the rest of our family.

Finally, I took my father's stone from the water: black, heavy and gleaming. Pressing it between my palms, then to my brow, I prayed.

Wahir let me stay this sea.

I returned to my desk and began sorting through the letters, the tasks. This time with focus, an eagerness. *I was the king.* Each time I thought it, an ease traveled through me, a soft tingling over my skin. Tomorrow, I would speak with Azim, Ekram, Nassar. Together we would put the soiled past behind us. We would move forward, with me as its leader and these men at my sides. It would take time, but I would earn my place as king.

As I worked through the inquiries, addressing this and that, finishing tasks that had long been waiting for my attention, things seemed to shift back into place. At the bottom of the pile I found an old letter from Helena's father indicating when they would be arriving for the wedding. The parchment was soft, of a fine quality, and my fingertips brushed against it absently as I read the words over and over.

Footsteps. Mariam bustled in to fuel the fire.

"Do you need someone to sleep?" she asked, glancing at my work with ill-veiled surprise.

Shaking out my aching hand, I handed her the completed letters. She set them on a chair before moving to the fire. I considered her offer. Tonight, though, Dima was not what I wanted. I glanced at the letter in front of me again. Helena's name stretched toward me like eager arms.

"Not tonight, Mariam. How is the child?"

She prodded the fire. "She was inconsolable, reaching for everything and becoming more upset when she couldn't find it. Emel came in with a bag of dates, which helped. Finally, Bilara's asleep. I don't understand how we lost her box. She never let it go."

"Should I have a new one made?"

Mariam stood slowly, rubbing her lower back. "No," she said, lifting the letters from the chair. "She must learn to live without it."

When Mariam was gone, I rose from the desk and began to undress. Beside my wardrobe, I saw the polished boots that had been set out for the wedding, kicked to the side in a frantic exit.

There she was again. *Helena.*

Kneeling, I set the boots beside my sword that leaned sheathed against the wall. My father's sword, now mine.

Too long I had sat upon the wall dividing my lives, thinking I could keep a foot on both, but I could not. I was not a child who dreamed of holding a sword.

I was a *king.* It was time I acted as one.

I looked at the boots again and nodded, committing to my decision.

I was a king. A king married a princess.

I wrote my letter to Helena's father.

I was a king. I was no boy.

These words did not buoy me as they had moments before. Not when this goodbye loomed so near.

The moon had not yet risen high. It was not too late.

Moving down the stairs, the finality of my decision terrified me. Saying goodbye to that part of my life . . . to that tapestry of my future, nearly made me turn back. To say *no* to her. I sat down, nausea rising in my throat. Taking heavy breaths, I stood and continued down the stairs.

"My lord," the soldier said, pushing off the wall he leaned against.

"I will return soon."

"Do you need an escort?"

I shook my head and went down the hall, unable to utter another word for fear I would have him stop me, fearing that I would have him pull Nassar from his bed to seek his counsel. But it was a decision I had to make. I knew it was the right one.

I was up the stairs of the guest tower standing outside the doorway. Hesitating, I looked back down the stairs. No, this could not wait. She would need to decide what she wanted to do, where she wanted to go. Again, nausea unfurled through me. It felt like a whole part of my past was being loosed, a ship's mooring snapped.

"Emel?" I called out, voice tremoring like a child's. Pathetic. Clearing my throat, I pushed the door open wider and called again when she did not respond.

Still nothing, so I stepped into the room. It was well-lit, the torches and fire blazing. It appeared as if Mariam had just been there as well.

Where had she gone after dinner, if not here? Traitorous relief told me that I could tell her some other time. It did not have to be now.

It felt like trespassing, stepping into the room, but it *was* my palace, after all. The space was untouched, the bedding smooth as stone. There was nothing in the room that told me Emel was staying here.

Unless she was not staying here? My hands dropped to my side, limp. Had she left for good?

I threw open the wardrobe and exhaled. Drooping fabric was suspended from hooks and settled into shallow wooden boxes. Her clothes. Something bright caught my eye in the back of the wardrobe.

Her pack.

It was sagging open, gold glinting at me. Gold? Why had she been carrying around gold all this time? The pack was surprisingly light but noisy as I moved it to the bed.

"Emel?" I called again, looking toward the bathing room.

Nothing.

The metal was cold when I touched it, and though I wanted to examine all the contents in the sack, I let it go and walked away from the bed.

Wind brushed in, and I followed it out to the balcony. Orange-lit windows glowed throughout the city, the clouds still smothering any light from the sky. The rain had stopped, but the stone below was still slick with it. Leaning against the rail, the water cold beneath my fingers, I thought of the people that lived here. They slept, worked, loved because they trusted me and my father before me. That we would protect them, serve to anchor and shelter their lives. Today Kassim had attempted to shake that trust. He failed, but what if Emel had not been here? That was a future I prepared to face.

"Saalim?"

My pulse quickened, and I turned to Emel.

"What are you doing here?" she asked, sounding nervous as she stepped toward me. "My things . . ." she said, glancing behind her.

"I did not go through them," I said.

Though I wanted to reach out to her, to hold her face in my palm, my arms were fast at my side. "I needed to talk to you."

"It is late."

"It could not wait."

She led me back into the room, and we found ourselves in front of the fire, Emel forgoing the chair to sit upon the rug. She was already reaching out her hands to the flames, warming them, when I sat.

Leaning my elbows on my knees, I watched her face. "I have made a decision."

She waited, glancing at me only briefly before watching the flames again. She pressed her lips together.

I said, "There is a chair that sits in the throne room. It is empty, and it needs a queen. There is a crown that is cold. It belongs on the brow of a woman who is strong enough to hold it." I hesitated, looking down at my clenched hands. "There is a king who sits in front of a woman—a once ahira, a healer's apprentice, a freer of jinn—who is equally alone."

Her eyes met mine, mouth parting slightly.

I said, "My father chose the crown over his heart. He chose wrong. I will not do the same." I knelt down before her, taking her warm hand carefully. "I choose both." I took a breath, then said, "Would the daughter of the Salt King deign to wed the son of a salt chaser?"

Her eyes were so dark, I saw nothing in their depths. So many secrets she could hide in them. What would she say?

She pulled her scarf away from her neck, then folded her fingers into a fist. "Me?" she asked, eyes glistening. "You are choosing me?"

The way she looked, the way she said it, I could almost convince myself she was saying—

"Yes, Saalim," she breathed. "Yes."

Sons, there it was. That word like an anchor. A heavy, comforting weight that pulled me to the ground and held me there. *She* was holding me there— holding me home. Reaching out, I pressed my hand against her cheek. She leaned into it, and almost unconsciously, pressed her hand over mine. It was like she had done it one hundred times before. And apparently she had.

I said, "Since I went to your settlement, I've felt a void within myself. I always thought it was grief for my family. But *you* have filled it." How could I describe it to her without sounding mad? "Like I was a musician who had found his hands." I took both of her hands in mine.

She smiled knowingly. "A nomad who has found his feet?"

"Yes," I said, laughing. That was exactly it. "I am a bird, and now I have wind." I dropped my gaze to the ground. "If she will have me?"

"How many times must I say that I am already yours?" She rose to her knees and brought her face near mine. So close, I could almost feel each exhalation against my skin. Her lips so close, I could see them bow like an eagle's wings.

Slowly, I moved my hand across her back, feeling the rise and fall of the bones of her shoulders, how they moved just a little under my touch. I wrapped my arm around her, pulling her toward me. A tacit request for more. Heat pooled, and all I wanted was her lips against mine, our bodies crashing together on the bed.

But Emel stilled. "Saalim," she said. "There can be no secrets."

"No," I agreed. I would have agreed to anything in that moment.

"Then—" she pushed off me and hurried to the bed, bringing back her sack. Without explanation, she dumped the contents onto the ground. A glass vessel filled with sand rolled toward me. It was etched with the symbols of Almulihi. Two golden—?

"Cuffs," Emel said when she saw my face. "These were yours."

"Mine?" My breath paused, and I lifted one. It was so heavy.

"When you were a jinni."

Jinni. I swallowed. Edala had said as much, and Emel, too. But seeing it in front of me felt unbelievable. Those had once been around my wrists? Emel held out the glass and told me it was my vessel. Then she showed me a moon jasmine with bright white petals, alive despite being plucked from the ground.

"You gave this to me when we visited Almulihi together." She watched the flower swirl between her fingertips.

"We came here?"

She nodded, explaining it all. She showed me a tile that I was sure had come from the palace. Emel confirmed it had, that I had given it to her. "I often wonder if there is a missing tile somewhere."

"There must be many."

Emel showed me the map I knew she carried with her, a necklace I had many times seen around her neck, and finally, a half of a wooden soldier.

"You have this?" I was incredulous, thinking of its other half tucked away on a shelf.

She explained that, too. It would never be easy, knowing there was a past that Emel claimed to have memory of that I knew nothing about. What were we like? What was I like? How did I compare to the man she fell in love with? Perhaps Masira covering her tracks was not so wrong. Magic warped sanity, and I would have been better off not knowing this in such detail.

"I show you this," Emel said, "because I will hide nothing from you. And that includes this." She pulled out the wrinkled parchment. "The letter from Edala."

The one I had thrown aside. I thought it had been lost forever. It the last thing I would have from my sister. Greedily, I reached for it. The wax seal had been broken already.

"I read it," Emel said. Her voice was low, eyelashes brushing her cheek. "I know I shouldn't have, but you threw it aside, and I thought you might never read it and if you . . ." She stopped herself. "Well, go ahead."

Saalim,

This letter gives me as much joy to write as it does sorrow. If you are reading this, then Masira has taken me.

I feel it is the second time I have chosen death. Only this time, it was not for selfish gain. Though it grieves me to admit it, I see wisdom in a desert without magic. A life without divine meddling.

Emel seems to be the last piece in the puzzle of our entanglement with the gods. She was placed to bring us all together, so that in one final rent, we would be pulled apart again. Only this time with finality. And this time, without the goddess having her say in how it unfolds.

Father was wrong. You do not have to wed for blood, Saalim. There are few whom I would view as your equal, as worthy of your love, of Mother's crown. Emel is one of the few. She is a sister I would be proud to have.

Almost as proud as I am to have you as my brother. I thank the Sons every day for our father's decision, because it brought us you. As a foolish child, I did not see it. Now, I see that none could hold this city on their back as well as you.

I hope that you have already learned all of this for yourself, but if you are unsure and care to know the past, you will find a drink I have left you behind the portraits in my room.

Finally, if you choose to take the drink, please give Tamam the portraits.

With so much love,
Edala

Confused, I looked up. Emel held a small clear vial in her hand.

Inside, there was a small amount of liquid—one swallow at most.

"I know I should not have read it, I should not have gotten this, but—"

"What is it?" I asked, uncaring of what she had done. What had Edala left me?

"I do not know."

I took the vial, peering closely at it through the firelight. "It is not safe to drink."

"Do you trust Edala?"

I nodded. *Know the past.*

I held out my hand. Emel took it in hers. Nothing felt as right as these moments with her. So far, nothing with her had been wrong.

Tipping the vial into my mouth, I swallowed the tasteless liquid.

Then, like the sand of an hourglass, memories seeped in.

The pull of fire on my hands, my voice speaking words I did not want to say.

Trapped under the sun.

An angry man.

Trapped in the coolest water.

A monster's mind, a demon's wish.

Trapped in foul conscience.

A girl, a woman.

Emel.

Freedom, but not quite. Warping minds, changing hands.

Dead strewn like pillows in a harem.

A woman—Emel.

And she was there, and there, and there some more. We were together. When we weren't, still she was with me.

Her mouth on another. Her hands on another. Man after man.

Of Almulihi, broken and vacant.

Her naked body pressed against mine.

Agony, desperation, grief like I had never felt.

And there was a bending of time. Of two lives that blurred into one.

Traveling to Alfaar's, being ripped from the oasis. My memories colliding like waves in the deep sea. The merging and tearing of time made me sick.

Then I was back in the guest tower, sitting in front of Emel. I saw it all: the suitors I had swayed, death around us, her hands in mine, her lips against my neck, selfish desire, our bodies together, the cruelty from her father, her life as a slave. All of it because of me.

Clearer than the vial I held in my hand, I saw it all.

Everything I had done before crashing into everything I was now.

32

EMEL

Saalim shook his head, looked at me, then shook his head again.

"What happened?" I asked. "Are you all right?"

He was changed. The way he looked at me, the way he spoke to me. The way he *wouldn't* look at me.

"All of it is there," he stammered. "I see it all." His head hung between his knees.

"All of it?" I said, hopeful. Did he see us?

"Yes." He looked at me briefly, turning away like there was something foul. What about the past was so appalling?

Then, it struck me like a hand. My past with the muhamis, my life as an ahira. He knew about it before, but now, he saw it all with sickening clarity. I had not considered that possibility when giving him the vial.

"Me," I said, willing myself to hold my head high.

Saalim did not look at me.

The rejection spread like venom. He had seen our past together, and he wanted none of it. So this was it. My future with Saalim gone as quickly as it came. The utter joy there only moments before, stripped in a rush, and I was left stinging.

I reeled.

"The guilt," Saalim groaned, rubbing his brow. "It is unbearable." I followed his gaze. The stars were bright, the moon—a sharp sliver peaking in through the window—the brightest among them. "I am a man made insane. To have these memories, this understanding that no one else can have. Of two lives lived separately." He turned to me. "But this is how it has been for you this entire time."

"I do not quite have two lives, but I have grown used to having a past no one knows." I held myself away from him, terrified of what he would say next.

"It explains everything. All of these thoughts I had, this confusion and unexplained confidence about . . ." He looked at his hands. "Then there's Nassar . . . Zahar . . . Omar." He looked at me, disgusted. I recoiled. "And Almulihi." He almost whimpered when he said the last word. "And then there was you."

I held my breath, chest aching. I waited.

"You were the shortest part of my impossibly long life as a jinni." He stumbled on those words, picking up a golden cuff, then the vessel. He looked at them with a new understanding. "But the memories with you are so vivid, so *real* compared to others." He set the vessel down. "I need to step outside. Please, come with me."

Warily, I followed him onto the balcony. He did not take my hand, he did not look at me. He went to the edge, leaned against the rail. Just as I had found him not long ago. My insides gnawed themselves to pulp as I waited for an explanation.

Finally, he said, "I can barely look at you without seeing everything I have done." He folded his arms across his chest, staring at the ground far below. "Your entire life—all the suffering—was because of me."

That was unexpected. "You're not making sense."

He shook his head in the darkness. "I was greedy—"

"Greedy?"

"What if I had let the first suitor who wanted to wed you do so? Years ago, you would have been free of Alfaar's court." He pushed away and paced. "All the suitors, the years trapped in that tent . . . your father's savagery, the parties . . ."

The pain in his voice nearly convinced me that he was right, that my life had been worse because of what he had done. But when I looked around me, I knew he was wrong.

"Saalim, look at what you have given me. The sea, Madinat Almulihi, a whole world I would not have had otherwise. The beauty here, this life . . . it is unparalleled."

He scoffed.

"You have read the Litab Almuq?" I asked.

"Of course."

"Eiqab apologizes to Wahir for drying his pools. Do you remember?"

"Yes."

"Wahir tells him that without Eiqab's sun, he would not have made pools. If Eiqab had not dried the pools, Wahir would not have learned to make them deep and plentiful.

"Though you feel like you took my choices from me, pulled me from what seemed the obvious path of my life, you did no such thing. You allowed me my choice, Saalim.

"That girl who escaped the palace again and again? That was me searching for a path I could choose, desperate to forge a life that I had some control over. By taking the suitors from me, you took from me my father's control.

"If I had not wanted you, I could have turned you away while I was imprisoned. You remember that now, don't you?"

"I do." He glanced at my back, then back to the city below.

How odd it was to have memories we shared again. Memories of that life. I took his hand, pressing it to mine. I no longer tiptoed around a past none could know of except me.

Saalim said, "I thought it was the strangest answer, you know, when I asked you about the scars."

I remembered that night on the balcony. Dazed from being so high off the ground, still baffled by differences between Madinat Almulihi and my home, stunned from the isolation of my memories. The man I loved stood before me and asked me about wounds he had healed with his own hands.

"'He is,' you said, when I asked you if they were worth it."

We were silent, watching each other.

"You are," I said finally. "No matter what you feel like you've done or caused." I reached for his hand. "You are."

He did not let go.

Turning to him, I held our hands in front of us. "This," I said, "is worth everything to me. So stop your guilt, Saalim."

He jerked his head up at my insistence. Taking my hand between both of his, he brushed his lips across my knuckles.

He said, "You're perilously close to the edge, you know." He raised his eyebrows, smirking. His tone had changed. He sounded almost happy.

"I trust you," I said, though I edged away from the railing. He did not miss my movement.

"I don't think you do." Then, in one swift movement his arms were wrapped around my waist and my feet were lifted off the ground. I squealed. He ran into the bedroom and tossed me onto the bed.

This was the Saalim I longed for. The one who was carefree, who smiled and played and laughed. Beaming at him, I said, "So, you have not changed your mind then?"

He leaned forward. "My mind has been made up for a long time; I just couldn't see clearly before." Crawling over me, he said, "Sons, how I have longed to have you in my bed. Since the moment I saw you, in this life and the last."

Wrapping my fingers around his neck, I pulled him toward me. No more talking, no more remembering. I wanted to just have him as I did before. Have him like I always dreamed: freely, no secrets.

Our mouths met in furious need. He lowered himself onto me, pressing me into the soft bed as he had pressed me into the soft sand. Everything was surreal, and I simultaneously wanted to stop time so that I might grasp every detail, hold onto every moment, and rush forward to have it all.

"There is a bath . . . Mariam prepared," I whispered as he kissed my temple, my cheek, my neck. "Last time we never . . . But perhaps . . . it is unnecessary . . ."

He laughed quietly into my neck, breathing me in. Dragging his lips down my skin, he said, "A bath sounds nice."

He pulled his tunic over his head and led me to the bath. Mariam had the enormous basin filled and warmed every evening, and each night I lounged in it, soaking in the luxury. The water inside was impossibly warm, the low fire beneath having only just recently waned. Steam rose from the water's surface, blowing with each cool gust of wind. The stone was cold against my feet, so I stepped onto the large pelt beside the basin.

"It's no oasis pool," Saalim said as if it were somehow disappointing.

"You have high expectations, eh?" I dipped my fingers into the warm water, wondering which oasis pool he was remembering.

Suddenly Saalim's hands were on my sides, and he was pulling the fustan over my head.

With a new understanding, he peered at the scars on my back. "Do you wish they were gone?" he asked.

"I don't *wish* for anything," I said, turning to him.

His gaze dropped to my chest, to the smudge of gold on my skin.

"Now that I know to look for it, I see it there," he said quietly. "Still bright after all this time."

"It will be that way forever, I think."

We lowered ourselves into the bath.

Saalim pulled me to him, and I curled into him. Saying nothing, he wrapped his arms around me. My head lay against his chest, his heart a tabla drumming in my ear. His body was tense, his arms tight around me as if he was worried this moment was fleeting.

There was just the sound of the ocean wind outside, the crackle of burning wood in the fire, and the soft splash of water licking up the sides of the basin.

"I hope," Saalim said, his voice vibrating through me. "That this will be forever, too."

My face turned up to his. His eyes were soft with pleasure, the muted gold of being human. Once more, our mouths met, and like waves to a shore, we fell into each other. We were a tangle of limbs, a sharing of life.

Home. Finally, I was home.

⌒〜〜〜⌒

"Where were you last night, when I first came looking for you?" Saalim asked the next morning. The sun had barely risen, and Saalim had risen with it. I would have been mad that he woke me, too, but his lips against my skin snuffed the irritation like sand on flame. The fire had long ago died, and it was cold in the room. I pulled the blankets up to my chin and curled into Saalim.

"To see Zahar."

He stiffened. "In the prison? Why?" He pulled away, immediately suspicious.

"There was more I needed to understand."

"And you understand now?"

I nodded. I was not sure how I would tell him what I had learned from my conversation with the healer, but he had dragged her into bed with us, so now I felt as if I must say everything. "Do you know who she is?"

"Zahar?" He looked beyond me at the gray dawn, the gulls that dove down to the fish-strewn docks.

My mouth struggled to form the right words. Finally, I said, "Your birth mother was her sister."

Saalim's eyes shot to mine. "That cannot be."

I told him everything. His hands on my skin were like stone.

"I suppose it is sad," I said after a long silence. "That someone could loathe themselves so much that they would destroy everyone around them. Sabra was like that. I hated her for it, at first. But now that she is dead, I realize that everything I despised about her, she despised even more."

"I wish I could say the same for Kassim." Saalim's fist curled against my hip. "It does not matter. About Kassim, nor about Zahar."

"How quickly your anger is gone," I said.

He nodded. "Zahar does not realize that had she left me alone to rule in my father's absence, I would have ruined Almulihi on my own. But by making me a jinni, she taught me much—the ache of a slave, the perception of a tyrant, the pervasiveness of weakness." He looked at me. "I will be a better ruler from my time as jinni. I will be a better ruler with you at my side."

I stroked his wrist with my fingers, remembering how warm the cuff was that had once been fastened there.

Finally, Saalim asked, "What do we do with Zahar?"

"If Edala was correct, Zahar is the only one who remains to join us to Masira. I think there is little choice in what happens to Zahar. Magic serves no good."

"I agree. She must be destroyed."

I told him my plan.

"I will talk to Nassar, and we will arrange it." Pressing his lips to my brow, he rose from bed, dressed himself, and made me promise to find him for midday meal. "I will tell them about us."

Moths fluttered. *Us.*

Though the city was unchanged, everything felt different. I walked through the streets seeing the people, the homes, the shops anew. Soon, I would look after them as Saalim did. Soon, I would be their queen.

For now, I enjoyed the anonymity and the freedom that came with it.

The baytahira appeared remarkably untouched after Kassim's fire and Edala's flooding. Aside from smudges left from the flames and a few remaining piles of sodden furniture, it looked the same. Edala mended much before she died.

I found the jalsa tadhat as I expected it to be: quiet and empty. When I nudged the door open, I was surprised to see the front room was swept clean, a table with chairs in the place of sand, fire, and cushions. The many people seated at the table turned to me at my entrance.

Odham scooted back from the table and approached. "We are closed."

He did not appear to recognize me, and for that I was grateful. "I am looking for Firoz."

Odham moved to the side, pointing behind him.

"Emel," a nearly unrecognizable man said, rising from the table.

"Firoz?" I could not believe it. His hair was covered by a turban, his face was clean, beard groomed. He looked rested and sounded clearheaded. This was not the same Firoz I had seen in the street, blinking away the fog of magic and drink, not long ago.

"What is this?" I plucked at his soft tunic. "Your mother would have nothing to complain about!"

His eyes softened and he laughed, excusing us as he led me upstairs. He did not take me to his room, as I expected. Instead, he took me to the roof.

"You've been up here?" he sounded surprised. When I told him of the time Rashid brought me up there, he confessed he did not remember.

"After that arwah," he said, "nothing has been the same. We tried, you know, having more. It's good coin, of course. But there was no . . ." He wiggled his fingers in the air. "There was nothing from the spirits. None of us could tell if it was because we all felt a bit funny from it all, or if it was because something had changed."

Above us, a trio of gulls swarmed greedily, thinking we might have an easy meal. I wondered if it was the loss of the jinni or of the si'la that had left the jalsa tadhat quiet.

Firoz said, "I realized you were right."

I coiled my hair around my fingers, trying not to gloat when he was already offering me as much of an apology as I suspected I would get.

He set his palm against my knee. When I went to place my hand on his, I startled.

"Firoz! What happened?" Pale, shining burns arced across his hands and disappeared up his sleeve. "The fire?" Saalim had not told me he was injured.

"I heard about plans to burn the palace the night of the Falsa Mawk, to make it seem as though it was the healer's errant flame," he continued. "I worried about you." Firoz told me how he went to the palace, prepared to beg a soldier to post at the healer's, but found the palace unguarded completely. "I walked right in." It certainly had been Kassim's magic that sent the guards away.

"Saalim told me you saved my life." I took his scarred hand and leaned against him. "I didn't realize what harm had come to you in doing so."

"The king?"

I nodded. "I owe you so much. Especially after how I've treated you . . ."

Embarrassed, he shrugged me away. "What is it between you two? He seemed very worried."

Finally, I did not have to lie. "He and I will be wed."

"Emel?" Firoz gasped. He had the most disbelieving look on his face, I was nearly offended. "You, a queen?!" Then he settled and seemed to consider it. "It would be you. You have always been able to make something of nothing, to find salt in the sand."

Warmth touched my cheeks. "You, too, Firoz. Look at what you've found here." I did not elaborate, unsure of what exactly he'd found. I watched the sun rise behind low clouds, the sky settling into blue with each breath that passed.

He shook his head. "I thought I needed to leave my family, to be out of the settlement, but I was wrong."

I tore my gaze away from the man who swept outside his shop. The same one who hadn't so much as blinked at Firoz's unconscious form on the street.

"I have come here and experienced everything I wanted to. But Rashid and I have both realized that what we have gained living here—all the freedom and extravagance and wealth of the city—has not been worth what we lost by leaving behind our friends and our family. And now that the Salt King is dead." He cringed at the word. "Sorry . . ."

"It's all right," I said. "He deserved his fate."

"Now that there is a new leader, I wonder if I wouldn't be happier there."

"What are you saying?"

"As soon as I have the coin, I am going to go home."

The confession did not hurt like I would have suspected. "This is why . . ." I pointed at his clothes, his turban.

He nodded. "I miss Mama, my brother and sisters. I want to go home to them, and to be a brother they can be proud of. I lost myself in all of this, and I didn't like it."

"Back to the marketplace, eh?"

He smiled and nodded.

"And Rashid will go?"

"He will."

"Then I am happy."

His shoulders dropped. "That is a relief."

"You won't leave without goodbye?"

"I promise."

I took his hand in mine, our fingers interlocking. With my head against his shoulder, we watched the morning turn to day.

"Queen Emel," Firoz whispered. "I hope this Saalim knows the extent you've been trained to sway muhami. He has no chance!"

Laughing loudly, I confessed Saalim had some idea.

"Tell me one thing," Firoz said, lowering his voice. I looked him expectantly, waiting. "Is his snake long?"

With the widest smile on my face, I nearly pushed him from the roof.

<hr />

Tavi would not stop hugging me. Well, she would stop to wipe her face, but then she would grab me again, mumbling between cries that she was so happy for me.

"I can't believe *my* sister will be a queen!" She held my face with her hands, stroking my cheeks with her thumbs like our mother used to.

"And you can come live in the palace!" I said excitedly, seeing a future where we stole bread from the kitchens, kicked each other under the table at fancy dinners. I imagined nights in front of the fire in the guest tower—Tavi's tower—telling each other stories of our former life, each story more unbelievable. "*Can you believe we used to bathe only once or twice a moon?*" The two of us living in a palace of stone as free as birds. It was nearly as exciting as wedding Saalim.

Tavi's brightness was gone like a cloud covering the sun. "Oh," was all she said.

"You wouldn't want to come? Live in the palace?" I was hurt. I knew that she had found a life that satisfied her with Saira, but surely she wouldn't want to live with them forever?

Tavi shook her head. "It isn't that. It's just—" She looked at the boat drifting by, and when she saw who passed, she waved. "I think someday soon I might go to live with Yakub. Marry him."

"But you hardly know him!" It was a pathetic argument, but the idea that she might marry someone *I* did not know scared me.

"I've known him as long as you've known the king," she said.

I held my tongue and looked down at our sandaled feet, hanging over the edge of the canal like two children. I could not dislike Yakub because she would not live in the palace with me. Because she would choose him over her family.

After all, I had done the same.

I finally said, "When?"

Tavi kicked her feet through the air. "I don't know, but Saira has asked little questions here and there about how I feel for Yakub and what I think of that part of the city." Flicking a small leaf into the water, she said, "I think he is going to ask me to wed him, and Saira and Josef are the only ones he can ask for permission since, well . . ."

"We don't have a mother and father."

"Right. Josef loves him. Saira seems happier than I've ever seen her."

Standing, I said, "Come, show me where he lives. I might not be your mother, but I am your sister and want to approve of this myself."

Tavi clucked her tongue just like Hadiyah used to, and led me along the canal toward his home. It was warm now that it was nearing midday. I would need to return to Saalim soon. The idea excited me, making it easy to find happiness for Tavi. Return *home*.

"You can still have me to the palace as often as you want, you know," Tavi said as we walked.

"Oh, I can?" I raised my eyebrows and folded my arms.

She hummed a confirmation, explaining, "I have heard that at each meal, the food is piled so high it's taller than me. And if you're any indication, I would bet those rumors are true." She pinched my midsection, and I pushed her away, giggling.

"Let me tell you, the food is piled even higher."

"Praise the Sons for that!" She grew serious. "But you will be inviting me for meals, won't you? At least one a day, or I might reconsider this." She gestured between us, like our being sisters was some sort of choice.

"I knew you only cared about me for the food."

She pushed her braid over her shoulder and sauntered away, leaving me to trot after her.

We crept by Yakub's home, snorting with delight at our attempts to be quiet.

"He can't know I suspect!" she hissed, and we cackled even louder.

We said goodbye, and I floated on a river of glee back to the palace.

33

SAALIM

"I t will be ill-received so soon after Helena," Nassar said. "They will want some explanation." Though I could see his irritation, even he knew this was a matter he could not argue. Emel is who I wanted, and I was the king.

Emel picked at the fish, her eyes trained on her meal. This was an uncomfortable discussion, to be sure, but if she was to be queen, she would sit through worse. She had known what to expect when she met me here.

"The answer is power, of course," she said, lifting her gaze to Nassar's. "You ask the people who is the greater threat? Those in the north, or the *salt chasers* to the south?"

Behind his beard, Nassar's lips pursed. Emel leaned back as though bored. Perhaps I was wrong about her.

She seemed a natural at this table.

Emel added, "I should clarify: who is the *perceived* threat." She nodded to Kofi, who sat at the end of the table glaring at nothing. The entire time I had known him, he had hated those born from the desert.

Nassar shook his head, turning to Azim. Suddenly, I missed Amir, Masira carry his soul. He would have had us laughing about something or other, determining ways for us to move forward without tumult from the people.

While the two bent their heads in discussion, I leaned over to Emel. "What is it like for you?" I whispered, tipping my head to Nassar. "I see a loyal advisor, then I see your father's sycophantic vizier."

"I have grown used to it," she said into my ear. "But do not let me in a room with him alone." She glanced at him. "I might have things to say."

"I really don't want you alone in a room with any man. Unless you've a dagger of sorts."

One corner of her lip curled, and she raised an eyebrow. "Saalim, you don't need to worry about me." Slowly she dragged her finger up my thigh, and the room began to fade away.

Sons.

I snatched her hand from my—

"Saalim," Nassar repeated.

"I am listening," I said, setting my heel across my knee and leaning forward. Emel was the portrait of perfect behavior beside me.

Azim and Nassar glanced at each other. Nassar said, "The wedding will be in seven days. That gives us time to spread word. After, we will take the journey. A tour and introduction of the queen, if you will." He sighed. I think he wanted to travel with the caravan even less than I did.

"Emel?" I asked.

She nodded. "It suits."

Our meal finished in alternating waves of silence and discussion, Nassar and Azim offering suggestions by turn for this and that aspect of our upcoming ceremony and journey that followed. Occasionally, I would look up and see Emel watching me. I would reach forward and press my hand to her wrist, to her arm. Everything was changed and everything was right, because she was here with me.

The ceremony was small at Emel's request, and I agreed. It seemed, in many ways, premature to have a large celebration so close on the heels of Kassim, and Zahar still lingered like a poison plant in the ground. When the roots were pulled, and we had returned from our journey, we could travel the city to let the people celebrate the new queen. Until then, peace was not yet ours.

We were wed in Wahir's temple, standing side by side in the pool, water above our ankles.

People caught word of the wedding and clustered around the temple, trying to peak in through the columns. But I could only think of them for a moment, because each time Emel breathed, with each sweep of her fingers against the silk dress, my attention was pulled to her again. There was no shining sword, no sun over the sea, no ship with full sails that was more beautiful. Blue and gold cascaded down her shoulders, swirling in the pool around us.

And seeing my mother's crown on her head. I could barely look at it for the overwhelming pride I felt seeing it on Emel. My mother would have been pleased with her successor.

See, father? Sometimes we are wrong. Look at this beautiful queen.

When the cleric asked us to kneel in the pool, when he touched our brows with the pads of his fingers, when he committed us as wed under the will of Wahir, Emel smiled so brightly I had to look away. And still, like a flame, I saw her smile as I closed my eyes.

My chest ached with the cry I held back. My throat, even, was sore. As if she knew my turmoil, I felt a squeeze of my hand. Clutching her hand tightly, I pulled it to my lips. I held it there, breathing her in.

"Are these tears?" Emel whispered when we were told to face each other, when we were declared wed by the hands of Wahir.

I blinked, unable to speak for fear that more may come. I smiled and shook my head.

"That silly jinni in that story. All he did was swoon after the ahira. Pathetic, wasn't he?" Her eyes glistened, and then she pressed her mouth to mine.

Sons, how did I ever come to deserve such fortune?

Emel in my arms, in Almulihi.

Once slaves with a bound and bleak future, now freed and wed in love.

I tasted tears, but I did not know if they were hers or mine.

We went into the desert for the last time—I hoped—for a long time. Our caravan was sturdier, nearly triple the guards we'd brought with us on our previous journey. How long ago that felt, but it had barely been one moon.

Now, Zahar came with us.

"This is not how I imagined spending my first nights wed to you," I said to Emel as we rolled our packs in preparation for yet another evening journey. She looked so tired and though I knew she wanted to take this journey more than anyone, I wished she would have stayed home. I did not want her out here anymore than she had to be—the risk of nomads, of illness, and one wrong turn haunting me with each step we took away from Almulihi.

Still, the journey so far had proved to be useful. The people loved Emel, as I knew they would. They loved that they saw someone like them beside me. The Hayali were overjoyed—as much as they would show joy to someone like me. Liika sent us away with an entire camel packed with gifts. "I have seen so much of you recently. Perhaps we should make it a tradition. I like this queen," she said with a calculated smile as her slave handed over the reins of the camel.

I said, "Ah, but doesn't the Litab teach that distance feeds affection?"

She waved her hand at me, mumbling about fools with the Litab. "We don't need a book to tell us how to live."

When we parted, the child Dyah sprinted out to Emel, clasping her hand, insisting she would take the journey with her. Emel knelt down and explained why it could not be, but Dyah followed us so far that I was forced to send one of my men to escort—well, carry—her home so that she did not lose her way in the fast-approaching night.

Zahar joined us on those journeys to the settlements, but she remained outside them, posted with three guards. The people who lingered on the edge of their city to see our caravan would watch her curiously. At the first stop she tried to coax a man to come near, and Tamam nearly killed her on the spot.

He was no longer asked to guard her.

Zahar was kept tightly bound by chains of which only I had the key. Even when we were not visiting settlements, she was constantly surrounded by guards, and she remained as far away as possible from me. I did not want to hear her or see her, fearing I would behave the same as Tamam.

Emel insisted Zahar's end should be Zahar's choice, but that neither choice resulted in life. Emel said simply ending her swiftly was a kindness far too great for someone who had caused so much destruction. So it would be, I agreed, when Emel said she was to be taken to the sands. It was a task we could trust with no one else. A manipulative healer who could make jinn of men was far too enticing for most people to be trusted with.

So we journeyed, the handful of civilians who joined our caravan dropping off person by person as we reached their desired settlements. Even Emel's friends had joined us, though they would be the last to leave. It felt like our own hourglass, marking the passage of time as their numbers diminished. Each day felt longer than the last, but this time it was not because I was eager to get home to protect the city. Now, I was eager to get home with Emel, to show my people their queen.

Under the blanket of night, I found Tamam.

"What do you need?" he asked.

"To travel beside my best soldier. To ask him how he fares." Emel had told me the details of his parting with Edala, but if she had not, I would never have suspected the depth of his grief. He was the same: quiet, loyal, alone. His face, the carriage of his shoulders, his work, all unchanged. How many secrets did he hide?

The tack rattled through the silence.

"I would have left the army for her," Tamam said at last.

Tamam would have left the guard for Edala? "You would have stayed your hand," I said, an echo of what he long ago told me.

He looked at me briefly. "I would have even left Almulihi if she asked."

The moon cast so little light, the only things that could tell me sand from sky were the stars. "She would not hear it, would she?"

"She said she could not live knowing it was her fault. As if it was something she forced me to do. As if I didn't offer because it was something I wanted." I could nearly feel his fist clench around the reins. "For her, it was worth it."

"You cannot carry that regret. You know Edala was headstrong. You have to live with her decision, and she left you the greater burden." Bringing Farasa close beside him, I lowered my voice. "Tell me what you want now." Did he want to take leave to work in the hot houses preparing flowers for the Falsa Mawk? Or did he want to be a sea man, go out to sail with the clippers? Whatever it was, he could have it. He deserved that much.

"I have considered this often since . . ." He turned his face away from me.

Tamam, I thought, *it is too dark to see your tears.*

"I want only Edala."

⌐◡◠◡◠⌐

Emel was bent over a map with Kofi and Parvaz, and as I watched them discuss the people in the next settlement, I wondered if it was a mistake to leave Nassar in Almulihi. I had found him in the aviary the day before we were to leave.

"What are you doing?" I asked.

"Ah, giving them a final treat. Haris doesn't spoil them like I do." He loved those birds.

"Anisa is lazy because of you." I gestured to my eagle. Her golden eyes flashed to me, then back to the carcass in Nassar's hand.

He was unapologetic as he tossed it to her.

"I want you to stay here when we leave tomorrow."

His hand dropped, and he peered up at me with disgust. What Nassar lacked in height he made up for in impertinence. "I will not."

"I insist."

"What have I done?" He pulled the leather glove from his arm and angrily hung it on the nearby hook, the birds ignored.

"Nothing that is wrong." I hesitated. "The journey will be long, and you have already made it many times."

"No more than you," he said. That was not true, but of course I could not explain that to him.

"I cannot risk losing you on this journey. You have too much to teach me." He looked beyond me and nodded.

"Stay home this time. Ekram has said on multiple occasions that a soldier shouldn't be at the docks. Let's avoid battle between he and Azim, eh?"

Though I didn't think it possible without copious amounts of drink, Nassar actually smiled. He tapped his fingertips together and said, "And about Emel. What she said I did . . . handed her father the whip? I—"

"You have nothing to apologize for. Least of all a past you cannot remember. You have been very loyal, Nassar." I thought of those years he spent with the Salt King. The offense to his principles as he supported Alfaar, the grit of the life he led in his earnest attempt to find me, to resurrect his home. Though he could recall none of it, in that reality I was shown the depth of his loyalty.

"Thank you, Saalim."

I knocked his shoulder. "*King* Saalim, don't you mean?"

Now I smiled, remembering how pleased—really, relieved—he was.

Back in the desert, as I recalled this, Emel watched me. "Something funny, eh?"

I shook my head, sending away thoughts of home, of Nassar. I asked, "Where did you get this map? Was it Amir's?"

Sadness flashed across her eyes as I know it did mine, but she reassured me it was not his. Emel had taken her map to Kahina as a gift before we left. She said it had made the baytahira proprietress happy to know what hope it had given Emel.

And even more, it pleased her to see how Emel had marked it, filling it in how she thought the desert lay. In return, Kahina gave Emel the completed map we used to guide us now.

Parvaz stood. "At dawn we will leave the prisoner."

Son of the Salt Chaser

I looked to Emel for confirmation. She nodded.

Under the high quarter-moon, I approached Zahar with Emel. Kofi stood by, preparing to intervene if needed. Her feet were tightly bound, so she would not run anywhere yet. And when she was unbound, Kofi would still not be needed. There was nothing around for Zahar to use. There was nothing around for her to live.

"So you plan to leave me out here like some animal?" she said. Her voice was hoarse, and I was not sure when she had spoken last. We had been traveling for so long already. She peered around. The moon was just bright enough to light the sands, to reveal a long stretch of nothing in all directions.

Emel stepped forward. "No, not like an animal, because an animal, at least, might adapt. You are being left out here like a prisoner. Only there will be no chains, no boundaries. You are free to do whatever you please."

Zahar was unimpressed by the generosity. "I will die out here." Her voice tremored.

"You will," Emel said. "It is your choice how quickly."

The healer raised an eyebrow, then wiped hair from her brow, pulling the veil more carefully over her eyes. What was it she hid? Surely not feelings of sadness or remorse. Those were things I did not think her capable of.

From her pack, Emel pulled a small vial. It did not appear so different from the one Edala had given me.

"The only drink you will be left with. Should you choose it," Emel said, handing her the vial. "This will bring you to Masira—if she will have you—more swiftly."

Zahar opened the vial and sniffed it. Then, she let out a crackling, mirthless laugh. "Oh child, you had so much potential!"

Emel's expression did not change. I looked between Zahar and Emel, wondering what exactly Emel had given the healer.

As if she knew my thoughts, Zahar turned to me and showed me the vial. "For dhitah. It's what should have killed your father."

I stiffened, my hand finding the hilt of my blade. I wanted to be done with her.

"If your brother hadn't been so daft and simply given him the entire tonic in one drink like I told him to, it *would* have!" She turned away, taking mincing steps through the sand in a circle. "And it should have killed you! I thought those idiots had finally done something right, putting the tonic in your water. They refused to kill, you know. They were weak. But I convinced them of this." She held the vial to me. "But then I heard you smashed the damn pitcher and all the dhitah in it!"

The day I found the Darkafa in my room, they had poisoned my water?

Zahar went on. "It's why I should never task anything to anyone else! Just do it myself . . . it will, at least, be done right."

My heart pounded all the way to the tips of my fingers. I would kill her. Right then, I would kill her.

Emel leaned just slightly into me. "Zahar, you will not win an easy death by goading Saalim." The healer and Emel stared at the shadows in each other's eyes, and I wondered what they saw there. "Your end will right the desert. A worthy death, wouldn't you agree?"

Zahar spat at Emel's feet, and I could not resist my fury, I shoved Zahar hard, and she fell into the sand.

"Monster!" Zahar croaked at me.

"Fool!" Emel shouted at her. "Waste what precious water you have left because you are angry? You are no survivor." Now, Emel knelt down, leaning closer to Zahar than I wanted her to be. Kofi had neared, ready to protect his queen just as I was. "You think you are strong because you can take someone else's gifts, take magic"—Emel waved her hands around—"and use them to fight your troubles. But Zahar, your strength is weak, because it relies on another.

"I am strong," Emel continued. "Because I see your magic and say, *I don't need it.* I am enough." Emel stood. "You told me that comfort and power are bred from wealth. You are wrong. They are bred from suffering. And there is nothing the desert has taught me if not how to endure hardship." Emel gestured to me to unlock the bindings. "I am a salt chaser," Emel said proudly, looking back to Zahar once more. "You are nothing."

We left Zahar with only the hatif as her companion. It made me uneasy. What if a traveler crossed her path? What if she found an oasis we didn't realize existed? The map told that the nearest water was over a day's travel, and that was if she traveled in the right direction. Without water, the chances were nearly impossible that she would make it, but I wished we did not have to take them at all.

Emel insisted, though, that her death must be her choice.

My concern faded the farther from her we traveled.

It was the following dusk, not even a full day turned, when we felt it.

We were still sitting around on our mats, finding reprieve in the dimming sun. There were no trees to shade us through sleep that day, so none of us found great rest despite the lean-tos.

It felt like I was dropped, like my gut was suddenly in my throat, like I had been cut free of something high above me, and now was grounded. It was indescribable, because I had experienced nothing like it before.

Clutching my stomach, I looked at Emel. She did the same as she stared at me, wide-eyed and worried. The soldiers around us looked similarly perplexed. Those that had been standing had crouched but quickly stood upright.

Had the sand been so smooth before? I could have sworn it had been more rippled. And what of those dunes? Were they not taller a moment ago?

"What happened?" Emel asked.

I shook my head, helping her to stand.

Walking to the nearest group of soldiers, I asked if they were all right. They nodded, and I moved quickly through the caravan, asking after everyone's well-being. By the time I reached the last group of travelers, they looked at me as if I were daft. Nothing had happened, of course they were fine.

I went to Tamam sitting at the periphery of the group, watching the horizon.

"Did you feel it?" I asked when he stood.

Tamam nodded, his eyes sweeping the landscape around us. Then, "Magic."

Emel appeared beside me, staring at Tamam. "You are right." She took several long breaths. "She is dead."

Emel turned in a slow circle, understanding washing over her. "The desert has been restored. Can't you feel it?" She smiled and pointed at the sky. "Masira is only there. At last, we are free."

No, I did not feel it perhaps like Emel did, but there was an ease of breath, the clearing of mind. Like I had awoken from a satisfying sleep or was at sea with only the wind at my back.

Taking Emel's hand in mine, I said, "Nearly free."

A shadow crossed her eyes before she nodded, and she went to pack her things.

34

EMEL

I t was simply there, like it had always been, ready for me to step into it if
only my feet would take me. But they did not want to take me.

Saalim nudged my back, telling me it was all right. It was not permanent. I would not stay. *He* was not there. But when I looked at the sea of tents
with white peaks surfacing at their center, I only saw the Salt King. He was in
everything that was there. I felt the clutch of my lungs, the stepping on glass,
the hold of my tongue when I was around him. The silk chains that weighed
more than any iron cuff pulled me down, and the scars across my back stung as
I stared at what used to be my home.

"I don't think . . ." I began, my throat tight. I did not want to return, I
could not do it. It was a past I could not face.

"Emel," Saalim said. "You wanted this."

The day before we left Madinat Almulihi, I had told him of Firoz wanting
to return home.

"Could we bring Firoz and Rashid on the journey? I know you said other
people would join the caravan."

"Yes, but others are traveling to places we will be stopping in. Your home
is much farther than we need to travel," he said, the crease between his brow
deepening.

Smoothing it with my finger, I said, "Of course. I knew that." I began to turn, disappointment at war with relief. His arm hooked around my middle, and he turned me so I faced him again. He studied my face, trying to know my thoughts.

"You want to return?" he asked.

I chewed my cheek, sorting through what I did want. "One last time. To see . . ."

"To heal."

Our eyes met.

I said, "Tamam visits the docks every day." I nodded toward the basin of water that Saalim prayed to, carrying his family from its depth to the clusters of incense. "You move stones every day."

"We will make the journey. But not for Firoz and Rashid. We will do it for you." He brushed his thumb over my cheek. "Usman should be checked on anyway."

Now that we were here, I feared I had made a mistake, and a costly one. It was days and days added to our journey to arrive, and I did not want to step into the settlement.

I did not want to see any part of that life I had led.

Firoz was soon at my side. He and Rashid had been so glad to take the journey with us. When I told Firoz it was a gift, and he owed no coin, he cried.

"We can't hide from it forever," Firoz said now. "Do you know what Mama told me when I told her I was leaving for Almulihi?"

Tearing my gaze away from my father's palace, I looked at my friend. I watched the muscles in his jaw clench, his eyes reflecting the light of the morning sun.

"'Another's feast may look grander, but who sits at the table?' I told her she knew nothing of Almulihi." He laughed. "But here I am, coming back to her. I want my family at my table." He took my hand in his, squeezing gently. Saalim was on my other side, towering over both of us, his hand on my back. Why couldn't I just stay here? Between the people I loved. Firoz said, "We left together. Shall we return the same?"

So with Saalim and Firoz, I stepped into a past to which I had hoped never to return.

The winding lanes of tents—people's homes!—were so small, so narrow. I peered at them closely. Most were open, people inside leaning against cushions or shuffling around, doing this and that.

When we passed by the marketplace, I was staggered by its mediocrity. I once thought I could get lost here? Everything was so small, so feeble. The voices were not, though, and they shouted loudly at us as we passed, sensing the salt and coin carried in our purses.

The people in the lanes were quiet and curious, watching us just as I remembered being watched in the palace finding my way to a muhami. They looked like me, these people. They dressed like me, too, but when they understood who we were and kneeled, I could see that more separated us than the turn of moons.

Queen. I was their queen, yet like a child I wanted to cower away from them, from the memories this place stoked. It was all around me. Too bright. I could not close my eyes against it.

Saalim tightened his grip on my hand as we reached the palace edge. There it was. The prison where I had lived my whole life. The place where I had learned to search for my freedom, where I had found my love. The place that took as much as it gave.

Did Saalim feel me falling apart? Did he feel me split, my pieces tumbling to the ground?

I stared at that which was my whole world, my father the god and myself his supplicant. Each memory of my blindness, my horrid misunderstanding of what life and happiness and love were was a piece of me that splintered and fell.

With a shaking hand, I wiped at my cheeks.

"Emel?" Saalim asked, turning toward me.

His face, his voice, that life. It was all too much. I thought I was freed, and now I was here again. My memories crashed together, my understanding blurred.

"I can't," I cried, falling into him, uncaring who watched.

Clutching me close, Saalim walked me into the palace. I kept my eyes closed, letting him lead. I did not want to see it. I did not want to be there. Step after step after step, and though I did not open my eyes, I knew by each turn where I was. By each sound what was near me.

We were inside the palace tents, seated on a long bench I had never sat upon before. One that had been reserved for the muhamis. Even the same cushions were around us—the ones the ahiran lounged on as we watched my father draw yet another jackal onto the leash.

Usman spoke with Saalim. My tears had stopped, and I stared numbly at the room and servants around us. Some I recognized, but most were unfamiliar. Did any recognize me?

Then, "Emel?"

I stood, spinning around. Where was she? There! There! Coming in from the hall, she was running toward me. *Hadiyah!*

She cried, "They said she looked like an ahira! Someone said it was you! I did not dare believe!" Hadiyah was holding me to her. She was full of softness and warmth and memories of safety and care.

Mama. Oh, I missed Mama.

Hadiyah was wiping her face. She held me away from her, taking a long look at me. I did the same to her. She looked no different, no worse. She looked, in fact, happy.

"Can I take you to the harem?" she asked softly, her eyes darting from me to Saalim and back again. "They will want to see you. To know everything."

With assurances to Saalim I would be fine, I followed Hadiyah. There, more motherly embraces, long presses of palms to my back, of fingers on my cheeks and hair. They all spoke at once, telling me that they had been well, that Usman had been kind, to stop worrying about them. What about me? Tell them about Madinat Almulihi. Was it true I had become a queen?

Sitting at their feet, unable to stare at one place too long for the memories it pulled of my mother, I told them of life.

"Isra knew," one said, "that you would find great things."

I looked at her, begging her to tell me more of my mother.

"She always said you would leave, you would find your own life. She said she hoped it of all her children, but for you, she knew she did not have to hope."

Hadiyah brushed her palm across my shoulders. "Masira carry her soul." The others echoed her words.

It was not so hard seeing them. And I felt that, just a little, they helped to smooth the roughness of my memories.

That night Saalim and I lay together in a tent I had never been in. One that had been reserved for guests. I imagined it was unchanged since my father had ruled. The carpets the same as all the others, the fabric spun above us the same. I trembled, remembering him. Remembering my life under his rule. Saalim took heavy breaths beside me. Had he already fallen asleep? I shifted.

"I am awake," he said, slurring his words. He had not been. We had barely slept that day, and I knew he was more tired than me, but still he said, "I promise, I will wait until you sleep."

I did not want to be the only one awake while all others slept. Alone with my thoughts. To ease the clattering worries of my past, I told him of my visit to my mothers and, after, to my sisters. Everyone was happy, none had been forced out of the palace like we had assumed. They worked, many of them, and those who didn't found ways to assist in the palace. They were free to come and go. Many had left the palace only briefly, with their brothers at their sides. They told me my brother Lateef had left the settlement with a caravan that traveled east. So all of Isra's children had fled, then. Just as she dreamed we would.

My sisters could not stop telling me about the things in our village as if I had never been there myself. I listened, amazed by the ways they had changed and the ways they had not. They showed me the coin they had earned, the salt they saved. Small earnings compared to what I had as the healer's apprentice, but they were so proud that I warmed with pride, too.

Saalim said, "I was not sure how it would feel to return. It makes real again so many memories I wanted to believe were false."

His eyes were shadowed in the torch light, but I saw the brightness there. My gaze traveled around his face, remembering when I thought I looked at him for the last time, when I committed every detail to memory so that I would never forget him. Now, he was beside me. Forever.

He continued. "But I find I am in awe."

Rearing my head, I said, "Awe?"

"Of you. Of the people here. I think I finally understand what you mean about the desert. That it is not all bad. It is made better by the people who live in it. Your people—our people—are not to be pitied because they have a home that falls to fire and wind, nor because they have to hide their skin from their hostile land. They are not savage because they fight for their needs rather than trade for it. They are a product of the sand and sun.

"I did not understand it before, but traveling here with you, I see it now. Salt chasers, those of the sand, whatever you want to call them—" He raised himself up on his elbow, his words smooth. "They are resilient, Emel. Look at the moon-jasmine that grows from the sand that has learned to cover herself from the sun. Such a beautiful flower . . ."

I smiled, thinking of those white-petaled blooms that poked up from the ground through every crack in Almulihi's stone streets.

"My point," Saalim said with chagrin, "is that you will remember your past. It may shake you and try to cripple you, but it can't pull you apart, Emel, because it is what has put you together. See the past, and know that because of it, you are here now." He traced an invisible crown around my head, and with his voice low, he said, "It cannot defeat you, because with it, you have won."

⁓

We left my settlement after we had toured and saw and shared and celebrated, like we did at every place on our tour of the desert. Each place had welcomed Saalim and me like family, but there, I *was* family. Even Saalim laughed with real joy, confessed he smiled so much it hurt. Though the food was dull compared to that in Almulihi, the people who sat at the table were brilliant.

Even through my own pleasure at being amongst those that I knew best, there were the cracks that let in the throb of hurt, the ache of my darkest memories. Time, Saalim reminded me. It would take time for the pain to soften completely, for the light to clear the shadow.

After a day of tearful goodbyes to Firoz, to my mothers and sisters, to Hadi-yah, Adilah, and the servants who had known me from infancy, we left.

When the cluster of tents was behind us, I turned and looked to the place that birthed me, that raised me. Still, there was the tightening of sadness and shame, but it was small. Instead, I saw that which had given me strength.

Eiqab, Mama, Tavi, Raheemah, Firoz, Sabra.

I looked to the man at my side.

Saalim.

Kneeling down, I took a fistful of sand and poured it into my sack.

"Let's go home," I said.

⌁

Madinat Almulihi greeted us like an oasis: shining in the sun, welcoming in its promised shade. I felt Saalim stiffen the closer we got. I understood now: He faced an unpleasant past here just as I did at the settlement. I cooed the same words to him as he had to me.

When our caravan finally arrived at the palace, we both stopped.

"What . . . ?" I stammered, staring at the tall walls that surrounded the palace and its courtyard.

Instead of the white-washed walls that had bordered the steps were walls now filled with bright colors. Designs and patterns and images were there that had never been before. The guards around us seemed undisturbed, continuing their walk to the stables for the horses, handing their packs to the servants as though nothing was amiss. The people who walked the streets around us were the same. How could they ignore this?

Where had it come from?

On the steps, we touched the walls, inspecting them closely. The images were made up of the smallest tiles arranged so carefully it was as if they were painted. They were beautiful, but they did not look new. Some of the tiles had the smallest chips at the edges. I stepped back, trying to take in the picture completely.

A man with golden cuffs coming out of a cloud of golden smoke. A woman in blue with a chained veil across her face, jewels around her fingers and belly.

"A jinni and an ahira," Saalim whispered, touching the black tiles of the ahira's hair. We moved to the opposite side of the stairs to better view the other image. A white palace over the backdrop of night. A crystal-blue sea at its side reflected the bright moon.

There, amongst the waves, was a missing tile.

"How could they know?" I asked nervously as I touched the empty space where I knew my tile belonged.

When we went inside the palace, we were greeted by Mariam and a cluster of other servants. Bilara, dressed like any other child in the city, played on the stairs behind her.

"Who did the mosaic?" Saalim asked.

Mariam seemed confused by the question. "I can't say. It has been there since long before my arrival here."

"Ah," Saalim said, understanding just as I did. This was magic. Something with the desert shifting one final time.

"I've always wondered what it means," I said. "I was just looking at it . . ."

Tilting her head, Mariam said, "It tells the legend of the ahira and the jinni, of course."

I asked her to remind me. Salt chasers did not share the same legends, see.

"The trapped ahira who found and fell in love with a jinni. With a wish for freedom, she freed the jinni, and Madinat Almulihi was born." She said it slowly, like I was a touch crazed.

"Oh, yes," I said in a rush. "I think I've seen children act out that one in the marketplace."

As we passed through the throne room, Saalim stopped me again. He pointed to the tapestry that had been gifted to him at the Falsa Mawk.

No longer was there a woman in pale pink with long straight hair at the king's side. Now, the silhouette of the woman was soft red with a deeper shaded veil that covered her hair and face. At the head of the woman was a golden crown, and at her heart was a golden flower.

"Emel," he said, his voice hushed. "It is you."

Indeed, it was.

～～～～〕〔～～～

That night an enormous party was held for the return of the king and queen. People ate and drank to our names throughout the night.

Tavi and Yakub were there with Saira's family, the children running around in feral glee. Others were there, too. Kahina and her son, Rafal. Saalim's men: Tamam, Nassar, Kofi, Parvaz, and so many more. People both wealthy and common. With deep satisfaction, I watched the people revel in our halls, Saalim at my side, my hand in his.

Suddenly, Gaffar was in front of me. All night he had broken into song no matter how many times Saalim told him to be quiet so the musicians he hired could do their job. But alas, he was unstoppable. "May I sing a tune for the new queen? In the tradition of an Almulihi welcome."

Reluctantly, Saalim nodded. I giggled at his exasperation, leaning forward eagerly to hear.

Gaffar jumped onto a chair, calling the attention of the guests. Then, he began:

> '*Ahira! Ahira! Flee with me,*
> *Back to my home beside the sea,*'
> *The heartsick jinni did implore*
> *Of the shackled daughter of the sand*
> *Her chain wrapped round her father's hand*
> *Free to dream, though nothing more.*

> '*I cannot flee, and nor can you*
> *For my father is your master, too,*'

Sighed the ahira in resigned repose.
But nurtured by Wahir's fair hand
Love struggled up from Eiqab's sands
A defiant and desperate desert rose.

The wishes that the jinn bestow,
Like the sea, conceal an undertow,
For dangerous is Masira's guile.
The ahira wished the lovers freed,
The goddess twisted desperate need
And threw them into cruel exile.

The ahira fled across the dunes
Her path lit by Wahir's fair moon.
She found a kingdom by the sea,
No map contained, no seer could scry
That fair land of Almulihi
Where there, her jinni crowned as King,

Took the ahira as his queen.

Gazing around the room, I saw that the people smiled, the women wiped their eyes. As if this was some legend their ancestors knew.

Quickly, I turned to Saalim. He remembered still, didn't he? I was not alone once more?

Leaning toward me, his mouth brushed my ear before he whispered, "Masira is cunning, isn't she?"

"What does it mean?"

"I'm afraid it means that neither of us had any choice with this." He gestured between us. "We have been puppets on strings."

"Then it is well that I like you."

"Do you like me, or is it this?" He tapped the crown on my head.

I pretended to consider it. "Really, it's the dune of salt bricks."

He grew serious, his brow furrowing. "After all, you are a salt chaser."

"As are you."

Leaning into his neck, I smiled and breathed him in. Would I ever tire of him? Would I tire of us? Or would we be like the mosaic on the walls of the palace, our love captured forever?

Of course, I knew the answer to that already.

Like the legends, the stories, the songs: We would endure.

ACKNOWLEDGMENTS

This book would not be in your hands if it were not for the CamCat team who supported it. Thank you Sue Arroyo for continuing to allow my dream to be a reality. To Bridget McFadden and Helga Schier, thank you for pushing me when I needed it. I was not easy to work with, so know your patience was much appreciated. To all of those behind the scenes, thank you: Maryann, Maia, Bill, Laura, and the many others.

Thank you to Cassandra Farrin for everything you did with *Daughter of the Salt King*, as it carried so heavily into the second, and thank you for all you did with *Son of the Salt Chaser*.

The biggest thank you must be reserved for my husband. I began drafting this book two weeks after my daughter was born. Never again do I want to write a book on a deadline with a newborn! This was the hardest thing I have ever done, and it would not have been possible if my husband had not been so incredibly supportive. Words cannot do my gratitude justice.

An author in the sequel slog can only be fueled on imagination for so long. After a while, the encouragement and support of fans proves to be much more effective at providing momentum. To every reader who raved about *Daughter of the Salt King*, who reached out to tell me how much my book meant to them, who forced it into their friends' hands—thank you, thank you, thank you.

To my Veterinary Moms Book Club crew: Your fangirling and relentless support often brought me happy tears (often after I was crying frustrated tears) and gave me the nudge I needed to keep going.

How lucky I am to have found you all.

ABOUT THE AUTHOR

A. S. Thornton is the author of the award-winning *Daughter of the Salt King* (CamCat Books, 2021), the first book in the Salt Chasers duology. She has evolved from book blogger to author with a particular fondness for writing forbidden love in ancient deserts. She lives with her family in Northern California. When not writing, she's taking care of dogs and cats as a veterinarian. You'll never find animals at the center of her writing, though. Those fictional worlds don't have veterinarians and her literal brain can't accept that the poor critters would be without parasite prevention.

Learn more about her on
IG @as_thornton
and visit her website
www.asthornton.com.

If you've enjoyed

A. S. Thornton's *Son of the Salt Chaser,*

you'll enjoy

Brandon Ying Kit Boey's *Karma of the Sun.*

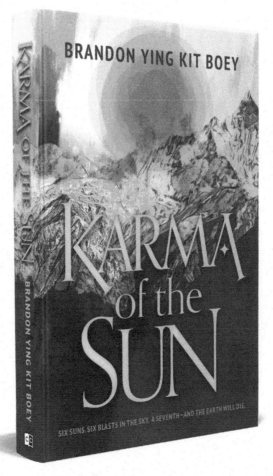

1

THE YAK

K arma knows it is a bad omen.

He feels it in his body. A sudden chill in the summer air. A passing shadow in the white Tibetan sky. A hush in the rustle of the yellow grasses.

One moment, the yak calf had been with the herd. Now it is gone—the gift for the shaman on his visit. The benefaction. Their offering. Missing.

Karma hastens frantically up the rise, climbing hill and dune as he searches, the little boy beside him scampering to keep up, three little steps for every one of his.

Bad omen. Bad luck.

This day, of all days.

The shaman is to arrive at the village tonight. Soon, the fathers of the valley will bring their sons, and the mothers their daughters, to have their fortunes told, the spirits consulted.

It is Karma's turn to graze the herd. His lot. His fate.

His fault.

Karma's heart pounds as he scales the last hill. The tattered prayer flags of the village outskirts come into view, trembling slightly in the uneven wind. They have been placed here purposely, auspiciously, adorning the rusted ruins of the iron wreckage said to have once been able to fly, a stupa to a miracle of the time before the destruction known only by the name of "the Six Suns"—six fires said to have consumed all the earth, leaving only the barrens of this remote hinterland. Now the cloth images of the Four Dignities float like ghosts against the sinking of the western sun: the snow lion, the tiger, the phoenix, and the dragon—chained to the east, south, west, and north.

An incongruous form catches the corner of Karma's eye, only paces away from the wreckage like some offering delivered before the stupa: white fur. No movement, except for the fluttering of a few woolen strands. His heart plummets. Before he can even fully comprehend what he is seeing, he already knows it is something terrible.

The calfling.

It lies on its side. Coming down the dune, Karma flinches at the sight of the animal's belly. A large hole gapes from sternum to flank. A jumble of intestines bulge out like a heap of spilled rope from a sack. The ground is a patch of blood so dark it looks black. Karma is paralyzed at the sight, as if it were his own lifeblood drained to the earth.

No . . . it can't be. Not the shaman's offering . . .

Only hours ago, it was alive and with the herd. Now it is a bloody carcass, viscera baking in the sun.

"What . . . happened?" a boy's voice gasps behind him.

Karma startles. It is his little cousin Lobsang. Karma moves to shield the boy from the sight, but the child is too far out of reach, or perhaps it is only Karma's legs that are too numb.

"It . . . it was probably wolves," Karma mumbles. "Maybe a pack of them, or something . . ."

His voice trails. True, there have been more sightings of wild animals, but his instinct tells him this is something else. None of the meat has been touched. The yak was a calf but by no means small. Looking at the sheer size of the wound, nothing on four legs could have done damage that looks like this.

A swarm of horseflies buzzes fiercely, as if to defend their quarry. A feeling comes over him, even more fearful than before. He has been afraid for the yak. But now that he's found it, he is afraid for the village.

If not animals . . . then bandits?

Karma's gaze flickers to the distance, to the flat horizon, the mountains long gone, where the border bandits are known to dwell. Lobsang mirrors his gaze. The vista is empty, but he knows the bandits prefer the night anyway, the better to avoid being shot by the villagers' matchlock rifles. Still, if it had been them, wouldn't they have stolen the calf, not wasted it? As depraved as they are, they are more deprived of food, no different from the rest of the Four Rivers and Six Ranges.

But if neither animals nor bandits . . .

Little Lobsang seems to read his thoughts. "Could it be a *migoi*?" he asks in a hushed voice, invoking the name for the supernatural creature that, thus far, to Karma was nothing but a child's figment. "My father says that in the end, the cursed become even more savage because they know that their doom is near. It's like the ghosts who mourn at night because they will never be reborn—"

Karma cannot help a shudder. First the missing yak, then the mutilation. Now talk of migoi, ghosts, and the coming of the Seventh Sun. The day is going from inauspicious to downright ominous.

"That's quite enough, Lobsang. We shouldn't speak of such things."

The wind stirs, and the stink of slowly fouling meat hits them. Karma's little cousin buries his nose in his sleeve, tangling his arm in the necklace of amber and coral that the boy's father has given him that day.

"We should ask my father what to do," Lobsang says, muffled behind his sleeve.

It is a perfectly reasonable course of action. Karma has the same urge, to leave this scene and go back to the village. But he feels as if he cannot. He is seventeen, not a child. This has happened on his watch. He cannot go back empty-handed. The bones and the hide. The hooves, the fat, and the tendons. He cannot lose the rest to wild animals overnight. As the son of the scoundrel—it would be unforgivable.

Karma makes up his mind. "There isn't enough time. The shaman's ceremony will be starting soon. We'll have to drag it back with us. Salvage what we can there." He could ask his mother to help him. He meets his cousin's skeptical gaze. "The meat's already turned," he explains. "If I lose the offal . . ."

Your father will lash me for sure, is what he wants to say, but doesn't need to. Lobsang seems to understand the logic. A look of sympathy crosses the boy's face, and Karma wonders if his cousin, young as he is, actually understands a lot more. If so, he has never shown it. To him, Karma is not the cursed Sherpa's boy, not the son of the scoundrel. He is just Karma—and for that, Karma has always loved him.

As they begin dragging the carcass away, Karma glances back over his shoulder. The sun is already beginning its descent behind the dusty horizon. Something about the light, the angle of his gaze—and a memory floods him, searing in its suddenness: An image of his father in this exact place, ten years ago. The entire village was there too. His mother, his aunt, his uncle the headman. And a caravan . . . waiting. But not Karma.

He was only seven years old then, but the memory is clear. He turns his face away.

Father's farewell.

"Are you alright, Karma?"

Karma blinks and the memory vanishes, leaving in its place the empty western landscape, the fluttering prayer flags the only thing stirring. A strand of the pennants has come untethered and is snaking now in the air like a loose kite string, whistling as it whips back and forth, back and forth.

His little cousin's head is cocked, watching him. "What is it?"

"It's . . . nothing," Karma says. "Nothing at all."

He nods to resume their movement. But though they continue onward to the village, something lingers in the air, sticks to them like the scent of the fouling meat they carry, certain only to ripen even more. A feeling of some ill-fated consequence of the past now finding its way back home.

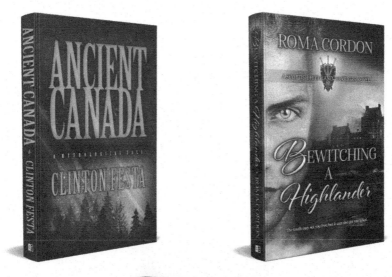
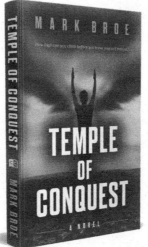

CamCat
Books

VISIT US ONLINE FOR MORE BOOKS TO LIVE IN:
CAMCATBOOKS.COM

SIGN UP FOR CAMCAT'S FICTION NEWSLETTER FOR
COVER REVEALS, EBOOK DEALS, AND MORE EXCLUSIVE CONTENT.

CamCatBooks   @CamCatBooks   @CamCat_Books   @CamCatBooks